THE KEY TO DAMOCLES

JAMES DANIEL ROSS

Winter Wolf PUBLICATIONS

| Cincinnati Ohio

Copyright © 2024, James Daniel Ross
Cover Art © 2024, Tithi Laudthong
Cover Design © 2024, Miriam Chowdhury
Edited by Danielle McPhail
Interior Design by Tracy Ross

Published by Copper Fox Books,
An imprint of Winter Wolf Publications, LLC

Previously published by Mundania Press, 2009

ISBN: 978-1-945039-32-4 (paperback)

DEDICATION

Thank you to all the fans, the family, the coworkers and the compatriots. Special thanks has to go to Russell Akred, Mike Chiseck, Mike Ritzmann, Joe Cowles, John Wicket, Joe Blanco, the McPhails, and Mr. Henderson. Most of all, thank you to Tracy Ross, my wife. You keep me writing,

–James Daniel Ross

CONTENTS

"There is always an easy solution to every human problem— neat, plausible, and wrong."

—H.L. Mencken

BOOK ONE:

MISDIRECTION

CHAPTER 1: FROM YOUR MOUTH...

Fire, gas, and lead leapt from the barrel of a gun. The bullet flashed, too fast for the eye to follow, becoming a bright red period marking the end to a scant twelve years of life. A scream erupted from an already dead mouth, flying outward in all directions, ricocheting off of the walls, shattering against the stained-glass windows, and fluttering to die at the base of the altar. Whimpers, like mourners, limped from the cowering crowd amongst the pews. They echoed inside the walls and settled across the bleeding body of a young boy beneath a carved icon of the crucified Christ. Beyond the light, beyond the hallowed walls, dark shapes moved with deadly purpose. Invisible voices flitted through the air, speaking only to those with ears to hear. "Another one. We have three down. Repeat: three down."

From darkened corners and through intervening walls my voice flew stealthily back to the first. "Hold and report."

People imagine war as an extended action scene splashed with blood and fire. They think of the sound of plasma guns hissing, of chemical lasers huffing out burnt focus gasses, of mechanized beasts churning blood into the soil, and of shouted orders drowning in the crash of exploding bombs. What people don't know is that the worst parts of war, the deepest, dirtiest parts of any conflict, are always much quieter than that. I've been there, and usually the worst stories are written in sentences composed of a single scream punctuated by gunfire. It happens on nights like this one, in wars like this, with sounds such as these.

The boy's father broke free of the crowd and shouldered aside a thug holding an automatic weapon. He cradled the cooling body of his offspring as he screamed his impotent rage at the armed men all around. "You cruel bastard! You piece of *grit*! How could you? He was just a boy! You took him from me! You took him from me!"

The murderer was still for only a second or two before the pure rush of power evident in his rictus grin was corroded by the weeping of the distraught father. His next words were ladled out scathingly. "Yes, how could I be so cruel?"

Another shot rang out and father joined son on the faux marble floor, his brains splashing across the open Bible like the vomit of a demon. The murderer ejected his magazine in the deafening quiet of the Ninth Street Cathlist Church and loaded a fresh one. The weapon clicked and clattered like a bug feasting on a corpse. "All right, now... who's going to put an end to this?"

Again, the silent watcher reported. "Now four down. Best move people, or–"

My angry reply cut him off. "No commentary, Archer, just hold and report."

Across the packed hall of worshipers, collection plates were passed to take everything of value. Criminals, like deacons, accepted the tribute to their leader, a false and bloody god. Chains dangled from their ragged clothes, clinking like bells as they walked among the flock. They shared smiles at the sheer terror of their charges, laughing at one another as they bragged about which mothers and daughters they would rape should the opportunity arise. Their leader began sauntering along the altar dais like a carnival showman, kicking up his heels and waving his gun like a sick combination between a fairy godmother's wand and grim reaper's scythe.

"Ladies and gentleman, my name is Juan and I'll be your host for the evening. Be quiet and we won't kill you all." At those words the congregation shivered, glancing guiltily at one another, obviously wondering not if anyone else would die, but how many and who. Juan smiled, breathing deeply of their fear as his burning eyes, and his aim, settled on the elderly priest. Standing at the foot of the two freshest martyrs to enter God's Kingdom, the holy man appeared at the verge of collapse. "Now, Padre, I know that Maria Ortega sent your church ten grand. The banks are down, so it had to come in as cash. The IgBank has frozen account creation from Persephone, and so it still has to be in the building. We are here to collect that cash. We want it, and we want it now."

Unnoticed words flashed back and forth in the air, colored in a multitude of voices. "Pair Two on over-watch. Pair Three on over-watch. Pair Four stacked and packed. Pair Five stacked and packed. Pair Six in position, target sighted."

My breathless reply soundlessly echoed back. "Pair One and Actual *en route*. Hold for my action order."

Back on the floor of the church, the weeping Father Gallego looked out upon his terrified congregation. He flung a silent prayer from inside his soul and took a deep breath to steady his voice. "My son, there is no money."

Those dangerous words hung in the air, threatening to descend in a lead rain and turn the church into a mausoleum. The gangers scattered throughout the nave shuffled uncomfortably. Juan scratched his head with the cheap, polymer-frame pistol, face screwed up with the effort of making rusty mental gears crunch against his hunger, rage, and the dregs of his last drug high.

"Bull*grit*." He raised the gun and blindly pulled the trigger. A nine-millimeter bullet rocketed outward and slammed into the breastbone of Lucia Fernandez. Gallego moaned as the wispy, plain young woman looked at the spreading dark stain on her chest. She tried to speak, but only let loose a spray of bloody foam as parishioners on every side simultaneously tried to catch her and take cover in the pews. Without even a further glance in the direction of Lucia, Juan leveled the smoking barrel of his weapon directly at the priest. "Tell me something I want to hear, Padre."

"I'm telling you there is no money, sir. Brother DeMarco and I accepted the donation and took it to the spaceport where we purchased food, clothing, blankets, and heaters to help the congregation during this time—"

Juan sneered and continued to stare into Gallego's eyes as he pointed the gun outward and pulled the trigger in three, unaimed shots. The congregation stifled screams and one man gasped as a bullet bit at his arm.

Tears streamed freely down Father Gallego's face as his hands kneaded his prayer beads into knots. Sweat beaded his brow, and his face was drained of color, but his voice barely wavered as he tried desperately for neutral tones. "You've got to believe me. Go see for yourself! The supplies are in the basement. You could take them. You could sell them!"

The gunman fired blindly again, eliciting a yelp from one of his own crewmembers near the point of impact. Unnoticed or uncaring, Juan never looked away from the holy man even as he pressed the smoking weapon against the priest's chest. "You are not proving to be as useful as I had hoped, Padre."

Father Gallego shut his eyes, trembling as tears peaked from the corners of his lids. Then, without warning, his face calmed. Subtle ripples washed away the fear and terror from him, leading his entire being into a state of almost supernatural calm. The priest walked to the center of the dais and raised his arms. He looked at the frightened faces, most of whom he knew as well as if they were his own children. There was only one gift he could give them. "My brethren, let us pray…"

Together, the people of the Ninth Street Cathlist Church bowed their heads, closed their eyes, and spoke as one, beseeching heaven in voices desperate and afraid. "Our Father, Who art in Heaven, hallowed be Thy name…"

Juan saw his control over the situation fading, his chance to make the big score dwindling. All the fine things, all the big plans for that money slipping through his fingers. "Goddammit."

From on high, Archer's voice whispered, "Boss, this guy's getting unstable."

"…Thy Kingdom come, Thy will be done, on Earth as it is in Heaven."

"Goddammit," Juan said again, the word gaining momentum inside his chest. A lifetime of cheap booze and rampant drug use flashed across seared neurons, shorting out paths like acid snipping steel threads.

Archer watched the gunman's face contort in the throes of approximated thought, obviously going nowhere fast. "Boss, he's about to lose it."

"Give us this day, our daily bread…"

Every option led to failure and every face mocked this fiasco. Years of degradation provided twisted paths that spun back upon themselves in serpentine knots, all leading into a funnel that began to spark like a nuclear furnace, radiating pure hatred. "GODDAMMIT!"

"Captain…"

"…and forgive us our debts, as we forgive our debtors…"

Juan placed the hot barrel to the back of the priest's head, his entire universe of opportunities squandered, and bad decisions embraced, collapsing down to be personified in the body of this holy man. "GOD DAMN YOU PEOPLE TO HELL!"

His finger tightened on the trigger-

"Lead us not unto temptation..."

Lungs burning, legs aching, we reached the door and I screamed, "ACTION! ACTION! ACTION!"

Four flash-bangs were lobbed, hissing and spitting, into the room.

"...but deliver us from evil-"

Two rifles whispered, spitting steel-jacketed lead bullets at just under the speed of sound. The hooligan by the altar jerked violently as one projectile blew through his skin, his ribcage, his heart, and his spine. His automatic rifle fell from limp fingers, clattering loudly against the desperate prayers. The sound distracted Juan just before the second bullet entered his right temple and ruptured his skull like a ripe fruit.

The explosive canisters detonated just as the corpse of Juan collapsed to the fake marble floor. Light flooded every corner of the room, burning eyes even as an impossibly loud concussion punished every ear.

"BREACH! BREACH! BREACH!" Then both light and sound vanished. In the void left behind, black clad bulky shapes crashed through doors, splintering frames and unleashing death in tightly controlled bursts.

The scattered thugs moved their hands from the needles jabbing at their eyes to clutch their chests as ten-millimeter bullets found their marks like curses from the grave. A silver giant bounded out from a door in the east aisle and swung his hand like a racket, hammering into the back of a criminal's skull and sending the whole distended mass flying over the pews. I moved behind him, sighting over my weapon and quickly acquiring a target. My hands locked around the gun, controlling its jump as three bullets streaked forth and carved out the heart of a blinded ganger. Two more sniping whispers sucked the life from two more criminals as the suppressed ten-millimeter machine carbines huffed like angry bulls. Looking through the sight on my weapon with one eye, I scanned with the other, left and right, ready to fire.

Then over the communications link came the voices of the *Radiation Angels* as each team checked in.

"Clear!"

"Clear!"

The Key to Damocles

"Clear!"

"Clear!"

"Clear!"

I finished my sweep, finding nothing more than huddled victims and dead enemies. "Clear."

And like that, it was over.

I checked the chronograph in the upper right corner of my HUD. The entire breach had taken fifteen seconds.

The assigned mercenaries moved to the exits and kept watch as Pair Five came in from outside, having just killed the three criminals keeping watch on the getaway vehicles. The people shuffled and moved only slightly as Logan walked among them, his silvery metallic chassis towering above them like the avatar of a saint. At four meters in height, the cyborg could simply step over the pews, his eyes, scanners, and detectors sweeping over the huddled parishioners, looking for weapons. It was unlikely that a street gang would have the brainpower to put a sleeper agent in the crowd to assassinate anyone coming to the rescue; after all, they hadn't thought anyone was coming. Much more likely at the moment was someone getting the idea of being a hero and attacking one of their rescuers in a misguided attempt to overcome guilt or shame. Still, I'd rather be too cautious than too dead.

To my right, the priest moved forward tentatively. "My son, there is no need for that now—"

I felt bad about it, but I trained my gun on him for just a moment, stopping him in his tracks. I tongued on the external speaker to the C^2 helmet. "Father: please stand very, very still."

To his credit, he stood very still.

My weapon's angry muzzle scanned back over the cowering congregation, who even now were wondering what worse fate had descended upon them from the night. Logan reached the center aisle and paused only a moment before giving a thumbs-up. I barked a quick order over the commlink, sending Ortega out to join Logan. Once there, the Electronic Warfare Officer set up a small backpack on self-extending legs. Switches sounded like tiny firecrackers in the absolute silence of the church and the signal booster device began to hum with life. Then Ortega plugged a cord into his shovel-like scanner. Four seconds later, the electronic ensemble confirmed that the people of Ninth

Street Cathlist Church and my team were the only people for hundreds of yards in any direction. There were no primed energy weapons in the crowd. No unaccounted-for explosives, including propellants used in firearms. Ortega lifted his visor to expose his face and signaled all clear.

I called for our medics before tonguing the external speaker up to a hefty volume setting and addressing the crowd. "Ladies and gentlemen, my name is Captain Todd Rook. We are *The Radiation Angels*. We were sent by the Ortega family to help, so you are safe. Try to stay calm and this will be over very soon. Now, if you are sitting by a wounded person, raise your hand and some of my team members will come out to begin first aid. Otherwise, remain where you are for a few moments so the medics can move quickly and easily to reach the wounded."

Hands went up, acting as signposts for the medics: Ansef and Tsang. The two moved awkwardly because of the bulk of their heavily laden surgical kits, but the flock shifted to the side and let them pass without comment. Pent up fear began to rush out of the room, being replaced with a hesitant hope as families took several seconds to hold one another and relish the idea of being alive. I cut the external feed to the communication system and ordered Pair Three to guard the street in front and sent Four out back. The rest were tasked with collecting the criminals' weapons or helping Ansef or Tsang as they judged which victims were in most dire need of medical attention.

The priest approached from my left, his hands in plain view and held slightly out to each side. Realizing that I still had my damn rifle out, I quickly placed it on 'safe' and slung it over my shoulder. I savaged myself inside my own head. *That's how friendly fire happens, grithead.*

The priest relaxed even more and awkwardly held out his hands, caught between seeking a handshake and an embrace.

"My son, bless you and your men." His words expanded inside his throat as the pressure on his mind was released. He glanced about at the left-over carnage and tears sprang anew from his eyes. Then he looked at his feet and saw the glassy eyes of a twelve-year-old boy. "I had almost lost...lost faith...that...Oh, God."

Everyone's reaction to war is different in the details, but it always strikes to the core of their being. Some are elated at being alive, while some are torn with guilt at having lived. Others

19

The Key to Damocles

become enraged at the injustice, and others collapse into emotionally dead black holes. Some of us develop coping skills that allow us to function, to contain the psychological wreckage until later when it could be hammered out with the help of friends or shrinks. Some never manage to make sense of it all, and have to simply drown the ruined memories in alcohol, or sear them away with even stronger stuff. Say what you want, but you can't make it out of a war zone without a scratch. Nobody leaves untouched.

I reached out and took the priest by the arm, steadying him just as his legs looked like they would give way. I led him away from the altar over to the empty choir loft where he could sit and we could talk away from the others. I took a little longer than necessary to crack the seals on the C^2 helmet. Partially, it gave him a moment to compose himself, and partially I wasn't quite done mentally whipping myself for having an unsecured weapon pointed at people who weren't targets. I pulled out a ring on the rear of the right shoulder plate of my articulated armor, exposing a small hook upon which I placed the helmet. I finished and turned back to the holy man who was staring at me like I had two heads.

"You're black," he said.

I am really beginning to hate this fragging planet. I forced a good-natured smirk and stifled a sigh as I moved a stray dreadlock out of my face and tucked it into the tied-back mass behind my head. "Yes, Father."

He floundered for a second. "Oh, I'm sorry, my son, I just assumed when you said you were sent by the Ortegas-"

I shook my head and dismissed the subject. "*De nada*, *Padre*. But I do need a favor... can you direct me to where we can call the police, er, *policia*?"

He blinked at me, clearly nonplussed. "Sir, we can call them, but I don't think they will come."

We were both distracted as one man erupted into screams as Ansef worked on him. The medic waved at Logan who placed his two massive hands on the patient and, by expending the tiniest fraction of his strength, held him in place as if he was nailed to the floor. As much as I hate to see anyone suffer, at least it was acting as a macabre distraction from the priest and me. About a quarter of the congregation had already seen me, and none of them were very happy to see a 'black' man in their church.

I closed my eyes and tried to sweep aside the exhaustion that lurked there. The *Angels* had landed on Persephone at 13:20 local time and had been running to take care of this emergency ever since. Between interrogating the snitch at the Ortega home, fruitlessly tracking the gangers through their usual hangouts, and finally planning the assault on the church, we had burned three days' worth of sleep and a hundred liters of adrenaline in a matter of hours. I don't remember sitting down, but when I opened my eyes, I was in a chair next to the mournful priest, my helmet on my lap. A weeping grandmother came forward, speaking to the priest in rapid-fire Spanish. His tears abated immediately as he snapped into the role of comforter, something he obviously had a great deal of practice with. I really needed some information from the priest, but I didn't feel like I could horn in on this particular conversation.

I only knew a few dozen phrases and terms in Spanish, enough to be able to speak the more common Spanish/English hybrid, called MexiCali for some reason, but not nearly enough to keep up with either of them when they spoke the unmixed language. My adrenaline petered out, leaving my blood thin and weak. I barely fought off a yawn, shoved my head into the electronics laden helmet to get it off my lap, crossed my arms, and closed my eyes again.

Just for a second…

CHAPTER 2: FIVE WEEKS AGO

Planet Lucia Sanchez 7,
Peaceful, 12:31, 9/24/2662

I was going to hit the guy on my left first. It was only fair; he was the largest and smelliest.

The guy behind me, 'Squeaky', was nearly urinating on himself, so I tagged him for a sendoff kick, but only after I had taken 'Stinky' down, and after I had enveloped the leader in front of me, 'Moustache', in a joint lock. All that was left after that was to decide whether 'Joe Average' to my right would get a little pain, or a lot, and whether it would be before I came close to breaking the arm of his boss, or after.

Decisions, decisions.

I didn't contemplate drawing the slim-line concealable laser pistol at the small of my back, not unless this got a lot uglier than I thought it would. That was the problem with having a deadly weapon; if the situation didn't come under control immediately once you pulled it, you had to use it. Otherwise, you ran the very real possibility of having it taken away and turned upon you. The point of having a deadly weapon was not to pull it when you didn't intend to use it, but to pull it only when there was no other choice. It shouldn't come to that. After all, these were nonviolent people. They were just forgetting that fact at the moment. My name is Todd Rook. I am a violent person, and that makes me the perfect person to remind them.

The leader leaned in closer, narrowing his eyes and twitching his moustache at me in irritation. "I told you to leave, mercenary. We don't want you in Peaceful."

The owner of Peaceful World Market, Tim Robbins, was frozen in place behind the counter, hoping and praying that his store wasn't about to become the scene of a beating. I reached between Moustache and Average and took a soft drink from the pile of supplies I had collected on the counter. I forced a casual pace as I twisted off the cap and drained a few swallows. "Just so I know what my options are, let's say I decide to complete buying what I came into town for, load up my flier, and leave in my own good time. What happens then?"

Stinky smiled a bit and cracked walnut-sized knuckles. Squeaky behind me let slip a strange, high-pitched worried noise. Average tensed a bit and Moustache replied in what was supposed to be a dangerous whisper. "Then we four will toss you out on your ass and have your vehicle impounded."

I took another pull on the mostly full soda, gripping the hard plastic bottle by the base so it could be used to bean Average in the head just before I arm-locked his boss. "You seem pretty certain of yourself for a people dedicated to the principles of nonviolence."

"Not all of us have always been nonviolent."

"Really? This nonviolent, well, semi-nonviolent, philosophy of yours is fascinating." It was time to change tactics. These guys were still too confident. I had a hunch that if I hurt one of them a little, I wouldn't have to hurt them all a lot. "Perhaps you could explain it to me?"

I set down the soda on the counter and began to push my way past Stinky to reach the grain-products isle. "I mean, is it possible for you to actually hurt someone, just as long as no real damage is done? I only ask because I'd hate to be thought of as a miscreant..."

I was almost past Stinky when he reached out a hand and clamped it onto my shoulder. Casually, slowly, apparently effortlessly, I took hold of his thumb and twisted hard. The burly thug melted to the floor like a block of Styrofoam splashed with gasoline, gasping and twitching in pain. All good humor fled from my voice, "...and that information will be critical over the next ten seconds."

I twisted a little farther, and moved Stinky's wrist backward while my other hand casually picked over a few loaves of fresh bread. The front door chime sung, and I hoped it wasn't backup for the Stooges. "I mean, how do extremely painful but fairly harmless little things, like a joint lock, fit into the legal system here? And how exactly do you expect to force someone to back down once you realize that he has about a decade of real-world combat experience on you?"

"They call the Marshal," a deep, rich voice called out from behind them, "who happens to have some training in that area."

I'm something of a connoisseur of pre-Exile cowboy movies and I swear to God that, minus the hint of country drawl, this guy had John Wayne's voice. He was a huge man, at least a decimeter taller than me, and I'm not a short guy. Once powerful arms and legs had softened with age, however, and lines had begun to creep across his face. Still, his eyes were hard with resolve, Nubian features set in what I had come to think of as a 'command scowl'. Like a shaven-head African version of Patton, he shouldered past Moustache and Average and rested a large hand on a push pistol like he knew how to use it. He took a second or two to size up the situation, which made him smarter than I gave him credit for. "Sir, would you mind letting go of Hank?"

"Oh, sure." I let Stinky/Hank go and he hissed and scuttled away in a fair imitation of a roach.

The Marshal ushered the four goons out, and I continued my shopping experience relatively undisturbed. I picked over the perishables I would need for my trip, leaving behind the heavy canned and expensive preserved goods. I had removed all fresh fruits, vegetables, nuts, and grains from my ship months beforehand, but I had plenty of prepackaged preserved staples aboard already. Preserved, packaged in plastic, and irradiated to kill off bacteria, the stuff would stay edible for a decade. Unfortunately, it still tasted like grainy cardboard.

I assembled a respectably sized pile on the counter and Tim, the proprietor, stopped staring at his feet and began running the food over an imager. The little machine looked at the item, categorized it, and charged the card slotted into the register which in turn deducted the credits from my obscenely sized DeBiers Intergalactic Bank account. Hands working like lightning, Tim soon had my purchases bagged without ever having to look up at me.

I dialed in as much sincerity as I could muster. "Sorry about the trouble, Tim."

He stole a quick look in my eyes before dropping his gaze back to my belt buckle and shrugging. "No trouble, Mr. Rook."

Unspoken words hung in the air, second after second, like a grotesquely strong fart in an elevator. Slowly, with some finality, I picked up the first two bags and ferried them outside to the military surplus personnel flier at the curb. Tim made no move to help, which he had always done before. Across the street, the Marshal was quietly berating the four goons and drawing a crowd of onlookers to boot. I went back inside to grab the next

25

The Key to Damocles

load, chased by the angry stares and dirty looks of Peaceful town folk.

It really wasn't my fault. When the real estate agent sold me half of the northern continent on Lucia Sanchez 7, he didn't say that my next-door neighbors would be a group of people dedicated to nonviolence, people to whom I, as a mercenary, would be a pariah. I grabbed the next few bags and went back outside.

Every year, movements like this one happen. They are all from high-crime planets: fuzzyheaded people too afraid to be able to fight, too religious to consider fighting, or too rich to have to fight the plague of criminal behavior. These upper-middle class types sell off most of their lives, pack up whatever's left, and catch a colony ship to the closest dirtball on which they can buy a significant stake. It's very much like living in an American 'old west' town... if one squints enough to disguise the water purification plants, air conditioner units, personal fliers, and robot laborers that is. Settlers like these dream of a life far away from violence and set up communities made of dirt roads, prefabricated homes, and whatever lunatic laws they can envision.

The problem is, it never works. Violence may be a noun, but it isn't a thing you can run away from. It resides inside the soul of every human, and no matter how carefully you screen your fellow colonists, it will boil to the surface like tar.

Most never learn this fact because they starve to death at the first hard drought, are scoured clean by pirates, or are raided and taken by slavers. Hardship doesn't care how moral you think you are, and criminals have always preferred disarmed prey. Not that any of this matters. Like hard-core socialists, anarchists, or communists, these people have based their lives around a political theory that has become a religion offered up by a charismatic prophet. It may be disproved time and again, but facts have very little effect on something

I finished loading the flier and shut the cargo door in the back. It was a good beast: boxy, dented, and ugly, but willing to work at a moment's notice without a hint of hesitation. I climbed into the cab and started the preflight sequence as the Marshal flagged me down. I shut down the systems and stepped down to

26

the street, fingers instinctively patting at my pockets for a smoke. They found nothing, but it didn't stop them from looking.

The Marshal walked over from the sizable crowd on the opposite side of the street. His gait was measured and slow, brave but cautious. His eyes were scanning my vehicle and me for trouble, and his shoulders were tight. I saw that his pushgun's retaining strap had been unsnapped. It was clear that he was about to tell me something I wasn't going to like and was bracing for a fight. I checked my watch and determined it would probably be about five minutes before his backup could get here from the outlying communities or another town. I opened a hatch on my flier and slipped into a covertly armored vest. Maybe he recognized the brand, or perhaps just guessed at its purpose, but this gave him pause before he finished sauntering up. I readied myself and reined in my temper as far as I could.

He stopped just out of reach and addressed me like the very picture of a small-town cop. "Rook, I think we need to have a talk."

"Really, Marshal? Do you need me to testify against those four men?"

This knocked the wind out his sails a bit, forcing him to rethink this entire encounter. "Well, I don't think there's any need for that, besides they never touched you. In fact, you might be facing some charges…"

Well, either he was lying or he had bought the lies of Dopey, Dippy, Dingleberry and Dumbshit. Stinky/Hank had touched me first, and that classified what I did as self-defense in any sane justice system. While he blathered on, I checked the street. Still no deputies. I was sure that if he was going to press the matter of my arrest, then he was just stalling for time until they got here. Waiting for backup was wise for him, and stupid of me. It was time to end the conversation. "Are you arresting me, Marshal?"

This stopped him for a second and he looked back and forth, searching the streets for the exact same thing I had. "Well, no…no, I'm not."

At least not without backup, huh Marshal? "Well then this is the obligatory 'We don't like your type in this here town' speech."

"You've got quite a mouth on you, don't you, Mercenary?"

The Key to Damocles

Despite my best efforts, I could feel my skin prickle with heat as blood began to pound in my temples. "Marshal, a little more than a year ago, I was targeted by a megalomaniac admiral in control of a military, the resources of an industrialized planet, and access to any mercenaries he could buy." *More or less.* "He chased me across the known galaxy, looking for my blood. How much do you think a few pacifist villagers scare me?"

He gave me an appraising look. I don't know what he saw, but his hand moved slowly away from his weapon. I reached up to the cab of the flier and pulled myself in. "If you aren't going to arrest me, then we are done here."

He called after me, "It chills me to think what would have happened if you had been wearing a gun in that store."

I thought about the self-defense laser pistol concealed in the holster at the small of my back under my shirt, unseen, untouched, and unused. "Marshal, you don't know what you're talking about."

And I slammed the door shut in his face. Thirty seconds later, I had cleared preflight. The computer checked to make sure there was no one dangerously close to the vehicle, de-chalked the engines, and fed aeroline into the burn chamber in screaming gulps. Dust rushed out from beneath the heavy beast, and the ground smoked from the exhaust just before the flier leapt straight into the sky. The high efficiency engines roared as they drank in the highly volatile fuel, propelling the boxy flier upward into the clouds, leaving the Marshal and his crowd of murmuring gawkers behind.

At this point, a good cigarette would have been just what the doctor ordered. Well, maybe not an M.D., but definitely a psychiatrist. I quit ten years ago, but in times of high stress, the cravings always return. The last one I tried had nearly made me puke, but the desire, almost a physical need, remained. I quit so that I could keep up with the heavily physical job I do. Well… did. Once I retired, however, I felt that I should be allowed to take up the habit where I left off.

Sometimes, you just can't go back again.

That thought hit me with almost physical force, and I winced. A growl started up in my chest as I jerked the control yoke to the left, bringing the craft around to true north, and punched the throttle. The airspeed indicator crept up to 500kph as land gave way to sea, and sea to shore, and then shore to hilly plains. Almost an hour later, I had circled part of the immense perimeter of my property before being able to pull into a massive canyon on the western edge. I slowed down and piloted roughly down the center, wary of the walls rising two kilometers high and one kilometer to either side. A few lazy turns led to a three hundred kilometer, straight-as-an-arrow trench where the canyon terminated in a massive cave.

I cut the throttle even more and redirected the jet thrust downward, hovering in place as I found an area clear of strewn supplies or scurrying bots to set the craft down. I snapped buttons and toggles, cutting power to the beast. I hopped down from the cab and summoned over a labor robot and gave it very clear instructions to take the food to the galley. The planet that exported this model must have a strong Japanese influence because it bowed its human-shaped head and torso deeply—a strange programmed-in social quirk I had never bothered to override—and rolled off on tank-like rubber treads.

Behind me, a heavily synthesized bass voice threaded itself through the mechanical sounds of crackling welders, clacking toolbots, and clanging laborers. "So, how did it go, Captain?"

"You don't have to call me Captain yet, Logan," I tossed over my shoulder, a little too acidly.

His massive shoulders pumped up and down once. "I don't want to train myself out of a good habit, Captain."

"How's the refueling going?"

"By the book, sir. The protective layers inside the fuel pods seem to have done their job and the shielding on the fueling lines is containing the radiation just fine. We should be full in about an hour." His bare feet clanked on the floor, shattering any bits of gravel trapped underneath as he came closer. "But you didn't answer my question."

I reached under the seat in the cab, pulling out the pistol-length, double-barreled, gauss flechette weapon. I broke open the breech of the barrels and pulled out the two plastic shells—sixteen tiny darts wrapped in a plastic sabot—and dropped them into my vest pocket. "Badly, Logan. It went very badly, like it always does."

The Key to Damocles

I flipped the pistol closed savagely. He watched me store the weapon in a lock box in the back of the beast. "I should have come with you, sir."

I turned to look at Logan, taking in every detail. I had fought and bled with him for years, so I figured that I knew as much about Logan as any man alive, and I knew very little. I guessed that he was an Earther, a first-generation Exile who had once stood on humanity's home planet before being tossed off for any number of crazy reasons. Since then, he had ceased to be human in much anything but shape and mind.

There are thirteen types of cyborgs, robot parts, pieces or whole bodies into which a human nervous system can be installed. Type ones are most basic, involving barely functional abbreviated appendages used on low tech or frontier worlds where nothing else is available. Type twos are functionally human in almost every respect. Type threes begin replacing limbs with tools or weapons that interact with the human brain through translator chips. This melding of cybernetics and bionics give these tools the finesse of a natural appendage. The further toward the magic number thirteen you go, the less human cyborgs become until you actually reach the thirteens. These are indistinguishable from humans in any way, and most people don't even believe they exist. I do because I've seen one. To be honest, I saw two.

Logan was a type two. Which is not to say that he could be mistaken as a human, only that he functioned as one. He had two arms, two legs, a head and torso, but after that, the similarities began to blur. His hide was a composite laminate of titanium, ceramics, polymers, and alloys over a four-meter tall, high-density skeleton. His internal organs had been replaced a long time ago, leaving spaces available for detection electronics, a holographic sonar unit, equipment hatches and at least one sidearm holster. He could lift over two tons, run at a little under seventy kilometers per hour, and bend steel bars with his thumb the way school children snap pencils. Of all his features, his head was least human. It was a featureless plate interrupted only by small clusters of electronic eyes set in a 'T'-shaped opening. Instead of ears, he had two wings, like the flared decorations on a knight's helm. They moved back and forth as the internal electronics scanned for any number of signals. I had to believe that this was purposeful; his was a two-hundred-year-old design called a 'Templar model'.

Some people, including the population of Peaceful, would argue that he was no longer human at all, but an engine of destruction made for nothing but war. That was nothing but fear and ignorance, the principal components of all bigotry. I have never known a more dedicated soldier, a truer moral compass, or a more loyal friend. Logan was the oldest living member of *The Radiation Angels* and that bought him a lot of privacy about his past. He had pulled my fat out of the fire on too many cases to count and that's what mattered. I shook my head and chuckled at him, feeling the tension and anger escape from me. "Yeah, I'm sure they would have loved you in town."

He cocked his head to the side, becoming the very picture of innocence. "Captain, I am a very likable person."

"Of course you are, but I think they'd be more concerned that you are a very likable person who happens to be bulletproof."

"There is nothing offensive about being bulletproof."

I ground my teeth a little. "That depends on how helpless you like your neighbors."

Electronic Warfare Officer Ortega appeared out of the fueling shed where he had been monitoring the pressure gauges. His coveralls were spattered with oils, fluids, and dirt, testifying to how hard he had been working at getting the ship operational. "*Hola*, Captain. How'd it go?"

My father had all but trained me out of rolling my eyes, with the help of his menacingly large leather belt, but at times like this I almost let one slip. I hiked my thumb over my shoulder. "Fresh produce is being loaded now. We should be off planet by nightfall."

Ortega, a small, stoutly built Latino-extraction guy, had picked up quite a few more kilos during the last year of peace, but for a second he looked like the lean, competent Electronic Warfare Officer I had led into battle for nearly two years. His eyes drank in the form of the leviathan behind us, and we turned to join his gaze.

"Man, I missed this ship," he murmured.

Servos quietly whined as Logan nodded in agreement. "She is beautiful."

The Key to Damocles

Which just goes to show you that beauty is at least nine parts familiarity to one part aesthetics. Well, maybe seven to three. As spacecraft go, she did have her own kind of style. But beauty? She resembled nothing so much as an oversized submarine with a massive bank of nuclear reaction drive engines affixed to the back. Relatively tiny wings, or planes, were placed on the engines, a sensor tower at the top, and near the nose. These provided some aerodynamic maneuverability and lift in an atmosphere but still looked like a hasty afterthought to me. At forty meters tall, sixty-five meters wide, and a hair over eight hundred and fifty meters long, her size and soft curving lines belied her deadly purpose. From the front, she looked like a slightly flattened oval studded with banks of man-sized laser cannons, Logan-sized plasma cannons, four innocuously small torpedo banks, and several stubby defensive-shot canister cannons.

On the forward right panel of the spacecraft was her one decoration. A beautiful blonde seraph stood straight and strong, the very picture of righteous determination. Aloft, she held a massive silver sword shining with the light of vengeance. In her left hand was a small round shield painted with the furnace symbol that designated a nuclear threat. Above her, emblazoned in proud letters, was the name of the craft: *Deadly Heaven*. Beneath her in slightly larger letters, as befitting their importance, was the name of the mercenary crew she faithfully served: *The Radiation Angels*.

I don't know why, I'm not overtly religious after all, but the sight of her has always moved me. After a day like this, it was enough to moisten my eyes. I cleared my throat and blinked at the tears as I moved toward the craft. "You two are getting maudlin. I'm going to need help getting that tug attached to the front landing gear so we can pull this hulk out for liftoff. Now, come on! We need to get this craft ready for flight to *Haven*."

Ortega acted like I had sucker punched him. *"Haven?"*

I got onboard a small, wheeled cart and started the electric engine with the flip of a switch. "Yep."

"Captain, we need to get to Persephone, now!"

I turned to face the *EWO* and molded my features into my very best 'I am not *gritting* you' face. "Ortega, I know you are

32

worried, and that things are bad, but we are going to need backup... at least one team, maybe two."

"What about all the other *Angels?*"

I turned away from him and took a datapad from a waiting bot. I checked off the list one by one. "All of them are retired except for Reeves and O'Leary, and they are already on scene."

"They'd come if you asked, sir."

I wrote down another set of orders on the pad and gave it back to the mechanical engineer. "Even if I managed to rally four or five, which I doubt would happen, it won't be enough. We need to put out a call, vet soldiers, and train them up like a real crew. We can't go in all *cowboy* and figure on coming back."

His face twisted into tortured lines at hearing the truth. "Really? It worked out pretty well on Mars."

I clenched my jaw and sighed. "That was different."

"How?"

Logan came close to both of us and laid a hand on Ortega's shoulder. "He knew the situation on the ground, Ortega. He knew where he was going and who he was fighting. He had a plan."

Ortega nodded and moved off toward the fueling shack. I tossed Logan a thank you wink and drove toward *Deadly Heaven*. He had saved me from having to either slap down Ortega, or lie to him. I hadn't been blowing smoke at the Marshal in Peaceful: a megalomaniac Admiral had come after the *Angels*, and me personally.

I had planned to play it *cowboy,* dropping onto Mars alone to delay the enemy long enough for the cavalry to arrive. I couldn't ask the team to come along. In large part it was because too many of my soldiers had died on that mission for me to ask them to risk their lives again... partly because I felt, as captain, it was my job to make sure everything worked. It had been stupid. It had been wrong. It was a plan that had made us all multi-millionaires, but it could have also made us all very dead. There were enough dead already. If Logan, O'Leary, and Reeves hadn't hijacked my secret plot and horned in, I would never have come home. It was for that very reason that these two situations couldn't be held up as similar; back then, I really wasn't planning on coming home.

The Key to Damocles

But, that's not something I can say to a subordinate, even an ex-subordinate, even a year later. I shut my eyes, pinched the bridge of my nose, and tried to forget the faces of the dead.

CHAPTER 3: THE LAY OF THE LAND

The voice was too close and too synthetic to be Ortega's, but it was his just the same. My eyes snapped open like twin shutters, but it took a moment before I could swim out through sleep and begin funneling input from my ears to my brain. I tongued on my mic. "Repeat, Ortega."

Even over the radio, I could tell he was not happy. "Ambulances have arrived, Captain, but there's no sign of *policia*."

Something clicked and whirred inside my head, spinning faster and faster as if a motor ran without any belt attached. I flicked my eyes up at the mission clock. I still hadn't gotten to call for local law enforcement, but still, by this time... "Haven't they been called?"

"You better believe it, *Jefe*. My sensors are picking up at least twenty-five different currently active communication units connecting to *Respuesta de la Emergencia*. I checked a few of them; they are still on hold. My non-scientific poll shows about half of these people called the cops, but no one ever answered their call, just an automated hold message."

That made no sense. We had staged from the Ortega Compound less than an hour before. It was located in Mezzo-Americana, another megacity to the north. While it was tense, with reports of a few riots and bombings, the police there were still on duty. Why would things be so bad here, in the capital of Persephone? "Can we reach them?"

"Standard emergency number puts us on hold, and a call on their private *freqs* has gotten me threatened with jail time for improper use of police equipment or something. New California police in this area are a no-show, and the Justice Center has been completely shut down."

"Understood. Wait one." I stared at the holographic tapestries on the walls, each showing different scenes from the Bible. The one across from me was showing the ascension of Jesus to heaven. It struck me how much of a motivation it was to have someone untouchable on high looking over one's shoulder. And that, of course, was the solution to my problem. "Ortega, call up the news stations and let them know a little of what's happened. Set the bad guys' body-bags outside and line up the comm units inside on the first table you see. Leave them on and open so the news crews can see where they are calling."

Ortega's laugh came out as a raw bark. "Yes sir, Captain."

I stood smartly, grasped the rifle near my legs, and slung it over my back. I took a few seconds and stretched to loosen up the tightness that had settled in on my torso. Pins and needles poked at my chest as the cybernetic plates of hardened armor pinched off fibers of muscle that had grown between them since last I did this. A year ago, I had shattered my ribcage and had the armor installed to replace them. While the plate would stop bullets and knives from reaching my organs, and you could hardly see the implantation scars anymore, there were always reminders that a part of me had been broken and replaced. Uncomfortable reminder or not, I needed that excuse to pause and to take in what was going on around me. The disorientation of leaving sleep coupled with the unfamiliar setting made me want to come up shouting orders. For that very reason, I clamped my mouth firmly shut, took off my helmet, and just watched what was going on.

Many years ago, my old boss, Captain Arthur, had told me that sometimes you could do a lot more damage with a hasty order than with a little bit of shut-up. I don't know how much frustration it has saved my men, but it's saved my credibility dozens of times over. As mercenaries, a little faith in a commander is worth a bucket of blood, and if you think that's poetic license, think about it a little longer.

The *Angels* were spread out at the perimeter of the church, with a few grouped at the front doors where the wounded were even now being loaded onto stretchers. Logan was in the center of the room, keeping an eye on everything at once, while Ortega scurried about using a few men for manual labor. Archer was field stripping and cleaning the captured weapons. He was probably wasting his time, but at least it kept him quiet.

The congregation had split up into self-appointed groups. Some sat with those mourning lost loved ones, others had disappeared into the kitchen downstairs to fix soup, coffee, and sandwiches. A group of twenty had taken it upon themselves to clean up the pools of excrement, urine, and blood left by the dead. I thought about stopping them, but I remembered that apparently the *policia* were *de nada*, and thus any evidence they destroyed wouldn't be sought by anyone anyway. Logan caught my eye and gave a minimal thumbs-up. It was just his way of saying *Everything's under control, Captain.*

I nodded back, proud and a little ashamed. Three weeks ago, I had handpicked a single team of twelve men and women, trained them to work together in grueling twenty-hour shifts during the flight, and transported them here where they were exceeding my expectations at every turn. Though I knew as the brains of the outfit it was of paramount importance that I be rested, it still seemed like they were doing the real work while I took a nap.

"You look better." I nearly jumped. The priest had come out of nowhere to offer a steaming cup of coffee. I removed my helmet and hung it on the armor's pop-up hook before I took the mug and smiled a thanks. The taste was hollow and slightly greasy, a sure sign that it was cheap synthetic food. On the bright side, it was wet, hot, and contained not only a quarter of my daily nutritional needs, but enough caffeine to kill a bull elephant.

"*Gracias*, Father…?"

"Gallego, my son." He joined me, shoulder to shoulder, in keeping watch from the altar dais. "And don't beat yourself up over the nap; you needed it." I was about to ask the obvious question when he answered it. "In my profession, you see people punishing themselves all the time for sins, both real and imagined. You needed that nap; it did your soul *mucho bueno*."

To be completely honest, it would do my soul a heap of good to hear just one person say—

"Oh, and thank you, my son." And the priest embraced me, somewhat awkwardly since I was wearing twenty kilos of gear and carrying a mostly full coffee mug. Still, what it lacked in grace, it made up in authenticity. "I should have known the Lord our God would send… angels to our rescue."

He smiled, a warm glow beginning to smooth his worn edges. That is, until he looked behind him and saw the outline of the church's holy book on the altar; a void of brain matter and blood. He appeared to sink back toward guilt and depression, but a deep breath buoyed him up again. He was a strong one, and he would help the others here survive just fine. His travel up and down did leave a few seconds of uncomfortable silence between us. "Sorry I had you at gunpoint, Father Gallego."

He shrugged and smirked tiredly. "I think I understand. It seems like a whole other life when I saw police make a dynamic entry, up close and personal. As I remember, they were fairly cautious too, and with good reason."

That was an answer begging for a question. The thing about it was that I'm a mercenary, and I work with unsavory types all the time. His past was his own business and he had probably told me everything he thought I needed to know already. I stifled my curiosity with a whole different question. "Father, I need your advice. The police aren't coming, and I really don't have any use for those pistols the thugs brought with them. At the same time, your people were a little..." I panicked inside as I searched for the kindest word I could use, "...exposed tonight. I imagine they could use a little personal defense. If I leave the gangers' guns, do you think your flock might...?"

"I don't know. Our interpretation of the scriptures is very rigid, but after tonight..." He tiredly shrugged his shoulders. No one seemed very good at finishing unwelcome thoughts today.

In any case, the wounded were finally being airlifted to a mercy station, and the bad guys were stacked up outside awaiting the coroner, the garbage man, or wild dogs; whichever came first. Considering the ransacked condition of the New California streets, I was betting on the latter. This meant our job here was done and it was time to go. I stuffed my head back into the C^2 helmet and called the team to a rally-point outside. I gave orders to Archer over the comm to begin distributing the weapons discreetly. This was easier than expected since everyone wanted a chance to say goodbye to the *Angels*.

It was done slowly, with many hugs and well-wishes from a grateful congregation. A gaggle of children swarmed over Ansef, giggling despite the horror of this night. There would be weeks, if not years, of nightmares from this ordeal, but eventually they would either cope or forget. Children are especially good at that. Logan stood at the corner of the building, probing the shadows with senses beyond human; he caused a few furrowed brows to smooth when they saw him. They would feel afraid when he had gone but would remember him and watch the shadows themselves, which is a good habit for everyone to get into.

Archer stopped to give a few pointers on handgun use to one old, determined man. A few others listened closely, tightly cradling their own weapons, symbols of newfound security in an uncertain world. The talk about shot placement and the concept of a 'double tap' sent shivers of revulsion through the most of the crowd. We may have saved their lives, but we left a peaceful people torn with doubt about their choices, their future, and, worst yet, their faith. The only fact that softened the blow was that had we not come, the result would have been far worse.

That's the way it usually is for mercenaries.

Milling at the edge of the crowd, a few soldiers sat mostly untouched in the outpouring of thanks. Each one, helmet removed, was noticeably of African descent. Considering the situation on Persephone it was to be expected, but it was still a crappy thing to do to someone who had risked death to save you.

No one said it was a fair universe. I pressed a button on my integrated forearm pad which signaled that we were ready for pick up.

Lieutenant/Flight John—I *grit* you not—Doe appeared in the air moments later, bringing in the armored urban exploratory craft. I hired him into the *Angels* because he had the resume— rap sheet actually—of an illegal urban flier aficionado. As I had hoped, he was turning out to be an ace urban combat pilot. The aeroline driven engines whined as he banked tightly just over the tops of the buildings and sank like a stone to street level. The boxy, armored craft retracted its short wings and pointed its engines downward, halting its fall only feet before the cruel fist of gravity deformed the flier on the concrete. The craft spun like a grazed piñata and then settled into an empty space between burnt out crawlers and fliers, hitting the turf the instant the landing gear reached full extension and not a moment before. His voice came in clearly over the comm channel. "Hell yeah, *Angels.* Yon *Cherubic* chariot awaits."

Then again, his military manner could use some work. Logan and I shared a look and he just shook his head. We waved to the crowd again and boarded *The Cherub.* Its engines roared to life, showing off the diapered, cigar smoking, nuclear bomb riding, stubby-winged angel painted on the side. Don't ask me, I don't know where Logan comes up with the ideas for nose art. And speaking of Logan, I really had something to talk to him about, and I was hoping it wouldn't get unpleasant.

There was a feeling of disorientation, extreme pressure, and constipation as the craft jumped from the asphalt. Seconds later, *The Cherub* was speeding at rooftop level across New California toward home base in the city of Mezzo-Americana. Only once the team had settled down did I toggle on the radio.

"Logan?" From across the crowded jump seats, he looked at me. "Tac-freq nine."

Some of the *Angels* looked around at each other, since they didn't know what 'Tac-freq nine', pronounced 'tack-freak nine', and properly Tactical Frequency number Nine, was. This was good since I needed to talk to Logan alone, and in a crowded urban flier, there really was no other way to yell at him discreetly except via encrypted radio transmission. "Master Sergeant?"

"Will it help if I say I'm sorry, Captain?"

"Sorry for what, Master Sergeant?"

"I don't know, but the last time you called me only by rank, I had just finished saving your life."

"When was that?"

"Haverson 4."

"Isn't that when you 'saved me' by crashing a half a million-credit flier into an enemy bunker?"

"Some people have no gratitude."

Say what you want, but Logan is a hell of a straight man. I stifled a laugh, then tried to harden my voice a little, let him know this wasn't a social call. "Tell me about the ganger, Logan."

"Which ganger, sir?"

"The one you played volleyball with."

There was the slightest pause. "I neutralized him immediately, Captain."

Don't dodge my question, Logan. "You decapitated him with the flat of your fragging hand. That's not tactical advantage, a stealthy kill, or anything else. It's unprofessional and that's not like you. I need you to be as much like you as possible right now, Master Sergeant. So, are you having a psychotic episode I should be aware of, or what?"

40

Logan's posture shifted, all of his flat motors tightening, bringing his joints in close. If he was human, I'd say he looked tense. "I am sorry, sir."

"Sorry really doesn't cut it. I need to know if you have personal issues, here."

Another pause. "No...no, sir."

"I don't believe you."

"Then would you believe me if I said I had issues, but I can get a handle on them?"

It took me a long time to answer. "Yes, Master Sergeant. But only because it's you."

Across from me, the cyborg turned his head, pointing his visual sensors out the window where the moon shone upon the tops of broken buildings. "Thank you, Captain."

"Logan, if you need to talk—"

"No. No thank you, Captain Rook. I would if I could, but..."

Like I said, no one seemed very good at finishing unwelcome thoughts today. I wondered about how much I didn't know about the silver sentinel that seemed more a part of the *Angel's* name and ethos than even myself. It only took half an hour to fly to the Ortega Compound after that, it just seemed like forever.

CHAPTER 4: CONSCIOUSNESS INTERRUPTUS

Maria Ortega, mother of Electronic Warfare Officer Manuel Ortega, was a towering and fiery colossus distilled into a dumpy matron's body. We were in what Maria Ortega had taken to calling the sitting room. During my career, I've been in more than one home of the fantastically rich, and I've only seen shadowed, low-table-strewn, off-the-beaten-path rooms like this one used for privately taking drugs, having sex, or both. I just thought it would be rude to mention it to Ortega's mother.

Not that she'd notice right now.

She was yelling at me like a veteran drill sergeant, and gesticulating like a woman with a foot stuck in a wasp's nest. I caught every third word or so as she slowed down to breathe. I had almost convinced myself she had evolved past the need. Such is just one of the many skills developed by the mother of a dozen children.

She railed on, using her uncomfortable son as a translator, as I sipped at a small crystal cup full of chilled lemon-lime gin. The citrus and the juniper blended in ways that seemed unnaturally fluid. I picked up the teddy bear shaped bottle and checked the back. It took me serious effort to mentally cut and paste Spanish to English. As I thought, the gin was made from genetically engineered plants, '*Blending the beautiful tart of lemon and lime with the traditional pleasure of juniper—*'

Maria took the bottle from me and set it gingerly down upon the table before folding her arms across her ample chest. She glared at me with practiced disapproval. My mother used to fix me with that same glare, and I'd shrink under it. *That was a long time ago.* I stood. "Ortega, explain this to your mother…"

He only got those words out before things got better for me. Granted, it was because she began yelling at him instead, but I am a practical man; I take what victories I can. He tried to put it to her gently, but she would have nothing of it. Manuel tried one more time, but only managed to get us thrown out of the sitting room. *Oh my, a briar patch, whatever shall I do?*

The Key to Damocles

I had a hundred different things going on in my mind, but foremost at this second was whether or not Ortega had the ability to control his mother. I felt bad for her, I ready did, but I was not about to take another tongue lashing for the sake of her mental health. She was rich now; she could afford a head-shrink like everybody else.

He fell into step with me as I crossed deserted halls that were just beginning to show signs of life. The *EWO* started to say something twice before he cleared his throat and shot me a sheepish glance. "Sorry about that, Captain. I'm not really sure what that was all about."

"You don't?" I drained the rest of the gin out of the cup, still marveling at the smoothness, and set it the empty rocks glass deftly in the kitchen sink. He smiled self-consciously and shook his head. I tried not to look too disappointed. "What was she yelling about?"

"The dead thugs at the church."

"And she's upset about that?"

"Well, I mean *mia madre* has always hated gangsters, so I can't see why she's so upset."

"How did you feel the first time you killed another human being?"

Ortega looked like he'd been slapped in the face. "Wait a minute, Capitan, it's not like my mom shot anyone."

I saw a chance coming up, so I grabbed the *EWO* and took him into a small cubbyhole where we could talk in low tones. "Look, Ortega, how do you think she feels about it?"

"She can't—"

"She can and she does." I searched his eyes, but it was clear he just didn't get it. "Ortega, she is used to seeing this in movies. She wanted us to go, get there in time, and keep everyone safe. She's never seen a dynamic entry, and I can guarantee that the news coverage was probably as gruesome as it could get."

"Oh yeah, that may have been a mistake. Have you seen the news sites?"

I could feel him trying to shift the conversation. "No."

"Might want to keep an eye on it."

"Sure, but listen, she's going to be a little volatile for a while. She's lived poor for most of her life, and now she has money, and money is power. The first time she exercised her power, people died." He started to interrupt, but I rolled right over him. "She said, 'go' and we went. We did what we do and now she's living with that order. She's thinking about the deaths she thinks she caused and not the lives she saved. The best thing you can do for her is to get the members of her old church to write her some flowery messages of thanks. Until then, she'll be fine just as long she doesn't begin to transfer her guilt onto us. If that happens, things will get much more complicated."

"I'll have my sister keep an eye on her."

"See that you do, Ortega." We left the nook and continued out into the courtyard.

Our steps were stilted, weighed down with the possibility of an uncomfortable stay at the Compound. Ortega did what he always does when things get a little too heavy for him, he chuckled, "You're lucky she didn't throw things."

"I thought that was an Irish thing."

"My mother is very multicultural."

"Is that why she only speaks Spanish?"

"She only yells in Spanish; she speaks MexiCali. Besides, *Capitan*, on Persephone you're a *gringo* and Spanish is the language of poets and philosophers."

"I'll keep that in mind. I'll be in the communications center if you need me."

He shot me a 'thumbs up' and jogged off toward the barracks.

It struck me that Ortega was really a good soldier, if a little too shortsighted to be a combat leader. I never had to tell him that he was to stay with the troops instead of inside his palatial bedroom. That was no mean feat, considering the place that Ortega had bought for his family with his part of the chimerium funds.

The Ortega Compound had once been a joke, a nickname given to a sizable estate purchased by the former mercenary. After our last mission, the one that had netted each of the rank-and-file *Angels* millions of credits, he had returned to his home planet of Persephone to do the honorable thing. He had often mentioned his family in the old days, how they lived in relative poverty amid the movie stars of the universe. I can't say all of us believed his stories... At least I didn't until I finally landed on this rock. In any case, for the Ortegas, the days of menial service jobs and a drafty tenement in New California were a long-gone memory. He had bought one of the smaller homes of a movie magnate in the city of Mezzo-Americana and set to moving his dirt-poor family into the sixty-four bedroom, sixty-eight bath, three kitchen, four garage, two pool mansion. The ex-owner movie magnate apparently needed to sell fast in order to settle some legal bills. This, in addition to the fact the house was completely out of style for the ultra chic crowd, sent the price spiraling into the pavement. I'm sure all Ortega cared about was the price was more than a steal, and it was located in the safest city, surrounded by the best schools, next to the richest neighbors. As near as we could figure, he had his entire extended family of seventy living there right now with another fifty living on the property in trailers and campers brought in since the 'revolution' started.

And since the 'revolution', Ortega had bought a massive earthworks 'bot and put it to good use. He had it dig a moat behind the original, mostly decorative, wall. He had built another wall, backed with sandbags to create firing positions over top. Impromptu bunkers had been installed at all the chokepoints, as well as eight state-of-the-art, autonomous anti-air laser turrets that were programmed to bring down anything from a rocket, low flying flier, or Molotov cocktail. He had done a passable job turning the place into an actual military compound. He had even added a dozen second-hand trailers in which the *Angel's Apostles* were currently barracked.

Compared to their seventy-five men, the *Radiation Angels* were little more than a footnote. In fact, I was confused to find out that that Ortega had hired our former teammates and yet was still so adamant that I come in.

When I had signed up for this pooch-screw, Ortega told me it involved civil unrest. After some searching, I found that the planet appeared to be in the throws of a revolution. Either crisis would have been fine, but it turned out that the entire planet was battered by continuous violence and was reacting in unpredictable, nearly schizophrenic, ways. The capital city, New California, was drowning in uncontrolled anarchy, while other megacities were becoming independent sovereign states whose political climates ranged from commune-style anarchy to militant police-states. What was worse was the entire setup reeked of convenient stupidity, incidental catastrophe, and

46

canned speeches. Every bone in my body told me that this was a setup, but neither my bones nor any other part of me knew exactly who was being set up.

It turned out that his family had all but insisted that I be contacted. Ortega had spent months since we disbanded telling his family war stories about the *Angels* and, in particular, his near precognitient commander, Captain Todd Rook. I had been told I was coming to try to shore up the defenses of the compound and coordinate the work of nearby mercenary teams. When seventy members of the Ortega Clan, plus sixty off-duty *Apostles*, greeted me this morning, it was like waking up in the body of a rock star. Suddenly, I wasn't here to coordinate *grit*; they truly believed that I could to bring an end to a planet full of lawlessness, rioting, and murder.

I was in a small trailer that acted as the command center, where all the security camera feeds were piped. Two muted entertainment screens, bolted into the ceiling, were tuned into live newsfeeds off the planetary net. I paid them scant attention as I used my datapads to scan information from news services, and made hopeless requests to police organizations to get updates on the current situation. From all I could see, the unrest was a massive case of civil disobedience and near revolution. No other merc teams really wanted to work together, and neither local nor planetary police appeared to be answering my calls right now. It would take months for a dozen brigades to get control of the cities, though the rural areas appeared pretty stable. Unfortunately, I didn't have brigades; in fact, all I had was one reinforced mobile squad. One team made up of six pairs, a Templar-model cyborg, and myself, to put down widespread unrest across twelve megacity complexes.

Where do these people get the idea that I walk on *fragging* water? Might as well ask me to turn aside a tornado with a lasso and harsh language. Before I could get control of it, my temper towered like a solar flare inside my skull. I slammed a fist into the metal desk, making the monitors wobble.

"Problems, Captain?" I spun in my seat, hand racing for my sidearm before the automatic reaction to draw was aborted by information from my senses. The speaker let out a disturbingly girlish giggle as she shut the door behind her. She swayed her thin hips just a little too much as she crossed the space from the back of the command trailer to my chair. "Oooh, and you're feeling feisty."

Corporal—*oops*—Captain Kei O'Leary stood with one hand on her hip and the other hanging a little too casually on the filing cabinet. The indigo bodysuit looked as if it was put on with a paintbrush, and though the loose-fitting white blouse hung low enough to save a great deal of her modesty, the overall effect was still striking. *Yeah, that's it, striking—like a sledgehammer.* I had to concentrate to breathe, and found myself thanking God that I'm African extraction. Dark skin makes it harder to see when we blush.

"Wow, O'Leary—um, Captain. Just… well, wow." *Smooth, Rook, real smooth*.

O'Leary's grandfather had been European extraction, Irish to be exact, though she had an otherwise unbroken Asian lineage going back to the Exile. It seemed that the two bloodlines had managed to create something of exceptional functionality and beauty, not to mention lethality.

"I've got the day off, so I want to go out dancing tonight with some of the guys."

O'Leary was admittedly drawn to danger, but she usually wasn't this stupid. "You're going clubbing during a civil war?"

"Look, Captain, other than some elevated criminal activity, Mezzo-Americana is very safe. Most of the problems are in New California, so stop worrying. Do you like it?" She spun in a circle like a girl going out to prom. Her body had always run toward a certain level of athletic muscle overlaid with subtly feminine curves, and financial success had only allowed her to buy outfits that accentuated every feature. She had let her hair grow out over the last year, making her look less like her warrior-self and more like a woman… not that she hadn't been pretty. O'Leary was certainly pretty, but she was still the same woman I had to discipline for taping grenades to the crotches of male prisoners and leading them around by the pin. I have seen her smile as she slit throats, chuckle as she emptied full clips into oncoming troops, and laugh out loud at any chance to use high explosives. She was beautiful, but there was definitely something not right with her.

Perhaps it was a year alone on my farm, or the fact that I usually saw her in bulky fatigues, but even though I picked out at least three concealed weapons on her person, I couldn't help notice the curve of her buttocks, hips, and scant flash of cleavage from within the ruffled neckline of her blouse. One half of me said, *Because she's no longer under your command?* The other half wisely replied, *Shut the hell up, soldier.* "You look gorgeous, Captain."

She paused, a half-second hiccup in the dialogue, and I felt like I missed something important. It was like I was conversing in a language I didn't fully understand, fumbling with a limited vocabulary, screwing up my tenses and clauses. She closed the distance between us with strong steps and pulled me from my seat. Face to face, I could see details I had missed even though I had known her for four years now. Her eyes faded from a rich brown to a bright emerald green at the iris, and fate had sprinkled her with perhaps a dozen tiny freckles at the corners of her eyes. I felt something inside me shift and thump pushing at my artificial ribcage with almost painful intensity. I fought the urge to back up. Handling O'Leary was often like dealing with a wolf, and I wondered if she was going to knee me in the crotch or kiss me. There was only a slight pause before she wrapped me in her arms and held me close. Much too close.

"Thanks, Todd." Clumsily, I hugged back, and as she nuzzled into my chest, felt slightly self-conscious that I might stink after the night's exertions. She pulled back to stare at me again. "I missed you, Captain."

And then she left. I was almost shaking as the door shut behind her, and I'll be damned if was able to articulate a single word. All I could think as the scent of her orange-and-ginger perfume dispersed through the air conditioning was, *WHAT IN HOLY HELL JUST HAPPENED?*

I sat heavily in my chair and flicked my gaze across the monitors, each one flashing across various camera angles, keeping an eye on the *Apostle* soldiers on the walls of the Ortega Compound and the small groups of people moving hurriedly through the grand boulevards outside.

Since it didn't appear that we were under attack, I snatched up my scattered thoughts and picked up the datapad to resume my study of the current geopolitical crisis on Persephone. I scanned the contents of the file, and figured the entire situation could be summed up in one word: *Fragged.* Riots had turned into looting, and then bombings, and now near-anarchy. The problem was that none of it made much of any sense. Perhaps I was just tired. I stretched again, and felt the metal plates in my chest pinch a stray muscle fiber.

We had made planet-fall last night but had only managed to unload our equipment before Lopez had walked into the Ortega mansion kitchen and heard one of the maids calling her gangster boyfriend, telling him about the ten thousand credit donation to the church.

And that was another problem. Currently, she was being held in her room with an armed guard outside. Technically under the Laws of War, she was a spy and could be executed, but I would have preferred to hand her over to the authorities to be tried for 'conspiracy to do something sleazy' or whatever. Unfortunately, there were few police forces left working on the planet with the jurisdiction to take her.

Then a thought hit me like a charging tank... *Did O'Leary just call me Todd?*

Another bit of theoretical paper rocketed into my electronic inbox. Normally, I'd have shuffled it into the slush file with all the others but this one looked important. It was from the planetary police agency, signed Director Saracho, no less. Quite short, and very specific in its tone, it stated that apparently they weren't happy that I had killed so many 'citizens of New California', which is how you say 'armed thug' on this planet, I suppose, and it reminded me I had no official powers whatsoever in this instance. *Blah blah blah...* cease and desist... *Blah blah blah... legal ramifications...Well if you want me to stop saving people, then you better come out and do the fragging job for me.* I hit delete as the door opened and blew that train of thought all to hell.

O'Leary was athletic and svelte; Reeves was anything but. At a few centimeters under two meters, his tall frame was layered with over a hundred kilos of hard-won muscle and reddish blond hair. He had served under me for five years, and as long as I have known him, he always enters every room as if he's stomping into a bar where he first intends to drink, then to brawl. His uniform was ruffled, slightly stained, and showing signs of frequent wear. His beard, always closely cropped as a member of the *Angels,* had grown over a hand's length from his chin. He looked like a Viking raider more than ever before.

Though rough around the edges, his manner was crisp and cool. He drew himself up to his full, formidable height and addressed me like a true soldier. "Captain."

I studiously blanked my face and flicked my eyes to his chest, where the half-buttoned shirt held badges of rank and a few notable medals. I saluted. "General."

He saluted back, a perfect snap, half count, then return to his side. The moment elongated as we each sized up the other, possibly friends, possibly enemies in the grand game of galactic war.

Then, without preamble, he charged me with a roar and swept me into a bear hug. We jostled about for a few minutes, with the requisite arm punching and hand squeezing to prove that over the last year neither had gone soft.

As with O'Leary, I picked up on minute changes in him. There were lines around his eyes from lack of sleep, and a bit of a beer belly beginning where he had too often given himself the day off from physical training. His uniform was not quite as ramshackle as I had first imagined since the edges were blurred and smudged by the dot and slash urban camouflage he had adopted as the uniform of the *Apostles.* Still, it could have used a fresh washing and pressing. "Holy *grit*, Todd, I half expected you to show up here as a three-hundred-kilogram pudding snack with a dozen Nubian girls fanning you."

I chuckled at the jibe, and at my ex-subordinates giving my first name a thorough workout. Conflicting emotions in my chest released their grip. "Not likely. I might be able to get one fan-girl, but with a face like this, she'd better be blind..." We both laughed, until I added my own thrust, "...sir."

Reeves roared at that. "Now, don't you start that *grit—*"

"Hey, don't blame me. You're the one who went and frocked yourself as a general."

The big man grinned from ear to ear as he spun a chair on its central post and sat on it ass-backwards. "Hey, I got expenses."

I sat down next to him, pursing my lips and raising an eyebrow. Mercenary companies were as varied as the number of colonies, and thus all had their own way of keeping track of rank. The one thing that stayed constant was the higher the rank, the more shares of pay. By making himself a full general, he had established a pay scale far above the lieutenants, corporals, and privates under his command. It was a way to squeeze out more than a few extra credits for himself. That was typical of Reeves, but I had hoped for more of him. "Speaking of expenses, how are things running here?"

My old teammate raised his eyebrows and leaned back in the office chair, affecting a light tone as he retrieved a cigar and a pocket lighter. "Well, I was wondering when you'd get around to talking to me. I just thought it would be before you took command."

I waved my hand, dismissing his annoyance. "Look, I'm not here to crap in your boots. In fact, I'm not even sure why I'm really here. It seems like Ortega's family thinks—"

"—That you can actually do something about this mess?" he interrupted. "Yeah, well you're a victim of your own success. Hell, the quarter of my men on duty last night woke the rest of them just so they could watch you land." His friendly tone had faded at the edges, gaining barbs as flecks of jealousy began showing through. Reeves took a draw from the cigar, filling the air with thick, pungent smoke. "They whisper about you in the barracks. They think you drink whiskey and piss napalm."

I waved again, partially speaking with my hands but mostly parting the smoke. Though it smelled like a burning dog turd, it still set off a deep craving inside me. I think Reeves knew it would. My voice gained its own ragged edge. "And whose fault is that?"

Reeves' eyes became flinty points beneath his heavy brows before a long, slow, deep breath washed his entire face clean of anger. "Yeah, well I guess I did some of that damage myself."

We sat across from one another, each taking the new measure of the other. I guess we both looked frazzled, tired, and a little older than we had any right to be. He had used my apparent 'legend' to prop himself up to his men, never thinking that the statue he had erected of me would one day come to life and move to overshadow him. For my part, I would have liked to break his nose for making me into some sort of Samson. I had enough stress without everyone thinking I can do miracles.

I got up and walked across the room to the soda machine in the corner. I punched two buttons, retrieving a cola for Reeves and a ginger ale for myself. I tossed him his drink and took my seat. He checked the brand, found that it was his favorite, and smiled a thanks. We made up the way most men do, without a word said or apology made. It may sound crazy, but that's the way it's done. The proper thing to do at this point was change the subject. "So, what can you tell me about what's going on here?"

He took a deep breath. "Captain, I don't think anyone really knows."

Reeves punched at a keyboard in the command room, turning one of the monitors from the cameras outside to its internal processors. He brought up maps of Persephone, turning the screen so that I could see more clearly. For a planet with a population of over three hundred million, there were surprisingly few cities. He droned on haphazardly, pointing to each in roughly chronological order and giving me updates on important events. The problem was he was giving me details without telling me what was really happening.

Planet Persephone had been colonized by a massed emigration of Latino-descendants anxious to escape Mars and protect their heritage. They landed on an uninhabited planet and set to building massive cities fed by a few agricultural mega-plantations. These cities sprawled across the landscape: unplanned, unchecked, and filled with living things. The people of Persephone lived easy, lazy lives, punctuated by siestas—a necessity not only because of heat but also because of the thirty-two hour days—and promises of work done *mañana*, tomorrow. To a desperate people fresh from the crowded battleground of Mars, Persephone was a paradise.

But, as the population grew by leaps and bounds, more vehicles crowded into the roads and sky-ways. The unintentional sprawl of homesteads were sold off and built up. This not only robbed the grandest metropolises of their pastoral air, but turned the choked urban centers into blinding mazes. Companies sprang up to create more automated farms and plantations to feed the additional bodies, but the economy stuttered, unable to provide fresh jobs to those that needed them. Purchasing power dwindled, the economy declined, and seventy-five years after it was colonized, Persephone was teetering on the edge of ruin.

This is when L/V/D Productions first made a movie here.

The Key to Damocles

Lionel, Vincent, and Davidson was, and is, one of the premier movie houses of all time. At first, they were drawn to Persephone because of a looming deadline in filming *The Lion of Mars*. The idea of having sixteen to twenty hours of light in which to work was extremely attractive. Once here, L/V/D executives were stunned by the variety of inexpensive goods, cheap land, and amicable politicians. Within a year, L/V/D had bought millions of acres across Persephone from the local populous and governments. These self-contained movie-making cities, called flat-towns for some archaic reason, were to be used for on-location shots and were in as varied climates and terrains as could be found anywhere. L/V/D built flat cities, fourteen completely functional ghost towns from different time periods, used only to stage shots on various projects. Computer generated images were fine for flat screen movies, or even full definition displays, but in mind screen theaters, nothing but the real thing can fool the human brain on its own turf.

L/V/D contracted with dozens more construction companies. Within two years, offices had been built, as well as hundreds of homes for movie executives, their stable of stars, and the thousands of other personnel needed to make a film come together. Single handedly, the film company revitalized the economy of Persephone. Then, they did what they always did. They made movies.

Since the invention of digital recording devices, entertainment has always been the most portable of goods and this trend became ever more exaggerated as time went on. From a merchant's perspective, it was almost perfect. Entertainment has an intrinsic value all its own; it can be transmitted as data to be made into concrete recordings at the final sales location, and gains value only through the use of unique talents beholden to usually lifelong contracts within the industry. Whether you were watching a Jonathan Krace action movie, a Katie Ranner suspense film, a Carter Banks romance, or a Lolly Brown comedy— whether it is set in the old west, medieval Europe, nineteenth century Japan, some mythical realm of elves and fairies, or some future time or place… it was all written, filmed, produced, and edited on Persephone.

Then the finished product was super-encrypted and broadcast on seven secret channels over the quantum bands to thousands of planets where it's received, decrypted, reassembled, and then seen in mind screen theaters by hundreds of billions of people, for about ten credits a person. All that adds up to some pretty serious money, transmitted automatically to accounts in the DeBiers Intergalactic Bank. It rains down upon this planet in torrents where it was spent on needed supplies, gigantic luxuries, and little necessities.

The influx of money had done nearly as much damage to the economy of Persephone as two decades of squalor and decay, pricing even basic goods higher and higher in a never-ending spiral. But this inflation was only the lesser cause of unrest on the planet.

Depending on whom you believed, through the hand of fate, random chance, or by design of racists, the majority of Exiles from Earth were of African extraction. An axiom in the entertainment business was that people want to see what they can identify with. This means that nine out of ten movies produced were English speaking, African extraction stars. Most casts were almost completely of African descent brought in from off planet and housed here to create the illusion of being somewhere else. In the meantime, the native Persephonites were trained as gaffers and cameramen. They worked on scripts, costume, and makeup. They were everywhere behind the camera, and gained some of that endless waterfall of money in their own hands. But they were conspicuously absent from leading roles. For over a decade, a tide of resentment had been building against the movie industry and African-extraction people in general.

For five years, it was nothing but protests, petitions, and marches, but over the last six months, things had turned really ugly. Petitions were abandoned for threats of violence. Protests had given way to riots. Marches had finally evolved into bomb hoaxes and then bombings themselves. Apparently, the friction between the movie industry and the people it had both saved and damned had finally created enough heat to ignite into violence. It all seemed like a perfect evolution in everyone's mind, but it still didn't make any sense to me.

Reeves punched a few more keys, bringing up a muted video of a college-age Latino. His surroundings were nondescript, white on white on white, with no windows, nothing on the desk in front of him, no shadows, cobwebs, and only a simple folding chair for furniture. Dressed in a plain black sweater, the speaker still managed to fill the screen with his presence. I soaked in every detail of his unlined face: the proud moustache, vibrant features, and angry brows.

Reeves settled back and relit his cigar. "This is *El Toro*, The Bull. He began making videotaped announcements and sending them into the local newsfeeds. They were picked up by pirate sites on the planetary network and repeated all over the place. This started after the first few weeks of bombings. He and his group of followers have taken credit for almost every act of terrorism to hit Persephone since. He's becoming a media icon, something in between a rock star and a serial killer. Hell, the bastard doesn't even bother to cover up his face anymore."

I leaned toward the screen studying the face there. "Who is he?"

"The major news networks don't know. The best people to identify him would be the planetary police, but of course they closed down, so they aren't looking. If the local police know, they just aren't talking."

"Military?"

A bitter laugh jerked from his throat. "Oh, they're doing a whole lot of nothing. They've recused themselves from the mess, sighting a 'conflict of interest' or some such. Here." And he tossed me a fax sheet.

I scanned it briefly. 'Because the civilian government to which we are beholden has ceased to exist, it has become clear that we cannot take sides in the chaos of Persephone. It would be immoral to visit death upon our countrymen and even more vile to unleash several hundred thousand armed marines upon a planet with no guiding influence...' I stopped reading and began scanning. 'Keeping station at the edge of Persephone space... Holding clear threats at bay until the government can be reconstituted...' I tossed the thing aside. "You're telling me that this guy shows up out of nowhere, claims to have started a planetary civil war, and no one knows who the *frag* he is?"

Reeves shrugged wide shoulders. "That's about the long and short of it, Cap- Todd."

I finished my soda, crumpled the can, and sunk it perfectly into the trashcan at the far end of the room. "I don't understand that. It doesn't seem to—"

The speaker in the wall, hooked into the radio frequencies of both the *Angels* and *Apostles*, barked without warning. "Captain Rook!"

Hands moving like lightning, I hit the reply button on the console. "Rook here, report!"

Pilot Sichak aboard *Deadly Heaven* dutifully rattled off information. "Captain, there's been another bombing over in New California. The local police department there is begging for any assistance. You asked to be informed."

I reached for the integrated command armband on my forearm, but found I hadn't put the damn thing on. I brought up my command voice. "Alert the team. Everyone is to be suited up in equipment load out 'Riot 2', and ready to move in ten minutes. Wake up Doe and have him warm up *The Cherub*. I want to be in the air in twelve minutes."

As clear as a bell, Sichak confirmed my orders back to me. "Team on Alert, Equipment load out Riot 2, I say again: Riot 2, Doe to warm up *Cherub*, ready for transit in twelve."

"Roger-Roger."

"Out, Captain." A half second later, the MercTool in the pocket of every *Angel* in the compound chirped and began to relay my orders.

I sprang to my feet and made it out the door, Reeves hot on my heels. "Captain, what in the hell are you doing?"

"Tornado sighting," I tossed over my shoulder. "I don't suppose you have a lasso?"

My rhetorical question stopped him in his tracks, confused. Ahead, the weary *Angels* were scattering throughout the barracks, gathering the gear they would need for this new, unexpected mission. I took out my MercTool and checked the tiny screen just to make sure everything was relayed correctly.

My ex-Lieutenant-turned-self-proclaimed-General called up to me, "What are you doing, Rook? That megacity is a thousand kilometers north. The Ortegas are here."

"I wasn't hired to defend the Ortegas; you were," I shot back. Over the din of shouting men, I could hear the whine of turbine engines spooling to full speed. Out of nowhere, Logan appeared, my equipment looking like black plastic doll clothes in his oversized chrome arms. "I'm supposed to be able to end this mess, remember?"

With purposeful strides, I left Reeves behind. By the time I walked into *The Cherub*, I had pulled on my armor, web gear, pack, and sidearm. I secured the elastic cuff holding my forearm tactical pad, slung a pushgun over my shoulder and then jammed the C^2 helmet on my head. The visor HUD came to life as the last member of the team ran aboard. The ramp began to close. The engines de-chalked and inertia yanked at every *Angel* as the craft launched into the clear, bright day.

I opened the comm to L/F Doe. "Captain, here. Burn the sky."

I could hear the ear-to-ear smile from the cockpit. "Aye, aye Cappy. Full thrust it is."

The g-forces twisted and hammered at the team as *The Cherub* oriented on our target and left bright contrails in its wake. Most tried to sleep during transit; I just turned my armband to a civilian channel and listed to the newsfeeds give a play-by-play of the chaos. I needed to know what I was facing when we landed.

CHAPTER 5: CROWD CONTROL

On the west side of New California, Los Angeles Street was burning.

The Cherub lurched, dove, and came in along the four-lane road. *The Succubus*, still sitting safely back at the Ortega Compound, was a fine dropship, but in the tight confines of urban warfare bringing her down safely would be like trying to drive a car down the rows of a crowded theater. *The Cherub*, while nowhere near as large, sleek, or fast as *The Succubus*, was nimble, well armored, and packed a whole array of specialty weapons just for occasions such as this. I had bought it on *Haven* on impulse, and I had yet to regret it.

Thick black clouds rose into the sky like monstrous serpents, coil after coil belching from homes, vehicles, and businesses set alight. Beneath the manmade clouds, a surf of flesh crashed against the police station, lapped against the lampposts, slapped against cars, smashed through storefronts, and turned against itself. Baseball bats, wood axes, and improvised clubs waved in the air next to signs proclaiming the virtues of *El Toro*. Molotov cocktails streaked like burning moths over the crowd toward the hated symbol of authority. Every once in a while, there was the sound of gunplay, and as *The Cherub* dove down into the streets, random shots became more aimed and purposeful.

Doe's voice sounded more offended than concerned in my ear. "We're taking small arms fire."

I have to remind myself that most people have no idea what war looks like. In fact, whenever they see real war on the newsfeeds from across their world, or from a whole other world, they shake their heads. They make noises, and speak platitudes, and wonder aloud at what must be wrong with those people. They never imagine that it could happen in their own back yard, on the street right outside their door, until it does. Then, more often than not, they simply join in.

The crowd below had been living in fear for weeks. The constant pressure of worrying if the train-ride to work would end in fire, or if the office building would crumble into a cairnstone tomb, had built up in them. They had seen the lawlessness firsthand, and everyone knew someone who had been scarred by the encroaching hand of anarchy. Most were out of work, out of money, and probably out of food. Fear is a horrible motivator, but it only takes a slight push to go from sheer terror to raw animal rage.

The violence is terrible at first, but then it changes. It becomes a blanket of warmth, a comforting shield to hold the fear at bay, and then it starts to become fun. A person can rage against all the injustice of the universe and personify it in a target. Then, he can let his wrath flow, given license and anonymity by the crowd. Get enough people to make that transition from fear to rage to wrath all at once at one place, and a riot is born— hundreds of people, each individual simply going along with the crowd for fear of being ground under its feet.

It wasn't the hundreds that really worried me, though. For centuries, if you wanted to know the mind of a riot, wanted to find the true believers amongst the cattle, then you had to look for those who were there for a reason. Luckily, it wasn't hard; they always carried signs. Banners, written in red paint so it looked like blood, pulsed up and down in time with anarchistic chants. I practiced my Spanish by translating their short messages inside my head.

For love of El Toro.
Toro will rescue us.
El Toro = Truth.
Down with the oppression.
Free Persephone.
The Police are the arm of the Elite.
L/V/D kills our culture.

The monitors inside *The Cherub* caught details from the crowd. Near the police station, two cruisers smoldered, the officers dragged from inside hours before. Their bodies now hung from streetlamps where they had been beaten until their limbs fell off. Small pockets of rioters fought each other while the great mass of them broke windows, threw trash, and screamed profanities. At the mouth of one alley, a woman was being gang-raped by a group of men. Those not involved in general chaos, or self-serving theft or abuse, were piled behind makeshift barriers where they directed fire at the front of the police station. A clear blast pattern showed where a bomb had failed to do much to the building except strip off any external cameras or weaponry.

That didn't mean there were no witnesses. Hidden in shadowed corners, cameras were positioned: inside of armored vans, on rooftops, and inside sturdy buildings. They watched passionlessly, recording the events without passing judgment. Like vultures, they were just waiting to feast their lidless eyes on the dead after the crowd dispersed. There were dozens, seeing for millions.

I clicked on the comm. "Spice them."

In the cockpit, Doe snickered. "Hell yeah, Cap!"

Doe flipped a set of switches, arming munitions on the bottom of the craft and unlocking the safeties that held them in place. Most of the crowd below was just noticing us as he pushed four buttons in quick succession, allowing the thigh-sized canisters to fall free. Thirty feet above the ground, the simple computer inside each cylinder opened the valves on compressed nitrogen tanks, allowing the gas to sneeze out kilo after kilo of rusty red powder.

Made from a wide variety of finely-ground, genetically-engineered peppers, the canisters vomited this powder into the air and out across the crowd as they bounced off of the pavement. Profanities took on new urgency and shouts turned to screams as the clawing, acidic pepper dust ate at eyes, noses, mouths, and lungs. Some protestors ran, some fell over and choked, many staggered and screamed. It created the 'three C's' we needed: chaos, confusion, and cover.

I reactivated the comm. "*Angels*: seal suits; open drop doors; prepare for fast rope."

Soldiers moved to both sides of the interior of *The Cherub*. They hooked C-clamps into anchor points on the ceiling. From these clamps, rope threaded through a specialized climbing harness and terminated at pre-loaded bags around their left ankles. There was a second or two pause as they looked to me for any last second orders. Every possible catastrophe gut-punched me again and again, sending my intestines slithering: broken legs, snapped lines, fatal gusts of wind that could push *The Cherub* off course and slam us all into a building. I looked from visor to visor and saw through the bulletproof plastic to reveal titanic hearts, surging with courage and excitement.

61

The Key to Damocles

These were *Angels*, and they were chomping at the bit to do their jobs. "All right, let's move like we have a purpose. Pairs Six and Four, you're first."

Two Pairs backed up to the opening and jumped into space. Normally, fast roping from a hovering craft was like rappelling using a swing set, but with John Doe's hands at the controls, the craft acted as if it had been nailed into place midair. Four men saluted and flashed down the cables to the ground. As they cleared the ropes at the bottom, I ordered Pairs Two and Five to stack and rope down. As they made their descent, I looked over at Logan and tapped my head and held up nine fingers. We switched to preset frequency number nine. "Can you get that woman?"

He didn't even have to ask which one. "I will get her to the police station."

I nodded at him, ordered up Pair One, Logan and Ortega, Pair Three, and Actual: myself. I grabbed onto the speed control for my descent and backed out of *The Cherub*, leaving the safety of the armored hull behind. The cable whirred through the climbing rings with the sound of polymer gears grinding together. My stomach lurched, and I spun slightly, enveloped in brick red particles of pepper smoke that were being flash fried into embers by the aeroline engines of the armored personnel flier. I tightened my grip on the device that controlled the cable, halting my fall only a meter above the asphalt road.

Even though the canisters were well emptied, the silt-fine particles created a sandstorm in *The Cherub's* jet wash and reduced our line of sight to a mere handful of meters. Even the holo-sonar was useless, sonically blinded by the deafening roar of the craft above and reducing the battle to the equivalent of a knife fight with guns. This suited our purpose just fine since there were more of them than there were of us.

I yanked the rest of the cable through the harness and cleared the landing pad so the rest could disembark. Logan launched himself out into the burning fog. I ordered the team to switch to thermal sights. It added a few meters to our visibility, but it was still like swimming through a sewer. Pushguns came off our shoulders, and the *Angels* began fighting their way to the police station, or at least what was left of it.

"Captain!"

The tone of Logan's synthesized voice burned an icy trail through my guts and loosened my bladder. I've seen Logan charge main battle tanks, stand alone in front of oncoming hordes, and wade through storms of lead and steel without thought for his safety. Inside his voice, I heard something as rare as a black pearl or a blue moon. He was afraid. "Report!"

"Captain, there are men out here in light armor. They are putting on full respirators."

My feet were suddenly glued to place, refusing to rise at my command. Pushguns thudded quietly, sending out small packets of electrons like baseballs made of air, hitting those protestors that came too close and dropping them with the kinetic force of a martial artist on a steroid bender. Everything appeared to be going according to plan, but now I knew that something was very, very wrong. "Say again?"

"There are several sets of protestors out here putting on protective gear. They are arming themselves with rifles."

We were wearing top-shelf riot armor, but while it would stop handgun ammunition, the chances of stopping a high-power rifle round were perhaps fifty-fifty. The rest of men were listening on the team frequency and more than a few glanced nervously at me. I could have whispered and they would have heard me, but adrenaline surged from my glands to my throat and had me yelling like an idiot. "Logan, get back here, NOW. Rook to *Cherub*, retreat to safe distance and orbit for pickup. *Angels,* forget the niceties. Make a *fragging* road into that police station, now!"

A chorus of assents came over the comm, just as the unmistakable sound of high explosives fell on us from above. Shrapnel rained down and the electronically muffled roar of our armored flier hiccupped and coughed. Doe's voice was in my ear. "Captain! *Cherub* is hit. *Cherub* is hit. One engine is down."

"Weapons free! Weapons free! Spike that *fragging* grit-licker!" *Oh, yeah, this is exactly what an ambush feels like.* "Assault formation! Into the station! MOVE! MOVE! MOVE!"

Struggling to keep the craft in the air, Doe flipped the safety cover over a big red button and pressed it with relish. Automated guns took a few microseconds to assess the situation, talk with the sensor array of *The Cherub*, and a few microseconds later decided who deserved to die. Pulse plasma cannons fluttered their magnetic bottles to release streams of light as if from the eyes of Satan himself. A two-man team on the roof across from us became blazing beacons, dying before they could even release a scream.

Angels formed a wedge and ran up the steps to the police station, dodging the burning pools left behind from improvised incendiaries, tripping on rubble from thrown rocks and broken pieces of the station. Doe yanked his collective control yolk and disappeared over the western line of buildings just as we began taking automatic fire from out of the swirling shadows. Enemy fire spanged off the concrete steps and crashed into bulletproof windows. One shot grazed Ansef's leg to my right, and another ricocheted off of Archer's helmet. Over the comm, the news got worse. A string of rapid-fire Spanish curses identified the next speaker as Ortega. "Captain, the door is locked and barricaded!"

I looked left and right, realizing we were three meters above the ground, and there was absolutely no cover to be had. A quick glance up gave snatches of the bright blue sky, a sure sign that the silty pepper was falling to earth and robbing us of cover. In a few seconds, we would be exposed, and there would be aimed fire and dead *Angels*. "Sichak, get a hold of the P.D. and tell them we need them to open this *fragging* door, NOW!"

Sichak called back in my ear. "Captain, the P.D. band is now being jammed."

Jammed? Crap. Crap. Crap.

Then, a basso synthetic voice echoed from behind us and over the comm. "MAKE WAY!"

Obediently, every one of us crowded to the sides of the wide staircase as Logan came barreling upward as a juggernaut. He moved like a silver battering ram, his feet cracking the steps and shattering rubble beneath him even as he gently cradled a huddled body in his arms. Ansef had to be pulled out of his way as the cyborg spun, protecting the defenseless woman with the bulk of his body as his back did the brutal work of twisting the metal framed door. The makeshift wall groaned for half a heartbeat and then ruptured with the sound of a metal avalanche. Titanium and polymer laminate skin snapped the locks like matchsticks, sundered hastily welded crossbars from their moorings, and battered the desks piled up to secure the barrier.

James Daniel Ross

There was a peppering of gunfire and the sound of pushguns discharging from inside. Before we were even able to get through the breech, Logan had rolled up into a ball to protect the woman in his arms, shotgun pellets and electron packets alike bouncing harmlessly off his cyborg body.

He ratcheted up the volume on his loudspeaker to deafening levels. "Hold your fire! We're the *Angels*! Hold your fire!"

To their credit, they did stop trying to kill us as we piled inside and tried in vain to secure the wrecked front door. Automatic fire rained into the opening, starring and chipping the remaining glass. Shotgun and pushgun wielding police officers dressed in light riot gear—even thinner, scanter armor than ours—stood up in the doorways of the main corridor where they had taken up firing positions. The thirteen of us walked past them toward booking where a massive, multi part booking desk had become impromptu cover for those officers armed with precious few automatic rifles. An older European extraction officer, dressed in a cheap suit the same gray as his hair, walked forward from behind the desk and off of the raised platform to meet us on our way.

He had obviously never been a tall man, but nonetheless had a commanding presence that echoed great physical power from years ago. Certainly, his shoulders were wide enough, and his hands bulky enough, to suggest that he had once been in prime physical condition. Now age was coming onto him and had softened his arms and legs, expanding his belly over his belt and up into his chest. It gave him the appearance of an anthropomorphic barrel, or a muscular Santa Claus. His appearance might just be comical if not for the police belt holding two pistols, a bandoleer of shotgun shells, and the short-barreled riot shotgun in his stubby left paw. He said something in Spanish before coughing and switching to flawless English. "Captain Lomen, Acting Station Chief. Thank God you're here."

"Captain Rook, *Radiation Angels*." I met his hand halfway with mine. His grip was firm, "Do you have a trauma station here?"

His eyes flicked behind me, and without further hesitation he nodded. "Fourth floor, left side. Use whatever you need."

I sent the *Angels* down one corridor to stack up and prepare to defend the front door if it was breached. Without being told,

The Key to Damocles

Logan took Medic Tsang, the rape victim, and the wounded Medic Ansef upstairs to the medical center. Ortega busied himself unpacking and assembling his scanner. The damn things were notoriously temperamental, and I had ordered the item safely packed for the fast rope descent. I had been counting on using *The Cherub's* sensors during the drop, but now that plan was *cracked* beyond salvage. Mentally I beat slave drums to get the robust Latino to work faster, but assembling and calibrating the shovel-shaped device would take precious minutes whether I loomed over his shoulder and glowered or not. That being the case, I moved over to the booking desk and glanced at the security monitors angled up from knee level.

I wouldn't admit it, but I felt naked with nothing but police officers covering the one exit I knew about, and who knew who guarding the others I didn't. Perhaps I wasn't being fair, but while the cops might look competent, they were not mercenaries. Lomen moved up beside me as a quick glance at the screens showed ten stories of mostly empty building. All the most important cameras, those showing the front of the building, had been stripped off by the car bomb.

My thoughts started racing. "Captain, how many men do you have?"

"Fifteen on shift, sixty-seven total." I was wearing a tinted helmet, but he must have read something in my body language because he spread his hands and shrugged. "City stopped paying us about two months ago. These guys are the most dedicated officers I've got. I'm lucky they're still here."

Two months. That explained the lack of response at the Ninth Street Church. It was further into the poor quarter, and the officers there had probably been burnt out or driven off first. I let my eyes linger on the cops, their weapons riveted on the doors which were still taking sporadic fire, and felt a twinge of guilt for thinking so little of them. "How many exits to the building?"

"It's an old, retrofitted building, so there are only two: one here, one in back. I've got two officers back there, but all the action has been up here so far."

"Windows?"

"Armored. Paxzen plastic—"

He was missing the point. "Do they open?"

"No. They are all sealed, first three floors and last three floors have bars."

I moved over to the wall and looked at the emergency map on the wall. "Escape routes?"

"Fire escapes… but the doors are sealed unless they are manually activated or automatically by the fire suppression… system…." Lomen trailed off and looked behind him, down the corridor.

The incoming fire had stopped.

I spun on my EWO. "Ortega!"

The last parts clicked together and the device began chirping as it calibrated. "Thirty seconds!"

Good to his word, thirty seconds later, Ortega ran a full spectrum scan on everything within a kilometer in every direction. "The jamming is gone. I've got various small arms out there, lots of people… Heart rates indicate distress. They're moving away from us. I've got twenty-five separate signals in surrounding buildings… Bandwidth usage from those spots indicates that these are probably our newsies. The operators are still manning their cameras… Heart rates indicate they missed most of the spicing, but they are not happy campers. There are some explosives on the roof across the street, but no living people within ten meters of them. No armor grade alloys or plastics except in and on this building…

"They're gone Captain."

A few minutes later, we were out on the street.

CHAPTER 6:
KINDRED SPIRITS

The police had spread out to cordon off the area, *Angels* positioned at alleyways. One or two protestors, those with a genetic predisposition of weakness to the active ingredient in the crowd-spicing pepper, were still thrashing on the ground. Tsang moved from one to another, using canned chemical mist to diffuse the burning capsicum in eyes, noses, throats and lungs. The Asian extraction paramedic was surprisingly gentle and soothing to his patients, even though the officers that took them into custody were less than friendly to the rioters.

Cameras focused in on us as Lomen and I walked on what appeared to be a carpet of granulated blood. Dozens of bullet-riddled bodies were sprawled around the entrance to the police station, contorted in agony even in death. It looked like the dead were dissolving into red dust, remembered only by angry signs discarded during the incident. Across the street, a few men were being hauled, screaming, to their feet so they could be taken inside, booked, and thrown into a jail cell. Logan-sized footprints were clear on their pants. One in particular had his leggings around his ankles, showing off his pain-shrunken penis and the twisted ruins of his knees. If I didn't miss my guess, 'The Pantsless Avenger' and the rest of his mob were the rapists I'd spotted during the fly in.

I sighed, but though it was unprofessional, I couldn't quite muster any anger at Logan this time. I see enough rape in wartime, and I had a feeling that these 'men' would never run down and beat a woman into submission ever again, jail time or no. That was a good thing. In fact, if the police captain wasn't standing right here, I'd probably download the stored images from *The Cherub*, match their faces to the data, and then hang each and every one of them from the light poles. Perhaps that would be too good for them. After all, we had just cut down the bodies of police officers who had given their lives in service to their community. Those poles had held heroes, and hanging rapists from them seemed like using a flag as toilet paper.

The Key to Damocles

I deadened the loudspeaker on the C^2 and dialed up Doe aboard *The Cherub*. "Doe, report."

His voice held its usual aplomb, but the quality was strained. "Well, *Cherub* ain't dead, but she's definitely not happy. Fire suppression and automatic fuel shutoff saved her, and I can keep in the air with three engines, but I'm pushing the red lines on all of them. It's possible to get home empty, but not with all of you—especially not the Master Sergeant—aboard."

I don't know how long I stood there in silence, watching flies buzz into and out of a young woman's open mouth. The day was getting hotter, and I tried to focus on the fact that we had better do something about these bodies soon rather than dwell on the fact that these corpses had been living people just an hour before. "Get to the local spaceport. Land and get repaired. Contact Sichak about funds from our onboard computer vault."

"So how are you going to get home, Captain?"

I caught the flash of the afternoon—I checked the time clock on my HUD and was surprised to find out how young of an afternoon it was —sun on a camera lens. I met its stare unflinchingly even as Lomen kept his head tilted down. It was easy for me; I had a tinted helmet on so I could be bold. Anonymity is a powerful drug. *Plus, I don't live here.* "We don't. So, make it fast."

"Aye, Aye."

I touched Captain Lomen on the shoulder and we went back inside through the dreary corridors and up to his office. We rode the elevator to the fourth floor in silence, staring at the mirrored doors the way people ride elevators the universe over. Part of it was we really didn't know anything about each other. Part of it was honest exhaustion. Entering combat, any combat, throws switches in the back of a human brain that send it into overdrive. After the bullets stop flying, the brain loses all thrust. Like a boat out of gas, it drifts wherever the tide of events takes it. It's very easy to get caught in all of the fatigue; convincing oneself that everything can wait until later or, worse yet, that things that can wait need to get done right now.

Tony broke the silence first. "So, Captain, what exactly was that stuff?"

"*Fuerpeppar* powder. It's just finely ground pepper innards."

He hooked his thumb to his right, which I took to be the front of the building. "And it does that to people?"

"Well, have you ever bit into a raw hot pepper? Or rub your eye after eating one as finger food?"

Tony winced. "Ouch, yeah. So why not use CS gas or normal pepper spray solutions?"

I chuckled. "Well, on some planets both of those are considered chemical agents and constitute chemical warfare. This stuff is just as effective and it's legal most everywhere."

"How strong is it?"

"Well as I understand it, there is a scale for hotness. A Jalapeno is about fifty-five thousand. I think a Habañero is around three hundred thousand. The crowd spicer is genetically engineered to be hotter. Much hotter."

Lomen gaped. "How hot?"

"It'll bleach your brain... from the outside." Tony's eyes said he was taking me at face value. I waved his concerns off. "It doesn't kill you; it just makes you wish it did."

We stepped out of the elevator, and he led me in the direction of his office. He stopped for a moment in front of the trauma station, looking through the glass walls with sad eyes. Inside the first aid station and emergency operating room, two women talked. Medic Ansef had taken off her bulky armor, exposing an antiseptic white bandage around her thigh. Her Arabian features were normally rather plain, but right now they were set in a beautiful smile that shone from her deep brown eyes. Behind the soundproof glass, she was talking with the short, dumpy woman Logan had saved from the alleyway. Bruises roiled underneath her brown skin, still blackening and expanding with blood. Someone, probably Ansef or Tsang, had given her a lab-coat and a few blankets, which she wore like armor of her own over several fresh bandages and a splinted foot. Even from here, I could see the red film of broken capillaries in her right eye. Amazingly enough, she was already smiling a little.

Lomen shook his head. "Bastards."

The young woman looked up and saw the two of us. As if someone pulled a plug, all emotion inside her died.

"And then some." We started moving again, leaving Ansef to heal what wounds she could. "You know, I could take them for 'storage at the Ortega complex' and toss them out somewhere between four thousand and five thousand."

"Kilometers high, or kilometers per hour?"

He opened the door and ushered me in as I gave him his answer. "Both."

He didn't laugh, but once inside he gave me a savage smile and a rocks glass of tequila. We clinked them musically. "Wish it were possible."

I guess that is the difference between a cop and a merc.

He quickly downed one glass and poured himself another. He rubbed his eyes with one pudgy hand and sighed at the ceiling. "More than that, I wish the rains would come. It's months late, and the weather's much hotter than it should be. Making everyone *loco*." I pulled off the C^2 helmet and set the comm to sound off through the loud speaker if there was anything coming in. I reached back with a utility knife and cut the zip-ties holding my hair at bay, letting it free down past my shoulders and releasing the heat trapped against my scalp. At that he chuckled, his blue eyes sparkling. "That's not any kind of regulation haircut."

I smiled, sheepishly. "Well, no. Helps throw off the snipers."

Lomen eased himself down into his chair. "Huh?"

I took a polite sip of tequila and managed to hide the grimace at the bitter liquor. At least I thought I had until Captain Lomen grinned at my discomfort. "If you saw two guys through your scope, and one had hair like this, who's in charge?"

"Ah... but isn't that hard on the hired help?"

"Yes, it is, but it's a matter of odds." I took another sip. "If I die in a combat zone, then the chances of anyone making it home drop by seventy-five percent."

"Seventy-five?"

"Believe it or not, *Haven* actually keeps studies on these things. Anyway, I started growing it long when I was lieutenant, but I never got around to cutting it when I got the job of captain. It's become something of a symbol of authority in the team."

"We usually carry around badges for that."

Again, I found myself laughing. "I guess that could work too."

I saw Lomen visibly consider pouring himself another, then twist the cap back on the bottle and shove it into a mini-fridge behind his desk. I heard other bottles clinking inside, and caught the whiff of slightly decaying food. As he worked to find space for the tequila, I glanced across the office.

I was surprised at how small it was. The medium-sized desk took up much of the space. With just enough room to walk around every side, it felt much more like a cubicle than office of a station chief. The half-glass walls were blotted from view, covered up with maps, rap sheets, mug shots, and hand written notes. His desk was similarly strewn with reports and printouts, and the only clear spot was over the pop-up screen in the desk surface. What was here told as much of a story as what was not. For all of the cases this paperwork indicated, there were no flowers, no pictures of loved ones, no riotball memorabilia, nothing of himself except his work. Then one sheet caught my eye. In the corner was written 11/01/2662.

"Captain, you said you have not been paid in two months?"

"Oh, yeah." Lomen settled back into the chair and touched a button, popping up the monitor from the surface of his desk. "The bombings caused the mobilization of every cop, firefighter, and government agent on twenty-hour shifts, seven days a week, for months. Then there were several failed levies, and tax schemes tried to pay for all the manpower. And then there was this massive movement five months ago to stop paying taxes. Some charismatic and popular people were arrested to prove no one was above the law, but all it did was turn it into a real brushfire movement really, really fast.

"The City and Planetary government buildings of New California are now ghost towns. The Justice Center was shut down completely, and all the prisoners released. Police, fire, emergency medical, only a handful of people are left in any one area. The Planetaries are mostly funded, but only by the movie house. If the Planetaries want to stay funded, they do what L/V/D says, when they say it. After all the rhetoric over the last few weeks, I don't think the movie executives care too much what happens on the streets of the regular, residential neighborhoods."

"But you're still working?"

"Murderers don't go on strike."

"Captain, if you ever want a job, I'll give you one in an instant."

The Key to Damocles

"I'm a little old to go tromping through trenches. Besides, I have a job." We shared a moment in silence, each taking a fresh measure of the other. "We should go check on the troops."

"Agreed." I put my helmet back on. It was time for work.

The captain held out his hand to me. "Oh, and call me Tony."

I took it and shook it firmly, honestly. "Todd."

Ten *Angels* were working security, cordoning off the entire area as the police did work they were much better trained for. Pictures were being taken, objects catalogued and bagged. Notes were written. Ortega had set up shop in the center of the street, keeping guard with his sensor unit. Logan walked the line of police tape, keeping the sparse crowd back and ignoring questions hurled by the reporters. Lomen's radio chirped, and he answered in code. He took his leave and rushed back upstairs. I walked the perimeter, giving advice and praise to my men over the radio. The news crews had been here since the riot and even now were shouting questions, focusing in on our identical, black padded armor suits and featureless black-tinted helmets, looking for who was in charge. Seeing me with Tony and not on station like the rest of the team let them know precisely who that was. Not that I answered, but the tone of the questions was getting nasty.

A pretty young woman, face contorted in frustration, shouted, "How many people did you murder in this raid?"

None.

"Colonel," That one trying to give me a promotion, "why did you open fire on defenseless protestors?"

Defenseless? I don't often mistake pistols for flowers.

Another one was much more professional, but no less persistent. "How do you plan to defend yourself against the inevitable lawsuits that will follow?"

Lawsuits? Good luck with that considering the court system has been abandoned for six weeks.

"Were you the team that murdered twenty-seven young boys at the Ninth Street Cathlist Church last night?" Bolts of electricity ran up and down my legs as blood thumped in my ears. Only the greatest effort allowed me to keep moving past the reporter without depositing one well-aimed fist.

Question: What does it take to turn a murdering band of thieves into revered saints?

Answer: One hundred hollow point 10mm rounds, four flash-bang grenades, and one news crew.

Whenever possible, I ignored the press on any given world I worked on. The reasons are simple: sometimes, they were dirt bags, other times, they were apologists for philosophies looking to draw strength from the blood of mercenaries. The good ones, and there are a lot of ethical members of the media, were simply too nosy. Battle plans need to be kept secret. Identities on the vidscreen become targets for the enemy. I told them as little as possible, as often as possible. Sometimes, however, it was worth it to listen to their questions because it would tell you things your enemy might be wondering. This time, their questions told me they had been checking up on us. They were all speaking English.

Within six hours, all the evidence had been gathered and we all pulled back to the police station. The cops had filtered off in ones and twos; others had taken their places, but apparently there was only one guy willing to come back to work that was qualified to look at it all. Despite what they show in the entertainment feeds, it takes pretty intense skills to correctly process all the details of an investigation, so one lonely officer was working the evidence, of which we had truckloads. While she had to process prints, bag shells, and set inventory of everything on her own, the least we could do is look up the weaponry on the massive computerized database aboard *Deadly Heaven*. In return, we got to use some of the empty police station, which worked out just fine. There were plenty of lockers, showers, and bunks for the *Angels* in the unused SWAT on-call rooms. While the *Angels* showered and settled down, the police reopened the station for business. Our one problem as unexpected guests was food, so I would soon have to send someone out to a local market. Considering the rioters probably lived within walking distance, sending men out alone on the streets was out of the question. There were more pressing matters at the moment, however.

I made my way to Evidence, and what I saw chilled my blood. A map on the wall showed the hiding places of the rocket-team, as well as where Logan's downloaded artificial memory said the riflemen had appeared with their masks on. Red stickers showed where the camera crews had been stationed. Enlarged pictures of the automatic rifles used by the attackers hung on the wall, cross-referenced with factory specifications, cost, and ballistic properties. In the center of the table, like the skeletal remains of Grendel, were the half-melted rocket tubes, unused rockets, two rifles, fourteen magazines, and six miraculously intact grenades.

Lomen was there, talking with the police evidence processor. She wore a badge marked A. Inez. Things immediately became awkward when the conversation stuttered to a halt as I walked into the room. I scanned the positions on the roof and on the street as well as the equipment on the table with no small amount of interest, but it wasn't until I got to the grenades that everything fit together.

"Please don't touch anything," Inez said.

Never mind that none of this was going to see the inside of a court. Never mind that every piece of equipment was wrapped in transparent plastic. Never mind that my hands had been behind my back the whole time. Swallowing all of my 'never-minds', I tried to keep my face blank and nodded. She grinned a bit, but it wasn't a nice grin, nor did it melt the frost in her eyes.

Tony cleared his throat. "There is one thing I don't understand. How did they know you were coming?"

I shrugged. "All of this is at least upper middle shelf mercenary equipment. Those Walther & Wesson assault rifles alone are a grand apiece; the rockets are even more expensive. Those are 'MuRRs', multi-role rockets, meant to set off an armor piercing charge to the front, while an anti-personnel charge sends out shrapnel to the sides and rear. These grenades—"

Icy Inez crossed her arms and leaned against a stool. "We know all this. We looked it up in your database."

I decided to be a little less genial. One or two wisps of fire exited my eyes in her general direction. "My point is that if they have this level of equipment, then they can certainly have decoding software beefy enough to crack our signals to *Deadly Heaven.*"

And if they can break my encryption, yours wouldn't even slow them down, I thought…loudly.

Tony nodded slightly, like a poker player tasting an opponent's face card. "Could they crack the encryption soon enough to set up an ambush?"

"Set it up?"

James Daniel Ross

"Yeah, they had to set up or hear about the riot. Hear our call for help," He held his hands out, surveying the evidence. "I know that's no huge thing to a mercenary team, but they still had to get here, position the riflemen, and prep the rockets for launch."

"You think they were coming for us? You think the *Angels* brought this attack on?" Inez smirked behind Captain Lomen's shoulder, enjoying this way too much. He pursed his lips and half nodded. Inside, my head, gears whirled without catching for a moment. "Tony, this was an ambush, but they didn't want us."

My words made Tony smirk and Inez huff. The Captain *cum* Station Chief moved over to me and picked up one of the rifles in its plastic cocoon. "How do you figure?"

I pulled up a stool of my own and plopped down. "One question... when were you issued firearms?"

Tony chuckled, but if Inez were a cat, her tail would be bottle-brushed. "We weren't. We had police-standard issue PPG-149e pushguns. When the riots and bombings started at other stations, I broke out confiscated firearms out of the evidence locker."

I sat back, apparently lost in thought, but really I was counting thirty ticks of the clock on the wall, mentally laughing a tad that the purely electronic device had to have a bit inside to make it 'tick' and 'tock'. It was odd; no matter how advanced humanity gets, there are some things humanity wants because they grow up expecting things to be that way. Expensive electronics are heavy, laser guns make noise, digital cameras whirr to advance theoretical film, and clocks tick to tell time. Nowadays, electronics are weighted with lead plates, civilian laser pistols and cameras often have a sound chip installed to produce a noise, and clocks tick because they have a speaker to make them do so. Then I realized that half a minute was a really long time when nothing was being said. That was the point, really, making them wait so they listened when I finally spoke.

"They set what looks like a car bomb to blow outside of the building, blinding cameras and stripping off the external defenses. Then they either waited for a riot, or more likely incited one. Next, they set up across the street, and waited for things to get nasty." My eyes swept across the map on the wall and over the equipment. "At the right time, the riflemen take out the news crews..."

The Key to Damocles

I stood up and brushed past Inez, who recoiled from me. I picked up a nearby marker and drew lines across the map. Each was short, no more than ten meters, each was straight, with nothing to block their line of sight. When I was done, each of the enemy rifle teams was accounted for. "With the witnesses dead, they'd pop off a MuRR at the front doors—blowing apart your barricade and shredding any nearby protestors, toss in grenades, and sweep the building, killing everyone in their path."

"That's insane!" Inez put the evidence table between her and I, tossing her doubts over her shoulder. "They'd be beaten to a pulp by officers with pushguns before they ever made to the booking desk."

"Wrong." Specifically ignoring her previous order, I reached onto the table and tossed one baseball-sized object at her. "Ion dust grenade. It throws up a cloud of ionized dust that obscures certain kinds of sensors, fragments low power transmissions..." Inez tried to interrupt so I raised my voice to roll over her, "...and what the official corporate write up on it doesn't say is that it completely disrupts the electron packet projectiles of pushguns." I let that thought hang in the air. "If they had decided to come in, it would have been bloody because they were obviously not expecting you to be armed with firearms. Even so, with their numbers and equipment, they had better than even chances of wiping you all out."

Inez looked as if she were choosing an orifice of mine in which to place a grenade *sans* pin. Tony mimed applause at me, looking as proud as a teacher with a prized student. "Todd, you would have made a good detective. Now you just have to tell us why."

I shook my head. "I don't know. But I will."

Tony hopped up, putting an arm around my shoulder and guiding me out of the evidence room. "And that deserves a toast. Inez, keep on working. If you need me, you know where to reach me."

Behind me, just as the door closed, I heard the room's last occupant whisper a single word: an ancient, ugly word. My stride faltered, but Tony's arm pushed me onward. We got to his office where he reused our glasses from earlier to pour another round of tequila. We sat in silence for a minute that refused to die. It seemed to hang in the air like the stink of uninvited guests. Tony poured himself another. "Sorry, Captain. Luckily enough for me, it just so happens this is one of the best places in the universe to be a white guy. Most of the Latin population has a pretty nasty opinion of blacks, though…"

I really wanted to change topics, but the next words out of my mouth surprised even me. "Do you have any patrol cruisers?"

"Yeah, we have a dozen in the underground garage. I've kept them under wraps, though. We lost five since this whole thing began due to ground fire from rioters and gangs. Plus, they've been flying for two months without regular maintenance, and I'm worried. I don't have any mechanics to clear them for flight and regulations say they need checked every week."

I hadn't even thought of that. Fliers required regular maintenance and with no mechanics… "Are they armed?"

"Yes. Nothing like you're used to, but a pack of them could take down a military craft."

I filed that away for later. "I need a uniform."

"Captain, impersonating an officer of the law is a serious offense that carries the penalty of a ten year… Yeah, go ahead. Take anything you need from supply."

I drained the glass, nodded my thanks, and left. I rode the elevator to the basement and walked past the empty cage where whatever cops called a master-of-arms would normally sit. Inside, I performed many paperless requisitions including a uniform, light armor, sidearm, boots, duty belt, and radio. Then I stopped by the evidence lockup. Similarly deserted, there was no one to protest my fingering through the computer someone had conveniently left logged into the network. In five minutes, I had a badge.

I made a call over my forearm command pad to Logan. His response was immediate. "Yes sir?"

"I'm 'going independent', Logan."

"Is that wise, sir?"

"I hope so. Send out two pairs for food using their issued funds. Side arms only. Make haste."

"Aye, aye, Captain. Take care."

"Will do. Rook Out."

It was time to do some recon.

CHAPTER 7: EMPTY STREETS

There are many kinds of commander. Each has benefits and drawbacks. The first type is the absentee commander. They usually preside over teams that are sent out on their own, teams that get the job done in the mud and filth while the commander fills out paperwork. They bring no experience to the table, only a name and funding. Without anything useful to do, they exert control over their teams by creating tons of rules and regulations that clog up how mercenaries function. These are the kind of superiors that get men killed.

Captain Arthur, my first and only commander, the man who died and willed to me *The Radiation Angels*, was what mercs call a bridge commander. He needed to be away, on high, like an ancient god. He would sit above it all watching over helmet cameras and shipboard sensors, directing his men like a symphony. In the end there is no safe place in battle, but fighting a ground war from three dozen kilometers above the soil, surrounded by semi-intelligent anti-ship weapon systems, torpedo and bomb launchers, and several thousand metric tons of armor does extend some manner of security as well as perspective.

I don't know why, but I can't work that way. For good or for ill, I am the kind of man who has to feel the flow of the wind. I need to be there, touching the soil and hearing the snap of the bullets. From on high, I can't sense the ambushes. I can see what the other side wants me to see, but can't feel what they wish to hide. I have to be out on the sharp end. This means I risk death—and thereby the death of my troops—but it is the only way I can operate. It also leaves me doing a lot of dirty grunt work that, by rights, I should have been able to pass off to someone much junior on the team. By dirty grunt work I mean walking down a hot street, sweating in a police uniform, with nothing more offensive than a pushpistol on my hip. Well, I still had my slim-line laser pistol, but I was hoping I didn't have to pull it.

Two pairs exited the police station, decked out in full martial gear. They pushed through the few remaining reporters playing

The Key to Damocles

stake-out and ignored their questions. I had to suppress a smile because I'll be damned if they didn't look like death itself. Black helmets, black armor, black jumpsuits, each emblazoned with only one visible symbol: the wing, sword and nuclear furnace insignia of the *Angels*. On their helmets were personal markers that glowed when viewed through our visors so we could tell who was who, but to the casual eye they were dressed identically. While this meant none of them could be specifically targeted, I had to watch them move, examine gait, mannerisms, and level of awareness, in order to take my best guess at who was who.

The one who spotted me first was probably Thompson. I know she saw me first because when the next man in line, clearly her spotter Lopez, started to point at me, she nearly broke his arm pulling it behind him and steering him down the street before kicking him playfully in the rump. To anyone who just glanced, they appeared to be just horsing around. An experienced eye would probably see a senior officer covering up for the gaffe of a talented novice. Behind those two was most certainly Pair Six, their hulking frames marking them as the heavy weapon officers Richardson and King. The *Angels* immediately spread out, making sure no automatic weapon fire could take more than one of them at a time with a short burst. From that point, not one of them so much as glanced again in my direction as we walked fourteen blocks to the nearest open shop.

The whole charade wasn't just good field craft, it was currently a matter of my survival. I was a combatant dressed as a civilian in a war zone. If I were captured in this condition, I would be considered a spy. I could be held without legal council, tortured, and executed. So, it goes without saying that it behooved me to avoid notice, let alone capture.

I tied up my dreadlocks in the tightest ponytail I could and hoped that anyone who took notice thought I had been undercover recently or something. It was only then, out alone on the street, that a cold chill stole over me despite the heat of the day. I was the only African extraction on the sparsely populated streets. African extractions make up a huge majority of the universe, so I'm used to being able to blend in most anywhere. Still, it was too late to do anything but carry on. Thankfully, there were no mobs in evidence. In fact, the streets were nearly barren.

People on this planet should have finished their *siestas* hours ago, their metabolisms dialed into a thirty-two hour day. I was beginning to feel the ragged edges of fatigue rubbing at me like burrs in my clothing, sleep tugging at my awareness like a persistent child. Even though it was 19:00 hours, near bedtime for my twenty-four hour timed body, it was only the very last bits of afternoon on Persephone. I wondered for a half second at how they meshed the local thirty-two hour day, five hundred twelve day year with the Earth Standard the rest of the galaxy uses. Most planets were a little off, but this was ridiculous. Did they have leap years where whole months were skipped? And how do birthdays work when time is so out of whack? Did they fold time into a hot year and then a cold year rather than seasons?

Pay attention, soldier. If you only play spy, then you won't only have to play dead. And with that cheerful thought, I returned to the matter at hand.

The sun stole nearly any place I could become unobtrusive, but I don't think it would have mattered in any case; the streets were nearly deserted. It has always been my experience that after a major event, like the putdown of a riot, people want to talk about it. They sit out on their porches, in bars, outside of laundromats. They give each other the play-by-play of events, swap rumors, and place blame. These were lower-middle-class urban houses, packed next to one another like slices of bread. There should have been no end of chatting neighbors, but instead there were mostly empty streets and nervous pedestrians. The only groups were situated in knots around buildings, arms full of electronics, portable media, lamps, clothes, and even furniture. They looked around furtively, watching me with angry eyes as I strolled past. I watched them as respectfully as I could, taking mental notes.

None of them looked anywhere near middle class. There were too many pairs of worn shoes, cheap clothing, missing teeth, and scars. Even allowing for the idea that these were locals dressing down to avoid being mugged, nobody gives themselves seams. More than that, nobody who could afford to live in this neighborhood would put up with scars that could be taken care of as simply and cheaply as filling a tooth. Only mercenaries keep seams, especially facial scars. It isn't a badge of pride or anything; it's just that mercenaries have more important things to buy than vanity. These were poor folks, picking over empty houses to make their lives more livable. The whole thing had an air of a grand scale looting in slow motion.

The grocery store was a massive disappointment, with only a few scattered cans of hideously overpriced goods and loads of non-perishable snack foods. I did mark at least three local toughs acting as armed guards with what had to be nominally illegal weaponry.

I followed the *Angels* back to the precinct station house, and it took a few minutes to find Captain Lomen. He turned out to be at his computer in his office, stubby but expert fingers snapping at the keys as he entered reports. Immediately, I felt a dull chill in the air and noticed his eyes didn't focus quite right. Either someone had brained him with a mallet in my absence, or he had been at his stock of tequila again. He only glanced at me before returning to his work. "Looks good on you, but I didn't say you could have a badge."

"I improvised."

His keystrokes became crisper, harder. "Give it up, Rook."

I took off the badge and set it beside him. "The area around here is almost deserted."

"Of course it is."

"Why is that?" My only answer was the double fast clicking of the keys and the building staccato of my heartbeat. Blood began to swell up my neck and across my face, churning with heat and waspish intensity. "Why, Captain?"

With the sweep of one arm, Tony noisily cleared the desk in front of him onto the floor. Eyes wild, he swept up a clipboard off of the table with one, meaty hand and whipped it into the clear plastic half-wall of the cubicle. Police reports fluttered like an explosion of propaganda, but the wall was merely scratched, the clipboard similarly unharmed as it clattered into a corner. I clamped on temptations and vile, violent urges as he yanked a lamp from the desk and hurled it as well, failing to even ding the fake glass but coming ever closer to me. My hands itched, burned, ached for the cool, comforting caress of the weapon on my hip, but I stayed them, reining them in like a trembling horse. His eyes bulged and sweat beaded on his brow, but his exertions seemed to only build as each item went flying, one by one, closer and closer to my head.

Eye to eye, I met him with nothing but absolute stillness.

Face beet red, an inhuman grunt gathering strength from deep inside his chest, Lomen grabbed his ceramic coffee mug from the table and aimed it like a missile at my face.

My hand rocketed upward, guided by skills from a life, long past, until the empty mug slapped wetly into my outstretched palm. I took a step forward, exhaled as much of my temper as I could, and gently gave his mug back to him. In a voice barely a whisper, I asked a different question, though using the same mantra. "Why?"

Tony blinked, blinked again and wiped his unshaven face on his sleeve. He nodded and regained a bit of his composure as deep breaths cleansed him of his personal tempest. This close, I could smell the alcohol on him as he said, "Come on."

And he led the way upwards.

I could see why Tony didn't take the old station chief's office. The damn thing was pretentious as hell. The room was easily ten meters to a side. The desk was three times the size of Lomen's downstairs, and it was devoid of anything even vaguely approximating work. Thick, fresh carpeting, expensive wood paneling, and numerous heavy duty power outlets told that this room was more often used to greet news crews for official announcements than actually doing any kind of productive job. I picked up a family photo off of the table and gazed into the vacant, vapid, bureaucratic face there. It was a telling testament that the man who worked here had fled when those under his command continued to work in three-meter, cubed hovels. He held onto his wife and daughter, proclaiming *These are things I have made*. I tossed the picture onto the desk and the glass cracked. *Pity*.

Tony hit hidden controls next to the desk, and a riot of noise erupted behind me as wooden panels spun on hidden swivels to reveal flat-panel monitors. As each turned, it came to life, each showing expensively-dressed talking heads doing their best to regurgitate the prompting copy burned into their brains by the computer systems at the various news networks. The words moving across their brains varied in tone, in rhythm, in style, passionately delivered but strangely monotone all the same. It was all in Spanish, but then Lomen set the smartchip translators in the screens to English. The voices were remodulated into words I could understand, in their original voices, but out of sync with the lips that produced them.

—And tonight on Action 311 we have striking news from New California as a mercenary team called *The Radiation Angels* attacked protestors outside of the police station at—

It became a kind of *sans artiste* music, the kind you buy out of a box in the shopping mall.

—Channel 99 was there when death descended on fiery wings upon a peaceful group of protestors supporting *El Toro*—

It always seems like a good idea, custom-ordering computer simulated tunes, synched and synthed together to precisely your specifications. No royalties, supposedly unique, no contracts, egos, overdoses, or stars. No waiting.

—dropping what appeared to be some unknown biological agent upon the crowd. Kim Panocho was there for News 11 and—

The problem is, without someone behind the notes, the music always comes out the same. Sometimes we need someone objective to put something in our laps that resonates inside of us simply because it is from outside our experiences, but eerily the same.

—scene here was devastating, Julio. I don't know what that red dust was, but local doctors say it could have easily been a bioweapon, outlawed in every civilized system in the colonies—

—apparently the same group of mercenaries that killed over twenty young men at the Ninth Street Cathlist church yesterday—

There was nothing objective, here.

—And it is clear that this rogue mercenary band was welcomed with open arms by the acting Station Chief Antonio Lomen—

Anyone with a keyboard and an attitude could create *grit* like this. Then again, the more appropriate tool for moving it onto the airwaves might be a shovel.

—unclear as to whether the team has taken over this section of New California for their own, but it is certain that the people of this community are waiting for guidance from *El Toro* as to how they should respond to this latest abuse by the rich upon the common citizenry—

More monitors popped up, and text began pouring across them. Again, tiny chips stared at the grammar and syntax, sucking in the Spanish or MexiCali, and spitting out English.

Fr: West Lot Station   To: North End Station

—Tony, dear God, we're running out of food. You have got to send your mercenary team here with supplies. I've had rioters outside for two weeks. You have got to get them to help us.—

And it looked like even Tony's peers were buying into the media blitz.

—Captain Lomen, I don't know what you think you are doing, but allying yourself with murderers is not going to help the situation. When this is all over, I will use every ounce of my influence to bring you to trial—

I had made Tony a rich man amongst paupers, eliciting hate, envy, and pleading from every police force in the city, and beyond.

—Be assured that the director of Planetary Investigation Services has been informed, and while I do not want to sound sensationalistic, the word traitor is being used behind closed doors. The Director himself is considering issuing a warrant for your arrest—

—It is unknown if the puppet government and their L/V/D backers will retaliate for this expression of discontent as they have in the past—

And the newsies were working overtime to define the new equation. Faster and faster they came, soon flipping through as if fired from a machinegun.

—men are so tired—

—complicity of the police—

It wasn't about the truth.

—Tony, I had control of my precinct until you started this crap—

It really never even had to be about the truth.

—savage mercenaries—

—riots all over New California and beyond—

—must get relief soon—

—spreading to other metropoli—

—fault lay not only with the mercenary invaders, but with traitors within the ranks of the police—

The Key to Damocles

It was about news. It was about perception. I had done more than just save him. I had turned Tony into the focal point for the newsies to gorge upon. Since the people had cannibalized the body politic, there was no one looking over the shoulder of the news agencies except the sponsors. These same sponsors, faced with dropping revenue and an unstable market, needed to increase sales in any way they could. Their credits would be desperately needed by the news agencies for the same reasons, and now competition was so fierce that the news sites would say anything, do anything, to keep and gain ratings. They would burn Lomen at the stake for taking us in.

It was a great irony that newscasters couldn't do anything themselves, really. They could only shine the light upon wrong, make it too embarrassing for anyone to continue, but couldn't step in themselves. At times, this is a good thing, allowing for an objective observer to tell the truth when both sides of an argument began hurling lies. At times, it was disgusting, like when two healthy, athletic adults film a child drowning in a river wondering in a 'live from the scene voice-over' why no one comes to the rescue.

—This reporter watched in horror as mercenaries used apparently lethal force to clear the way into the police station—

The situation escalates once they stop looking for the truth and believe the truth is whatever they say, slanting words to fit preconceived notions and predetermined outcomes. Evidence to the contrary is not deemed newsworthy. On some planets, they call this 'spin'. My father called it lying and remedied it with a thick, leather belt.

—This just in, we have another message from *El Toro*—

They were kingmakers, and they wanted *El Toro* as king.

—Yes, we have this coming in, another proclamation from the rebel leader *El Toro*—

—and we will bring it to you in just a moment, after a word from these sponsors. Stay tuned to Action News 311—

—Stay tuned to News Center 142—

—Channel 99 News will be right back with—

They may have been objective once, but their opinions had crept in like a hit man and began killing everyone in the path of their agenda.

Brighter teeth and building supplies and home security devices and cheaper defensive arms, new news programs, medical kits, food and carsandtransportandsurvivalgearand findingloveanddetergentandcarsanddefensivearmsandsecurity devicesandbodyguardsandnewsshowsandmedicalkitsandtravel offplanetand...

—Welcome back to Action 311 News—

The bad guys in this fracas were the people of Persephone, the ones who had decided that instead of fighting the chaos they would run, hide, or join in. They had sold out their entire planet in order to settle some petty grievances, but these were the same people who bought the products displayed on the news channel feeds. Telling them they were naughty, naughty people was not likely to get them to buy the offered goods.

—And thank you for staying with Channel 99 as we bring you the newest transmission from—

—message from—

—edict from—

And there he was, their symbol.

"I am *El Toro*, and I am here to tell you that the time for plowshares is over. Take up your swords and fight against the oppressors and their black-clad executioners..."

I didn't think I could give them another symbol.

"My people, you have suffered long, and your voices have risen in anguish to the gilded pillars of justice only to be ignored."

But as I looked into his eyes, I didn't see a revolutionary leader. I didn't see a genius, nor a guerilla.

"You deserve a primary role on your own home world. So far, you have been denied glory, security and prosperity by those who even now act to eradicate you and breed you out of existence. My people, I can stop them..."

I saw an empty, little man, and that meant I sure as hell could take this symbol away.

"...I swear it..."

—Please—

"...but the revolution needs your donations..."

—help—

"...I know you will give, and give generously, my people."

The Key to Damocles

And then, with the push of a button, my ears rang with quiet. Talking heads mouthed in their boxes, words still scrolled across screens, but their accusatory posture recoiled as Tony digitally slit their throats.

"They *fragged* you, Rook."

I felt weakened, drained. I had to take a few steps back and lean against the *grande* desk to keep my legs from shaking.

"That's what you mercenaries say, right? They *fragged* you and me both." His voice dropped to an angry murmur. "Come on, Goddammit. I know you have something in here for photo ops, you bastard..."

There was the sound of a seal being broken, tearing foil, a hiss of celebration. My mind raced along paths into the future, finding blood and death at each one. Behind me, there was the tinkle of crystal, then a loud pop. A cork thumped against the wall in front of me as I heard the sound of soft, fizzing liquid pouring. "Everyone's going to turn you into a criminal, and me into some kind of Vichy capitulator. I've had fifteen walk-outs since the riot and there will be more."

A spark caught inside of me as the bitter fruit smell of alcohol tickled at my senses. I turned and saw his glazed eyes lingering lovingly inside the swirling cloud of liquid bubbles. He raised the crystal cup to his lips. When it came down, I was standing right in front of him, my arm already in motion. I clapped the glass from him, sending it into the wall where it shattered into stardust. Tony bounced to his feet, bristling as he drew himself up to put his face as close to my face as he could. I could sense the gathering storm and everything inside me tensed to be punched.

Then, abruptly, his ire was smothered by despair. He collapsed into the chair and kicked closed the mini-fridge behind the desk. The life, the hope, was out of him. "We're both dead men."

I moved back to the front of the desk and pulled a plush chair close. "Do the same people run the news networks and the movie house?"

Tony snapped up the bottle of champagne off the table. "No. Years ago, they were forbidden by law from owning any part of the news stations. No one company can have more than one station at one time... anti-monopoly laws."

"So why do they speak with one voice?"

Tony looked at me, then at the bottle for a good long time. "They know what the people want to hear, and they know how to tell a good story."

"So, what kind of retaliation can you expect?"

"Riots? Hell, I don't know. They made a good start of it last time they probably won't have too much trouble finishing the job if they try again."

"Raise a militia."

"Jesus, you would have made a lousy cop! Militias have been outlawed for a hundred years. Besides, no one is going to follow someone colluding with a 'black-clad executioner'."

I wanted to tell him that I didn't give a rat's ass for what was illegal, but I couldn't say that to a man who had given his entire life over to the law. He considered the size of the bottle, the heft of the glass and the tint of the liquor inside. My voice must have been like a far away echo to him. "Who is *El Toro*?"

"I don't know; nobody really knows." He began to raise the bottle to his lips.

"Where is he?" A shrug. "Where can he be found?"

"He can't."

"How does he gain followers?"

"Don't know."

"Who does he give interviews to?"

"Nobody, he makes pirate broadcasts."

"Where was his last rally?"

"I don't think he's ever had one."

"No rallies? How does he get soldiers?"

"Don't know, Rook. What's more, I don't think I care anymore."

"Dammit, Tony! What kind of explosives do his people use?"

"All kinds. Mostly high explosives, but they've used everything from fertilizer to homemade gunpowder and nitro."

Tony was there, right in front of me, sitting in the same room, in the same building, on the same planet, but as I asked him questions, I could see that he had no interest in the way the facts didn't fit. There was something heavy on his mind, the obvious thing. "Do you really think they'll kill you?"

My question stopped him. "Yeah, the media will call for my head, and someone will listen and come and kill me and everyone who looks like me."

91

The Key to Damocles

I stood, feeling complex emotions kicking into the sump of my belly, churning into acid and doubt. I turned to face the screens and saw something that shouldn't have been there. I walked over and glared at the image, feeling hate and hurt welling up inside as I read the letters parading underneath *El Toro's* face. It was time to go. I walked for the door, sensing Tony's hunger for the bottle rising again. "Denounce us."

"What?"

I reached out for the handle, resting cold clammy skin on the cool plasticized metal. "Denounce us. Call up the news and tell them you were tricked. Tell them we took you hostage. In any case, we'll go and you can tell them anything you want."

"You helped us, Todd. You and your men saved our lives."

"That really doesn't matter. What good is saving your life if you let these people tear you apart because I'm here? *The Radiation Angels* are leaving West Lot immediately, so go grab a camera and tell them what they want to hear and you'll be fine."

"You can't go now. Your aircraft is damaged, your men are exhausted, and you're outgunned on the streets."

Enough. "You know what, Captain? I am seriously tired of everyone and their mother on this *fragging* planet telling me what can't be done, what they can't do, and what I can't do." I couldn't turn, couldn't face him, though I felt his eyes on my shoulders like two-ton weights. "Like it or not, the moment a professional, well-armed mercenary team—and make no mistake, the people trying to kill you were a mercenary team—entered into this on both sides, it ceased to be a civil action and instantly became a real war.

"In a war there is only one thing to do: survive. I don't know much about police work, but I know about leading men into battle." I had to take a deep breath. "Among all humans, there have always been three types: those who hide, those who fight, and those who lead. The people downstairs may have sworn to uphold the law, but they believe in you. They want you. They need you. Without you, they will become a disorganized mass, a group that can be harried, picked off, and disbanded.

"So, you need to figure out, right here, right now, what is indeed possible and what is too costly to contemplate." I opened the door. "You do whatever you need to in order to survive, so either give up and get out, or trust them."

"They already trust you."

I walked through, and closed the door gently behind me. My legs were shaky, and it took two tries to hit the button for the elevator. Soundlessly, the magnetic tube pulled the metal-framed carriage upwards and locked it into position outside the floor. The doors slid open and I nearly fell in. The doors closed behind me, and left me alone with my despair.

What I just told Tony, I myself had been told in a stinking bar, in a little town, on a forgettable rock spinning in a careless void. Captain Arthur laid it down in no uncertain terms, telling me that I would have to be strong enough to carry on forever, or strong enough to walk away to give up leading men into battle. It was a lot like facing into a mirror and admitting to addiction, a childhood abuse, or any other life-threatening secret that would change how a person interacts with the rest of the universe for all time. He would either get control of his mercurial nature, or the enormity of the path ahead would surely break him.

I hit the button and marshaled my self-control to push the last twenty hours of effort down deep inside me. I collected my warrior ethos around me like a blanket, and used it to stop my body from shaking, my thoughts from squabbling. This would be a long night as it stood and I needed to focus to be effective.

I just needed to hold it together.

CHAPTER 8: THE LONG WALK

I stripped out of the police uniform and back into our basic black riot armor. Tony stopped by for a few minutes, watching me pack and dress. I didn't greet him, and he didn't say goodbye when he left.

I woke the bulk of the *Angels* in the SWAT ready-room. I don't remember what I said to them; I was too damn tired. I do know that shoulders were slumped and heads were lowered when they began collecting their equipment from around the room. I retired to the bathroom where I put on my helmet and got in contact with Sichak aboard *Deadly Heaven*.

It took half an hour before Sichak—still on a twenty-four-hour sleep schedule—could wake up, get to the control room, reorient the vessel in orbit and then send overhead pictures to my C^2. The route was a long haul, almost forty kilometers from the police station to join John Doe at the spaceport. All of it would have to be done on foot. I took off the helmet and rubbed my eyes which were already stinging from lack of sleep. Fully loaded, armed, and armored soldiers could make the forty-kilometer trek easily if they were fresh. The *Angels* were not. Considering there were no alligator pits, quicksand, or magma flows, misfortune was really losing its touch.

I balanced my helmet on my hip and went back to collect my men. Together, we took the stairs down to the trauma station where Logan and Ansef were saying goodbye to the woman inside. Behind soundproof panes, she smiled weakly and nodded, trying to be brave for her savior and her newfound confidant. They came out, joined the rest of the team, and started to filter into the stairwell. The woman inside the station backed herself into a corner and pulled up the blanket like a wall against the world. A hand with a thin remote-card poked out for a second before snaking back inside.

I felt Logan's feather light, yet rock hard, touch on my shoulder. I glanced back at my Master Sergeant's featureless chrome face. As always, it was as blank and nonjudgmental as a wall. I felt my guilt reflected and magnified in the chrome surface nonetheless.

The Key to Damocles

I'm not a psychologist, but I know that the first few days for a rape survivor are the hardest. That's when all the questions have no answers, dreams bring back the horrors denied during the day, and every shadow is seen as a pronounced danger. That's when they usually crumble, trying to escape the pain by any means necessary. She had maybe a 50/50 chance of living out the week on her own now that I was taking the only visible means of psychological support she had.

Dammit! Logan wasn't trying to make me feel like *grit*, he was trying to let me know that there was no shame in doing nothing if there is nothing that can be done. At least that's what they say. Which just goes to show that 'they' don't know a whole *frag* of a lot.

I handed him my helmet and motioned him to follow the *Angels*. Then I took two deep breaths and opened the door to the trauma station. Her eyes widened and she tensed visibly even under the formless blanket igloo. Some newscaster or another was bloviating about the situation on the streets. There was a movement from the blanket, and the screen positioned in one corner of the ceiling went mute. I held up my hands and moved slowly, giving the smell of pain time to leech into my brain.

No matter where you go in the galaxy, it is the same. Walk into a place of healing and the smell hits you like a brick wall because no matter how often it is scrubbed, no matter how deeply it is cleansed, once someone suffers unimaginable agony in any place, the smell of the screams soaks into the walls, floors, and ceilings. It wafts out as single molecules and floats in the air, waiting for someone to walk in. Then it enters the nose, travels through the bloodstream until it latches onto the lizard brain, and pushes buttons until you throw up or go insane.

Truly, that's why I'm always nervous in hospital settings. Invisible panic particles. It's not because every time I'm in one of these places someone I care for, or I myself, is usually bleeding all over the place. That's my story and I'm sticking to it.

The woman—I hadn't even found out her name—was still watching me, eyes darting toward the doors, measuring chances for escape if things got dicey.

"Ah, uh…" and that was as far as I got. The silence stretched out between us, pulsing with the passing of each heartbeat. "I am sorry we have to go."

96

Her frightened eyes were my only reply.

"Look, I am sorry we have to go, but things are getting really dangerous here. They're getting more dangerous because of us, so we have to go…" And then I stuttered out again.

The silence filled the room like hot water, darkening my face and making me uncomfortable inside my own skin. In fact, in the absence of sound, all I could hear was a crowd of corpses screaming: people I have killed and people I could not save.

I had to get out. Now.

I moved to the door, wondering if it would be more or less awkward to say goodbye. Her voice, a tiny hook as brittle as a mouse bone and colored by her native MexiCali, stopped me. "You're not bad, like they say."

Well, since there was a working television in the room, I didn't have to ask who 'they' were. I turned to her and shrugged. "Thank you."

She snuggled back into her fortress, but her eyes had gone from frightened to hoping, waiting for something, anything. "Logan said that you gave the order to get me."

I leaned back against the wall, crossing my arms in front of me. Orders or not, Logan would have gone after her, but it seemed better to keep things simple for now. "Yes, I did."

"Why?"

"Because what was happening to you was wrong."

She digested that for a few seconds. "Everything that's going on now is wrong."

I sighed and shrugged, trying desperately to be realistic but not sound bitter. "I can't do anything about that. I'm just one man."

Her voice became strained and cracked. "Then why do anything at all?"

I looked at the wall. This young woman was asking much more than her words would indicate, and I wasn't sure if I even wanted to answer her. But there she sat, unwilling to ask a diluted substitute or have it go unanswered. Her eyes just bored into me, hoping to gain something from me to help her through the next day. Then, abruptly, it came out. "Because my father always said that the purpose of strength is to protect the weak. And he said that standing by is in many ways worse than participating."

The Key to Damocles

Her lips upturned, but it was more of a sob than a smile. "You've got to do what you can?"

I nodded slowly. "Yeah, that's about it."

She thought on that before gingerly coming out of her corner. She moved delicately, despite her larger than average size, every move echoing her stiffness and pain. She left her blanket behind, but she was still masked in the sickening aroma of topical anesthetics and antiseptics. For a moment, just a split second, she stood taller than I. "You are a hero, Rook."

Her words slammed into me like a physical force. I tried my hardest to merge with the surface of the door behind me while my own words punched back at her. "Oh, no. Ah, no, miss. I am not. I am sorry."

Wounded, spurned, she turned away and leaned on the counter. "Then how long will this go on? How can any of us live through this without heroes?"

I had a stray thought slip across my brain. I dismissed it, but it came back. It multiplied and swarmed around, clogging my mind until it was all I could think of. I slipped my hands around my back, pulled up my armored BDU shirt, and grasped what lay concealed there.

"Look, I'm a mercenary. People pay me to show up and do damage. I work for my client's interests, I get paid, and I go home. Sometimes, things go wrong…" I looked down at the flat, black plastic shape in my hands. "I have seen soldiers hold a line to the last man because their friends are helpless somewhere behind or beside them. I have seen them dive onto live grenades because their comrades are in danger. I have seen mercenaries fly into enemy territory and hold an exposed position for days in order to protect teammates who were unable to escape when the battle lines shifted. All heroes are born in places like that, at times like that. All the heroes I know have done something for more than money… and usually, it gets them killed.

"They are at the time, at the place, where things go horribly wrong. I can try all I can, the police can try all they can, but none of us can be everywhere at once. We can't be here if you need us. We won't be there the next time something happens. So, if you want a hero, miss, I'm afraid you are going to have to be it." She turned to face me, and I handed her my slim-line laser pistol.

She looked at it like a venomous snake, eyes full of fear and fascination. She ran one finger along an oily black surface. She smiled bitterly. "Is this for being a hero?"

"No. This is for being human. If you want to be a hero, leave it holstered. Talk. Talk until you are certain talking won't help at all. Then, if things get dangerous, pull your gun." I took her hand and slid it along the weapon, placing it firmly on the grip. "Just remember that it isn't a magic wand. You really can't do good things with a gun; you can only make sure a bad situation doesn't get worse."

"Is that the reason to have one?"

"There is no other reason that matters, and no other reason necessary." I shrugged and stepped back from her to put my back against the door again. "What if you had owned one yesterday?"

My only reply was another bitter, short-lived smile. She sighted down the barrel incorrectly, one eye closed like they did in the movies. "They said I shouldn't be alone. Ansef and Logan said I would hurt myself."

"Yeah, that's what the textbooks say." I took a deep breath. I guess it was my day to be the bearer of bad news. "Look, you're a human being. You have every right to walk in the night without fear. You have every right to see a doctor, to see a councilor, to stay somewhere safe. The problem is, this world is in the middle of a revolution, and it doesn't look like you are going to get any of those things."

She looked at me, her face the very picture of doom. Tears peeked out of her eyes and then ran helter-skelter for the floor over her homely features.

"So, here it is... whether you survive is all up to you. The world is without support or sense, and I'm guessing that if you had any friends or family nearby they would have picked you up by now. So, gun or not, there's a million ways to kill yourself, from jumping off a building, drinking drain cleaner, slitting your wrists—" *What are you doing, moron? Giving her a suicide shopping-list?* "My point is, if you are going to kill yourself, you're going to do it, gun or not. If you don't have it, you will be alone and defenseless. With a gun, you'll be able to make yourself a little bit safer. Remember, it isn't magic; you have to aim it. You have to be aware of your surroundings for it to do you any good.

The Key to Damocles

You have to be willing to use it if it comes down to that, because once you pull it, you have to use it or things will get even worse."

Her eyes locked in on mine. Deep within her, I saw something flicker. "Show me."

The slim-line was a very simple, low power, self-defense pistol. It had no protruding pieces, one power level indicator, one red light to let the operator know to change the focus gasses—every hundred shots or so—and one three kilo trigger. I gave her a quick overview, and the normal safety rules for dealing with any such weapon. Afterwards, the silence returned, and I knew I had to leave. There was really only one question I could ask, and it was the obvious one. "Are you going to make it?"

She tucked the gun under her blankets and went back to her corner. Even more stiffly, she slid herself up onto the table and rebuilt her blanket/igloo. "I guess we'll see."

And that was that.

I left quietly, heading downward one level to where the team waited. Every step nagged me with doubt, every second screaming that I had just killed that poor woman. By the time I arrived, I exuded a grim finality of guilt from every pore. Without complaint, without even a word, they took to their feet. I couldn't talk without choking on barely contained tears so I simply motioned them to action.

We took the stairs to avoid the front desk, where maybe a dozen unwashed newsies kept constant watch, fearful if they left they wouldn't get to spit yours truly on their handcrafted accusations. The whole world was a danger to us, now. We'd have to operate quickly, quietly, and well away from the biased banter of the media elite. The *Angels* stacked by the rear exit, which was mysteriously clear of police or cameramen, as Ortega swept the surrounding areas with his sensor unit. He appeared a bit bewildered, shrugged and clicked the 'all clear' over his radio. Immediately, we jogged out into an empty back street, turned east, and dissolved into the shadows of the coming night.

Tired, with at least two of us nearly dead on their feet from fatigue and one limping badly, we still ran our escape as a military operation. As far as I was concerned, we were in enemy territory, so every weapon was primed and ready, every eye cast outwards. Sensor sweeps were constant and every precaution was taken. We crossed streets only when there was no traffic, shot out streetlights and lamps, and slowly, slowly, crawled across the glowing map on our HUDs toward the spaceport. It seemed a little too easy to be considered a real foray into dangerous ground, but the thoughts buzzing through the back of my head gave me constant reminders of what would happen if we were surrounded by a mob. There was no doubt that a lot of civilians would die, but Logan was the only one with a possibility of escaping with his life. Our best chance was to keep focused and avoid the situation completely, but focus was hard to come by after a full day of fighting, stress, dull inaction, and then a forced march. None of that seemed to be an issue yet, because the West Side was still a *fragging* ghost town and, if possible, getting ghostier and townier with every step. Despite constant worries of danger, my mind kept wading into all of the information I had collected so far, trying to lay out the chaos of Persephone into a coherent storyboard.

Every conflict in human history can be understood. Some occur to gain more living space, reduce a population, or distract said population from internal problems of the society. The nasty wars, the really nasty ones, are waged because people are led to believe they have to fight in order to preserve ideals, cultures, or the power of the ruling class. These are the wars where people get hung from lampposts, girls barely into puberty are brutally forced into motherhood, dead are left in the streets as political statements, and victims are hacked to death with machetes in order to save bullets. People will do the most awful things when they feel their way of life is threatened. So far, this war had some of the hallmarks of an ideological war against the forces of the incumbent power in the movie house. My problem was it was missing the most vital pieces, and those it had were the wrong shape.

They, whoever in the hell 'they' really were, had a leader, *El Toro*, who had managed to shut down the government for weeks but had not stepped up to take over. In my experience, revolutionary leaders cannot wait to leave their underground hideaways in order to snatch the reigns from the departing regime. Revolutionary leaders feed off the love of their people, and even if he didn't need new soldiers, *El Toro* would have watering holes and meeting halls where he could bask in the worship of the people who believe in him. These guys love the limelight, especially when they're winning. As of yet, though, no public meetings.

More incredibly, despite being blessed with a media so infatuated with him that they might raise a statue to him all on their own, he had given no interviews. He had supposedly inspired hundreds of bombing attacks and assassinations in a dozen distant cities, but had no recruitment runs among the populous. Even successful revolutionary campaigns hemorrhage dead bodies. Captured operatives and dead comrades are the rule rather than the exception, yet he had been at work for six months and had not looked for new soldiers to shore up his numbers. Neither had there been public executions for his captured accomplices. If there is anything an established government loves, it is executing terrorists and telling everyone how and why it was done.

The screen in the luxury office upstairs had just released information on how to get money to *El Toro* through various on-planet banks. That was unexpected of any revolutionary leaders who deal exclusively in cash since any electronic money trail was sure to lead the authorities to their doorsteps. Unless he wasn't a revolutionary leader. Unless the authorities weren't looking for him.

Unless this whole thing was bogus beyond belief.

Each bomb was different, with different materials, positions and targets. Bombers are generally very committed to a single type of explosive and detonator. The reason is simple: it is easier to become familiar with the quirks and nuances of one kind of explosive device than to be perfectly proficient in all kinds. If this seems odd, remember it is a business where making one mistake with a substance that goes BOOM will usually spread word of your demise over several hundred square feet almost instantly.

No public appearances. No interviews. No recruiting drives. No loss of revolutionaries. No fixed explosive device. All of this meant was that what everyone was seeing was not, in fact, what was happening. There was one last bit of evidence I needed to see with my own eyes in order to completely destroy the fallacy. I could only hope it would also lead to the truth.

I shook off the cobwebs as a small glob of heat caught my attention on the pavement. It was a very partial boot print and was cooling even as I watched with the thermographic overlay. I called a halt and followed the splatters until I came face-to-face with Ansef. Even only looking at her posture, weapon muzzle drooped as she leaned heavily against the alley wall, I could tell she was more than simply fatigued. I called Tsang over. He said she had ripped open her stitches some kilometers back. A few quick orders and a few mumbled protests later, Logan swept Ansef into his arms. The rest of the team was not much better, only the cyborg was unaffected by exertion and lack of sleep. We had twenty more kilometers to go and it didn't look like we were going to make it. I hated doing it, but I gave the order to take their *venom*.

A few complied happily, others reluctantly, but each in turn unzipped a thigh pouch, took out a small foil pack, tore it open, and dumped two large yellow pills into their hands. Visors came up, and canteens were passed around to wash them down. I took out my own *ASPs*, Anti-Sleep Pills, and wondered again if it was really worth it.

There were hundreds of pharmaceuticals used by mercenaries, most benign, but many were seriously dangerous. *ASPs* were somewhere in the middle. Each one was stuffed with concentrated caffeine, synthetic sugar, proteins, electrolytes, and a dozen other miscellaneous ingredients to redline mental activity, kill muscle fatigue, and hold off sleep. Most of the ingredients were not dangerous alone, but together it amounted to hard-chugging three pots of coffee, mowing through an entire case of chocolate bars, and blowing through a handful of bronchial dilators. Taking them upped the performance of tired troops, but afterwards...

I opened my visor, accepted the canteen, and swallowed the medication. It took two tries to get them both down. "Alright people, let's move like we have a purpose."

And move we did, at first slowly, but constantly gaining speed. I used the forearm pad to set a mission clock for four hours, starting the numbers spinning downward. When it reached zero, the team would come down off of the *venom* and likely fall asleep standing up. If that happened, our chances of survival would approach nil. I pushed them hard, whipping them with harsh words and quiet encouragement. The world seemed caught in deep water, struggling against the currents of time while we slid through the dark, clutching streets of New California like sharks.

Within twenty minutes, the team was buzzing, running, almost slipping through the streets and alleys beyond the clutches of mere friction. Power slid along every vein as virile as lava, tunneling into our brains and boiling away our thoughts, wants, and needs and leaving nothing but each individual second, which slowly withered and died to be replaced with the next in line. Each moment held only more brick buildings, more empty streets, papers frozen in midair, trash forgotten in overflowing dumpsters, burned out vehicles, and lines of spray-paint decrying the end of the world. Hidden in dark corners, abandoned bodies rotted like repressed memories. There were not many, but their presence served to galvanize the team, reminding them that the city was without law, without backup, and without mercy.

The stores had it the worst. Crawlers had been driven into the doors and the shelves stripped bare. Despite the mental enhancers, my attentiveness was chipping and dulling on reality all around me with no threats to whet upon. Then we crossed over New Vegas Boulevard, crested a hill, and gained a great view of the valley where the spaceport was located.

Archer must have had his comm unit on because I heard him barely whisper, "*Frag* me."

We had found the people missing from the homes and streets.

The megacity of New California sat in a chain of mountains, nestled in a string of highland desert valleys running from southwest to northeast. Sunline Street was a main thoroughfare, perhaps the main artery for New California. It jogged back and forth, cutting each valley in half and descending through each mountain pass down to the next in turn. The lowest, northern- and easternmost valley contained the sprawling, concrete walled spaceport.

I had expected there to be dozens of starships, dropships, and hundreds of vehicles to be in evidence. After all, times of turmoil across any planet mean both great physical danger and financial opportunity. It doesn't end there because the ships that come in empty can leave full, packed full of refugees that can afford whatever blinding cost the tradesmen *cum* smugglers charge. I had expected to find knots of people in the poor apartment buildings and seedy hotels that ring the spaceport. I hadn't expected the sheer volume of people to fill these buildings to capacity and then overflow like a mudslide into the streets.

Ortega nudged me. "How many, do you think, Captain?"

The sheer scale of the answer numbed my mind, and I hadn't even gathered a vague guesstimate when Logan's deep synthetic voice poured into my ears like molten chocolate. "One million, eight hundred, ninety thousand...assuming over-full capacity in the apartment buildings."

Logan glanced down at the rest of the team and then performed a picture-perfect double take when he noticed every *Angel* was staring at him. He shrugged, and said by way of explanation. "Numismatics program linked to my visual sensors."

And for just a second, I forgot that part of Logan was still human under all of that metal. I shook off the feeling as the scrolling numbers on the HUD focused me fully on the task ahead. "Alright, *Angels*, let's move. Double time. Weapons up and on safe—"

Though I couldn't see his face, I could see Archer shake his head and heard him whisper, "On safe?"

He snapped up straight when my voice cracked at him. "Yes Archer, on safe. We're going into a massive crowd down there. I don't want someone grabbing for your gun and having it go off into my ass when you try to wrestle it away."

His disposition changed quickly from embarrassment to hostility. "So, are we going to just walk on down there like we own the place?"

I could feel my own temper sizzle and begin to burn. *Goddamned venom, everyone's getting short.* "Yes, Archer. That's exactly what we are going to do. Ortega, put away that sensor. Logan, you're on point so clear us a path. Tsang, get out the stretcher. You and Richardson get to sling your weapons and carry Ansef in the center of the formation. Long, you're in the rear.

"Look people, we can do this. If we jog down there like we could take on the devil himself, then they will take one look at the big armor and big weapons, and they will believe it." I tried to douse the heat in my voice and at least seem rational to my team. "Remember that most people can't identify any weapons

The Key to Damocles

not used by their local police. We will look like a group of well-armed, well-armored warriors. Those people down there are scared, probably hungry and thirsty, but we don't have anything worth dying for. Just walk tall, and we'll be fine." I glanced from visor to visor, but I couldn't tell if they believed me or not. *Not as if it matters; time to go.* "Alright, move out."

The team members changed places, and with the final dregs of chemical energy leaking from our pores, we headed down the narrow pass and to the valley at a jog. I checked the time left on the venom, and we had little more than two hours. At least it was downhill.

Scenes like those we found are not uncommon, though most people would be surprised by that fact. On just about any planet, one can find an area rife with poverty brought on by military conflict, economic collapse, social strife, or oppressive regimes. Each one is different, but they are still all the same. Those not sleeping sat idly beside ramshackle, makeshift shacks, tattered tents, or vehicles turned into homes and watched us closely. It wasn't because of laziness, but because they have learned the necessity to conserve energy. Filthy children played quietly, staring with hollow eyes at passers-by without even the hopeful glimmer of receiving comfort.

In daylight, we would have been swarmed by beggars dressed in middle-class clothes turning to rags, everything of value auctioned off for a few more credits to buy food, medicine, or the Holy Grail: passage off world. These who remained on the street were the people most unprepared for the turmoil, either because they fled their homes empty handed or because they were less affluent to begin with. They begin to appear almost immediately at any camp, and as they die of exposure, dehydration, or starvation, others run out of supplies and join their ranks. They soon learn that mercy is in short supply, and many die in the throes of despair long before their body actually shuts down.

Within days, a few of those ill-prepared become very, very angry. They see the merciless new world as supremely unfair, and for whatever justification they can make to themselves, they begin robbing the other unfortunates on every side. Never trained for their new occupations, the thieves look for any corpses they can raid, or even some unguarded stash that can

106

be snatched to allow them to buy food, comfort, or their way free of Persephone.

The guards would develop next, from those genetically disposed to large, imposing bodies or pre-incident physical fitness buffs. They prowl the tents in their domain like alpha-wolves tending their pack because they believe it to be their moral duty, or because they are paid by their charges. Within a week of their appearance, the guards gather their people close into almost tribal societies and cooperative units relying upon one another for food, defense, and moral support. From there things just get worse.

A few of the angrier, beefier guys eyed us hungrily, but with Logan's footfalls announcing us to all for a hundred of meters in every direction, people saw us and universally shrunk into the shadows. To the minds of the refugees, we were an extra danger in a world already too full of them. As we continued to move briskly, I noticed that there were no child prostitutes, defensive arrangements, signs of tribal/gang warfare, pimps, black market peddlers, or corpses left unattended. That meant that the camp was only four to six weeks old, and the worst was yet to come.

The Angels came to the hundred-meter long, four-lane ramp at the base of the fortress-like walls of the spaceport. Originally designed to contain the shockwave, burning debris, and tumbling wreckage in case of a catastrophic starship crash, the wall now held back the massive tide of hard-packed humanity. At each entrance, well at least at this entrance, two armored personnel carriers splayed across the wheeled vehicle entrance. The guns on the boxy craft scanned back and forth, looking for threats. I was willing to bet they were tasked to send volleys at the least sign of a riot. Considering the sheer number of fliers being used as homes out in the camp behind us, I was certain that they would intercept aircraft as well. The guards on station weren't particularly alert, but they were lightly armored and armed with semiautomatic tactical shotguns with enlarged snail drum magazines. Bloodstains on the ramp showed they had used them at least once.

At least there was some good news. On the side of the craft was a symbol I recognized: two crossed laser carbines behind a skull. My heart leapt, and I strapped my rifle to my back and punched up their unsecured frequency from memory on the C^2.

The Key to Damocles

"*Lightwave Cyanide*, this is *The Radiation Angels*. We are requesting entry into the spaceport. On foot. Gate four."

"Roger your request, *Radiation Angels*. Please wait one." There was a brief pause, then the guards at the top of the ramp jumped to attention, presenting themselves as the very picture of a professional mercenary crew. Only after that did the unidentified operator come back to me. "*Radiation Angels*, you are clear to enter with your ordinance intact. Am I speaking to *Angels,* Actual?"

Actual is the leader of any group or mission. If you are talking to Actual, you are not talking to the radio operator or *EWO*, you are talking to the boss. "Affirmative, *Cyanide*."

"In that case I have been instructed to inform you that *Lightwave Cyanide* is providing security for the spaceport and if you don't come to see *Cyanide,* Actual, for a drink he will personally come down to your ship and kick your nasty ass all over the tarmac."

I was weary, cranky, and sore, but I still couldn't suppress a laugh. "*Five by Five, Lightwave Cyanide.* Let me have eight in a rack on my back, and I'll come by."

As we came up the base of the ramp, I waved my crew to shoulder their arms. The guards saluted respectfully, their weapons pointedly not aimed at us. The operator's voice smiled in my ear. "Roger, roger. Welcome to New California Spaceport, Captain Rook."

CHAPTER 9: SHIT, SHOWER, AND SLIPSTREAM

Planet Persephone,
New California, NC Spaceport 09:14, 11/04/2662

I was dreaming of the hill overlooking New California Spaceport. I knew it was a dream because everything was just right enough to be wrong, close enough to reality to require a second look.

Normally hot, the dry air blasted down from the sky like the angry furnace of God. Sweat was scorched from the pores before it appeared, rendering it stillborn underneath the skin. The buildings in the dream were not just run down, they were blasted hulks. The wind moaned through the skeletons of a civilization half absorbed by trash and sand. Cracked roads strewn with rusted vehicles full of discarded toys lined it like razor wire. Beneath me, in the heart of the valley, there was an island fortress surrounded by a churning sea. The whole scene had an unholy, unhealthy air as the water angrily crashed at the gates to the spaceport *cum* castle.

I began walking without wanting to. My hindbrain was violently rebelling, dumping adrenaline into my body and making it spasm with palsy, but as much as I shook and stumbled one foot kept falling in front of the other. My progress was marked by paranoia as hungry eyes watched from broken windows, and my steps ground against garbage that crackled and cried beneath my heels.

Dark dots barely masked by the frothing surf gained detail and mass until I could identify them as corpses. At the edge of the war of elements, rock and water gave way to graceless bleached pools full of lazily drifting bodies: women shielding cold children, old men wrestling young men, boys and girls locked in desperately dead embraces of murdered first love.

My heart was pounding, soaring blood pressure making my skin feel like an overfilled bladder even as some invisible force pulled me forward toward the monumental walls of the castle keep—no, wait—it was a spaceport. Wetness licked at my feet and I looked down to see sand squiggling through my toes like maggots. Water as clear as glass grasped at my ankles, knees, hips, and chest. It brought a frightening chill to my bones even as the dead brushed against me. Sightless, milky eyes seemed to follow me as I began to bob in the nearly invisible, pounding waves and every time the water enveloped my ears, screams clawed at me with physical force.

I gasped at the rarified air for scattered seconds in the troughs between hammering peaks. I almost had the timing when a hand grabbed my ankle and yanked me downward. Immediately catcalls, hateful begging, and desperate cries began reverberating hollowly in my brain. Corpses floated over me, at once unmoving and yet still managing to pull me down, drowning me with their very presence. The pain in my lungs built like the end of a symphony, moving from pain to panic and from red-hot, to white, to all-encompassing black.

I wanted to scream, but the frigid glass soup collapsed down my throat and filled my mouth like cold fire. It yanked me further away from the sky, chest burning as hands churned at the thick, blanket-like water. I urinated on myself, feeling that body-close heat that says even out of my dream I was peeing my bed.

I heard a fragile voice cut through the chaos of sound with a whisper, "You're a hero, Rook."

All of the floating bodies turned to look at me at once.

I took a deep breath and hot, stale air filled my lungs.

What—?

I woke with a start, heart pounding, chest heaving, sweat congealing into fat droplets at the end of my nose that promptly jumped to their deaths. I kicked the sheet off me, kicked myself off the cot, and kicked open the door to the head. I emptied buckets worth of burning bile into the toilet, thankful that military toilets didn't include a lid that had to be lifted. Cramps clutched at my midriff as my body lurched over and over, knocking the air from my lungs.

Calm. Stay Calm. It's just the venom. Just relax. It can't last forever. I gasped, belched and began coughing anew, then heaving, heaving, heaving...Nothing was coming out—and then the fist in my stomach let go. *Frag! Has anyone ever suffocated from puking in a toilet?*

All of the acidic brown and yellow swirling in the metal bottom of the commode let off a sickening stench that threatened to jumpstart my nausea again, but my grasping hands managed to find the flush button. The bottom of the toilet fell away and high-powered nozzles sprayed the internal surface beneath my face before the entire unit re-sealed. I took a double lungful of air and tried to let it out slowly. The smell still lingered, but I clamped down on my stomach and wiped my face with a piece of paper from the dispenser. I staggered out of the head just in time. Archer rushed past me and took up the usual position, emptying his own stomach. The sound nearly set me off again so I moved to the front of *The Cherub* and out onto the tarmac.

The sun stared angrily down at me. It caused me to break out into a sweat immediately and started the urine festering inside my jumpsuit. The sound of falling water stirred me from my vaguely doom-ridden thoughts. Behind *The Cherub,* someone deserving of a bonus check had hooked up the decontamination showers to the local water feed. Perhaps the nameless *Angel* deserved a generous bonus, since they had grabbed a map table from *The Cherub* and laid out towels caged from who-knows-where. King, the disturbingly muscled Heavy Weapons Officer, exited the tent and pulled a towel around him. His African features were ashy, his features drawn and lined with misery. I could have been a less muscular mirror image of him, though at least he managed a smile as I staggered toward the showers. His face twisted as he considered giving a thumbs-up or saying something. I knew from the moment I interviewed him that wit wasn't King's strong suit, still, he was honest and at least nominally friendly, so I was not surprised when he settled for clapping me on the shoulder as I passed him. "It's cold, sir."

"Thanks." I couldn't stop a shudder from dancing along my spine. The dream had been too real, and too unreal, to be dismissed in only five minutes. I left him behind as I clumsily rid myself of the piss-soaked jumpsuit and stepped up to a shower nozzle. The simple sensor in the tree-stand pole caught sight of me and told the head to begin stabbing me with water. Thankfully it was cool, but not cold, and washed away not only the uncomfortable warmth of urine but also the oven-like heat of the day. It poured over my skin, but it wasn't gentle. Decontamination showers were not used to get a person clean, they were supposed to remove chemical or biological agents from mercenaries' armor. I snatched one of the standard issue military soap tubes from a bucket in the corner—*perhaps a disgustingly generous bonus*—and soaped up before the water scythed the suds off of me. Even so, the hard stream of cool water pounded my front and back, hitting the muscle like a deep massage. I turned and turned, knowing I really should leave but not wanting to start a day with so many questions and so few answers.

"Wow, Captain." My eyes snapped open and I found Thompson just outside of the shower across from me. Stripped naked and soaped from neck to feet, I was acutely aware that she was definitely the first nude woman I had seen in the flesh in perhaps three years.

I was willing to work with women, but I believed in separate facilities. I have to admit I have been tempted myself to be unprofessional with some of the soldiers under my command. If you drop a human being into a war zone, redline their bodies, minds and emotions dozens of times a day, convince them every second may be their last, allow them to experience absolute adulation at their own survival, and then drop members of the opposite sex together… let's just say that sex does happen between *Angels*. As long as they keep it casual, consensual, infrequent, and reasonably covert, I pretend not to notice. On the other hand, I thought men and women naked together, alone in a hostile environment, was just asking too much of self-control.

I coughed and turned around. Thompson had a very kind laugh. "Oh, come on Captain. I asked Ortega and he said you were a pillar of restraint."

Thanks Ortega. "I'm just trying to be respectful, Sniper."

"Well, then, if you are trying to be respectful, then turn back around, take an honest look, and say something complementary." I knew it was a bad idea, but I turned around anyway and I took a look that turned into a lingering assessment. Beautiful brown flesh was taut over a lithe frame, tall legs flying from the ground to a set of oddly provocative hips. My eyes gasped for breath over her light breasts before sliding up her graceful neck that was set off by closely cropped hair. She giggled. "Wow, Captain. That's a good look."

No matter how old they get, women giggle and it's charming. I reach ten years old and *Wham!* All of a sudden, if I giggle I look like a *grithead*. It really isn't fair. As I looked past her body I sensed the tension siphoning out of the situation. "You have beautiful eyes. They're full of your strength."

She nodded at me, a little surprised, and said, "See? I knew you could do it. Now come here, you missed some urine at the small of your back."

"You can see that?" And then I felt stupid for saying it since I had seen her medical records and I knew she had—

She tapped a trimmed nail against an eyeball. There was a faint *tink-tink-tink*. "Targeting computer, starlight vision capable, motion detectors, zoom out to thirty-two times... They're the best that money can buy, and they catch some things that yours miss. C'mere."

I knew it was a bad idea, but I went. I felt her run lathered hands over my back, across my shoulders, and down my legs. I was comforted by the idea that she was being very businesslike until I realized that she must have confiscated the foam from her own body. She moved me into the range of her nozzle and turned me around to clean me off. Then she pushed me to the side and rinsed herself off.

I walked back under my own nozzle for a second. "Treat all your commanders like eight-year-olds?"

"Well, if you could wash yourself..." We left the shower stand, and she let her joke peter out. She picked up towels from the corner and handed me one. "Captain, can I make a suggestion?"

"Yes, Thompson."

"Give everyone a twenty-four-hour pass. Especially yourself. You've been wound real tight ever since we set foot on this planet, boss. You need some company..."

Well, advice may be all well and good, but I let her know under no uncertain terms that she was about to cross a line. "That will be all, Sniper."

Her eyes, normally clinical, caressed me gently and a little helplessly. "I've heard so much about you. I've read so much about you. You're one of the most inspired leaders I've ever seen, but you have to give yourself time to sort it all..."

The Key to Damocles

Thompson trailed off under my suddenly withering stare. Seconds fell together in a heap between us, creating a wall of silence. I wrapped the towel around myself and had almost made it to the flap in the tent before I decided to breech the gap with sound. "You're from Eureka."

"How did you know?"

"Let's just say growing up on a tropical world populated mostly by nudists tends to be obvious in certain situations." She laughed at that. "What I don't get is why someone would leave a paradise in order to become a sniper."

The light didn't die in her artificial eyes, but it did run and hide inside of her, "Even in paradise, bad things happen, Captain." I managed another step before she spoke again. "But you're not the only one that can play that game. You're from Roh."

It was as if my feet had been nailed into place. I was sure my face was blank, but the muscles on my exposed chest and back jumped to attention as apprehension rippled through them like electricity. I turned to her, but she stood straight under the weight of my temper without bending. *Brave woman...*

She was right, I really did need some extra time to think. I needed some distance from the everyday maintenance of the team. *Smart woman...*

"Whose idea was this shower?"

She hesitated just a second. "Mine, Captain."

"You're my new Lieutenant, Thompson. Go out into the spaceport and see if you can find a silver bar or two for your uniform. I'll announce it to the *Angels* when I get back." I had finally succeeded at putting her off her game. Her mouth flapped like a landed fish. She managed to grunt a few times, but no words emerged. "And this is the last time we will be naked in the same place and time ever again. Do you understand?"

Her mouth worked a little more before she said. "Don't you want to ask if I'm up to it?"

"If I had any doubt, I wouldn't have given it to you. So far, I've been burying myself in the details and trying to see the big picture at the same time and I just can't do it. You get the details from here on in." And with that I turned to leave. Conveniently, Archer was just staggering in. He dropped his clothes to his ankles but yelped and yanked his urine-filled jumpsuit back on when he saw Thompson standing naked behind me. I relished being able to growl at him. "Grow up, Archer. It's just a *fragging* shower."

I went back inside *The Cherub*, the scorched air sucking the moisture from my body in a little less than a minute. I grabbed my combat pack from a compartment as Lopez jerked awake. He looked relieved at the familiar surroundings, but then alarm erased all comfort. He dove off of the cot and I had to squeeze to the side of the narrow isle as he scrambled for the toilet and heaved.

It was going to be a glorious day for everyone concerned.

I took out my spare jumpsuit. This one better tailored, covertly armored, and covered in pockets. As I unrolled it from my pack, a small bundle fell out onto the cot with a dull thud. It was obviously a toy box that had been recycled to this new purpose, and at one point held something called a 'gAm3 LOOn', whatever the hell that was. There was a note taped to the top that said, "I was right the first time. You would have made a fine cop. -AL."

Inside of the box was a sacred bronze badge. It had a picture of an eagle grasping a clutch of arrows in one hand and a scale of justice in the other. It read: #888 Rook.

Suddenly, the clouds that had settled in around my brain and mood broke up and fled before the shiny piece of metal in my hand. A twenty-four hour, or rather thirty-two-hour, pass was a damn fine idea. In the past two days we had been tackling a nearly unending stream of crises, but my team had handled itself with professionalism, dignity, and competence. They deserved to take some time off, and Thompson was right; I needed to get some perspective. Everything was happening quickly and I needed to find out what was happening if I had any chance of stopping it. *And since when do you think you can do anything?*

I went to go get dressed, not completely done until I slipped a holster and a heavy plasma pistol appropriated from the abbreviated weapons locker. I checked in with Logan and took my C^2 forearm unit and an ear-bud radio. I had a meeting I had to keep.

The tarmac was like the front door of an oven, reflecting the collected heat of the high desert sun back into the sky like a middle finger. My black jumpsuit gathered every bit of excess radiation, and the cooling unit on my belt was quickly overwhelmed. Despite the light sweat, I kept my pace brisk even though I would have liked nothing more than to sit and marvel at the chaos of The New California Metropolitan Spaceport.

The tarmac was three kilometers wide, and was littered with a ragtag collection of spaceships that had landed and taken up the roles of a high-tech flea market. There were sleek, tiny cigarette starjumpers, meant to hold only a minimal crew as they bounced from planet to planet carrying light, expensive cargos such as medicines, gems, or contraband. Medium sized corvettes, about the size of *Deadly Heaven*, unloaded easily portable necessities or acted as the home base for one of dozens of mercenary companies, while titanic, clunky bulk freighters disgorged heavy cargo of all types. Most of the crews had set out cordons around their vessels to control access. In some cases, this was nothing more than self-standing fences of chain links. Others used heavy concrete blocks moved into place using huge robotic laborers. A few used ionic poles bolted into place that would beep when a trespasser got near, and arc out deadly bolts of lightning at anything that got between them. Whether used to keep crowds out, or pen in market animals for sale to the locals, the net effect was to turn each spacecraft into a fort surrounded by fields of concrete and radiation-resistant rubberized plates with squads of *Lightwave Cyanide* acting as copses of trees in the no-mans-land between.

There was a distant roar of engines as ships came in or left, but none of it was close enough to drown out the mindless babble of hundreds of thousands of people that came from just beyond the walls. It was morning, and business was brisk. Even as I watched, the gates were being 'opened' to allow refugees into the staging area. Once there, they were queued up into roped off stands where members of *Lightwave Cyanide* would check to see if they had money. If they didn't, they'd be ejected out back into the crowd. If they did, they'd be given access to the ships to try to buy food, clothing, and survival gear, or try to pay the huge cost of escaping into orbit and beyond. People also used fliers to come in, but since these customers were all nicely dressed, with personal bodyguards or even a small squad of mercs in attendance, I had to assume their trips were tightly regulated but expected. After all, the rich that were not fleeing their home-world needed to stock up just like everyone else.

116

As industrial centers shut down, mass produced goods become scarce. Canned foods, vehicles, clothing, bots, computers, and just about everything a modern society needs to function comfortably are built by large companies which are usually the first casualty of massed civil unrest. Supply drops, prices skyrocket, and suddenly it becomes profitable to ship heavy goods through Slipspace from one system to another.

Mercenaries add in their own market, and I could see a few of the craft were gypsy ships: light cargo craft converted into bars, dance clubs, and brothels. The scattered uniforms present around gypsy ships this early in the day could only mean that they were doing a booming business.

And of course, there were always refugees looking for space onboard to escape once the cargo was sold. I knew from past experience that about ten percent of the escapees, those that had paid the least, would be dumped out into space at first opportunity. It was simply cheaper than feeding them. Another ten to fifteen percent would be sold to slavers somewhere along the journey. From there they'd be carted off to one of any number of planets where human flesh still carried a price tag. They'd be broken, trained, and chained... usually with a behavioral implant. Even with bots in ready supply, there were some things AI couldn't do. I suppose there was always the possibility that some people just liked owning someone else. The rest— those that chose best, chose first, and paid the most— would reach a distant planet. There they would be friendless, creditless, starving, and afraid. Most of them probably wouldn't even speak the language, since MexiCali isn't really common across the colonies. Any way you cut it, they'd have a hard life ahead.

It only took a few realizations just like that one to make a mercenary a hard man. A person can really only take so much of other people's pain until shutting down all connection to them is simply a survival reflex. Psychologists call it disassociation, or dehumanization. Mercenaries call it being realistic. *There's no shame in doing nothing if there is nothing that can be done*.

I sighed as I reached one of the major thoroughfares. The street once served as a safe place for low-altitude fliers to travel without being turned into steel confetti by passing ships or each other. Today it acted like an arrow painted with the bodies of trudging refugees, and it pointed from the gate directly to the heart of the spaceport: the terminal. I moved into the currents of people, and was uncomfortably reminded of my night terror again. Far from pressing in, however, my size, my weapon, and my skin color guaranteed a large amount of leeway on every side. Even in the crowd, it was as if my power ensured my privacy as my impotency isolated me. I walked into the hulking, squared off shadow of the flight tower. For all practical purposes, the release from the grip of the sun heralded the beginning of my meeting, and so the commander in me woke up and dispelled all doubt.

Four members of *Lightwave Cyanide* stood guard outside of the main entrance. They saw me, saw my sidearm, and immediately tensed up. But by the time I had climbed the stairs, they had called to their command center for instruction, received confirmation of who I was, and were standing at a relaxed but respectful ease when I stepped up to the doors. One came forward and saluted. I returned the gesture as he said, "Captain Rook, if you will follow me, please?"

Without waiting for a reply, he walked through the automatic doors and began to wind his way through the terminal. I dutifully followed, keeping my eyes open but finding nothing unexpected. Like all terminals, it was a mixture of the cavernous and the labyrinthine. Huge areas were set aside to provide thousands of people access to check-in desks, security, luggage, cargo check in, and boarding. These areas were now in use as barracks, mess halls, communications, and briefing rooms by the three hundred members of *Lightwave Cyanide*. Past these well-lit, airy halls, security doors hid hundreds of hallways lined with tiny, windowless offices. This is where the real chore of keeping a spaceport working was done, but this section at least had been hijacked by the officers of *Cyanide*. In fact, I would not have been surprised in the least if the flight control tower was still in use, doing the exact same duty for the mercenaries as it had for civilians.

There were changes, to be sure: extra cameras, robotic guns linked to a pre-fabricated, drop-and-rock security system, new locks, cloth walls acting as partitions, a few defensive barricades made of armor-grade plastics and numerous Screamer-Chain™ locks set to deafen anyone who cut them and alert everyone else, closing off the areas *Lightwave* was not using. I was seeing everything I expected to, and though that made me a little nervous, I convinced myself that every once in a great while a horse is, indeed, a horse.

The—I checked his markings—lieutenant stopped in front of an elevator and pressed the call button. It took so long to arrive I began to wonder if there was a small team of carpenters inside the shaft, building the elevator to fit the number of waiting people.

"Um, Captain Rook?" I turned to the lieutenant. "May I ask a question?"

I looked him up and down. He was a young African-extraction man, perhaps in his early twenties, but he had suddenly become timid and this seemed to reduce him to infancy. I had a feel about what was coming next, but nodded anyway.

"Well, I have heard rumors and I was wondering... did you really kill one hundred and fifty men by yourself?"

The elevator dinged, the doors opened and we boarded. "No, not really."

"Oh, well, I'm sorry, sir, I had just heard...about Mars."

I glanced at his nametag. "No, I'm sorry, Lieutenant Miller, I did not kill one hundred and fifty men—" And I waited until the elevator churned its tortured way to our target floor. I made sure to wait until he was halfway out of the door before finishing. "It was only just over a hundred."

The lieutenant nearly tripped over himself trying to stare at me and watch where he was going at the same time. Miller pressed a button besides a door marked as 'The Orange Room' and ushered me in. He saluted crisply. I returned his salute before winking at him and adding, "And there were four of us."

Inside, reigning at the head of the table like a Greek god was Commander Mike Janchea. Wide-shouldered and all smiles, he welcomed me warmly to what turned out to be a daily thing for the mercenary commanders stationed in New California.

I had seen meetings like this one before, and it's all part of the business. Commanders leave their units with a small group of guards/aides to 'share intelligence' with other mercenary leaders. We all flew different flags, but finding true equals was hard for the leaders of a mercenary band, and these chat sessions gave everyone a chance to relax among peers. Or at least the peers he could trust enough to eat and drink around. It was once said that nations have no friends, only interests. Well, welcome to the world of a mercenary. Mostly it was a chance to blow off steam, have a few drinks, eat breakfast, and sometimes lose money playing Poker, Whiplash, or Suicide Kings. Once in a blue moon, information actually changes hands. Commander Janchea introduced me to the room and I immediately felt on display. It seemed it wasn't only lieutenants that had heard of me.

Rather than catching a bad case of hero worship, every commander saw me enter the room conspicuously alone and immediately checked on the position of their bodyguards. I was the man who had killed a century of men, and now I came out to a 'neutral ground' meeting carrying only a sidearm. It was a sidearm that could blow a fist-sized hole in a wall, but a sidearm nonetheless. To me, it was an uncomfortable necessity because of manpower constraints. To them, it was a definite display of confidence and power. Overall, I preferred their take on it, so I pushed all of my doubt and confusion deep inside and let my presence fill more than my fair share of the room. Mike may have been our host, but I sought to dominate the gathering by sheer will. Given weight by my legend, I found it terribly easy.

I'd spent a great deal of time with Mike, who knew me from when we had bought into our first basic training classes back on *Haven*, 'when Christ was a choir boy'. He made several loud comments about how he was better at most of basic than I. Honestly, he was. Mike was the kind of guy who flew through the obstacle courses, shot like a natural, seemed to have an innate mechanical ability, and could sleep standing up. I had just given up smoking for an obvious reason: I had to work very hard just to make the grade. That was a decade... well, thirteen years ago, but mentioning it now had the net effect of stealing bits of my legend for himself. He was giving hints to the others that he could do great things too, if only given the chance.

And, of course, everyone wanted to hear the complete story about Supreme Admiral Tomlinson, Ashley 9, and Mars. They made it hard to skimp on the details, and honestly it was a story I'd rather not remember that clearly. I could have told them about the ambushes, traps, and tricks that had eliminated the opposition without the need of exposing my own tender hide to damage. I could have told them I had faced third-rate teams, not professional soldiers. I could have told them a great deal to make the story seem less impressive, but I think it still would have come off as bragging. Besides, it may have been necessary, but snuffing out a hundred lives leaves a mark on a man. We talk about it lightly to one another because there's no point in wearing sackcloth and ashes and flagellating oneself over having survived a conflict. Everyone in this room who could afford it, saw a shrink. That alone means something.

After the heavily edited story, I could mingle among the other guests, eat breakfast, and begin pumping them for information. I received a whole lot of nothing, and little to no interest in helping me pursue my theories whatsoever.

Prime Fjorden of *Machinegun Valkeries*, whose forces were hired by an insurance company to guard select contracted objects and people, was completely disinterested in any talk about the goings on. Number One Beck of *Sherman's Children*, a group of cyborg soldiers guarding a collection of high-end apartment blocks, had dealt with minor disturbances, but everything he described amounted to little more than protests, vandalism, and attempted theft. He also had no need to talk about what really might have been really happening on Persephone. Colonel Kek was there with the simply named *Kek's,* and though he appeared to be freelancing wetwork, or at least dampwork, for various syndicates and corporations, he had not come across anything that would make it seem that this was anything other than civil war. Commander after commander looked at me askance and shrugged, uninterested and nonplussed.

It was as if none of them cared why everything was the way it was. And, I guess, that was just it. As long as Persephone was in chaos, they had work. As soon as things stabilized, they would be looking for a job again. Their contracts were held by hundreds of the most affluent and powerful people on the planet, but the jobs were typically short sighted and compartmentalized. Their employers were experienced at this kind of thing. They were being realistic. No one would expect them to be able to bring an end to the unrest. On the other hand, making things worse could land them in bad trouble with the Mercenary Guild and *Haven*, even make them unbondable. So, while they would not make things worse, they had no motivation to make things better.

The list went on, but the answers remained the same. None of them worked in New California except Commander Janchea, and he was the only one with horror stories of his own to tell. The only things in New California worth defending were the spaceport and the movie house; the rest was largely looted, burned, or abandoned. Apparently, the planetary federal agents had taken up as defenders of L/V/D; they hired no mercenaries.

And just like that, another part of the puzzle became a little clearer. I excused myself a little too early, but I had to get back to my ship. Lieutenant Miller was waiting to lead me out, and once we were in the elevator, I took my own turn to ask a few questions of him. "So, Miller, you've been working with the refugees?"

"Oh, yes sir. Every day."

"So why are they pouring out of New California so fast? It's not this bad everywhere, is it?"

He shrugged. "No, most of the rest of the planet's population is pretty stable, but then again, these people are trying to get away from ground zero. The rescue shelters in all the other cities are full, and turning people away. Most New Californians don't want to move to another city anyway since they don't know how long it will be before the unrest spreads."

"I don't understand."

"Well, when we first stationed here about two months ago and took over operations of the spaceport, the riots were really bad. Bombs began going off like popcorn. Not small ones, either. Big, spectacular ones on busses, at restaurants, in movie theaters, anywhere people gathered. So, people started staying home. Then people's homes were bombed. That's when most of them started showing up here because nowhere else was safe." He kept talking, but I stopped listening.

A constant in the mercenary world was the danger of an ambush. Most of the time the point of an ambush is to corral targets into a predetermined kill zone. You can do it with false signs of passage, explosives, or live bait, but the point is to get them into a place where all of your guns are aimed and all of theirs are holstered. Then you slaughter them without mercy. You kill most of them and break the spirit of the rest, and from that point you can mop up the survivors at your leisure. There would have been only one reason I wouldn't have killed the survivors: if I hadn't needed to. Once an enemy is dispirited, huddled, and out of your way, shooting at them further just risks turning fear into anger, or at best wastes valuable ammunition. I tuned back into the conversation just as we reached the front doors. Miller smiled, we saluted, and then shook hands.

Three hours later, the last repairs were completed on *The Cherub*. I announced Thompson's promotion, her shiny new bars winking in the unblinking sun. The crew took it well, and she accepted the traditional needling as well as the punch in her unit patch from each team member. Then, I told them that they each had a thirty-hour pass and a small bonus. I handed out some of our dwindling supply of hard currency to the crew and unleashed them onto the tarmac like a patch of especially dangerous children. Well, most of them.

Logan held back John Doe, making him last in line. He looked at me like I had just shot his puppy when he found out he wasn't going with the rest of the crew. I could empathize, but I needed my pilot. Besides, I wasn't getting a thirty-hour pass either; I had places to go.

Soon we were in the air, heading for L/V/D.

CHAPTER 10: BUSINESS

Planet Persephone,
New California, L/V/D Studio 13:33, 11/04/2662

Most people think of 'mercenary' and immediately make a mental list of the required talents:

#1) Kill people.
#2) Break things.
#3) Repeat as necessary.

To a certain extent this is true if all you ever want to do is pull triggers and chew mud. A leader, however, must be much more broadly defined. One must know how to make polite conversation, how to eat in cultured settings, how to read the media, make diplomatic overtures, and gather covert intelligence. In addition to everything else, a skilled mercenary leader is one part each: prince, public relations hack, ambassador, and spy.

"Captain Rook!" Opus Lionel and his entourage swept into the courtyard… tittering, bickering, and cooing all the while. He came forward and shook my hand warmly. "I have heard so much about you, Captain. In fact, I'm sure I could make you a very rich man if you could be convinced to tell me some of your stories."

I shook my head and applied firm pressure to his hand while focusing in on his eyes. "Thank you, Mr. Lionel, but I'm paid to do a job, not talk about it."

"Ah, pity, pity. I am sorry about this but we're going to have to have a working lunch."

"I would be delighted."

Lionel smiled and snapped his fingers like an emperor of old. Bots swarmed on every side of us, setting up tables, chairs, and laying down bundles of freshly prepared food. The hangers-on chose spaces dictated by secret-but-rigid rules of etiquette that I could scarcely fathom. The wordless power struggle to gain the attention of this, the most influential man on the planet, was giving me uncomfortable flashbacks to another who enjoyed the company of flunkies. It made my eyes flick to tactical locations around the lush gardens.

Covertly armed guards appeared in innocuous places in numerous niches and shadowed corners, setting off alarms at the back of my head. I tried to keep my breathing slow and regular, letting my eyes slip past them as if I didn't notice. The security was disturbing—especially since I had been disarmed upon landing—but not out of place for a head of state, *de facto* or not. Some people called him 'the second president of Persephone', others simply omitted 'the second' portion of the statement. Surprisingly, he looked like anybody else. He was just an average looking African/European mix with a few more kilos around the midsection and a bit more authority in his walk. At least he didn't look like one of the richest people in the known universe. I'm worth tens of millions even after buying most of a continent, but this man had enough money to fund his own government. In fact, he had done just that...twice.

The Lionel, Vincent, and Davidson Studio sat in the middle of New California. It was considered its own municipality of ten million, but it didn't save them any taxes. Though L/V/D directly employed less than half a percent of the population of the planet, it paid fifty-four percent of the taxes. About the only thing their status allowed them was to write, regulate, and enforce their own laws which mainly focused on contract law and employment regulations within their walls. This not only included harsher penalties for breaking contracts, and abolition of many restrictive child labor laws; it also allowed them to severely restrict media access. Since the collapse of the government, however, Lionel had apparently bought the ruling elite wholesale by employing the upper echelons of the planetary-level police agencies, the parliament, the president, and numerous judges.

He gestured, and I took my place graciously. The conversation was predictably light, and I got a chance to take a few bites of the food in front of me. He started by mentioning the hideously expensive air defense network—much like the one Ortega had installed around his home, just bigger—L/V/D had just purchased. Then he went on about how many thousands of ex-planetary agents he had working for him as security, and the internal roving patrols, the sensor systems, the thick outer walls...Lionel also kept me abreast of what I was eating, but to be honest, I wasn't listening. His body language was laid back and extravagant, non-threatening and jovial, so he wasn't saying anything important. His lackeys, however, were carrying on their own conversations. I sifted through their voices but if there was anything to hear worthy of the effort I missed it.

There are whole planets worth of idiots who feel they are smart enough to point out the shortcomings of someone else, and then standardize it to the whole race of humanity. I am not one of them. On the other hand, after a few days of wandering around cities populated by Latino-descendants, I would have to be blind not to notice that I was sitting in a sea of Africans like myself. The only two Latinos in the room sat at a table far removed from Lionel's seat of power. They were heavyset men in badly tailored suits who were trying to watch me without being too obvious.

The scent of fresh salmon hit me sideways from the tortilla wrapped vegetable thing, accented by a dish of cold pasta and vegetables in some kind of dill-based dressing. Cuts from a thick, leathery mushroom cap, the smell of garlic and onion weeping upwards, dissolved on my tongue like superb steak. Freshly squeezed juice, like the kiss of a beautiful woman, washed away the harsh tastes and accented the subtle melody of flavors. Each portion danced with the others, completely bereft of the oily aftertaste of synthetic food. The lunch was brief, then coffee was served. I had to force myself to slow down since real coffee had only a fraction of the bitter caffeine as the synthetic counterpart, and I had a tendency to gulp the real stuff like water. This was some kind of special blend: nutty, chocolaty, and minty without the use of a single creamer or syrup packet. *Nice.*

And that, of course, was when I found out the important conversation I had been searching for was the one I was supposed to be having. I shook my head. "I'm sorry, I missed that last part?"

"I said, so you can see, I really don't have need of your services. Although, the offer is quite tempting, even flattering." Lionel shrugged his shoulders and spread his hands wide while doing a fair imitation of the Cheshire cat. He sat back, cup firmly in his hands, eyes probing me from over the rim. I felt him relinquish the reigns of the conversation, and I leaned forward.

"Well, I appreciate that, Mr. Lionel..." I lifted the cup to my lips, taking a second to form the next thing out of my mouth. *Well, I guess he wasn't bragging about security; he was setting me up to be let down after I asked for a job. Now the question was, how could I say, I didn't want to work for you, anyway, mister*

The Key to Damocles

trillionaire, sir. More importantly, how could I say it politely? "Oh, that's good coffee. Well, I am, of course disappointed, but thankful that you took the time to see me."

He accepted the compliments with easy grace. "Well, to be honest, I wasn't going to; time is such a finite commodity for me since I took over the studio. But I was advised that your mercenary troupe can do some really impressive things and, well, it pays to be polite to people of your caliber."

He toasted me and I returned it. "I thank you, sir. Well, I guess that's it, then."

"Sorry to waste your time."

"Not at all." I took the opportunity to signal a robot *garcon* and get a refill, giving me perhaps five minutes of time in which to pry the answers I needed out of him. "I have looked at the local news reports since you took office, and I have to say I'm impressed."

"Oh, I hope not." Lionel sneered. He sat up and then hunched over, looking around the courtyard as if for assassins. "The damn press has made a devil of me, Captain Rook."

I leaned back a bit and raised a hand. "Oh, quite the contrary, Mr. Lionel. If one has enough objectivity to see past the obvious biases, you appear to be quite the philanthropist."

He blinked at me for a moment. "That's uncommonly kind of you, Captain."

"Todd, please."

He smiled, nodded, and ordered another coffee. "Opus then, Todd."

"I did notice that the local media loved to paint the studio, and you in particular, in the least flattering light possible."

"Of course. Gratitude is a disease of dogs, and all that. Only on Persephone can a company come in, revitalize the entire economy, invest trillions in development of the infrastructure, educate the entire public, and then be made a pariah for turning a profit." He nodded, grinding his teeth as if on a piece of gristle. I nodded sympathetically, apparently pulling a pin on a grenade that had been set long, long ago. He had been about ready to get up and leave, but I had brought up something that had gotten under his skin. If there was a trait shared by all men across all the colonized worlds, it was that they love to complain about things beyond their control. The more powerful the man, the

128

more he liked to complain. Lionel spent a half an hour rehashing everything I already knew about the situation on Persephone.

I finally got to interject a question. "Have you ever thought about trying to calm down the streets?"

Lionel slapped the table and brayed like a donkey, spilling a few droplets from his mug that a robot attendant instantly wiped up. "Todd, you know better than I what would happen if I tried to lend any more help to these ungrateful simpletons. Christ, Mohammad, and Buddha!

"It's not enough that we have to safeguard half the stars from psychotic fans. It's not enough that we have to keep the other half from being kidnapped by rival movie houses. It's not *WOCing* enough that we have to make sure they've been scrubbed of all loose DNA so that those self-same movie houses don't get a sample and grow their own mega star!" I had no idea what a *WOC* was, but when Opus spoke of DNA, he was talking about body swapping and talent cloning. Both were uncommon, but not unheard of, in the movie business. Either would— not could but would— cost billions to L/V/D, as look-alikes siphoned credits from those with the real talent. With no unifying government and no foreign judiciary interested in righting these wrongs, the chance of L/V/D recouping these stolen revenues was zero. They had a standing reward of ten million credits to recover any such breech in their security. Ten million, no questions asked. "But even with all these costs, at a time of such turmoil, we tried doing some good for this planet. When their own leaders were being picked off one by one—assassinated mind you! When I brought them into a protected environment, there were protests like you would not believe. Now we have to baby-sit them as well!"

His interviews at the time had said, 'in this time of crisis (he was) concerned for the safety of public servants who had done naught but good for Persephone'. That being said, taking in most of the high-ranking government officials and keeping them in a place where his word was law had the makings of a plot that would give Machiavelli an aneurysm. Could he keep them in their place? What leverage was he buying himself for the future? How long would they live if they became redundant assets?

"I had thousands of local staff quit! I had to get replacements—at great cost mind you—from other planets. Then, after the workers' homes were burnt, shot up, and bombed, I had to relocate them into the studio as well! It's hard enough to make movies when everything runs smoothly, but now we're running on a skeleton crew…" He tossed up his hands. "First, they quit their jobs and then the *WOCers* scream when they are replaced. It's just incomprehensible!

"At every turn, my grandfather, my uncle, and the other CEOs of L/V/D have tried to do right by this planet and this city. Every time, there's someone who pops up to slap them for it." He shook his head darkly, "And the thing that started it all? My grandfather was too acidic in his condemnation of a past president. Afterwards, he was accused of election tampering and other such *deadwood*. As part of the settlement, we stopped running our own news channels. I tell you, once the government forced us give up our voice in the public sector, we were doomed. The other media outlets came out from under our shadow and have never stopped biting at us."

I let him vent, his wrath bubbling away into the air. I waited until his face returned to a normal shade before I asked, "So, what are your plans now, if you don't mind me asking?"

Lionel shrugged. "We're just going to let this mess burn itself out. Just think of the studio as one big bomb shelter. Eventually, things will be broken long enough that people will flee off world, the violent dregs of society will kill them, or they'll starve. We will still be here: well defended, well rested, well fed, and we will gain our voice in the political process again."

His words were all the more chilling for their matter-of-fact tone. "Too bad about all those deaths."

"*WOC* them. If they wanted to live, they should have better control over their neighbors."

He stared at me, daring me to defy him, so I deflected the conversation a bit. "Walk them?"

"Hmm?" Lionel seemed to come to his senses, chuckling at his own outburst. "Oh, no. *WOC*. With Out Contract. It's an artist guild thing; they hate people who work outside the system."

WOC equals frag. Interesting. I nodded and stood. "Well sir, I hope things work out for you and your company."

He smiled like a man who had seen the weather reports and stocked up before the price gouging began. "Oh, they will. And I want to make it clear, Todd; I live here. I grew up here. This planet is my home. I just wish the rest of Persephone realized being African and speaking English doesn't make me an enemy."

"Yeah, I've run into that myself." I shook his hand warmly. "Just out of curiosity, did any of the government agents ever identify *El Toro?*"

"I asked *Servicios de la Investigación Planetarios*, that is Planetary Investigation Services, to check into it once, just before they came into the studio."

"And?"

"They didn't find a thing."

And that's what I needed to know. "Probably some professional rabble rouser from off planet."

"I don't know, Todd. His accent, his syntax, everything's perfect. And MexiCali is not a common language."

"Huh, you'd think someone would have a record of him, then. A student identification, a criminal record, a flier's license if nothing else."

"That's what I thought."

I filed that away for later. "Well, good luck, and if your situation changes, just let us know."

"I will certainly keep you in mind."

I took my leave. A robot dressed like a doorman but built like a wrestler walked me out. Its six legs clanged a semi-musical tune as I digested the important bits and new dangling threads of the conversation. In the hallway stood the two, middle aged Latinos from the dining garden. I don't know how they had gotten ahead of us, but there they were, glaring at me like I had given offense in some way. They carried themselves like bullies, thugs, or perhaps like mercenaries. Their bland, gray suits said they were used to mixing with the upper crust. Their posture said they were intimately familiar with violence and they would not shrink from proving it.

I could have puffed up my chest and glared as I went by. I could have gotten in their faces and started asked pointed, four-letter questions. I could have thrown them around the hallway, breaking bones until they answered unasked questions. Considering the time and place, I settled for smiling and waving at them like an exhibit in a zoo. Their scowls deepened until we turned a corner. I wondered what that was all about until my guide and I got to the landing pads that serviced the L/V/D fliers.

The Key to Damocles

There, Logan sat outside on the tarmac, playing cards with Doe. The giant reclined on the ground, and still had no trouble tossing coins into the center of the table where Doe sighed in abject exasperation. Logan was a mean card player. Without a face, tells were almost out of the question and his numismatics programs made counting cards child's play. *Though he does do that thing when he bluffs...*

Doe bowed out of the hand as gracefully as he could. "Hey boss!"

The wrestling butler hexapod reached into his chest and produced my pistol in one hand and the battery in the other. He handed them over impersonally and coldly wished me a good day. Logan came up behind me, casting enough shadow to cover me...and any three friends as long as we were posing for a picture. "How did it go?"

"Pretty well."

Doe shook his head as he tossed the folding map table and camp chair into *The Cherub*, "All due respect, Cap, but one day you're going to walk into a place alone and never come out again."

I shook my head and walked into the passenger compartment. "Not a chance. Remember what's in orbit and what's not?"

Doe looked at me like I had given him a math problem with an answer of 'cream cheese'. Logan secured the loose gear to the walls and whispered to him, "He means that we have a warship in orbit, and the Persephone military is AWOL."

"Oh." Doe looked between the Master Sergeant and me. "So, where to now?"

I shrugged. "You want the rest of that time at the gypsy ship?"

"Is the pope black?" Doe jumped up and almost ran to the cockpit. "Heeeeeeeeeeeell Yeeeee—"

"Well then, stop that immediately and get us in the air."

Doe coughed, grinned sheepishly, and began flipping switches like a madman. "Uh... aye, aye, Captain?"

"Better, *Angel*."

"Sure Cap, but don't call me *Angel*. Makes me sound like your girlfriend or something."

"Just fly the *fragging* ship, Doe."

The ride was short, but the facts were already forming a lattice in my mind, a net that I could cast out. It would let the lies, assumptions, and falsehoods fall through as the facts were caught in the web. There was just too much sewage pouring into my head, filling my mind until my eyes wanted to jump out of my skull. I needed someone who could assimilate disparate facts into an easily digestible form. What I needed was a lawyer, but my last lawyer, Lewis, had retired to write some kind of fantasy novel or something. I suppose I could call him, but no, I would be on the comm with him at all hours getting advice and opinions. He had earned his retirement, and he didn't need me barging in on it. On the other hand, most of the local types would be off planet already; the rest would be desperate refugees willing to tell me anything to get a job, or huddled behind guarded walls and unwilling to speak to a gun-toting knuckle dragger like me. None of this changed the situation. I needed someone unaffected by the current affair, intelligent, and most importantly, here and now so that updates could be gotten in real-time.

We landed at the spaceport and Logan stood guard over *The Cherub* while I sent Doe out with cash and a direct order to steer clear of any mind-altering substances. I checked the repair job on the craft myself to make sure it was holding up to Doe's abuse, and then walked onto the tarmac and into the storm of consumerism. While out amongst the stalls, I saw some crates of food being freshly unloaded. I bargained for a few minutes, then took the lot. I bypassed other stalls selling used and obsolete weaponry, illicit drugs, even slipshod cybernetic implants. There was enough of this kind of thing flying around to fund a hundred brushfire wars, and the sellers were not too picky about who was the customer.

Normally, I'm the first proponent for an armed society. Unfortunately, it also requires some form of government. I know dozens of theorists who worship at the altar of anarchy, the complete absence of government, but I've seen anarchy up close and I've seen the nail holes are faked. Too much government can do horrible damage to the people it is supposed to protect. Anarchy allows the people to do horrible damage to one another. Part of keeping oneself safe is to be armed… meaning the poor will never be as prepared as the rich, and the rich will always be outnumbered. There's a balance to that, and believe it or not, it works. But when one social, religious, or political group decides to target a minority social, religious, or political group, things will get nasty. The blood flows loud and fast without any government to stand up for the minority. This isn't to say governments are any good at it, but it is their responsibility. Guns or no guns, in a situation like this: no government, a hysterical media, and a stable of shadowy figures egging the populace on was a recipe for a bloodbath. If there is an unfairness for which we can hold God responsible, it is this. There are no perfect solutions.

I checked my MercTool and requested the present location of the *Angels*. Most of them were in a single gypsy ship across the tarmac, so I headed there.

If you take a three hundred shop mall, throw in a brothel, five restaurants, plus a dozen bars, then shoehorn them into a massive freighter the size of a football stadium you will have an approximation of a gypsy ship. Hugely muscled, often cybernetically augmented, armed guards circulated everywhere. Painfully perfect women and men danced on stages... employees, customers, or decoration I could not tell. I squinted as lights strobed in mesmerizing patterns clinically proven to lower inhibitions. Music thumped and whined behind my eyes, reverberating in my chest and pushing my pulse faster.

I found the *Angels* easily, and I was pleased that Thompson had already set drinking rules. Each of them had prepaid cards around their neck, allowing for only limited amounts of alcohol available from the automated bartender at set intervals. It allowed them to build a buzz and unwind, but kept them from descending into sloppy drunkenness. Doe was left out, completely dry in a room full of merriment, but at least he was busying himself gambling at a side kiosk playing Whiplash with Archer. I checked in, and then left as gracefully as possible. There was no way for them to relax with the boss around.

I stopped by a clearly marked exotic foods bar and ordered something tropical, a mix of fruit juices that washed away the sand and heat of New California. I searched until I came across a small side room with a viewscreen. I pressed buttons inset into the surface of the table until I came upon the newsfeeds. The screen showed signs of carnage outside as I swirled the fruit juice in my glass, relishing the cold, tart liquid. Then, a familiar face took up the entire screen, a small icon pulsed showing that the feed was 'live!' I trusted my gut enough to hurriedly dig out my bankcard and wave it over the center of the table. The microcomputer in the table talked with the card for less than a second then ejected a pair of lightweight, wireless headphones. I put them on, cutting off the outside noise. I pushed buttons, cycling through translator programs.

He was haggard, worn, almost drawn. His gray hair seemed whiter since last I saw him forty kilometers ago. He was standing behind a podium in front of his precinct house.

"Captain Lomen? I don't understand. Are you saying you let the murderers go free?" Reporters were everywhere, asking barbed questions...

...and getting harpoons for answers.

"I will say this again for the learning impaired among you. *The Radiation Angels* are not murderers. In the riot there were fourteen deaths. Two died from trampling of the crowd, two were knifed and apparently robbed, and ten died by gunshot wound. The *Angels* were armed with pushguns, similar to what police forces all across Persephone are armed with. These are defensive weapons and do not shoot bullets, and so it is impossible they murdered these civilians."

One of the fine-suited reporters thrust his hand in the air but didn't wait to be acknowledged. "But sir, what about the boys at the Ninth Street Cathlist Church?"

Tony fished a toothpick out of his pocket and clenched it between his teeth. "What's your definition of boy?"

The reporter looked like he had been slapped. "Excuse me?"

"I checked on that incident, which obviously none of you bothered to. If you had, you would have found that there were two gang members, aged sixteen. The rest were over eighteen, and three were over twenty-five. And before you ask another stupid question, I want to say that there were forty real children, under the age of thirteen, being held hostage in the church and one of them had just been murdered in cold blood." Tony popped the toothpick from between his teeth. "And since I'm supposed to be giving this as a press conference, I suppose it would be bad form for me to ask you which children's safety you think should have taken priority."

The Key to Damocles

The members of the media looked at one another, shaken and confused; this was not how this was supposed to go, not at all. "Officer Lomen, how can you stand by such a universally hated group?"

Tony huffed. "Hated? Of course they're hated. They're hated because you want them to be hated. Not because they should be. You've written the script to this movie. You've decided who wears black hats and who wears white hats, but I watched thirteen men and women risk their lives in order to save public servants who the people and the government had abandoned."

He held up a sheaf of papers. "I have a list of all the police officers who have died in the line of duty since the government of New California went into hiding. These men gave their lives for something bigger than themselves, and they are irreplaceable. We have to do something. We owe it to them to do something."

I was caught between cheering and crying as I watched Tony Lomen throw himself on his sword. "As of right now, this police station will no longer be prosecuting weapons violations amongst the citizenry. I cannot guarantee the response time of my police department. If I can't keep the people safe, then they will have to defend themselves. Secondly, without massive and substantial aid from the government, we cannot keep up the level of patrols needed to sustain even the most basic levels of public safety. To combat this, I am putting out a call to all able-bodied citizens in New California. I am requesting their aid in forming the first Citizen Militia in over a century. If enough people come forward, then we might just start to get on top of this garbage slide that has turned our community into a war zone. Make no mistake... there will be no pay. You will need your own equipment and your own ammunition. About all I can do is organize you and give you a little training, maybe a place to sleep. We will arrest the criminals we find in accordance with the law, and hold them for trial at a later date."

The reporters were stunned. The crowd behind them was stunned. Hell, I was stunned. There was a good ten seconds of dead air that sucked any residual warmth from the crowd. One of the reporters found her voice. "But Captain, how about the suspects' right to a speedy trial?"

Tony laughed at her, nastily. "Well, if you can find a judge that hasn't skipped planet or gone to live with the movie stars, I'd appreciate you pointing him or her in my direction so we can take care of that. I'm not a judge, people. I have no intention of pretending to be one. I'm a cop. I have no intention of pretending not to be one any longer."

Another came to the fore, edging past his verbally masticated colleague. "What authority do you have…?"

Tony slammed one, meaty fist into the podium. "I took an oath to protect and serve the people of Persephone and uphold the law. That oath gives me a responsibility that I intend to keep. I need help to do it and the people who have not fled or died are all I have left. I think it's time we stop treating the citizens like stupid cattle and give them back some control over what happens on their streets. I believe in them. With a little training and a lot of courage, they can help put us back on track. If someone wants to call me a traitor, or a usurper, let them come and hang me. For some reason, I don't think the Planetaries hiding behind the walls of L/V/D will be doing that anytime soon."

The feed clicked back to a shot of the Action 311 newsroom, where the anchorpersons looked visibly shaken by both Tony's announcements and his savage handling of the media. It looked like the first time anyone had ever treated the cameras as if he didn't *need* them to succeed. The nominal male ran a hand along his hair and found a faltering smile. "Those…shocking words from Captain Tony Lomen just now. What's your take, Maria?"

"Well, Enrique, I can hardly see how putting more guns on the street is going to stop all the violence. And in the hands of untrained civilians!"

I shut off the feed and replaced the headset. I ducked out of the gypsy ship, dodging two offers to play cards, three thrill seekers looking to have a virtual duel, and an attractive prostitute trolling for some credits. I went back outside, the heat baking the giddy fear from my brain.

I worried for him. People are seldom patted on the back for doing what they know is right in the face of public opinion. In addition, he had just made himself a convenient target for whoever tried to raid the police station once already. His only safety lay in my speedy hunt. I had an ally in my fight. Now I just needed was to find my prey. I left for the open-air mall of the tarmac.

I made some other purchases, and against my better judgment I procured one slightly used lawyer before I hit my MercTool and summoned everyone back to the landing pad. They arrived looking professional, with only a hint of alcohol impairment visible. They'd have time to burn it off prepping for transit. The food supplies arrived at our slip, and Logan loaded them into the craft without complaint. We made only one side-trip, over to the barricaded, besieged Eastside Police Station. John Doe's expert touch kept *The Cherub* hovering inches off the roof where we dropped off two crates of military prepackaged meals, three cases of emergency bar-rations, and two barrels of drinkable water. The whole lot of goods was worth two thousand credits at any supply store on any other planet, but here it cost ten grand. All things considered, it was pocket change well spent.

Two cautious police officers emerged from the building, but by that time we were already in the air and rocketing away.

Maybe I couldn't fix everything, but I could do something.

And that was worth something, after all.

CHAPTER 11: WHEN STRONG, APPEAR WEAK

Back at Ortega's home, we landed safely and without incident. If you think that's redundant, then I haven't sufficiently explained how John Doe flies *The Cherub*. I was able to give the *Angels* another day off, allowing them to unwind in a relatively safe city for a change. To tell the truth, that was an excuse to get them out of my hair while I faced a mounting pile of electronic paperwork. I ignored the screens showing the outer perimeter as I tried to consolidate everything and separate important data from meaningless noise. Most of the static was easy to eliminate, but there was still a huge mound of official looking electronic communications that required more than just a glance before being discarded. There were offers for work… both local and off planet, applications for employment, death threats, and cease and desist paperwork from the all but defunct planetary government. A full half of my electronic mailbox was eaten up with repeated requests for interviews from local news networks. Thankfully, I had something like a lawyer slash office assistant slash personal computer to take care of it, though he—/*l*—would never have been my first choice for the job. "Grisham?"

His voice was synthesized, but polite and proper. "Yes, sir?"

I waved at the computer screen inside the communications trailer. "Handle this. I need everything even slightly tactical in one folder on top, everything official from a government agency or company in another, and everything else thrown into like-minded subject folders. Anything looking to sell me goods and/or services can be deleted."

"Of course, sir." His flat motors whined as he moved forward, looking over my shoulder as if it mattered. I slowly turned my head to face him, my frown glaring back at me from his ivory-chrome finish. He looked like an upright man in a suit, with clean, straight lines and a compact but impressive frame. I doubt even a blind man would mistake him for a real person, since everything else about him was so mechanical. But even so, his designers had known their work. His face had two 'eyes', but they were made of liquid gold and blue crystals in hypnotic glass spheres. Shutters like eyelids held the eyes in a pose of perpetual sympathetic strength, but could be lowered to be unsettlingly hostile and accusatory. His mouth was a simple, neutral grid that seemed happy, angry, or calm depending on the posing of his eyes. I imagine that thousands of focus groups had given input to result in the flat dome of his head that made him look older, distinguished, and bald. He—*It! It! It! It! It! It! IT!*—it continued to loom over me.

"What are you doing?"

"I am accessing the files, sir."

"You have the access codes, quantum frequency of the modem, and port ID for the computer, you can access them from anywhere on the planet."

"Well yes, sir."

"Then don't crowd me, Grisham." I pushed the heavy, metallic man back. "And after you're done, open up the folder marked 'police' and send the file you find there to Tony Lomen at the email address noted. Then look through every historical resource on the planet. Sift the relevant data, build it into a timeline, and give me the last hundred years of Persephone's socio-political history in as few words as possible. I'm tired of working in the dark here."

I sipped on the steaming mug of coffee as the law unit took control of the computer and flipped through the files. Behind me the door opened to the communications trailer and Reeves stuck his head inside. "Capitan? Uh—what the hell is this?"

Grisham turned and nodded his mechanical head. "Hello, I am—"

I cut it off. "I bought a new robot."

Reeves smiled and shook his shaggy head. "I can see that. Why?"

"I needed a law expert, a researcher, an encyclopedia, and an automated presentation system. This thing fits the bill."

"But it's got an integrated personality!"

I could feel my jaw begin to ache from the constant pressure of my teeth grinding. "There weren't a whole lot of choices."

"Well, let's leave your new toy alone to work for a moment. Mrs. Ortega and some cops want to speak with you." That, of course, caught my attention. Reeves read my posture and shrugged. "It ain't anything good, that's for sure."

I sighed as I levered myself out of the chair. For once, just once, I wanted a few, short hours to figure out what was going on here. I slid on my forearm pad and followed it up with a skin-toned subvocal sticky mike and dermal speaker. If anything happened, Sichak, Logan or Grisham could reach me.

I have to admit that I moved slowly, resenting every step that took me further from my real work. I walked into the Ortega house, mind reeling from the clash of hard won and treasured possessions of a poor household against the cold and clean technological luxuries of the rich. We ducked through the halls, acutely aware that wherever we went the numerous members of the Ortega family were absent. No children played tag in the hallways, nobody was watching the entertainment units, and even more telling, there was nobody in the expansive kitchen cooking, lounging, or snacking. Clearly, we were headed for the sitting room and that meant somebody was going to get yelled at again. Given my history with Mrs. Ortega, it was probably me. Worse, I didn't think her son was around to shield me from her incomprehensible tirade.

Reeves walked in and ducked to the side, making way for a hurled picture frame that caught me full in the chest. My left hand batted the next hurled breakable out of the air as my right instinctively closed around the thick grip of my holstered plasma pistol.

"FREEZE!" And just like that, things got dangerous. "Alright Rook, drop the gun. Really slowly."

Nothing sharpens the mind and focuses the attention like looking down the barrel of a gun, let alone three. Reeves backed against the wall and let his hand dangle just to side of his laser pistol, but his desire to help me was balanced by the fact that we were outnumbered…plus the guns were pointed at me, not him, and he didn't really feel like drawing that kind of attention. I understood; after all, I didn't like it much, myself. In the corner, Ortega's mother stood, shocked. Her hands were still filled with knickknack ammunition she had intended to use to punctuate her shouts, but her mouth hung open at the scene of imminent death before her.

The Key to Damocles

I gently eased the bulky pistol out of the holster and dropped it to the carpeted floor.

"Kick it."

I did as I was ordered.

Each one of the strangers had the posture of a self-important bureaucrat with a distinct whiff of cop. That made them special agents: secret agents or planetary agents, lots of trouble with badges. I slowly, ever so delicately, lifted my hands into the air above my head. Two were young and scared, which made them smarter than the older agent, who only radiated smug confidence. Agent Young bent down and picked up the pistol, but it took him four tries to clear the weapon's capacitor and render it inert. He almost fired it twice, finger stupidly on the trigger, but since the muzzle was covering his boss I didn't feel it was my place to correct him. While Young was trying to commit manslaughter by negligent discharge, Agent Younger walked forward and relieved me of my forearm keypad. Then he holstered his weapon and roughly but expertly cuffed my wrists behind my back with a set of nasty *plasteel* ribbons. He fumbled in his pocket for the fuser, a little device made to clip off the ends and turn the ribbons into clean, form-fitted restraints.

I'm no Huang Lee, but I've studied unarmed combat. Mainly, I know ugly things: joint locks, breaking punches, and disarming maneuvers. In fact, I'm proficient in no less than three different moves from this position. Each one is a collection of martial arts attacks to simultaneously stun the guy behind me, provide me with his holstered sidearm, and give me a human shield to hide behind. I was confident I could beat Agent Old Fart's reflexes, plus Young and Younger had both put away their weapons to do their respective chores. Even with the element of surprise, my chances of survival were perhaps fifty/fifty. As much as it would have pleased me to crack a nose, smash an instep, and perhaps perform a nine-millimeter circumcision or three, these *gritheads* were from some government agency and I needed to talk to them. Still, I did have something to say right away. "Thanks for the heads up, Reeves."

He looked hurt. I didn't think it was an act. "The guys at the gate said there was a few policemen that wanted to talk to Mrs. Ortega. I thought these were detectives from a local PD or something."

"You let armed, unidentified men into the compound? You're a dumb shit." Reeves took the verbal slap about as well as could be expected. "You should have had snipers on these guys from the first second they were here. Then you should have come in ten minutes later with a huge sergeant as backup, fully prepared to escort them off the premises."

Reeves glared at me, but saluted as sarcastically as he could manage. While he was busy looking wounded, Younger came from behind me and pushed me down into a large, comfy chair. They paid no mind to how my arms would be strained while pinned behind me. I didn't complain; anything that made them complacent would work in my favor.

Old Fart holstered his weapon, not a pushgun but a Sy-Vine™ laser pistol. I was familiar with the brand, known more for its stylish lines than ruggedness or power. It was capable of putting an unarmored man on the ground, but it would be absorbed even by light armored plates. Besides, thirty seconds out in the muck and mud of a real battlefield, and the thing would be hopelessly clogged beyond use. It was the kind of expensive weapon chosen by people who spend a lot of time behind a desk trying to impress their superiors. Young and Younger moved to cover the windows and door, respectively, while Old Fart came forward to try to loom over me. Maybe it would have worked if he didn't look so much like a gray-haired scarecrow. His pricy suit simply hung on his wire hangar-shaped shoulders. Then again, maybe it was held up by the power of smug alone. "Well, well, well, Rook. It looks like you're not quite as clever as reported."

I smiled at Old Fart. I had spent long hours practicing that smile in front of a mirror, making sure it had the right mix of cold murder and feral rage. I was pleased to see Younger's hand stray a little closer to his holster. "Good afternoon, agent…?"

Old Fart retrieved a badge holder from inside his jacket and pushed his identification into my face. "I am Special Planetary Agent Gil Carlos, boy. From *Servicios de la Investigación Planetarios.*"

"Planetary Investigation Services. The men from PISs are here. I am all a-quiver." Carlos actually laughed as he took out an evil-looking, pronged device from his jacket pocket. I had seen them on battlefields the universe over, and knew exactly what it was. He turned the nerve manipulator over in his withered hands and considered it carefully, almost lovingly. I could see the numbing medical unit had at one time been opened and sloppily put back together. Carlos wasn't showing me a first aid device, but a *painbox*, an instrument of torture. He touched it to my arm.

There was no time, no breath, no need, and no thought, only complete and unimaginable agony. It was like being eaten away by acid, disintegrated by an inferno, torn to pieces by a million biting spiders. Reality spun away into a pinpoint and then impaled my brain with the force of a rail spike. Suddenly, I was light years away, decades ago. I was twelve, tied to a chair. Nicholas, my best friend, wept quietly next to me. He had to weep quietly, doing anything loud would just provoke them. Nick's brother, years older, and his friend were there. They passed a needle over a small torch, turning it white hot and passing it nearer and nearer my eyes. I strained at the ropes, pulled with all my might, screaming inside for a hero, any hero, to come and save me.

None came.

Then it ended. I was yanked back to the here and now. I spit on the carpet, adrenaline and barely remembered pain churning my stomach like a witch's cauldron. Tremors flooded through me. When I was able to look up, Carlos' shiny gold badge and picture ID were held at the end of my nose. I remembered what Doe said about going into places alone, and the back of my mind echoed with doubts that today he might just be proven right. I fought through new fear and old terror to force some levity between chattering teeth. "Ah, well, pleased to meet you. I'd show you my credentials, but my hands are a little restrained right now."

Carlos waved one hand while the other flipped the wallet shut and placed it back inside his jacket with practiced motions. "That won't be necessary. I think I know everything I need to know about you."

"Really?"

"Oh, yes." Carlos began to pace back and forth, but caught sight of Reeves and Maria. "We will be a few minutes; you may wait outside."

Reeves stared at me, so pale he was almost blue, as he ushered Maria Ortega out of her yelling room. A few seconds later, the door shut and I was left alone with the agent and his minions. "General Reeves doesn't really like you, does he?"

I shrugged. "There's been some friction."

"I can see why; you really are a colossal pain in the ass. No honor amongst thieves, or killers for that matter. Anyway, back to you." Agent Carlos sat down on the table in front of my chair and lit up a cigarette, smiling at the perfect nature of a universe in which he had complete control. He blew smoke at me, setting off distant cravings and setting a smoldering tinder dangerously close to my fuse. "You grew up on the cesspit called Roh. No serious convictions, though you were arrested for participating in illegal sporting events, and you had a few run-ins with the local gangs. Even wound up in the hospital once or twice. You joined up with the *Angels* at nineteen, and most of the rest of your life comes under the heading of 'confidential' or 'secret'. There is a Christmas Tree's worth of decorations, but most of them don't say for what."

"You have to understand my position." I leaned back further and tried to appear nonchalant and comfortable. A tremor in my right leg cracked the veneer of calm. "Most of my employers have a need for discretion."

"You are a murderer, Rook. You kill for money, and have done so on more than a hundred different planets over the course of a decade. You have an army of trained killers at your beck and call, but even thugs need a day off. I looked at your file, and I see a workaholic; so, you probably wouldn't take that time for yourself. We've been watching for this day, so that once you were alone, we could come and get you."

"Little old me? Mr. Lionel and I parted on good terms. I've broken no law within his enclave, and I haven't made any moves against L/V/D at all—."

"This really isn't about L/V/D or Mr. Lionel. This is about law, the law you're flaunting."

I just couldn't stop my mouth. "One: you mean flout, not flaunt. If I were flaunting the law I'd be wearing it like a brand-new tuxedo. Two: it is my understanding that there is no law on Persephone. Law died the day you ran and hid behind the ivory walls—."

The Key to Damocles

Carlos reached into his pocket and retrieved his *painbox*. He met my eyes with avuncular affection and then, without warning, he jabbed it at my chest.

My body tried to black out, but like a piece of cork dropped into the water the pain buoyed me back to the light. I didn't hear the click that started this endless hell, and I didn't hear the one that brought it to an end, but suddenly the pain was gone, leaving behind only a throbbing ghost behind. Everything pulsed in time to a snare drum solo, throwing me from my seat as my vision blurred. Rough hands hauled me up and set me into the plush chair. The soft fabric tingled against my skin, which expected nothing softer than shattered glass.

Carlos didn't bother to put the device away this time. He held it like a constant threat, the way some gang members play with pistols or knives. It remained a constant punctuation to his words and ideas. "Rook, I know that you are used to being in charge pretty much all the time, but it's time to re-evaluate your immediate future."

Even after a deep breath, my voice wavered weakly. "Fair enough, Agent. So, what part of the law am I *flaunting*?"

Sticking the cigarette into his mouth, he flicked nicotine-stained fingers in my face one by one. "First, you're bearing arms on the streets of Persephone, a category one felony. Second, you and your group have committed murder. Mass murder actually. First degree for sure. I could probably tack on conspiracy, kidnapping, reckless operation of a flier, and terrorism without too much of a stretch. You've even got lifetime police officers on live feeds denigrating the government and calling for a revolution!"

I wouldn't call organizing a heavily armed neighborhood watch a revolution, but it didn't seem the best time to contradict him. "All this effort for little old me. Tell me, Agent, if you're hungry to make your career on someone's bones, then why not go after *Toro*?"

Carlos barked, nearly losing his cigarette. "Oh, Rook, if I go catch the *Toro*, I will go down in history as a monster. If I bring you in, I become an instant hero."

"Plus, I'm willing to bet the pay is better, working for the movie house directly."

Carlos shot to his feet, "Don't you—!"

My voice plowed over his. "After all, if you catch the *Toro* and the crisis ends…"

"Don't you—!"

I smiled a little. "…you might have to go back to your public servant's salary."

"Don't. You. Dare." The agent waved the manipulator beneath my nose, his voice low and dangerous. "Mercenaries, pheh! You bastards dance amongst the stars, sowing chaos wherever you go. You call no man master, stay nowhere long, and leave behind nothing but hatred and misery."

Young and Younger watched in rapt fascination, unable to turn away from the spectacle of torture and yet repulsed by it. In stark contrast, Carlos was enjoying his grip on me, and every act of defiance allowed him to do what he really wanted to. Untold men had broken under his thumb, probably under the tender mercies of the same *painbox* with which he plied me. He probably enjoyed great success, since confessions would roll from lips as if greased. Without any marks to indicate abuse, they'd stand up in any court. I wondered idly how many innocent men he had sent to prison. As he continued, his eyes grew wide, glowing with almost religious fervor, "I have served the public for twenty years, but who do you serve, Rook? Only yourself. I know in most of the places you go, mercenaries are seen as something special. You bask in the adoration of the masses like some kind of movie star while I work myself into an early grave. I am an officer of the law, and I am more than you, Rook."

The thought of this *jacka* calling himself a lawman, comparing himself to someone like Lomen gave volcanic heat to my next four words. "But, am I right?"

By way of answer, Carlos touched the *painbox* to my chest and just left it there. I don't know how long it lasted, but I started screaming toward the end. When he turned it off, I saw that the ashtray had grown two more cigarette butts. I could clearly hear my heart in my ears, and it didn't sound normal. *Oh, yeah, I'm right.*

I took a few deep breaths, clamping down on the animal desire to panic, the base need to wrench at my bonds and try to be free. First, it wouldn't work. Second, a little whisper at the base of my ear told me it wasn't necessary. I took another breath for good measure and fixed Carlos with a stare that said, 'I will break you in half'.

He blew another cloud of smoke at me and chuckled. "Oh, it looks like you want another taste—"

It took every bit of discipline I could muster not to shrink away and scream. "Cut the *grit*, Agent. Since it looks like I don't have a right to remain silent on this planet, just ask what you came here to ask."

"Ask? Oh no, no, no, no. I have no questions. I'm just here to take you in. This little beauty," he waved the box at me, "is just meant to keep you compliant on the way."

"No."

"No? Mr. Rook, I don't think you understand the situation."

"Actually, I think that I am the only one who understands the situation." I spoke as if to the air. "Did you get it all?"

And then, as Fart's eyes grew wide, I appeared to listen to no one. He raked one smoke-smelling hand behind my left ear, singing my hair with his cigarette. He did it again on the other side, and peeled up the skin toned, self-adhesive speaker that had been feeding me updates from Logan and Reeves.

Instead of taking cover, Young spun and looked out the window. He immediately backed up a step and raised his hands in the air. Younger's breathing was approaching hyperventilation levels as he looked back and forth at his superiors. Carlos, on the other hand, was getting angry. I sat up straight, and began drawing up my booted foot.

"If the boy by the window moves, the sniper will kill him. If the boy by entrance moves, my cyborg sergeant will shoot him through the door." I continued addressing no one in particular, telling both the agents in here and the *Apostles* outside what I wanted to happen if...in fact all of their lives hung by the if's. "And if any of you does anything stupid, I'm going to make sure you leave here with a severe limp."

The gravity of the situation slipped through Carlos' fingers, and I saw his temper light off all at once. He punched at my nose, but I shifted in the chair and as his fist connected with my jaw, my cocked leg shot out like a lightning bolt. I felt two molars loosen and tasted blood, but the sound of his shin breaking under my steel reinforced boot was loud enough to rebound once from the walls before it was drowned out by his screams.

The door splintered as Logan shouldered it aside like tissue paper, flooding the room with mercs and guns.

Ten seconds after Logan and the *Apostles* made their entrance, the room was secure. The agents were taken down with brutal precision, tossed around like dangerous dogs. The *Apostles* disarmed the agents and freed me, then we used their own cuffing equipment to restrain our prisoners.

I stood over Carlos, who was breathing through his teeth to keep from whimpering too much. His eyes widened as I picked him up and sat him in the chair I had once occupied, hefting his favorite gadget with one hand as I rubbed my jaw with the other. I looked longingly at the stubs of cigarettes in the ashtray. My fingers itched to take one. I spit bloody saliva into it instead. Say what you want, but Carlos had practice hitting restrained men.

That thought festered inside of me, grabbing onto my reasoning brain, drawing up ancient beatings from my youth. The feeling of helplessness washed over me, dim memories of humiliation and pain brought up fresh like bodies bloating with decomposition gasses. Heat and hate belched from within me; it tried to dissolve my self-control. The weak little man in front of me became every boy, woman, or man who had ever wronged me. He personified the abuse of undeserved power. I hated him. I hated everyone like him.

I sat on his corner of the table and picked up the *painbox*. I cracked open the casing and fiddled with the insides. My words were cut short, my sentences bleeding disdain all over him. "You know, these were developed so that a medic could work on anyone, anywhere. They create a field that interrupts nerve conductivity. A non-chemical anesthetic: suddenly, you didn't have to worry about overmedicating a patient in the heat of battle. It's a wonder of the modern age. Weird things start to happen if you leave it on too long, but really it's a fair trade. It takes a special kind of bastard to turn it into a torture device."

I looked at him and saw a thin, shriveled, little man. I don't know how many times he had bent the rules to accommodate his ego. I don't know how many civil rights he had violated to ease the stress of his job. I knew it wasn't the first time because he did it like he had practice. Tired, frightened, and in pain, Gil Carlos sat at the mercy of a man he had wronged for the first time in his adult life. He debated in his head obviously, eyes slipping from object to object in the room. He was looking for hope, for an escape. "OK, Rook. What do you want to know?"

"I asked you one question, and the way you didn't answer me told me everything I wanted to know. *El Toro* is not a threat. So, who is he?"

Carlos' dusky Hispanic skin turned a horrible shade of tan. His mouth worked, but he shook his head as his voice ran and hid.

"You know what? Never mind. Everything else you said filled in all the blanks I needed from you. Well, everything else but one question. Who is the real threat? Who is starting all of this? Who is behind the chaos on Persephone?" I held the pain box nonchalantly, but his eyes followed it as if it were a golden watch in the hands of a hypnotist. He wasn't mesmerized. He was almost out of his mind. He had seen what this little thing had done to too many men... men who had been just as unable to give answers to questions. He was going into shock, partially from the severe break in his leg and partially because of his sheer terror of what I was about to do to him. He was useless.

I leaned forward with the little black box in my hand. Carlos began screaming at the top of his lungs, really bawling, and would not stop. I took up one of the plasteel restraints and used it to attach the box to his wounded leg. His cries went on and on, interrupted by sobs that wracked his ravaged frame. His choking gasps gave him pause, and then his panic died as he realized that his shin no longer hurt. He glanced down at the inhibitor, which was inhibiting instead of agitating, muting the complete agony of the shattered bone. I tapped it to draw his attention back to my face.

"That's what these are made for, asshole."

He looked left and right, gaining confidence and brewing rage with every second his pain was taken away. His questions were printed clearly on his face.

I could have told him that I cheated. He seemed to have a great amount of contempt for mercenaries, so I figured he would believe he could bully one into giving up another. But for all his reading of my file, he let Reeves leave instead of holding him hostage. He missed the fact that Reeves used to be in the *Angels*. I told my ex-lieutenant 'heads up', an old expression for 'pay attention'. The rest of the script wrote itself, but I didn't think that Old Fart Carlos would appreciate the lesson. Furthermore, I don't give free advice to an enemy.

"Now, you and your men are going to be escorted to my vehicle. You are coming with us as prisoners of war. You will receive medical attention in good time." The shin was well shattered, but I had no intention of spending our resources on putting it more right than the Laws of War required. I stood to leave, but decided to pause. While it shouldn't have to be said, I wasn't banking on Carlos being able to figure this out on his own. "You used torture on a soldier in a war zone. You are a war criminal, and the punishment for your crime is death. If you try to escape, you will be killed. If you make trouble, we will convene a military court and try you immediately."

Despite his near mental breakdown, Carlos managed to spit, "*Jimmy* yourself, Merc."

I didn't know what *jimmy* meant, but I could guess. I felt a need, as real and immediate as breathing, a need to hit him once.

In the face.

Hard.

My fists clenched so hard the knuckles cracked. Blood boiling up from my gut percolated in my ears in time with my heartbeat. I stood, legs shaking with the need to kick, to stomp, to inflict pain. *Once, just once.* Carlos licked his lips like a lizard and shrank from me.

I turned on my heels and walked out of the room. I left for the still abandoned kitchen. Seconds later, I had rifled through the cabinet, and found a bottle of vanilla rum that looked like it was going to fit the bill. I poured a glass over ice and sipped it slowly, relishing the sweet, chilled burn. I did it again, and once more, dousing the fire inside with alcohol instead of letting it run wild and free. I did it because there was no boxing ring handy, no firing range within easy reach, and no way I was going to hit a prisoner for any reason. Because no matter what you tell yourself, no matter the justification, you never just hit them once. You never just hit them. You never stop after just one time. Torture always escalates. The reasons will always become flimsier. Lastly, and most importantly, as much as torture changes the prisoner, it changes the torturer. *I hate you, Carlos, but not enough to give up my soul.*

The Key to Damocles

I stretched my chest, flexing the heavy subdermal armor plates, and tried not to think about cigarettes. I had a whole twenty minutes to myself before my *EWO* walked in with his mother.

Maria had been greatly deflated by the day's events, but she still projected a definite matronly presence into the room. Manuel translated her Spanish to my English. The really bad thing was as she went on, she was remembering why she was angry, and her voice gained momentum the more she spoke. Who was I to bring this violence into her home? She had been watching the newsfeeds, and she definitely did not like what she saw there about me. Like most of the people on Persephone, she had swallowed the propaganda whole.

To be honest, I wasn't listening. I had heard enough evictions to have the whole thing memorized. I held up a hand and he stopped. "Ortega, tell your mother *The Radiation Angels* will be lifting off in five hours. I need you to go start the packing and help me warm up *The Succubus.* We might be gone for a few weeks, so go and say goodbye to your family."

He did, and she decided she did not like that at all. I caught enough of her words to know she definitely did not like the idea of a villain like me giving her son orders to go anywhere. He turned to me, helplessly caught between the fury of a mother and the cold stone of his commanding officer. "Captain, I'm not sure if I can—"

My jaw still throbbed around the loosened teeth. My head thumped from unreleased violence and painful memories. My ears stung from the shrill tone of her abuse. Finally, my temper snapped. "Look, Ortega! You can come, or not. Now is the time to decide, because we are not coming back."

"Uh, Boss—"

"Stow it, *EWO*. I may be here to help your family, but I'll be damned if I'll be shit on while it happens."

I punched a few keys on the armband, summoning the *Angels* from their well-deserved rest. Across town, in many bars, restaurants, and theaters, MercTools chirped to life. At the 'Go' signal, the *Angels* dashed away from their distractions, moving at a run toward *The Cherub* where John Doe was already waiting. The engines spooled up, the armored transport raised over the low-level flyways, and began accelerating toward the compound.

By the time that happened, Logan and I were already outside the complex, gathering equipment and loading it into the cargo pod on *The Succubus*. Reeves exited the line of trees that screened the lawn from the house, his shoulders slumped and his gait less than commanding. He came to where I was snapping plastic cargo boxes closed and stood behind me. I sighed. "Don't worry about it, General."

"Don't 'General' me, Captain." I could hear it: the doubt, the pain of failure. "They looked like detectives, normal PD. I honestly didn't know—"

"It worked out, and you got to play cavalry, so don't sweat it. Next time, you'll know to look closer, so just learn from it and move on. You owe that to the men who have placed their lives under your command." I turned to him, and saw the sorrow lodged in his soul like bits of shrapnel. I snapped him a salute as the sound of *The Cherub's* engines faded in from the horizon. "You're a good soldier, but a fresh commander who has bitten off a large chunk to swallow. Chew more carefully, and you'll be fine."

"What about you?"

"I need time to think, so we're falling back to *Heaven*." I watched as *The Cherub* spun like a top, slid into position maybe a dozen yards away, and settled to the charred grass with little more than a thump. "Something's really wrong here. I'm going to find out what it is."

"Why? I mean you're on the outs with the Ortegas. Not only are you not getting paid, this whole thing must be costing you a mint. Why not just go home?"

I sighed and looked up at the sun, much milder at this latitude than in New California. I saw a homely brown face, puffy with bruises. Her eyes looked into me for something... "Because someone wanted to believe in me, and I wouldn't let her because I was afraid. I didn't like how she looked at me after that."

"You're the one who always said, 'Don't be a hero'."

"Yeah. I really don't know what to do about that." There was nothing more to say. Reeves shook my hand, said goodbye to Logan, and went back to his team. The *Angels* loaded up *The Succubus*, starting with the agent/prisoners and finishing with

The Key to Damocles

The Cherub, which was driven up directly into a cargo pod just before it was sealed. I went to the cockpit, and began running preflight routine using a checklist that was repeated three times. Doe was the best pilot I had ever seen for atmospheric craft, but transfer from high atmospheric travel to low orbit was tricky. I am not the most experienced flyer, but I had more stick-time in a suborbital craft than anyone else, including Doe, so I was the one to fly *The Succubus*. What I wouldn't do to have Macintosh, my old pilot, right now.

I was about to de-chalk the engines and shut the doors when another figure approached from the tree line. He was obviously as burdened as Reeves, his shoulders slumped and head bowed. He was carrying only a light rucksack, but it appeared as if he was a Latino Atlas, feet nearly dragging behind him as he fought years of familial ties and parental respect. He came to the front of the craft and dropped his load. Ortega looked up and caught my eyes in the pilot seat. Three heartbeats marked endless time until he snapped a picture-perfect salute, and stood there like the statue of a forgotten soldier, awaiting my answer.

I don't know how much of his home life he had just flushed away in order to be here. I remember making that same decision... walking away from everything your family said in order to do what you knew to be right. It wasn't like pissing off a friend, or torquing off an acquaintance, or even flipping the bird at a head of state. This was the kind of thing that would create rifts that were kilometers wide, and forever alter relationships begun in the womb.

Since the birth of civilization, humans have been taught that when all else crumbles, you will still have family. This is the kind of thing that could put an end to all that. It would begin endless arguments and uncomfortable silences, whispered rumors and disapproving looks. Eventually, it could even send a man wandering the universe, forever avoiding the place of his birth and those who share his blood.

But he had asked me to come and, out of love for him, I had. As he stood before me, he would be damned rather than leave me to finish this alone. I saluted back and popped the loading gate, allowing him aboard.

A damn fine soldier.

CHAPTER 12: PERSPECTIVE

Persephone hung in the window like a goddess attended by hundreds of fiery fae. Each moving star was a ship, mercenary or mercantile, bringing men and goods to the surface. Each one had an active standard quantum band transponder, read by every other ship and used to make sure several hundred thousand tons of metal didn't try to mate at speeds that defied imagination. Each one was a signal, and each one had to be weeded out.

From the bridge of *Deadly Heaven*, I watched Ortega type at the computer workstation, eliminating signals from the sensors' take. "That was the easy part."

He sensed my heavy stare over his shoulder and looked up at me with bloodshot eyes. I nodded at him, and he continued working without further comment. The visual display showed Persephone as a fuzzy globe caught in the grip of a manic electrical storm. Ortega followed a half-studied protocol, shutting off the receiver from commercial quantum communications signals. Modern broadcasts use quantum-state communications. They use laws of physics understood by perhaps a hundred people across all of colonized space. Well, maybe a hundred... if you fudge the numbers up a lot.

From what I remember from high school subatomic physics, if you alter the quantum state of one object, it can change the quantum state of other objects. In the regular world, macro-atomic if you will, we would expect that you change one then the other would follow. This is simple cause and effect.

Well, it appears in the subatomic world this isn't always true. Sometimes the causes and effects are simultaneous, and sometimes the effect precedes the cause by a few nanoseconds. Nevertheless, if you change one thing, another can change. It took humanity centuries of research and the best minds it had to offer to figure out how. Moreover, they discovered that if you can 'tune in' the right 'frequency', then you can instantly communicate with anyone, anywhere just by changing the quantum state of your unit. Only massive quantum disturbances, stars in a state of flux, nebulae, and purposeful jamming, can interrupt the call. All you need is the right 'frequency' and a clear 'pathway', and you can call family or friends all across the universe using a phone the size of a credit card.

Then again, finding the right frequency is whole other problem. Each communicator works off of a set of twenty-four atoms; each atom can be tuned to one of eight quantum states that determines the frequency, meaning the number of frequencies was...

I gave up on the mental math about the time my ears started to buzz. By then, Ortega had eliminated all of the low-band commercial communications such as phones, air traffic controls, robot communications, audio only entertainment channels, and the like and had begun working on the wide band stations: television, military data links, the planetary quantum net, and so forth. As each was deleted, the crazy, sparking became a little less furry and the planet became a little clearer. It was not a matter of minutes however; it was a process of hours. Pilot Sichak was able to help with the basics of the program, but beyond that was really work for a ship-board Electronic Warfare Officer. Thing was, we didn't have one. There simply had not been time to woo, vet, and hire one before making planet fall.

I busied myself at another station, slogging through the data Grisham had inexpertly culled for me once already. On the surface, this looked like a typical rebellion. On further examination, it came back to one, inescapable conclusion every time... there was something else entirely going on. These thoughts flitted away from me as I read report after report, tongue going over the teeth that had been freshly reseated by Bugs, our robotic doctor. A purposefully annoying chirp yelped from my pocket. I took out my MercTool and turned off the alarm. *Is it so late already?*

These devices were about a centimeter wide and deep by about five centimeters long. They contained a tiny camera, ceramic knife blade, three chemical torch fire starters, digital clock, calendar, flashlight, a quantum band communicator, and a dozen other micro-sized knickknacks... everything a mercenary on the go might need in an emergency. *Your mind's wandering, Captain.*

I set the computer to save, encrypt and lock up the newly sifted data in an offline storage module deep inside *Deadly Heaven*. I hooked a thumb at my electronic lawyer who had finally figured out that I was happiest when he was sitting in the corner quietly. "Come to bed, Ortega. Let Grisham do some of the work."

"Just a little while longer, Captain. I've got most of the hard ones. Grisham and the *Heaven* computer can handle the rest."

Ortega spun around on the affixed chair and stretched his back. Inside the silent bridge, the echoing sound of his vertebrae crackling made me wince. He had sat down at the console fifteen hours beforehand and had barely taken a break. I was getting worried about him. "It knows what to look for."

"Be fair, *Jefe*. This is a lot more involved than running a basic hand scanner. I haven't studied anything this touchy or complex. It's like going from a remote-control flier to the real thing. I've spent most of the time with the operators manual up on screen." He rubbed his eyes with the palms of his hands as if trying to press the blood out of the clearly veined whites. "Still, I have it looking, and it's been told to log all instances."

"It won't alert us on the PA?"

"I could, but we're going to have false alarms all over the place. There are too many extraneous signals that could reverb in the same way."

"Alright, alright. I've got to go get some shuteye. I'll see you in the morning." He waved over his shoulder, and I departed for my cabin. I opened the hatch, dogged it behind me, dropped my clothes to the floor and fell onto the bed.

Someone began hammering at the door to my room. My eyes shot open as Thompson flung open the hatch and dashed to the side of my bed. "Captain?"

"Lieutenant?" My voice sounded slurred, drunk, even to my own ears.

"Captain, you have to see this." And she reached for the control pad beside my head and turned on the wall-mounted viewscreen. The image woke me immediately, the way only a bucketful of adrenaline can.

"Get Logan and Ortega to the bridge."

She left, and I went to my private bathroom. The quiet closet was the ultimate proof of my position on this ship, a luxury that brought no comfort at the moment. I splashed icy water into my face, sparing a glare for the lying clock that claimed I had been asleep for over eight hours.

I surrendered the last wisps of sleep as I pulled on some clothes and began to jog toward the central spine hallway, and then back toward the bridge. The monitors were already on, and tuned to the streets, kilometers below us on Persephone.

I've seen this scene before. Many times before. Spanish words in bold fonts and glaring colors scrolled across the top and bottom of the screen. A talking head was set into a panel in the bottom right. Opposite her was a picture of me, age twenty. I flipped the next screen over to the cameras in the belly of *Deadly Heaven* and directed the electronic eyes southward.

In the heart of the city of Mezzo-Americana lay the Ortega Complex. It was dawn over the painstakingly groomed groves and avenues. Normally, it was as close to a pastoral setting as possible inside a city, but now it looked like a sandwich dropped on an anthill. The angry mob carried signs with my picture on it, the same outdated picture as on the news screen. It looked like an all-day event. The placards were covered with insulting slogans, harsh criticisms, and calls for my slow, tortured, death. I was even being burned in effigy. *How quaint.*

Fifty yards away from the crowd, a small knot of five police officers watched on. Even in Mezzo-Americana, where many people were still paying taxes, the police forces were stretched pretty thin. They were little more than a token force. The horrible thing was, from their posture you could tell they knew it.

Logan stood, implacable and unreadable, with the images on the screens reflecting off of his finish. Next to him was Ortega, feet set to the deck as if riveted there, his whole body leaning toward the screens as if to fall through and join his family. I backed up behind him as quietly as I could and stood at rest as the story unfolded. I waved off Sichak, who immediately got to his feet and beat a hasty retreat from the bridge. In seconds, we were alone with the drama hammering at us from the two, two-meter screens.

The reporters spoke in staccato sentences, interviewing angry protestors with leading questions. At every turn, the reporters spared no chance to remind the crowd why they were here, and egg them on. It became obvious that the news crews needed a story and there was nothing else going on today.

I felt something bigger was coming, and I didn't like the looks of it. I glanced over at the robot in the corner. "Grisham? Record this feed. Log it as if it were evidence."

"Yes, sir." Somewhere inside the metal man, independent and inviolate recorders began securing the data streams coming in from the news companies. It matched the data to a record of orbiting time/date/positioning satellites around the planet and his own time/date/location stamps, effectively turning it into a file admissible as evidence in any court in the universe.

Afterwards, silence pounced on the bridge again, broken only by the rattle of reporters on a mission that more resembled a feeding frenzy than a trial by jury. News cameras scanned the angry faces in the crowd for a second before focusing on the armed *Apostles* on the walls, then past the guardians to the windows of the Ortega mansion. There were faces looking through windows at the sea of hatred outside. They were frightened faces.

Finally, every tendon thrumming with suppressed rage and fear, Ortega began pacing with an almost stiff legged gait. "What do we do?"

I took a deep breath, using up long seconds to walk to my captain's chair and sink into the plush seat. The wasted time allowed him to stew, to run through the facts on his own, and to allow him to run through all the options in his head. "What would you do?"

"I would go down there and man the walls around my family!"

"What if that was your face on the screen?"

He looked over at the picture, obviously taken from my mercenary file on *Haven*. There were a thousand ways they could have gotten hold of it, and, to be honest, that really didn't matter anyway. "I wouldn't be afraid; I'd go anyway."

I took a deep breath and steepled my hands in front of my face. "And what happens to Reeves?"

"Reeves works for me. I've paid him—."

"You'd tell his entire mercenary crew that he can't handle his own command by charging in and taking over."

"Reeves works for me, and SO DO YOU!"

My muscles snapped, and I bolted to my feet. Heat ran along my skin in an almost visible aura as I came face to face with Ortega, fists clenched and nostrils flared. I felt the veins in my neck start to pulse as I put my nose millimeters from his. Ortega snapped to attention under the onslaught of my considerable personality, but he met my eyes bravely and refused to buckle under the storm of my ire. Mental bands harnessed my temper and rode it to a quiet walk as it exited from between bared teeth. "Don't, Ortega. Just don't. You may have bought his contract, but you did not buy the right to *frag* his team's morale into the sewer. He has access to five times our number to defend the grounds, and he is doing just fine at his job. Leave him the *frag* alone!"

My *EWO* developed a tic under his right eye as he swallowed a thousand barbed remarks and smoothed the wrinkles of machismo and fear from his voice. "So, what are we going to do…Captain?"

I backed off of him, rewarding his restraint with physical space. "We do what we came up here to do. What's the progress on the sensor sweeps?"

He shook his head. "Nothing yet. Thousands of extraneous signals."

I nodded. "Then we give the computer time to work."

Logan shifted. "Captain—"

Ortega and I fixated on the screen as gunfire erupted from the speakers. It was high pitched, acrid, and rapid… the sound of an automatic rifle. The camera jumped, blurring the picture as people began to bolt in every direction at once. The single rifle was joined by more. I placed a hand on Ortega's shoulder as the scene dissolved into utter chaos. Inside my head, so loud that I was sure everyone could hear it, words kept repeating: *Hold fire, Reeves. Take cover. Get your snipers into position.*

Sound erupted from the screen, a series of rapports so loud they caused the speakers to fuzz their output, losing a lot of definition. Even so, my ears picked out four separate guns. Ortega started to move, then jerked to a halt. He began to turn, but couldn't tear his eyes away. He balled up his fist, then let them go slack even as his legs began to tremble. I guided him to a chair and sat him down at the communication console. I reached past him and hit the PA system. An electronic boson's whistle presaged my words, drawing eyes to speakers across the ship. "*Angels*, this is the Captain. Begin prepping for descent. Load out, Combat One. Repeat: Load out, Combat One. You have five, zero-five, minutes. Go load up."

Prepping for a drop in five minutes was lunacy, and everyone would know it. You could imagine everyone on the ship dropping whatever was at hand and sprinting across *Deadly Heaven* for the Armories. Logan looked at me, his body posture asking the obvious question. I waved him out to ready the team. He paused as he passed me, looking down with hands spread. *Are we really going?*

I shrugged. How should I know? I make this up as I go.

Logan moved forward and put a hand on Ortega's shoulder. The cyborg murmured a few words pitched too low for me to hear. My curiosity piqued for a moment, but I figured if Logan thought I needed to hear, then he'd tell me. He left, footfalls heavy enough to echo through the airlock. On the ground, people started screaming again, and all but the most panic-stricken bolted down the wide, clean streets. Luckily, one of those too frightened to move was the news crew whose feed we were watching. The mob had scattered, and the scene was eerily quiet as the cameraman got back to his feet and scanned the streets in front of the Complex. Six bodies were not moving.

The cameraman staggered over and found that the first woman on the ground had simply fainted. Surrounded by a telltale pool of blood and bits of flesh, it was clear to all that the second woman had not. The reporter managed to catch up with his partner and begin spewing some tripe about an innocent woman gunned down by the villainous mercenaries when the cameraman took some initiative and hunkered down to get a good shot of the woman's slack face. He also caught a glimpse of something hard and metallic beneath her robe, the darkly reflective receiver of an automatic carbine. Caught up in the moment, the cameraman moved aside the woman's long robe revealing the unmistakable armadillo-hide texture of semi-stealthy combat armor. The correspondent, still going full throttle, hadn't noticed. That's when the door to the Ortega Complex opened, disgorging ten armed *Apostles* and Captain Kei O'Leary.

O'Leary gave the men terse orders over her headset, pointing to the four dead bodies. After the weapons were secured, the four bodies were dragged to the doors of the complex and their bulky, too hot for summer, clothes were opened to reveal identical sets of armor. She sent two medics over to revive the unconscious civilians. The camera closed in, and nobody stopped him. One *Apostle* flipped open one wallet, conveniently showing the camera that there was no identification as he pretended to search for one. A quick pat down revealed handfuls of cash, spare clips, fragmentation grenades, and MercTools.

The unblinking eye of the public did what he was trained, and he panned over the gore without remorse or relief until the reporter started asking questions. "Miss, uh, miss?"

I felt chilled as O'Leary glanced over her shoulder at him with eyes that could cut glass. Of the last ten minutes footage, this was the most dangerous. *God, O'Leary, keep it together.* "Captain."

"Excuse me?"

"Captain. I am Captain Kei O'Leary of the *Angel's Apostles.*"

"Oh, I apologize, Captain. I am Jorge Azila of Channel 311 Action News. Can you comment on the situation at hand?"

I was holding my breath. O'Leary was a good solider, but she tended to act violently without thinking. It made her an exceptionally effective assassin, scout, and sniper, but she was just as likely to kill this media shill as talk to him. "I think you should be ashamed of yourself."

The reporter looked like someone had just sucker punched him. He took a second to run a self-conscious hand thorough his thick, Latin hair. "Excuse me, Captain?"

"Ashamed. You should be ashamed. You made this happen."

The reporter started to flush beneath his dusky skin, obviously unused to being taken to task on live transmission. "And how do you think this is my fault?"

"Not just you, but all of you media vultures. You keep going on and on about how this revolutionary guy is the cure for all your ills, but where is the coverage of the bodies he leaves behind? Where is the outrage over the murders he commits?"

"*El Toro* has never been linked directly—" Azila backed up an unmanly step as O'Leary stalked forward and got in his face.

"And he won't be linked to this, either. But look!" She gestured, and the cameraman dutifully panned down to the bodies, faces blank, armor exposed. "What would have happened if we hadn't set up snipers with frangible ammunition to take these four down? What would have happened if we had just returned fire on the crowd?"

It was obvious he wanted to ask how the *Apostles* had known to set up snipers. He wanted to know where they had been stationed. He wanted to ask what frangible meant. He just didn't want to look ignorant, so instead he just sat there, not saying a thing and wound up looking stupid. His loss.

She plowed on. "You're dead; your cameraman's dead. That lady over there is dead. That guy? Dead!" The cameraman was trained not to look at his partner when he wasn't saying anything, so he followed O'Leary's finger and got a perfect shot of the revived male civilian shaking the hand of the mercenary medic who had tended him. I almost chuckled.

"Everybody's dead. We look like murderers, and in the chaos they slip away because, because unlike you," she kicked a body in the torso armor, "they came prepared for incoming fire!"

She continued, pressing closer to him to steal as much of the camera frame as possible. "You set up a revolutionary as a saint, and now he's trying to drum up more negative press for mercs on Persephone. To do it, he was willing to sacrifice you, your accomplices, and everyone in that crowd just to build up his political power. Now go away and let us do our jobs."

She turned away, leaving the newscaster flabbergasted and pale until the news station weenies finally figured out that they should have pulled the feed three minutes ago. They cut to the news station where the talking heads tried to recap the events while trying desperately to avoid blaming their golden *Toro*. In the corner of the screen was O'Leary's pretty face caught in a vicious sneer.

In one deft push, she had turned the tables on the reporter, the media, and *El Toro*. It was simple. It was elegant. It's precisely what I would have done. *But if they destroyed the original footage...*

The Key to Damocles

"Stop recording, Grisham. Log onto all public political information feed sites, message boards, and news services. Upload that recorded transmission, along with all authentication protocols. I want it everywhere."

The robot nodded and began to work without any obvious signs whatsoever.

Ortega cleared his throat, and the tension whooshed out of him in one, long breath. "She does a great impression of you, sir."

I smiled, "Yeah, I guess she does." *Who the frag taught you to be subtle, O'Leary?*

He stood up and walked around unsteadily, the unused adrenaline scorching his nervous system and making him clumsy. "So, what do we tell the team?"

I reached over and clicked on the PA. "Lieutenant Thompson! Is the team ready and assembled?"

"Sir! Everyone is on station and ready to drop except for Ortega, Sir!"

"Excellent. This has been a drill and I am pleased with the results. Take the *Angels* to the armory and exchange all ammunition for simulated ordinance. Report to port cargo bay and begin no-sensor urban combat drills with simulated ammunition in the current loadout. The Master Sergeant will give you scenarios and officiate scores. You have ten minutes."

"Without Ortega?"

"Yes, Lieutenant. He's still working on ferreting out our target."

There was a distinct pause before she replied, "Aye, aye, sir."

"Carry on." I cut off the mic.

Ortega cleared his throat. "A drill?"

"People will believe anything if it's reasonable enough."

"You think they believe you?"

"I'm the Captain," I sat heavily in my chair, "who gives a rusty *frag?*"

"Did you ever lie to me?"

"Constantly," I rubbed my eyes and laughed cynically, "but not about anything important."

He laughed too, hopelessly, pathetically, and then it almost dissolved into weeping. He took a few deep breaths, gathering up his shattered mental walls from behind cupped hands. He touched a few buttons and killed the prattle of the news companies trying to save face. He sat down like a bag of sand and held his head in his hands. I gave him a few moments to compose himself.

"Go to bed." He opened his mouth. "I don't care. Got to bed before I get Bugs to strap you in bed and put you under."

He nodded and stood.

"And Ortega? The next time you think you know better than me how to run this mission, I will walk and I take my toys with me. I do not work for you; I work for me. There's only room for one Captain."

"Captain, I'm—"

I held up a hand. "Stow it, *EWO*. You almost caused a real problem here because you are both contractor and subordinate. It can't work well and it never works for long, but I'm trying because you are a friend. Just don't do it again."

Ortega stood at attention and saluted.

"Dismissed."

I was left alone again with my thoughts. "Grisham, get close ups of the four corpses from your record. Do a level four trace through *Haven* and see if you can dig up the identities. Give the stated purpose as research so that felled enemies can be tagged for transport and burial in accordance with the Laws of War."

Grisham almost started a gesture, then stopped. His entire posture animated in frustrated ways before he straightened himself into a more robotic stance. I had no doubt that every break in his composure was completely calculated. "Don't hedge back and forth, Grisham. If you have a question, ask it."

"Um, I'm sorry sir, but won't General Reeves do such a search himself?"

"Probably, but not for a few hours. I need that info now." Because no matter what else had happened just now, O'Leary had lied. Those weren't revolutionaries. They were mercenaries.

"One other thing, sir. How am I supposed to know when I am supposed to ask and when am I supposed to um… be more robotic?"

I sighed and rolled my eyes. I silently cursed the first programmers who thought giving robots human quirks were cute. "Listen, Grisham. I have nothing against you, or against robots, but remember that you are equipment."

The Key to Damocles

"I don't understand."

I turned on the computer in the captain's chair and waited patiently as the screen deployed from around back and set itself for my use. "I have humans under my command. People. They have lives, dreams, and hopes. If it ever comes to it, I must weigh the loss of a person against the success of any mission. If possible, I will sacrifice equipment rather than a soldier because equipment can be replaced. You are a machine, a cunning machine but a machine, nonetheless. You may act like a man, but you are not. I must be ready to leave you behind at any moment if it means the life of one of my men. Anything that makes me think of you as a man will dull that instinct, and that is bad for the team. Do you understand?"

A human would have paused, hit by the immense realization that he or she was expendable. Grisham may well have paused as well, but it was a moment measured in microseconds as he digested this new data. "I apologize, Captain. I had no idea."

I gritted my teeth and affixed him with a cold stare.

"I did it again, didn't I? I am programmed to converse rather than just communicate. I will have to do some reprogramming on my subroutines." He straightened, washing out any empathy from his posture. "I understand, Captain."

"Ask if it's necessary for you to do your job." I nodded. "Now do the search."

"It's done, Captain. There are no matches."

"Use my credentials. Open the unbondable database and repeat the search."

There was a distinct pause. "I have matched four of four faces. Do you want their records pulled?"

"Yes, save them to files and I will look at them later."

"Captain, I am unable to find a satisfactory definition for the term 'unbondable' in any of my legal glossaries."

"Don't worry about it. Just start trolling the newscasts, start recording the feeds and cataloging them for later use."

After that, he left me alone.

I typed on the screen, bringing up the data sent to me by Lomen while I was being beat on by the special agent from PISs who was currently languishing in the brig. But I put it out of my mind to be dealt with later. I chuckled as I read Lomen's brief account of having a hacker show up to join his militia. The guy

166

had a rap sheet longer than Doe's, and he nearly fainted when the Captain ordered him to crack into various unmanned government computers. The bounty he had caged was downloaded to *Deadly Heaven's* computer banks in an instant, and then I started sifting the raw material. I now had the compiled crime data from every precinct in New California, and surprisingly, in the other megacities as well. With skills developed through years of use, I turned the distorted mess into charts, compiled spreadsheets, and then finally overlayed it on a map of Persephone. Then, and only then, it started to make sense.

I saved my progress, ran downstairs, and got into my battle gear. I went through a few hours of house-to-house drills with the team using the prefabricated units stored in the cargo bay. Afterwards, I handed out scores, with a lot of minor advice, and we hit the showers. All the while I was turning over the new evidence in my head, thinking of how the bomb patterns looked on the map of Persephone.

I stopped by the bunkroom Ortega shared with Lopez. My *EWO* was there in his underwear, apparently freshly awake from his six-hour nap. He looked up at me, eyes faded and empty as a wasteland. His body made it to attention, but his heart did not.

"Stand at ease. Get kitted up and come to get something to eat with me." He wanted to refuse, but I could see he had caught my tone and knew that I had not made a request. He nodded a surrender and I waited in the hallway while he got dressed.

We moved from the bridge to the spinal corridor, traditionally a hallway that ran the length of the ship, ritualistically unsealing each door in front of us and dogging them tightly behind. Robots of all kinds scurried out of our way as they went about the ship, monitoring systems, making repairs, and generally seeing to the care of *Deadly Heaven*. I led the way down the ladder to the 'living deck' where the library, recreation rooms, and the mess were. I was surprised to find out that there were five *Angels* already in the ship's kitchen. Lopez, Archer, and Richardson were playing cards. Most of the chips were in Archer's pot. King was stripped to the waist, his massive brown chest rippling with muscles as he broke down and cleaned his baby: a Walther and Wesson 'Harvester' heavy plasma pulse cannon. My eyes swept the table, and I was pleased that there were no power canisters for that weapon in the room. He had one of the viewscreens in the corner tuned to a Persephone newsfeed. At least the volume was low.

Lopez shot up to attention, making the others wonder if they should follow suit, but I smiled and waved them to their seats. "Anybody hungry?"

And at that, everyone looked back and forth wondering if general boss rule number one applied: if the boss asks you to eat, drink, or to change the news station, you say yes. They were also wondering who was going to be wrangled to cook. I chuckled for my audience even as I felt a little lonelier inside. "Cookie, I need breakfast."

Inside the kitchen, a massive metal octopus saluted and began preparing synthetic food with gusto. Clarifying agents, colors, and flavorings turned protein sludge into pancakes, bacon, eggs, and potatoes. Within minutes, the food was dished up on institutional trays. I hopped up and filled a plate high as one or two of the others followed suit.

Ortega sat down and threw himself into the card game, and by degrees, the situation became normal. I popped barely identifiable food into my mouth and winced. Over my year of retirement, I had become very fond of eating real food rather than the synthetic stuff mercenaries normally subsist on. Actual grown, gathered, or butchered food was nowhere near as healthy or nutritious; it was filled with fats, sugars, and cholesterol. And there was something indefinably satisfyingly primal about genuine food cooked from raw ingredients. I ate like a soldier, and as my mind chewed on the problems of Persephone, the plate magically cleared. I finished, wiped my mouth and got up to turn in my tray when my *EWO* met my eyes with steady pressure.

I'm afraid, but I believe in you, he was saying.

I nodded.

I hated to admit it, but I had missed more than the canned, greasy air of *Deadly Heaven*. For years, I had served in the *Radiation Angels* as an officer and then even longer as their leader. My predecessor and I had both struggled to institute an *esprit de corps*, a pride and trust in one another to forge the separate men of the company into a single machine. As the rest of the team began shuffling into the mess, I felt the missing final pieces I needed to turn them into the best team in the universe.

A few scant weeks ago, I had hired these people, sight unseen, based solely on resumes and applications. During the harried rush to Persephone, I hastily assigned jobs and ran them through simulation training across *Deadly Heaven*. We landed, and they fought for one hundred and fifty hours across a foreign land because the pay was right. They had proven themselves as professionals, and now I had to do the same.

Archer cleared his throat, and his eyes darted left and right before he continued. He looked like a man stepping out on the high board, looking down at the pool and wondering how hard the water would be. "Captain Rook, some of us were wondering…"

Thompson gave him a subtle nudge to shut him up, and I pretended not to notice as I scraped the tray clear. "Yes, Archer?"

"I, uhh…"

"Ask, Archer."

Archer sat straight, gathering pride in his posture as he made good use of his poker face. "Well, some of the team was wondering: this is beginning to feel like a martyr mission."

I gave Archer a long look, sensing the unusual discomfort in his green eyes. I could see why he was looking for a job when I found him. He was one of those people who cut corners whenever he could. He was insolent and in possession of no leadership skills whatsoever. He was also a shrewd judge of character and had an almost supernatural sense about when he was being lied to or bluffed. If nothing else, he was always brutally honest without the burdens of diplomacy or tact. I resented the timing of the near accusation, but he was probably the only one who would ask it to my face. I had to nod.

"Yeah, I can see why you'd think that. In fact, you are probably more than just half right." A shudder went through the *Angels*, and the quality of the meeting became strained. I glanced about. "Everyone, eat. We will have a briefing in an hour. I'll explain it better then."

CHAPTER 13: BRIEF IN BRIEF

Histories are full of martyr missions... armed conflicts begun with the best of intentions, but ending in absolute disaster. The Americans of the twentieth century were famous for them, then later the Anglo-French Union, and then even later the South American-Mexican Alliance. They start simply, usually with an order for soldiers to go into a foreign country and protect the populous from harm. Before long, soldiers are attacked and they respond with trained, deadly efficiency. There are always news crews around to show the bodies, and people unused to the sights of war scream for gentler, kinder armies to provide policing overseas.

The problem with this was that soldiers are not policemen, and should not try to be. Mercenaries are given far more training in this area, but we are still not perfect for the job of riot control. Mercenaries, and all true soldiers, are commissioned to kill people and break things. It is this at which we excel.

Policemen are tasked with a much harder job: keeping the peace even at the cost of their own lives. The differences between these two seemingly similar jobs have seen soldiers posted in foreign countries with weapons but without ammunition, with a defined mission objective which could never be finished, or fighting a war where the rules are defined by the public relations department. Martyr mission is shorthand for any job where a mercenary team was sent in to fix the unfixable, win the unwinnable, or protect something so ephemeral as an ideal. It usually winds up getting everyone killed.

I watched from my desk on the dais as the *Angels* filtered into the briefing room, some earlier than others. Someone had gotten word to Logan, who lumbered in and sat in what was obviously his chair in the front row. The *Angels* had plenty of time to find seats and get settled as I took my place at the podium and began retrieving the data I had been sifting all day and night. The briefing room was shaped like a small theater, racked seats allowing each and every person a good view of the raised dais and the 'altar' on top. It wasn't a real altar... it just looked like one. Set into the black, mirrored surface was a host of projectors, controls, computer banks, and a simple AI to control the presentation. I input my pass codes, unencrypted the data, and fed it to the screen imbedded in the surface.

I keyed up the information in the order I wanted, and then set the AI to listen for the cues in my voice. As I worked, Logan's tight posture kept snatching my attention from what I was doing. His arms were crossed, head bent. Even the flourishes that sprung from the side of his head seemed weighted down. I couldn't catch his eye, any one of the eight of them. He and I really needed to talk, and soon.

I started with a flat-cut globe map of Persephone. I flipped a switch. The lights dimmed, the map glowed into life on the wall behind the altar, and I took my seat at the front of my company.

"Alright *Angels*, what's going on?" Everyone looked at each other, sharing a collective shrug. "Come on, people! I hired you because you are bright, not because you're beautiful."

"Chaos, Captain. Revolution." That was Archer, course.

"In New California?"

"Of course."

"And Nuevo Aztecan?"

"Pretty much."

"In Mezzo-Americana?"

That took his thrust away. "Uhhh, not so much."

"Why?" There was another long pause from my crew. "I'm expecting something better from you."

But it was Ortega who spoke up. "Racial tensions. It's been a long time coming, boss. The movie houses film African extraction stars and the population is mostly Latin extraction. As long as I can remember, we've been angry that they film on our planet, eat our food, and take our tax breaks. All we get to do is clean out their toilets."

I stood up from my station and began pacing in front of the team. "Yep, that accounts for a great deal, but not everything. Not by a long shot. Map Overlay One."

The altar AI heard my cue, and began spattering the map with red, blue, and green dots, enough to completely obscure all twelve megacities on Persephone and provide disturbing stars across the remaining towns. "Alright, this is a track of every violent incident reported to the police or reported in the news."

Archer rubbed his eyes and slouched in his chair. "Looks like a revolution to me, sir."

"Exactly, but we aren't just looking for violence. We are looking for specific types of revolutionary activity. Look at this... Map Overlay One A." Dots disappeared from the countryside, but while they completely obscured New California, the other eleven megacities on Persephone only had a horrible case of acne. "This is every bombing."

Thompson leaned forward in her chair. "That doesn't tell us anything we didn't know."

"Yep. That's right. Show Big Twelve." I magnified the view on the areas with the cities, blotting out the view of the planet. They were still a disorganized mess. "Now, let's show them in chronological order, a day every second. Progression 1."

King snorted. "Damn."

"Damn, indeed." The first day, there were thirty-six bombings, three in each city. Two more bombings occurred per day, for several days after.

"And here," the number of bombings literally skyrocketed, "is just before *El Toro* made his first speech."

"So, *El Toro* is doing this?"

I shook my head. "I don't think so."

King shrugged. "Then why, Captain?"

"Lots of reasons: he's never done a recruitment drive, never tried to consolidate his power, never issued more than the most general of orders or edicts, never made personal appearance, and he just started asking for money."

And it was that moment that Logan decided to exit his funk and join the conversation. "He's looking to bolt soon."

Lopez looked around like a lost child. "Bolt? But..."

Archer reached down to the lower row and smacked him on the head. "*Toro's* a *fragging* con man. He's going to fleece a few million idiots of a few weeks' pay and then skip planet."

I nodded. "The most telling thing, however, is the variety of bombs. Disable All Other Overlays. Bomb Overlay 1."

The AI dutifully complied, showing a rainbow of colors.

"Here we can see fertilizer based, aeroline, chemical, traditional powder explosives, and..." I centered in on the black spots, "military grade explosives."

Lopez forgot he was the least experienced member of the team and asked the golden question. "Are they all the same kind of military explosives?"

I nodded. "Not only that, but I've got some scattered forensic reports from Captain Lomen and our friends that we fed at the Eastside Station. They pulled the stuff from police databases all across the planet. All the early ones—we don't have anything from after most of the police went off the grid—were not only the same explosive, they were from the precise same batch. It's all Compound XC-112, manufactured on Cyrus 2 and shipped to *Haven* twenty years ago. It was sold to the mercenary team *Der Jungen* a month later. Lost in combat later that year.

"Now, let's watch it with only the military grade hits. Run Progression 2."

Everyone leaned forward… now wanting to know, needing to see. Logan saw it first and he leaned back in his seat. Thompson was next. "It starts everywhere, but after that it's only in New California."

King nodded and grasped at the air. "It's like…um."

Archer cut in. "They were seeding the other cities, trying to cause unrest. Can we see all the bombings?"

"Progression One."

The bombings went on, black dots that were suddenly joined by a flourish of color, followed by a blossoming of color that almost blotted out entire sections of the map. Thompson almost jumped. "Wait!"

"Halt Progression."

"What was happening there, I mean then?"

I didn't have to check my charts; I had seen it too. "That's about three days after the governments of the megacities ran out of money for the fiscal year. Most police were shut down; others had their operations seriously scaled back."

"So, that's the actual revolution starting?"

I looked at them long and hard. "No."

Archer threw his hands in the air. "No? How can you say that? Look at the map!"

"Because a revolution would still make sense. Continue Progression." And the dots continued to march across the screen. "What's the target? Why are most of the bombings in residential areas, business parks, and high-end stores? Why the wildly different explosives?"

Archer smiled. "Different bombers taught by revolutionaries, of course, with different motivations."

Walt, the closest thing to an explosives expert on the team, shook his head. "Nope. Well, you are probably right about motivations, but the bombers are not linked. If you have one group teaching another how to make homemade bombs, then they're going to teach what they know best. Even down the line, as each revolutionary cell teaches others, then it will still be the same kind of bomb. This is a mix of everything, different groups, different explosives."

Lopez threw up his hands. "Fine, so what is it then?"

I shrugged. "Its cover."

Ansef, who had been quiet until now, nearly choked. "Cover?"

"Covering for heists, art thefts, jewelry theft, robbery, murder, industrial espionage." I nodded. "The rest of this is genuine fun. It's anarchy, rage, fear, a few scattered nut jobs, and criminal activity all rolled into one. Add in a charismatic leader driving people to acts of rage, and you get a combat pattern that looks like this."

Ansef spoke up, "So what can we do to eliminate *El Toro?*"

Archer laughed and drew his hand across his throat while sucking air wetly between his teeth.

I stood and went back to my podium. "Wrong. We can't kill him."

The entire team but Logan stared at me blankly. The cyborg only nodded. "Tell us, Captain."

"If we kill him, more black dots will still come and the media will make a martyr of *Toro*, ensuring another one just like him will pop up before too soon. I know this is not really what you want to hear, but this is going to have to be done very delicately. What you see on the map is evidence of anarchy, not revolution. The whole planet is tearing itself apart, and every time it tries to put itself back together, *El Toro* makes a speech. And if that doesn't do it, another black dot sprouts up. The megacities are busy trying to hold themselves together, and the planetary government of New California has gone into hiding completely. Those responsible for resolving this are largely scattered, disorganized, and unable to render assistance.

The Key to Damocles

"Someone's pushing this, and I need to find out who." My eyes speared Ortega to his seat, speaking to him alone for this moment. "I was brought here to stop this, and that's what I intend to do."

Archer shook his head and whispered none too quietly, "Martyr mission."

"Look," I changed the projection to show the layout of the Ninth Street Cathlist church, "with only twelve members, we raided a building with five exits. We took down half again our number in criminal thugs, and we did it without losing a hostage once operations began. That's saying something. We can do this. If you're all with me."

Thompson looked at her team, caught up in the realization that it was her place to answer for the *Angels*. "What's the plan, Captain?"

"Well, there isn't much of a plan right now except to find them and stop them."

Thompson shrugged. "Them, who is 'Them'?"

"They are unbondable."

The silence in the room was deafening. The team looked at each other, trying to draw strength from one another, unwilling to ask any more questions for fear of the next answer. Then Lopez, the only one with a blank expression, got fed up with being in the dark. "Sir, what is an unbondable?"

"When you signed on to the *Angels*, one of the forms you filled out was a background check. The other was a job description form, then an Oath of War, and a line of credit from the Igbank." I tried not to laugh, but the 'I did?' look on Lopez's face was priceless. I couldn't blame him; there is a lot of paperwork to sign when joining a mercenary team. "A background check was done, your information was sent to Igbank, and a bond was issued to you. In fact, one was issued to each of us."

I paused to walk to the podium and take a drink of water. Without missing a beat, Logan stood and walked up next to me, dwarfing everything else on the stage as he covered the break. "All mercenaries carry a bond issued by one of the intergalactic banks. It's like insurance, made to pay out to victims of any mistakes. If high wind pushes your artillery shells into the wrong building, if you accidentally catch a civilian while returning fire, if you are shot down and plow into a family home, if your mine turns into a dud for a few weeks until some local trips across it, then the bank pays out insurance money to the families to keep the populations from rising up against the mercenaries ostensibly there to help them. Accidents happen, everyone knows that, but the governments we work for need that guarantee: that we can be held accountable for negligence. Those mercenaries rendered unbondable are normally those that should never have been on the job in the first place. But that's not what we're dealing with."

Logan's metallic face and never blinking orbs rested heavily on me. I stared back at him and wished very hard that I could tell what he was thinking. It was a talent we had developed over the years, but since our year of retirement, I have been wondering if Logan's brain had been removed and replaced with someone else's. I stood straight and walked to the front of the stage area to reclaim the attention of my audience. "The guys on Persephone are not idiots. They aren't incompetent. That means their bonds were revoked because of war crimes. These people are torturers, raiders, slavers, rapists, and killers. They have no backup, no safety net. They are working as spies. If they are caught, they will expect to be executed. They're going to fight like hell and they're not going to follow any rules. Expect poison gas, radiation mines, macro-nanite infections…all the greatest nightmares."

Archer hid his face in his hands for a moment as the *Angels* exchanged worried looks. "Captain, why would we ever want to go anywhere near these people?"

"Three reasons." I ticked them off on my fingers. "Firstly, because the unbondable are mercenaries. It doesn't matter if you or I don't think of them that way; everyone else will. Every time we set down on a planet, tales of these people haunt us and turn us into dangerous psychopaths in the eyes of the populations we are there to protect. It makes the job of every mercenary harder to accomplish, causes all of our bonds to get more expensive, and sours entire planets who will never again hire mercenary troops because of the actions of a few.

"Secondly, because the unbondable are holding an entire planet hostage down there. The people of Persephone need help more desperately than they know. I am going to help because nobody else can.

"Lastly, a teammate asked me to come and help. I am not the kind of man to let a friend swing in the wind just because it may be rough going."

The team spent a few seconds in silence, digesting my speech. The first may have been generally a good idea, but it was not any reason to run off and get killed. The second was probably true, but also held little weight with men who were paid to fight. Getting emotionally involved gets mercenaries killed. Everyone knew it. The third, however, they could all grasp. Millions of light years from home, flying under a flag that stood for dozens instead of hundreds of thousands, often seen as an annoyance and as intruders wherever they go, you can only ever trust the man next to you for support. I was here to aid a brother in arms. That was something every one of them could understand and respect.

Thompson took in the faces of the men under her command and nodded at me. "We're with you, Captain."

I had not noticed the crushing weight across my shoulders until just now, when it lifted away.

Richardson flexed his muscled shoulders as if he felt it too. "But how do you hide an entire mercenary band on a planet without someone noticing?"

"Smuggle down a seed team with bombs to foment unrest. You set off bombs to destroy soft, civilian targets, neuter all nearby police forces and set off a panicked evacuation. If you happen to pick the city with the only spaceport capable of tracking all incoming vessels, it's pretty easy to bring down and hide the rest of the team."

Ortega spoke for all of them. "Son of a bitch! They're in—"

I brought up the map of New California behind me. "Oh yeah."

I immediately assigned a rigorous regimen for the *Angels*. The Heavy Weapons Officers, King and Richardson, along with Lopez, were sent to *Deadly Heaven's* Armory Alpha. I had them stripping, cleaning, testing, re-stripping, re-cleaning, and logging every weapon in the company's inventory. Considering the *Radiation Angels* was originally staffed with up to two hundred mercenaries, with multiple weapon load outs to handle different situations, this was an extensive project.

No less daunting, next door, Logan, Thompson, Archer, Walt, and Long were going over the numerous suits of battle armor in Armory Bravo. Ansef and Tsang were busy with prepping multiple medical packs, automated doctors, and personal aid kits. While there, Ansef was having her leg wound looked at by the robotic doctor to make sure the macro-nanite injections had repaired all the muscle damage.

Pilot Sichak was busy with space-based war simulations. Manning *Deadly Heaven* with a full complement of fifty flight officers was one thing, but his job was to fight a space battle with a ship crewed by robots. Lieutenant/Flight Doe had it no easier since he was learning how to fly *The Succubus* using the simulator one room over from Sichak. There were a disturbing number of virtual klaxons, explosions, and cursing coming from both chambers even through the bulkhead doors.

At that moment, I was envying the hell out of anyone else on *Deadly Heaven*. I would have traded any one of them their job in a second. I had spent several unproductive hours calling dozens of government officers, trying to find more allies on planet. The ones hiding in the L/V/D complex had no interest in the outside world and, looking back, I could see why. For years, the media had been especially critical of every regime, calling them puppets of L/V/D. How true it was before, I don't know, but it was very true now. The highest-ranking members of the government that hadn't fled space-side were living in the sprawling estate earning generous stipends. They had no interest in coming to the rescue of the population that had become the enemy, even though they were sworn to. Despite Lionel's protests to the contrary, I had the distinct feeling he was buying his own government, perhaps just to get the ban on L/V/D media access lifted, or maybe he wanted L/V/D to become a truly independent state on Persephone. In any case, it didn't matter; the reality of the situation was all that mattered. Hell, I couldn't even find anyone willing to claim my PISs(y) agents.

The Key to Damocles

Going beyond New California, I found stone walls of silence and apologetic nods of civility. Each of the megacities had already tried to send help to New California and Nuevo Aztecan, where violence was most endemic. Whether economic, political, or police related, the aid had set off 'unrest in their own cities', usually in the form of a few military style bombings. Rescue crews had come under fire and their aid stations set up in New California had been swarmed and destroyed by panic and greed. Most of the other megacities had set up underused refugee hospices in their own domains. Since there were several thousand kilometers between one megacity and another, only those who needed help least managed to reach them, which is typical of how governments offer assistance. What New California really needed was a leader, someone to stand up and take charge.

My core problem still remained. No one was willing to believe that an undocumented mercenary team was working on planet, and no one had time to help track them down. Even long-distance communications with the Persephone military, hovering at the edge of the system, achieved nothing more than officialese for 'We don't want to get involved'. Like the documented mercenaries, they had their own jobs to do, watching over their own asses, so it didn't occur to them that there were many, many more asses in the wind that needed saving.

Ortega was on the bridge, continuing to track and eliminate signals. I was right next to him, going over more data, running algorithms, sifting facts, and looking for any mistake that would let me know precisely where the unbondable were. I could turn a building into rubble from orbit with the press of a single button. Leveling a whole city just to flush them out wasn't something I was prepared to do.

After another hour of fruitless work, I got up and went back to my room. I changed into my running gear and went jogging around the ship. The numerous bots needed to keep *Deadly Heaven* in the sky moved silently out of my way as I ran up and down the spinal corridor. Within a few minutes, I had worked up a rhythm and my body shunted onto automatic.

I began withdrawing into my own mind, letting the towering theories and walls of facts begin melting into an egoless ocean. Shadows danced beneath the surface, frustratingly vague as I pushed myself further and further away from my own consciousness. Step after step fell behind me as I reached each end of the corridor and turned, jogging in a constant cadence. Step after step, turn upon turn, kilometer after kilometer parted around me as if I was standing still and the ship was moving around me. I tried to empty my mind, to forget, to let every fact become attached to every other in a massive spider web of thought. It washed over me, my mind's hands sifting through the waterfall to stare at disparate nuggets against the background of the whole. I threw in my team, the unknowns, Ortega's family, Reeves and his *Apostles*, Tony and his militia. Minutes bled into an hour... step after step after step. A trancelike oblivion swept across me until nothing was left but the metal grid of the deck plates and pipe lined ceilings—

WHAM!

I was off my feet, face down in the corridor. Blood coursed out of my nose like a fountain, the side of my face marred by the deck plates. My head spun and tiny crabs crawled along the muscle fibers of my legs to gnaw and pinch hungrily. A maintenance bot stopped and inquired if I required assistance.

I had been pushing too far, diving too deep into my subconscious to bring back the single pearl I needed. But there it was, glowing softly behind my eyes. Relishing its presence, I could only laugh at the bot's barely human metal face. I staggered into the medical bay a few minutes later, cackling like a madman as Tsang and Ansef stared. Bugs, our medical robot, popped out of his charging station and immediately began collecting reagents, macro-nanite infections, spray on bandages, and antibiotics to heal my hurts. Ansef crept closer to me as I heaved myself up on the exam table. "Captain... Captain are you—?"

The grin I gave her was positively feral. "I know how to catch them."

Before Bugs had even finished, I sent out orders over the PA system. Within minutes, bots were scurrying over *The Succubus* and *The Cherub*, readying them for landfall. Mayflower, the massive cargo robot, was tasked with gathering hundreds of guns and dozens of sets of light armor from the stores along with boxes of ultra-heavy assault equipment we hadn't used in years. I called for Logan and my lieutenant.

The Key to Damocles

Logan arrived first and waited respectfully as Bugs finished. A second later, Thompson walked in. She seemed self-conscious about her overalls spattered with oil and dirt until she saw the blood that covered the front of mine. "Buddha, Captain! What happened to you?"

I smiled. "Inspiration. Call the team up for loadout."

She gave me a face that said '*Right now?*' but uttered not a word as she made the announcement over the PA. For my part, I ran from medical and pulled *Deadly Heaven*'s pilot from his combat drills. "Sichak, move us into geosynchronous orbit over New California."

"Sir, that area is teeming with traffic. There are even a few heavy freighters stationed above the spaceport."

"There are an awful lot of guns on this boat, Pilot. They'll move." I unlocked the bulkhead door and waved him through to the bridge.

"Aye, sir."

Pressurized fuel squirted into the reaction chambers at the aft of *Deadly Heaven*. There, lasers burned away the stabilizing gel from the fissionable material, superheating it and forcing it to coalesce into a critical mass. The reaction began almost immediately, unleashing the fires of hell from the rear of the craft, pushing the multi thousand ton mass into position. I left Sichak to deal with the incoming comm traffic—most of which sounded like the kind of friendly banter one finds in hostile urban traffic—and called the rest of the team to the drop bay. Minutes later we were in freefall over New California.

I called Station Chief—everyone had dropped the acting title—Tony Lomen and had him clear the back lot behind the police station. It was big enough for me to land *The Succubus*, but just barely. John Doe watched from the copilot's seat, sweating bullets as he considered that next time it might be him at the helm. It takes skill to pilot an agile flier at top speeds, but landing a dropship was a slower, touchier affair than he was used to. Finally, after passing a dozen floors worth of sheer wall on every side, the pregnant-with-cargo-containers, dragonfly-shaped craft kissed the asphalt, leaving spreading cracks like lipstick prints.

I slapped the anchors for the cargo container on the left rear side and *The Cherub* on the right. Hydraulic jacks lowered both to the ground as the unloading doors disgorged *The Angels*. Even with so little warning, a crowd of a few dozen had arrived to watch us disembark.

Tony was at the fore, half smiling, half scowling, hands on his wide hips. "Well, this is going to cause a lot of heartburn for some people."

I shrugged and smiled like a giant African Santa. "But I bring gifts!"

Richardson came down the loading ramp, the handcuffed agents of PISs marched in front of him at gunpoint. The look Carlos shot me could have curdled milk. Lomen laughed, the sound reverberating honestly inside his chest. "I don't think that's going to calm matters any. Director Head Saracho has been writing us on a daily basis about how much he hates everything we've done here, and about you in particular."

"Really...?" I filed that away for later use. "Well, I need someplace to keep them, Tony, and I don't want to leave them on board my ship with only one guy up there. I have evidence of their war crimes if you need it."

"Well, it will help, but—" The Chief gaped. "Wait a minute...you have only one guy running an entire spaceship?"

"Well, him and a few dozen expert bots, but yeah."

"Kinda thin on manpower, eh?"

"Yeah, but you aren't."

"Sure enough." He rubbed at his chin, which managed to be pudgy and craggy at the same time. "I never thought we'd see you here again."

"You need help and it doesn't look like anyone else is stepping up to the plate." *And you covered my ass on live TV when ducking and running would have been much easier*, I didn't say.

Lomen's eyes bulged as he sighed. "More than you'd think. I've got more volunteers than I can deal with. We've run out of beds, uniforms, weapons, food. There were five thousand at last count, and they're still coming."

"No weapons?" I blinked innocently as Logan walked behind me, a massive crate over his shoulder marked 'Light-tech Armory: Danger! This crate contains class AAA weaponry'. "Well, we can't have that."

CHAPTER 14: OF TRAITORS AND TRADESMEN...

I forgot how hot it was down here. I wiped the sweat from my brow as my head took a beating from the noontime sun. Still, I had to be out here to see everything for myself. Lomen gave me a tour of the police station, but it was the surrounding buildings that told the real tale. I had to admit it though; Tony was right. There had to be five thousand people here if not more. Apartment blocks on every side of West End Station had been filled to overcapacity.

People from every walk of life were piled into rooms, each giving up comfort and privacy in exchange for the relative safety of numbers. I traveled the hallways, half listening to Lomen as he introduced me around, and I looked into a lot of eyes. The only thing that made the squalor bearable was the fact that while there were lots of live bodies, they were caring for the wounded and had carried off the dead. If they had let the dead lay, the situation would have been beyond salvage.

Most of these people had heard of me, though most had only seen my age-old picture on the newscasts, and none of them had been positive. I tried to be humble and nonthreatening, friendly and supportive, but I really wasn't welcome. All of that was bad on one hand, but very good on another. These people weren't frightened refugees huddling for warmth against a cold night. The ones who had heard Lomen's call were just as hungry and just as desperate as those they left behind at the spaceport. But they had one vital difference... these people were mad as hell. One or two got up in my face, screaming at me for the things I had done to 'their people'. I let Tony get in their way and send them off to do some menial task or another. All the while, I smiled inside. These people were itching for an enemy to fight. Luckily, I had one in mind.

Lomen motioned to rooms on either side as people parted the way like water before the prow of a boat. "We've got five lawyers, so we managed to set up a tribunal of judges, a prosecutor and a public defender. We've had some problems because our defender is much better than the prosecutor. The tribunal has already made one or two unpopular decisions, but overall, the people seem to know the moment they work to overthrow what little law we've managed to build, it will all come crumbling down."

"How's your medical situation?"

"Pretty bleak. I've got twelve paramedics, several dozen people who took first aid classes, sixteen nurses, and a veterinarian."

I shook my head. 'Bleak' just about covered it. "We brought supplies."

Tony smiled, but I saw something flicker to unwholesome life inside his skull. Thankfully he just came out and asked. "And what do you need in return?"

"Don't give up."

"Give up what?"

"I'll get to that in a bit. You have meetings with... what do you call them?"

"VIPs? Oh, yeah. They're 'department heads', and we have them twice a day. One's coming up here at twenty-nine hundred." He looked at me out of the corner of his eye. "Would you like to come?"

"Certainly. I might have some advice for your people. Maybe some intelligence, too."

"Intelligence? You think this is a military operation?"

"Militias are, by definition, military. Also, remember the bastards who are going to try to kill you are military all the way."

"Are you sure all of this is linked? Maybe it was just a high-tech gang trying to eliminate the police in West End?"

"Oh no Tony, they were military. And make no mistake, they were trying to kill you. You. Personally."

He had the good grace to turn pale.

Once we were back at the station, Tony ran off to oversee another facet of his new job as mayor/chief/tribal leader, and I called a meeting of the *Angels*. Everyone got their marching orders and scattered to the four winds. I checked the time, doing complex base thirty something hour conversion in my twenty-four hour head. I grabbed my laptop from *The Succubus* just before John Doe took the helm and lifted off.

I downloaded the same program I had used on the briefing altar. *I could use a cigarette.* Discipline swept aside the thought, and I got to work. I poured over it like a madman, looking for new patterns, holes in my theory, hidden secrets or little white lies that could give anything else away. Time trudged by as the screens flipped across my eyes. And suddenly, it was time. I picked up my computer and went up the stairs to the old station chief's office. Inside, Tony and his fifteen department heads were ready to sit down for their meeting. My presence caused a murmur to run amongst them like an unruly child. I pretended not to notice as I took a seat in the corner in the back, furthest from the display screens, and waited quietly. My cheeks were itchy, and I realized I hadn't shaved today.

This was the kind of meeting to give a spy a serious erection. They went over the minutiae of the militia camp in detail. Each department head laid out the problems they were having and gave anyone who might be listening a roadmap for how to break the back of this fragile community with the least effort. Of course, we were in the police station in one of the most secure parts of the facility with people Tony trusted implicitly. On the other hand, it was only a police station, not an intelligence agency, and only someone you trust can betray you. *You're getting paranoid in your old age.* I made notes in my laptop as best I could.

I noticed Lomen ignored me completely, acting as if I wasn't in the room, and the *Angels* weren't packed downstairs in the SWAT ready room like unwelcome relatives. He made no mention of the unbondable, the goods I had brought, or the soldiers waiting to defend this station. He was going to leave everything up to me. *Thanks, pal.*

I was impressed, though. Only seven days after his announcement, he had gathered not only five thousand people, but constructed a rudimentary government, gathered a staff, and was providing basic government services using the people under him. He had a crude medical team, security force, and scavenging teams looking for food and medicine from abandoned buildings across the mostly vacated city. I wanted to congratulate them, but from the hostile glares I was receiving it

The Key to Damocles

was clear they would take it as condescending prattle or naked pandering. Eventually, he turned the meeting over to me, and I walked to the front by the display screens. It still amazes me the weight a hostile stare carries.

"My name is Captain Todd Rook. I am here to help." One of the police officers in charge of security huffed loudly. I grabbed hold of my temper and wrestled it down the back of my throat into the pit of my stomach.

I punched a key and brought up the list on my laptop. Another key transmitted the data to the wallscreen behind me. "I have a list of goods we've brought from the hold aboard our ship. There isn't much, but at least—"

The Medical Officer leaned forward and squinted his eyes. "How many units of antibiotics?"

I checked the screen to make sure it was clear. It was. "Four crates. Five hundred units per case."

"And what are combat trauma kits? And autodocs?"

I reminded myself that this man was, in fact, a veterinarian, though he was acting like a kid in a candy store. Anytime else it would be endearing. Any time else. "I'll get you a list. Now, we have some issues with the security of your people—"

The same Security Officer mumbled something in MexiCali.

Lomen glowered at him from behind his desk. "In English, Jose."

Jose ground his teeth, looked me right in the eye and even felt the need to stand up. "I said, like the criminal bastard standing right in front of us?"

My hands clenched into fists that could create diamonds from carbon. *Calm. Be calm. No need to break his nose. No need at all.* "Do I know you, Jose?"

He took a step forward, coming tantalizingly within reach. "I know you! I've seen you. We all have, on the newsfeeds. We know what kind of guy you are."

You cannot be this stupid. And as I looked around, I knew it to be true. Even after everything that had happened, these idiots had made an opinion based on what they had seen in newscasts. I typed in commands into the laptop. Behind me on the screen, quotes began to blip into existence like wasps escaping a poisoned nest.

"...completely unregulated..."

188

"...loose cannons..."

"...murderers, tyrants, and thieves..."

"...irresponsible..."

The quotes continued, fragments of hate dancing behind my head like the fingers of angry cherubim.

"...unregulated..."

"...illegal..."

"...the greatest threat to the stability of Persephone."

"This is what you think of us," I stated.

Jose balled up his fists, ready for me to spring at him. He wasn't just waiting for me to, he was aching for me to. "*Si, dago.*"

Tony watched from behind his desk, arms folded, eyes at the floor. His expression was the same one my father got when my mother brought me before him for any number of childish crimes. It was contained rage. Directed at whom, I could not tell.

"This is from your own newsfeeds?" I clicked a few more keys, and the quotes listed the newscasters and stations that had burped them.

Jose nodded.

"And they speak the truth?"

Jose tossed his chair to the side and marched to get right in my face. "Si."

I touched another key, letting the quotes bloom into full, horrible life.

"A completely unregulated militia is nothing but a mob looking for a lynching."

"These people are loose cannons, devoid of honor or pride in our system of laws, and have instead of embracing civilization, crushed it."

"Tony Lomen has become a leader of a band of murderers, traitors, tyrants, and thieves. And now they have weapons."

"The formation of the militia is an irresponsible act, a fact that should be carved into stone tablets and hung around the necks of the participants before they are dropped into the sea."

"Militias have for centuries been the death knell of governments, and the birth cry of tyrants."

"Arming civilians may seem like the right thing to do, but it is most certainly illegal and therefore the wrong thing to do."

"Lomen's Rogues are the greatest threat to the stability of Persephone."

The Key to Damocles

Jose could only stand there, his precious think-for-you-box on the wall betraying him with every line.

Lomen came out of his shell. He called his head of security gently, almost sadly. "Jose? Sit down now."

"But Chief—!"

"Why do you think the newsfeeds were cut to this district after my first press conference?"

"Water, power, sanitation... everything's gone *loco*—"

"No, Jose, it was so that when they started condemning us, the people wouldn't hurt the reporters they sent in to 'observe'."

"Then why in the hell—"

"Because if we kicked them out it would look like we had something to hide. As long as they're making up things, they have to be hypothetical... as long as they don't have evidence, as long as evidence is conspicuously not denied them. They hate us, and they are afraid of what we are doing here."

"Why, we're just trying to help?"

Tony cut him off again as his voice sharpened to a distinct edge. Though he did not stand or shout, he seemed to grow behind the mammoth wood desk. "Because they are used to influencing everything they see and they do not like the idea of us not being under the control of a government that can be heckled into shutting us down. Now. Sit."

Jose walked back to his chair, uprighted it, and sat down.

I looked at everyone else in the room, and saw faces that registered shock, disbelief, or sad affirmation. L/V/D had saved the planet, but had been thought to be fixing an election. That made the government and corporations suspect. The only thing left to trust was the constant flow of information coming from smaller news sources that soon grew into titanic industries in their own right. They were raised on a planet that gave media the place of gods. Now these gods had declared them heretics because they were doing what they needed to survive. These were not traitors. They were tradesmen who had taken up arms to defend themselves and their loved ones in a place and at a time when no one could do it for them. This very well may have been the first time some of them had ever doubted their quantum pantheon.

I tried to darken my voice, slipping into the shadows of silence as unobtrusively as possible. "You have all done very well here, despite what the media have been saying about you. But trust me when I say they do not have all the answers. In fact, they haven't even looked for them. If they had, they would know there is an unbondable mercenary team working on Persephone, sowing unrest for months now."

The head of the tribunal steepled his fingers in front of his face and stared into my soul with his aged, Hispanic eyes. "Media bias notwithstanding, you can't expect us to take your word for it."

I hit another key, which started a flat screen version of the same presentation I gave the *Angels* on *Deadly Heaven*. "Nope."

The presentation had been updated, enhanced, and dumbed down since the first time I had delivered it. I went over the early attacks, the bombing of police stations, the rise of *El Toro*, and the attempt on Tony's life. I laid out the bomb schematics, and Tony vouched for the data he provided me from the police databanks. It was complete, visually simple, and graphically dynamic. It also proceeded at a snail's pace.

Military organizations approve of questions. Good leaders love questions. Questions mean thought. Questions mean the soldiers are involved, attentive, and trust their leaders to hear them out. The problem was, these were not soldiers. Civilian questions were much less to the point, sometimes couched to avoid conflict, and sometimes loaded to prove a point instead of gain guidance. I had to explain every detail, go over every incident three times, and then cover the entire theory from back to front repeatedly. I had to explain the concept of being unbondable twice. Perhaps I shouldn't complain; they were listening, after all.

Jose leaned back in his chair, rubbing at his eyes. I knew they were throbbing from staring at the viewscreen for three straight hours. I knew it because mine felt the same way. "So the only thing you haven't told us is why. Why are they here?"

I shrugged. "They have a definite target."

The judge leaned back in his chair. "What are they after?"

This was it, the point at which I lost them. Because no matter how much I read the data, I just didn't know what these bloody bastards were after. I turned away from them, losing myself in the picture of New California as it was now: dark splotches of lawlessness with bright bomb pimples spread through it.

The Key to Damocles

It was just then that I saw it.

There was a line, a dotted line only seen from an orbital shot of New California. It was ragged, because the targets didn't line up exactly, but only the spheres of influence overlapped. It did draw a haphazard trail across the megacity, from sector to sector. All of them were police stations, with Tony's right in the center. It turned into an indistinct arrow pointing to…

Dear God, they couldn't be that bold, one side of my brain said. Like their operation has been really low-key up until now, the other half muttered.

I reached down to my laptop and touched the red block on the menu bar. Then I drew a line of blood across the map. It extended from the worst areas of ghetto to the west, through Tony's precinct, and then on to the east, right up to the most secure patch of real estate on the planet. Their target was the L/V/D movie house.

I circled the huge unknown area where the unbondable were definitely hiding. Then I circled their target. The whole room erupted with curses, prayers, and denials.

The doctor/vet shook his head. "You have to be wrong."

I looked up at them, slipping on the angry face of the God of War. "I'm not."

Lomen had turned a greenish shade of pale. "But why start all the way out in the slums?"

"He's clear of the shipping lanes from the spaceport, away from major law enforcement stations, far enough from his target to be ready to skip planet the moment his mission is done." The more I thought about it, the more it was exactly what I would have done. That was bad because it meant my opposing number was at least as smart as I am. "And for them to get to their target, they have to go right through this area."

"But it would be suicide."

"Maybe. The price of this mission has to be astronomical, maybe enough to fade away into space and buy a whole new life."

"Astronomical?"

I pointed at the target on the map. "If you hit a business as big as L/V/D, they are going to hit you back. They're going to throw everything they can at you. If you don't disappear, they will find you and kill you. Or rather, they'd hire mercenaries to do it for them."

Lomen sat back and chuckled morbidly. "So, you better hire people with nothing to lose."

"Like unbondable, right."

The vet was slow on the uptake. "They're going to hit the movie house? Why?"

"There's only one thing that can be taken from a place like that." I sat down, exhausted but hungry for my enemy. "D.N.A. or one of their current stars."

The Housing Official, mostly quiet until now, shook her head and spoke up. "I don't get it. D.N.A.?"

The Judge nodded. "D.N.A. from old movie stars. They keep it in storage there for clones. Or did you think all of those names down the ages were actually from the same family of talent?"

She looked flabbergasted. "So, what do we do?"

I looked at Tony. Under thick, gray brows his eyes twinkled at me with violent glee. He stood up and thumped on the desk, causing everyone else to jump. "We *jimmy* them with their pants on."

I pointed my hand at him, miming a gun. "You betcha."

He grinned wolfishly. "How do we do it?"

It was as if the hand of God Himself had put a funnel in my ear and poured an epiphany in whole.

"I have an idea." I took a deep breath. "But you won't like it."

He didn't like it, not one bit.

After the others left, I slapped him on the back. "Celebratory drink?"

"I don't do that anymore, unless you mean *un agua*." He smiled and shook his head. "By the way, I had a question."

"Sure."

"Back in my office when I had my..."

"Tantrum?"

"Yeah, well. I gotta know... how did you catch that mug I threw at you?"

"I used to play riotball."

"Professional?"

I smirked. "No pads, fewer rules."

"Where'd you do that?"

The Key to Damocles

I looked out of the window, taking in the burnt-out hulks and dirty streets filled with lost, lonely people. "In a place not unlike this one. Well, at least how it is now."

Tony reached into the cooler hidden under the large, wooden desk and pulled out two bottles of water and handed me one. "What in the hell were you doing there?"

I shrugged. "Growing up."

CHAPTER 15: THREE CARD MONTY

My father used to say, "Don't be surprised by the inevitable". I wasn't sure what he meant until I was much older. Even so, I usually have to explain it to people, and it usually goes something like this: when you drop a glass, don't be surprised when it shatters on the floor. All you can really do once it's been dropped is either dive for it like an idiot, or prepare for it to shatter as best you can. Usually you can't do either one, but the principle is sound. It was with this in mind that I handed out the equipment to Tony's militia and began checking off things to do. After the briefing yesterday, I had sent the team out to train everyone they could in whatever would be useful. It was about that time Doe got back with *The Succubus* with Ortega's massive earthworks robot attached to the cargo pod latches. He set the craft, which was dangerously close to its weight limit, down surprisingly well. Once he appeared at the doorway, however, he was two different shades of green. I clapped him on the back and he ran off to an abandoned alleyway to vomit.

At least everything was all in one piece.

I let Tony go prepare his people as best he could. I gathered *The Radiation Angels* for the team briefing. I gave them their marching orders and then handed them small data sticks with their specific jobs on them. Each slotted it into their combat helmet, except for Logan who slotted his into his head. Each one jerked a bit as the information scrolled across their screens. Even Logan shifted where he stood. He dialed my private frequency with a thought.

His resonant voice cupped my brain gently. "Are you sure?"

I nodded slightly.

Lieutenant Thompson slapped her hands and sprung to her feet. "You have your orders. Dismissed."

I took the scant time alone to change into my dress uniform, with distinctive silver piping and name and rank displayed prominently to differentiate me from the rest of the team easily. Then I toured the facilities, making sure everyone saw me.

The Key to Damocles

Carried, implanted, or autonomous self-propelled cameras were everywhere, following vapid talking heads wearing tailored suits or dresses. They talked to the dirty refugees, seeking any hint of discontent or conspiracy. They found discontent, but now it was focused mainly at the news crews themselves. Word of what the media had said about this place had spread like wildfire. When they turned their attention to me, I simply walked by. Some followed me around for a while at a respectful distance until they figured out that I really wasn't going to go completely *loco*, draw my pistol, and kill everyone who looked at me funny. I do believe they were disappointed.

I caught sight of a few other reporters walking around, but these were different. They were dressed simply, in working class clothes. Some had a few bits of real camera gear, but others were using bulky makeshift systems obviously soldered together by hand. Others were making do with commercially available cameras, giving the impression that someone's dad was recording a particularly hellish vacation. Some behaved like a cross between sugar addicts and rock stars. Others tread softly, quietly documenting this brave new world. I stopped a local and asked about these rag-tag media-men. He shook his head. "Pirate media. Haven't seen their type in years."

Pirate media? This is getting interesting. I directed Ortega's earthworks bot to begin tearing up burnt-out cars, old dumpsters, and whatever rubble wasn't nailed down and begin creating a low wall around the buildings inhabited by the refugees. It worked quickly and efficiently, the multi-ton robot's artificial intelligence overcoming every complexity it came across. I made a mental note to purchase one for the team. *The team? You're retired. There is no team after this. You're a rancher now, aren't you?*

A hand grasped my elbow gently, and I shook off the warring thoughts in my head. I turned... and someone stole the *fragging* software for my mouth.

There she was. The last few days had done her body a world of good. The swelling of her ravaged face had gone away and the scrapes had scabbed over. The broken blood vessels in her eye and her wary stance were the only outward signs of her terrible ordeal. Her clothes were bulky and deemphasized her portly, though feminine, shape. She took a step back to stand a meter and change away, with her hands clasped in front of her, but she was here. She was alive. Her grin was less strained, her eyes brighter than I remember. "Hello Captain. You came back."

"Yeah, I guess I did." *And I left you behind. God, I am so sorry.* My body, without coherent direction from my brain, went immediately into 'at rest' with my hands clasped behind my back.

She motioned behind her to the refugee tenements. "I… I, uh, found some people who could help."

I felt my gut twist like snakes, and I wondered how bad the nights she had spent alone in the darkness had gotten. "That's good. I'm glad to see you, Miss."

"My name is Anita Cody."

I bobbed my head like a moron. "I'm glad you made it, Miss Cody."

She smiled, and I almost cried when I saw the seed of warmth spread from her mouth to fill up her big, brown eyes. "You're a little old fashioned, aren't you?"

"I suppose… a little, Miss." In reality, I was a bull, and this woman was one big china shop. I felt myself start to sweat more than the heat of the day accounted for. "Look, a…a…about that pistol—"

"No, no. I was alone in a war zone. It was the best of the bad choices you had to make." A shadow passed across her face. "And you were right. I went to stay with Mari and her two children, but that night someone came, and he was banging on the door…" She just trailed off for a moment but she took a deep breath and centered herself. *You're one tough lady, Miss Cody.* "But he's gone now. And once we heard about this place we came straight away. Everyone's been so supportive. There aren't any councilors, but there a lot of women who know how to help me deal with… with what happened. It's helped a lot. So, when I saw you, I thought I should bring this back to you." And with more class and discretion than I gave most civilians credit for, she passed my slim-line laser pistol back to me. Out of habit, I checked the ammo counter and saw two shots had been expended. It disappeared into my waistband.

"Uh, well, thank you. I appreciate it, but you could keep it…"

Gently, slowly, she stepped within my reach and laid a hand on my bicep. "No. I have the support I need now, and there are enough people to carry guns. I have a long way to go, and I think it's better to not have the temptation there."

"Of course. Of course." I nodded too quickly, head bobbing again like an idiot. "You know, Ansef is at the medical station and Logan is on the roof—"

She lunged forward and hugged me fiercely, muscles as tense as any woman jumping into a high orbital drop. I hugged her lightly, acknowledging the act even as I tried desperately not to confine her. She pulled back, and I let her without any resistance, hoping that the feeling of control would make the contact more bearable for her. Slowly, stiffly, she stepped away. She was so small, several heads shorter than I, and made of such soft flesh, but it was only a sheath over a solid steel soul.

"You are my hero, Captain Rook." She said that word again, and it slammed into me like the ghost of my father.

I felt tears well up and something swell inside my chest. "That's funny. You are mine, Miss Cody."

She turned and walked toward the tenements... not proudly, but not broken and never beaten. She had a long way to go before she was healed, but at least she was going in the right direction. She was stopped by one of the quieter pirate media members. The man asked her something and she nodded vigorously. I almost stepped in, but it looked like she was doing alright, and I didn't want to make her think I thought she couldn't handle herself. She needed that self-reliance too badly right now. Besides, I had things to do if she was going to live to realize a normal life.

From there, things started happening faster and faster.

I called *Deadly Heaven* and pulled down our beefiest scrambling software from the data vaults. I sent a copy to Reeves, and within minutes, we were talking in what I hoped was complete security. I asked, I begged, I cajoled and reasoned. Then I offered him money. Ten minutes later, I gave him a copy of his part of the plan and ended the call.

Next, I tried to contact Lionel at L/V/D. His secretary wouldn't put through my call. I made a mental note to call a dozen more times over the next few hours, hoping for the same results. *Sometimes plausible deniability is so easy to come by.*

At midmorning, I grabbed *The Succubus* and hauled the half empty containers from the back lot and dropped them onto the roof of the police station before parking the feisty girl again. Logan was waiting, and he immediately began unloading numerous three-hundred kilo armored crates. He plugged his data port into the machines within and downloaded their manuals and operating systems.

Half of the *Angels* began to work with Tony's security force to pass out chemical laser carbines and suits of light combat armor to nearly every able-bodied adult. To make things legal, we had to take precious time to remove all crests identifying the gear as belonging to *The Radiation Angels*. Then they had to train the civilians in their use. They went over small unit tactics, fields of fire, and proper use of cover, all in rushed, abbreviated classes so frugal that if they were clothing, they'd be made of dental floss. Frankly, passing the gear out was the easy part.

The medics started working with the available 'doctors' and began explaining the usage of all the drugs, trauma units, autodocs, and handheld equipment we had brought. They also got to explain true combat medicine, and work up procedures for the coming battle. The rest of the crew grabbed small fusion reactors off the cargo pods and made sure every building had a self-sufficient supply of power. It is amazing how much good will air conditioning can buy.

The whole time, the news crews were dogging everyone with unanswered questions.

"So, why the sudden military buildup in the West Lot Station? Are you planning to stage a coup of the government from here? How would you answer charges that you and your team are a bunch of murderers? Captain Rook, Captain Rook! You cannot seriously be considering arming these civilians to use them as cover?"

They were still loudly pooh-poohing the idea of an undocumented mercenary crew working on Persephone. They even wondered aloud, and often, if those gunned down—that's just how they put it: gunned down—at the Ortega complex were not *Angels*. I did my best to ignore them.

At around midday, I received a call on a highly encrypted frequency. It set the next series of events in motion.

Then I talked with Tony and he sent out teams of civilian scavengers. While, on the whole, the city had been picked clean, we were after items nobody thought of as high priority lootables.

The Key to Damocles

They went out in groups of twelve, the impromptu leaders shaking their heads over the lists in their hands. It was as if you could see the words written across their faces: *A thousand meters of polymer piping? Ten kilograms of brick screws? Twenty power drills, batteries and chargers? Two thousand screen doors? Fire extinguishers? Steel fire doors? Arial emergency flares? What can he possibly want with industrial-sized fans?*

They left mystified and came back heavily loaded with what I needed. Hidden among them, singles and pairs of strangers filtered in. This wasn't unusual; word had spread that Tony was making a safe zone in the middle of New California, and people were coming in at the rate of a handful an hour. If anyone had bothered to notice, some of these newcomers were very well fed, athletic, and carried themselves much more like predators than refugees. These predators eventually made their way to the back door of the Police Station. They were met by Archer and Richardson, and shuttled up to the SWAT ready room where dozens of whole, clearly blazoned *Radiation Angels* uniforms were kept. Nobody noticed, but a large part of that had to do with the salvage lists.

As each team brought back their bric-a-brac, a coherent plan began to take shape. Well, some kind of plan anyway. The captured screen doors and windows were being screwed to one-meter lengths of the polymer piping. Then, these cage-like devices were affixed outside the windows of every building, in effect making a screen just a bit away from the actual window. Of course, only the mercenaries in the crowd knew why. Next, I had them take up some plasma torches and began cutting holes in the armored glass windows behind the screens. By the time they had started this, I was already onto something else.

We cleared out select rooms on the top floor of each of the buildings occupied by refugees. The salvage teams were inflated with pride as they brought back industrial sized fans from various businesses across New California. Once they got them off the trucks, I brought in *The Succubus* and airlifted them onto the roofs. They were hooked into generators, pointed into the buildings, and set to force air into the massive tenements. From my seat in the cockpit, I could see Logan had already set up all his own heavy machinery, and was busy with final positioning and calibrations. Then we began installing steel fire doors with makeshift deadbolts throughout every building. There was no way they would stand up to a determined assault, but they would provide some delay for the defenders. Rooms were cleared. Firing positions were set up. Militia members and police officers were assigned areas of responsibility. We distributed fire extinguishers liberally.

New faces replaced the known faces of *The Radiation Angels*. These newcomers were wearing the correct armor, carried the same equipment, and deported themselves in much the same manner, and so were accepted by the refugees as part of the landscape. The familiar faces began to disappear, sneaking off into the police station, and from there into the belly of *The Succubus*. When people asked, they were told the other *Angels* were going to rest so they could pull guard duty in the middle of the night. Everyone had seen war movies, and so they instantly understood this… even the news crews, who failed to report such a mundane occurrence. I grabbed a few new faces and sent them to the underground lot beneath the police station with orders to get the dozen police fliers fully operational. I let a camera crew join them.

It was after this I disappeared into the station and emerged half an hour later, my familiar C^2 helmet and distinctive silver trimmed uniform in place. Or at least that's how it appeared.

After that, things got complex.

It was mid-afternoon when 'I' got into a loud, profane fight with Lieutenant/Flight John Doe. We did it in front of everybody. 'My' voice was somewhat unRookish, but it was being fed through the speakers on my C^2. 'I' asked him something, and he said something flippant. Within seconds, 'I' was dressing him down in full view of everyone, or at least most of everyone since 'I' drew a sizable crowd. He made a few, unprintable replies, and then took a swing. With authoritative precision, his commander appeared to put him on the ground with a few humiliatingly flashy moves. The cameras caught it all and dutifully broadcast it LIVE! With somewhat exaggerated motions, 'I' ordered Doe to return to his quarters and confine himself there. Doe stalked off without being dismissed. The crowd began to disperse, and the commentators talked with the anchors back at the station, supposing 'I' didn't have as good control over the situation as it appeared. Then everyone froze at the heavy, mechanical wail that screamed from between the buildings. It was the sound of *The Succubus'* engines spooling up.

Everyone bolted for the back lot of the police station. The crowd skidded to a halt in front of the pregnant dragonfly shape of our dropship. Doe made a profane gesture from the cockpit as the man in the silver trimmed uniform and C^2 helmet shook his fist in the air like a vaudevillian villain. The craft then picked itself up off the asphalt on aeroline driven turbines. It wobbled slightly, fought against a sudden draft, and then rocketed into the sky with all the grace of a rabbit hit with a cattle prod. The crowd stared at the receding shape in awe and even caught the outline of Logan watching from the rooftops. You could see the news crews titter at this greatly deserved misfortune even as the *Angels* ignored their questions. The man who was supposed to be Rook shook his head and stalked into the West Lot Station.

I, the actual I, that is me, reached from the crew compartment and patted Doe on his shoulder. "Pull back on the throttle, Flight. No need to burn the sky now."

Doe exhaled slowly as I squirmed forward and dropped into the co-pilot's seat. "Do you think we fooled anyone?"

I shook my head. "It doesn't matter what I think. It's done. Now we just have to pray we did."

Thompson came up behind us and giggled. "Wow, O'Leary wasn't kidding. That PFC could be your body double."

"The spare helmet helped."

"His head did look a little like a mushroom."

Silence slammed into the cockpit as we continued to climb skyward. Our thoughts seemed loud even against the rarified air rushing against the steel skin of *The Succubus.* Thompson finally gave voice to the silent chorus. "Do you think they'll be able to hold out?"

I dialed in to my command voice: strong, confident, and level. "*The Apostles* will do fine. We need to be elsewhere when this happens. Besides, Logan is worth a division of men all on his own and now he's plugged into half a ton of high-tech weaponry."

Thankfully, they took that at face value, but Doe had a question of his own as the numerous blips of the ships over New California started to show on sensors. "Do you want to dock this baby, Captain?"

I folded my arms and huffed, "No, you better do it. You're going to have to do it again really soon."

I was convinced he was going to vomit again, right there.

I adjusted the monitor on the right side, bringing up the view of the actual, real *Angels* in the crew compartment. I was about to lead them into a secret battle over a world that hates them, for people who misunderstood them, against an enemy without recourse and without mercy. All on the word of one man: me.

I closed my eyes and pretended to sleep. All the while, I began to run through the records of every example of hostile boarding of a ship in transit that I had ever read. Simultaneously, I reviewed the stocks of supplies on *Deadly Heaven*, formulating what we would need for the next step.

I was confident I could succeed, but how many of those riding skyward and those back at West Lot would have to die if I was wrong?

BOOK TWO:

THE KEY TO DAMOCLES

CHAPTER 16: WAR

Orbit around Planet Persephone,
Deadly Heaven, 01:02, 11/13/2662

Finally, the enemy came.

You could have set your watch by their appearance, precisely one hour after normal shift change at every police station in New California. Long enough for those going on shift to be scattered across the city and hip deep in their own problems. Long enough for those who left for the night to get home and go to sleep, slowing their response times if called back to duty. The idea was to cut off help from healthier police precincts surrounding West Lot Station as much as possible. Not that anyone thought that this was a huge possibility; the police hadn't been paid anywhere in New California for months and only the most dedicated were still doing their jobs. Still, whoever was in charge of the opposition was playing the odds on every angle he could.

The only surprise was it happened tonight and it was a surprise only because it was what I had been hoping for. I get precisely what I want so rarely that it almost caught me off guard. The *Angels* had been very visible in fortifying West Lot Station all day, and this was something which demanded a response. Within days, Tony would have enough officers and militia under his control to go sweeping the city for the unbondable. More importantly were the visuals of the police fliers being repaired, and anyone with any hint of military background would tell you it was be better to hit the *Angels* now instead of giving them more time to dig in. In fact, I had counted on it.

Kilometers above, the clear desert sky provided a lens through which the cameras of *Deadly Heaven* could watch the entire precinct with unblinking eyes. The quickly cooling air and ground gave a near perfect backdrop for the infrared cameras to pick up enemy movements. But even though they pooled in doorways, alleyways, and in abandoned lots, I could not find a cohesive stream leading back to their source. My opponent must have covertly stationed small teams all across the area in the last few days, allowing them to respond quickly without creating a glowing arrow pointing back to his base. There were abandoned buildings to spare, and nobody would notice one more gang wandering the street. *Clever.*

I hate clever enemies. I like them dumb, overconfident, naked, tied up, and asleep when I can get them. Fair fights are for those who do them as a hobby.

I encrypted a five hundred letter string and sent it to Logan. It didn't matter if the enemy broke the encryption, since the first eight letters were the only thing not random. They were: THYRCMNG

They are coming.

Almost instantly was the reply: CNUGIVMEFED

Can you give me a feed?

CMNGCHNINTNDCODIO

Coming, channel nineteen. Decode protocol iota.

I zoomed in as the Master Sergeant stood and moved to the center of the police station roof. He sat down crosslegged and picked up a bundle of plugs that fed into a central outlet. I could almost hear the metallic click as he seated the unit into the base of his neck. Then he looked up into the sky...and saluted.

LOTSOFTHMARNTTHR

I didn't need the translation of that one. I cleared the screen's message log. *Good luck, old friend.* The door opened behind me, and I heard four pairs of boots— six—eight pairs; I heard the entire crew come onto the bridge. They fanned out behind me and watched the main screen as I zoomed out. Two kilometers away from West Lot, man-sized red dots began moving, and wouldn't stop.

"*Frag* me. You never said there'd be so many."

Thompson probably spared him a nasty look. "Shut up, Archer."

I didn't look away. "Aren't you all supposed to be training for hostile boarding operations?"

Thompson walked forward and handed me a small printout. "We went through the simulations with the equipment, in full gear, in the cold bay. Four dozen repetitions, including the error runs and cross training. We started out as competent and got better each time. I have the scores here if you'd like to look at them, Captain."

The boarding gear was common to most crews: simple, and effective. Even so, the scores were very good, much better than I expected. I turned my chair to face them. "Is all of the gear ready to go?"

"Yes, Captain. We checked it, cross checked it, and packed it for fast action. All ammunition has been loaded and weapons are at the front of the lockers. *The Succubus* is fueled and Mayflower has changed out the weapons load. We are ready to go."

I stood and smiled at my crew, more for their benefit than anything. "Very well. Go get some rest, everyone. You will be on alert until it is time for us to enter into this."

Ortega stepped forward. "Captain, the program I hacked together may not work right without someone looking over its shoulder. I think I should stay here."

And then Doe. "Yeah, and Captain, I'm a little, uh, I think I should spend some more time in the simulator."

Richardson shrugged. "And there were a few of us that wanted to go over the manual charges for the boarding rig again just in case things don't go as planned."

Archer pursed his lips like a man who had found half a maggot in his food. "And I need a little range time on the small arms. My bursts are tracking high."

These were my men. Already pushed hard, up all day and worked all night. They wanted to do better, to work harder. I wanted to cry. I held up my hand to stop the rest. "You are at close liberty. Do what you like, but keep an ear out for the call."

Those leaving saluted and left. Thompson, Ortega and I were left behind, watching the spectacle on the ground. "How about you, Thompson? I'm sure you could use some sleep."

"I don't think I could, sir. Though that's what the manuals say we should do, I'm sure."

"Yeah, you got that right." But instead, we sat and watched the tide of the battle continue to build.

Ortega logged onto the sensor station and began sifting through the data, eliminating anything that looked legitimate, and giving closer scrutiny to any repeated signal that could be military in nature. He cursed and shook his head at me. Then he exclaimed, kicked the station, got up, and slammed his head into the bulkhead. Sichak, Thompson, and I could only stare in horrified fascination as he let loose with a positively volcanic string of Spanish. He dabbed at his forehead and it came away bloody. Thompson started to go to him, but I intercepted her and steered her toward another battle station. I tapped buttons over her shoulder and brought up the passive sensor read of the ships on every side of us. I slowly counted to thirty, letting Ortega calm down on his own. He left the bridge quietly.

Sichak swiveled his chair toward me. "What the *frag* was that?"

"Ortega has unreasonably high expectations of himself."

Thompson fixed me with a look that clearly said, *I wonder where he got them from?*

His mother, I didn't say. The *EWO* came back inside with a bandage on his head and sat down. He huffed twice and began to type. With a forced casual tone, as if his outburst hadn't happened, I spoke to Ortega without looking away from my panel. "So, *EWO*, what did you figure out?"

"These guys broke our encryption when we went to the police station. That means they're running really hefty software… mercenary quality software. I can't understand why they'd have it to break our codes and not use it for their own."

Sichak and I fixed him with a long stare.

Thompson threw up her hands. "OK, so what does that mean?" Sniper school wasn't heavy on Electronics Warfare and Signal Decryption classes.

"Up until now, it's just been looking for echoed signals, quantum transmissions that are repeated from place to place. We were hoping to be able to find some repeater stations that would be used to send and resend orders too quietly for others to hear unless we were listening real carefully. The problem is there are too many repeaters on the planet, too many signals from news stations, police, private communicators, and whatnot." Ortega continued to type with violent intent, the keys snapping like bullets. "The program is now looking for military style burst transmissions, packets of less than one tenth of a second. The news doesn't use them, the police don't use them, civilians don't use them, but mercenaries do."

"Good job, Ortega. How long to reset the parameters for your search?"

He continued typing. "It's done. Sending the overlay to the main screen now."

A seemingly random building in the 'dead zone' of the worst parts of the slums lit up.

Thompson leaned toward the screen from her station. "Is that where they—"

"No, first relay station. Look." Ortega made no apology for cutting her off. I noted that she seemed to know etiquette was trumped by his expertise right now. Another building was illuminated on the screen. And then another. "The packets are so small we can't roll up the network all at once. It has to track it backwards."

By the look of it, the line of repeaters was massive, and the orders were flying fast and free. The little red dots began tracking along buildings on their way toward West Lot Station. More importantly, isolated groups of enemy mercs disappeared into buildings. Thermal flares clearly highlighted engine startups. Fliers. Lots of them. Everyone on the bridge caught their collective breath.

"Should we warn the Master Sergeant?"

"Logan can see what we see. He's backed up by professional troops. He's an excellent soldier. He'll be fine." The fliers took to the air and more buildings turned red on the display as my nemesis continued to rally his troops. *Please Logan, be fine*.

CHAPTER 17: COMMITMENT

I watched from the bridge of *Deadly Heaven* with cameras that could read a newspaper over someone's shoulder from orbit. Over thirty thousand kilometers below, the enemy came within range of the West Lot complex. The bad guys put up their jamming net, and I pinpointed it onscreen, feeding the coordinates to the fire control computer just in case everything went wrong and we needed to destroy it. I prayed we didn't have to. We were supposed to be down there, after all. The red dots were converging, the fliers hovering at the edge of anti-aircraft range. The first shot was seconds away. I settled back into my chair and projected calm while my gut roiled with hot, bitter bile.

They were being confident but not stupid. They were expecting trouble. But the trouble they expected was a few police officers with beam weaponry, a few mercenaries bolstering the ranks. They expected the fire to be sporadic and disorganized. They expected to begin probing to find a blind spot in the defenses. What they got was a series of dark, fortified buildings.

Huge, ugly and angular, built under government contracts to house the poor, the darkness turned them into forbidden tombs hungry for blood. No guards patrolled the streets and no heads appeared in the windows. Nobody came out to spout rhetoric, hurl insults, make threats, or negotiate surrender.

Every mercenary team had fought against militia, and most of them were worse than amateurs. They would flee at the first sign of casualties and gave away their positions by opening fire far too early. They had no fire control, and so they often ran out of ammunition. It was no wonder; most governments had so restricted arms among the populous that militias fielded equipment centuries out of date. The worst governments marginalized those who trained to defend themselves and demonized them when they refused to be disarmed.

Persephone was no different. They had outlawed all but the most innocuous of arms a long time ago, disbanded all militias, and actively encouraged the people to rely on the government for protection. Without training or experienced members, the militia should be acting little better than a street gang. But they weren't.

A dozen or so mercs inside would not be able to control everyone inside the three tenements and the police station. They wouldn't be able to be at every entrance to repel attacks. The *Angels* simply wouldn't be able to be everywhere at once. And yet, as a few enemy soldiers crossed the streets at the edge of rifle range, nobody opened fire. The enemy took up positions inside the buildings across the four lane streets on every side, but they did not advance.

Then, out of one of the buildings further along the ragged line of repeaters, smack dead center of the slums, a massive thermal signature started up.

I'm not sure Sichak even knew he spoke aloud when he said, "That's no flier."

There you are. And I watched, thinking about commitment to the field of battle.

I grew up as an African extraction boy in a neighborhood of European extraction kids. Everything in the media painted 'my kind' as natural athletes and, as with anything else, kids like to test preconceived notions. That's how Kevin, Grant, Lacey, and I wound up on top of the Peterson's building, staring across five long meters to the roof of Kevin's apartment block.

Do it. Are you nuts? Hey, blacks are supposed to be natural athletes; jump it. What's that going to prove? None of you are jumping. So what if I make it? Anybody could. Fine, we all jump. Loser gives up his lunch tickets for a month. We didn't even stop to wonder how the loser would pay. We were twelve, and death was a very abstract concept.

Peer pressure is a weight that can turn coal into diamonds, and even the stupidest idea gains the glow of genius under the right conditions. We took a few steps back, and we sprinted. Kevin and I leapt, feeling thirty floors of nothing beneath us as the alley flashed below. Kevin landed hard on the other side. I landed flat, rolling away from the brink, laughing as the thrilling rush of being alive filled my soul. That's when I noticed we were alone.

Grant had skidded to a halt on the other side.

Lacey had tried to stop, and failed.

Her body had popped like a balloon with the impact, scattering blood and gore everywhere. We ran. The police never did figure out just who was there that day. We never spoke of it to anyone.

It seemed so stupid. Any of us could have physically made that jump. It was all about committing to a course of action. Either you went all out, or you did not. Going halfway was a great way to end up dead. I thought about Lacey's pulverized remains as the dropship lifted off from the north wing of some kind of governmental-style building in the slums. The metal roof, obviously an add-on by the unbondable, rolled to the side, allowing the mighty craft to climb into the air.

My enemy had committed all his forces to this one, big push. If he stopped now, I had him. If he continued on, he thought he might just succeed. He had no choice, now. It was like watching a natural disaster on the viewscreen. You could see the momentum building, see the worst case scenario unfold right there, but all you could do was wait.

"*Grit!* Captain, our decryption software can't even scratch their codes." Thompson shook her head, but her expression became awestruck as she watched the enemy dots on the screen. "Do you think they know we can see them?"

"It doesn't matter anymore." I took a deep breath. "Sichak, split the screen to follow that dropship wherever it goes. The second it begins to leave atmosphere I want to know where it's going."

"Aye, Captain."

Ortega wiped the sudden sweat from his face. "You mean after they get done with West Lot?"

"They're not going to stop anywhere near West Lot."

Surrounding the police station was a sound tactical move for leveling the buildings, but the dropship was now on the run and this stronghold had to be neutralized. It had to be, or else the plan would come crashing down.

I had told Tony the unbondable were after him, an idea equal parts lie and ignorance. Only once I saw their actual target did I realize in reality what they were after were his police cruisers. The reason they had struck police stations and shot down so many police craft was because the cruisers are armed.

The Key to Damocles

Police meant armed aircraft... armed aircraft that could chase down the dropship and cause trouble. Tony had even said enough of them could damage a dropship significantly. It was an unacceptable risk, and my opponent had spent three months trying to covertly destroy West Lot and every other police station within intercept range of his flight path. Unfortunately for them, Tony had stubbornly refused to give in, give up and go home. Then I came along and made things worse. Time was up. They had to kill the station to provide a clear lane of travel. They had to do it now.

More buildings lit up on my display as orders continued to come down from on high. I imagined them being angry, insistent. Isolated groups left the safety of the abandoned buildings and made a beeline for the nearest entrances to the compound. They advanced by the book, half the team covering the building while the other half advanced, each leapfrogging the other in turn. They were almost to the building when the streetlights came on.

Bright as hell, the lights hit the nailed-up screen doors and immediately turned the windows into metal blanks. You couldn't see in, but those inside could see out. The teams caught in the middle of the street froze like animals. That's when those inside opened fire.

The screens that stopped the human eye did nothing to stop the high wattage combat lasers from punching straight through. The enemy mercs were wearing light armor, allowing them to survive the first salvo of shots, and a few returned fire, but the majority of them retreated back across the street. Orders evidentially stopped them short of returning to cover, and then even more squads joined them in the kill zone as they began racing back toward the tenements. Their comrades in the building provided covering fire, but the small arms were being fired at blank screens. Behind the screens of the West Lot Station, we had cut small holes in the armored glass. Shots that normally would have hit those inside only bounced off, allowing them to put up a withering rain of accurate, coherent light. Those in the tenements were less lucky and had to move between volleys lest the blind fire find a chink in their invisibility and put a pinprick hole completely through them.

The groups caught in the street managed to get to the small retaining wall of crushed cars and rubble, leaving behind fifteen

216

dead and wounded. Once there, they found the windows in the compound were too high, and the defenders in the upper stories were still able to fire at them unless they were lying flat. Then the volume of fire increased. The men were pinned down and obviously screaming for backup, so my opponent sent in his fliers.

Aeroline engines screaming with the red-hot voices of the angry dead, the unbondable air support came burning in at two hundred kilometers per hour. None of these were military craft; they had obviously been stolen during the riots and retrofitted using time, a garbage dump, and a lot of welders. They sported tacked-on heavy squad weapons, but it was the improvised racks full of rockets that worried me. There were probably a few bombs onboard as well, held in makeshift cages where the rear passenger couch used to be, ready to be dropped from holes cut in the back floorboards. They raced along the empty streets below the tops of buildings, taking cover from any incidental fire that might come from the defenders. Four kilometers out, they split up and circled around, preparing for a one-two hit: one wave to come from the west and a second just after from the north. I watched them close in, pushing faster and faster toward their targets on glowing tongues of heat, confident in their ability to down at least one of the residential blocks instantly with the obvious plan of turning the police precinct into an island in a sea of rubble. The low-powered weapons that remained onboard afterward might not kill West Lot, but they would crack the walls and let the barbarians on the ground in to do the dirty work. The group to the west crested the tops of the buildings and fired. Rockets flew like thoughts of retribution—and that's where everything began to happen at the speed of electronic thought.

Logan, like an impossibly tall, metal Buddha, sat on the roof of the police station with his legs folded. He appeared to be meditating, arms slack on his knees, head bowed, the only movement of the giant being the constant flicker of his winged-helmet antennae. It was a lie, for beside him the routing box plugged into his head chugged though impossibly long lines of quantum computer code. It spun though the octinary language so fast it seemed to anticipate the next set of orders, turning normal human thoughts and movements into machine commands. He mentally flipped through menus the way a normal man might process familiar sounds… instantly and effortlessly.

Pairs of ten-centimeter rockets left the rails the moment the target was in sight, but at that same instant, a large anti-air RADAR, LIDAR, and quantum tracking shield sprang to life on the top of the police station. It was an active sensor, sending out waves of various types and measuring any return. It was not stealthy, and even from orbit it could not be missed, but it did provide precise targeting data to the vehicle-portable light defenses we had covertly installed in the compound. The dog-sized turrets glared menacingly from where they had been hidden beside the venting fans on the roofs of the buildings, but they were programmed to target intercept signals, so they tracked only the incoming fire. They turned ninety degrees on average, and took a quarter of a second to do so, but in that iota of time, the rockets had closed seventy meters toward the buildings.

The sensor net computer identified, prioritized, and assigned targets to each anti-air gun and then ordered them to open fire. The lasers charged and discharged, superheating the cone of the rockets into slag. The warheads were made of common military explosives, so heating it wouldn't make it detonate, but that could not be said for the aeroline-driven rocket engines. Concussions rocked the sky and beat against the ground with the speed of a string of fireworks. The anti-air laser turrets recycled five times per second, and were only just able to keep up with the incoming rockets.

Inside three seconds, forty rockets were released from ten fliers. By the time the clock moved again, thirty-nine of them were rapidly expanding clouds of vapor and metal. Only one made it through and impacted on the side of the westernmost residence. The explosion threw dust and rubble into the air, opening one hallway to the elements. The turrets went silent and waited for an eternity between orders as the humans caught up.

Only one flier reacted fast enough to the explosions and started to bank away when Logan activated the micro-missile battery sitting next to him. Three centimeters wide, half a meter long, the missiles didn't even have to see the fliers to find them. The trashcan sized multisensor pod whispered to the rockets of their enemy's position, and launched them in waves that created a white, toxic cloud on the roof of the station. Two more fliers saw the incoming fire and violently jerked at their control yokes while reaching for the makeshift button on the dashboard which enabled onboard countermeasures.

One of them almost made it.

Twenty friendly missiles were in the air, and they got to within one meter of their targets before the warheads exploded. Each explosion threw twenty, spinning, one-decimeter long tungsten rods out in a cone pattern. Normally used against light military craft, the *ad hoc* armor of the incoming fliers provided less protection than a dancer wrapped in tinfoil has against a shotgun. The craft split apart, and in eight cases, the fire suppression systems failed entirely. The onboard aeroline burned so fast it was nearly a detonation, raining red hot metal into the streets and along the residential blocks. Two came back down to ground in twisted heaps before their fuel tanks ruptured and ignited like the pyres of dead, forbidden gods. Timed precisely, the next wave came in, cresting the buildings to the north just as most of their compatriots disintegrated in midair.

It is at times like this that commitment matters. Of the twelve in the second wave, seven peeled off immediately and dove back for the safety of the streets. Of those, three failed to decelerate fast enough and crashed in a blinding set of explosions, setting unoccupied buildings alight. That left five pilots with nerves of steel. They came barreling in, launching everything in their arsenal.

The turrets on the roofs retasked and fired continuously, even as the micromissile launcher spun like a startled tiger and released multiple finned cylinders in a single roar. Pilots slapped the controls for their countermeasures and dumped lines of super hot flares and clouds of chaff. Haphazardly wrapped, magnesium-bright, cord-lights around the craft lit up, corrupting the light detection and ranging identification software. Missiles lost positive lock, some began to waver, and others veered wildly off target. That's when Logan's instincts took over.

Locked directly into the control unit for the entire operation, the cyborg did not so much command each individual missile in the nanosecond by nanosecond battle, but acted as a buffer through which the data was sifted. His brain easily disregarded the deceptions of the enemy, and righted the missiles on their paths. In less than a second, every flying object over West Lot became burning debris except two enemy rockets. One impacted the northernmost building, and one managed to bounce along the ground until it slammed into the base of the structure before it began leaking burning fuel.

I could only imagine the fear of those hiding in the bomb-shelter quality basements of the government-built buildings. Originally intended to house the tenants during a catastrophic natural disaster, now they were shaking with each crash or aimed hit. Inside, families were holding each other in the dark and wondering how much worse it would get.

I knew what was going through the minds of every defender at every window. I had been there many times, rejecting any hint of doubt or hope, living from second to second, knowing you were all that stood between those behind you and the death before you. It was the kind of hell that circled you like a snake, looking for any crack in your mind so it could burrow in and devour your sanity whole.

There were several minutes of silence as the fires quickly consumed their primary fuel and continued to gutter onward, eating rubber, plastic, and oil. The painfully dry but sparse grasses at the base of the north building provided insufficient to continue any kind of blaze, and the half dead rocket left naught but a black scorch on the building. I swept the camera over the holes in the residential blocks and was comforted that, so far, no bodies were apparent. The mercenary software loaded into *Deadly Heaven's* onboard systems immediately tallied the forty-three enemy soldiers dead in the street, and guesstimated five casualties—three dead—inside the buildings. One of the impact sites on the north building was smoking merrily, but the shadowed forms of armored defenders wielding fire extinguishers showed this too was coming under control. No bodies moved on the street, and the remaining fliers circled outside the range of the sensor pod until they popped above building-top level and rocketed upward at very steep angles.

The enemy dropship turned in a wide circle and lit off its aeroline engines. It was on an intercept course for the Station and L/V/D beyond it. The thing, for all its size, was moving at magnificent speeds. After accelerating to full on one set of engines, the pilot lit off the nuclear reaction space drive, leaving a wake of radiation over an entire swath of city.

Bastards! I clenched my hands in frustration, shattering the clear plastic facing of the main screen's remote control. I glanced up from the small, sparking device and saw everyone looking at me with wide eyes. I knew losing my temper was the wrong thing to do, but I just couldn't stop it. Showing emotion, any emotion, allows them license to feel and to think, often too much. Mercenary Rule #1, The Boss is Never Afraid.

I ordered everyone but Sichak off of the bridge and hit the alert. Klaxons blared from every corner of the ship, and *Angels* dropped whatever they were doing and rushed for the armories. I hit a button on the arm of my command chair, and my orders echoed through the halls like the voice of a god. "*Angels*, this is your Captain; prepare for combat launch. All mechanicals to battle stations. Begin warm up cycle on all weapons. Load all torpedo tubes. Straight board the ship. I repeat… a straight board throughout the ship. That is all."

Across the kilometer-long craft, all doors, even those usually allowed to stay open, were closed and dogged shut by mechanical hands. The handful of O's became horizontal dashes on the ship's status screen, confirming that every room was sealed from every other. Independent recyclers measured the level of carbon dioxide in any given room, struggling to keep up with the CO_2 to O_2 conversion without help from the main system. We were going into battle, and any hull breach now could only expose one room at a time.

I turned to Sichak and laid a firm hand on his shoulder. "Are you clear on this?"

He swallowed hard. "Yes, sir."

I affixed him with a serious stare.

He nodded and steeled his voice. "I can do this, sir."

All things considered, I'd rather have someone a little daring at the controls. If nothing else, they might do something unexpected and pull their own fat out of the fire if things got dicey. Unfortunately, Sichak was what I had and there was no percentage in making him feel unworthy. I spared him a lopsided smile. "I know you can. Just remember that no matter what you see on the screen, we have to stick to the plan. Go to it, Pilot."

The Key to Damocles

And I left for the Armory, opening, closing, and dogging every hatch I came to. I was getting suited up for the next ten minutes, and then on my way to *The Succubus* after, so I missed the next segment of The Battle of West Lot.

On a radio cue, the enemy fliers nosed over into a dive, adjusting their positions in the sky until they were coming down directly over West Lot Station, and Logan in particular. Logan saw them on the feed from *Deadly Heaven* and all of his weapons tracked upwards. Seconds later, unbondable rushed outward from the enemy staging buildings, snipers shot out streetlights from behind cover, and shoulder mounted missiles coughed from the windows. Launched from below the level of the turrets, there was nothing to stop them from slamming into the buildings with impunity. Some were aimed intelligently and caused child-sized gaps in the concrete walls. Many more were aimed stupidly, at the screen door cages covering windows. When they hit the tough metal screens, the armor piercing warheads went off, wasting the brunt of their fury on the empty air behind the screen. The police station's armored windows handled the residual blast easily, but civilian glass panes became a volcano of razors that scoured the halls inside. In either case, the screens remained largely intact with only fist-sized holes to show for all the abuse.

The fliers had become pinpoints to those on the ground when the rumbling thunder of the dropship built into a horrific roar. Those deep inside the building heard it go over, accompanied by a sonic boom that shattered more glass and deafened those unlucky enough to be without hearing protection or in a bomb shelter. It left behind a rattled and confused sensor network as the fliers activated all their countermeasures and launched their rockets at Logan and his missile base. They activated their forward mounted lasers at extreme range, causing sizzling spots on the roof like a rain of corrosive blood.

Unbondable infantry were pouring across the gap, eager to exploit both the distraction above and the near total darkness on the street. They came from their bunkers as a massed wave, looking to either blow apart doors or enter the few holes created by their heavy weapons officers. Laser fire was joined by plasma bolts from the street, as harder hitting weapons entered effective range in the fray. These bright lances of destruction proved a wonderful target, but otherwise the defenders were firing only sporadically into the dark.

Above, the turrets turned their domed heads toward the heavens and began to fire as soon as the rockets entered the sensor envelope. They had a lot more time to intercept the traces this time, but the radiation in the atmosphere played havoc with the targeting. Each turret recycled its charge as fast as it could, pouring energy into the air and raising the ambient temperature of the entire block by ten degrees at rooftop level. They acted without need to breathe, without need to second guess themselves, and without any concept of doubt. The fiery death of fifty rockets created even more debris in the air, impromptu chaff that confused the missile system. It immediately switched to LIDAR, but again the bright cords surrounding the craft confused the signal. RADAR was completely fuzzed from radiation and a sky of falling metal. Logan switched everything to passive infrared. The sensor system shut up and just watched the sky for telltale trails of extreme heat. The pilots were confident, since they were continuing to launch spurts of parachute mounted flares, but they realized too late that the flares were being left well behind at their current speeds. With the electronic equivalent of 'Oh, there you are,' the last ten missiles left the launcher.

Logan pulled the cord from his head, picked up a comically large rifle, and ran for the south edge of the roof.

Ten friendly missiles darted in a shallow arc and slammed into their targets, but with no human consciousness to guide them, their target acquisition was inefficient. The heavy level of electronic confusion affected them enough that four missiles homed in and obliterated one target. Another two fliers ate two each, and two ate one, which meant one got away without a scratch.

Logan jumped over the edge of the roof, reached back with mechanical precision, and closed his fist around the steel cable we had draped there. Huge metal staples groaned and bent as his weight and momentum tried to wrench them free. The heavy cable sung in pain as it arrested his forward momentum.

The untouched flier pulled out of his suicide dive, engines screaming his survival to the heavens.

The Key to Damocles

And then Logan loosened his grip. Gravity reached up and brought him down in a fall parallel with the wall.

The unbondable on the ground cheered for their lone survivor even as the broken wreckage of the rest crashed into the roof of West Lot Station and erased the sensor dome as well as the empty missile launcher. In a flash, a quarter of a million credit anti-air station was gone. The roof of the police station buckled and cracked but held as the aeroline burned it black.

Logan tightened his grip five stories later, and sparks shot out from his hand as his metal fist scoured away the steel. He slammed into the ground with enough force to liquefy the skeleton of a normal man, knees bending to absorb the shock with his cybernetic muscles rather than crumpling his titanium laminate frame. In a blink, he shouldered his massive rifle and made for the shadows.

The flier made three fast passes over the buildings, riddling the upper stories with burning holes. He kept too high, and too fast, for the troops inside to get a good shot at him and after the third round, he felt confident enough to start doing cheap acrobatics to inspire the troops to press forward.

He never got a chance to even register the silver form in the shadows that tracked his weapon in on the flier. He had no idea that a multimillion credit micro-computer was making love to a human brain, whispering not only where he was, but where he would be once a bullet traveled high enough to reach him. He never saw the muzzle flash of the gun as it went off.

All he knew was that both starboard engines flew to pieces within an instant of one another. He got to think about that for ten stories, but at a hundred kilometers per hour there was only time for surprise, not repentance nor regret. The cheers died as the spinning vehicle ground itself into a wave of fire on the roadway, churning dozens of unbondable into hamburger beneath it.

Forty kilometers away, the dropship had already arrived at L/V/D. It flew over the walls and hovered at the top of the huge string of luxury homes where the most valuable of the studio's stars were kept in comfortable confinement. Weapons meant to breach hardened naval armor vaporized every AA gun in range, then concentrated on the west wall of one fortress/home. The craft landed with the pounce of a predator and unbondable poured out of the ship's gullet.

They rushed inside, guns blazing.

Back at West Lot, unbondable at street level planted explosives on doors that ripped them from their hinges like a giant having at a dollhouse. They pulled the pins on small canisters and tossed them into lobbies and into breaches in the wall. The few fools who tried to put them into windows realized that the metal screens stopped those too. The canisters burped, belched, and begin to exude thick, harsh, green smoke.

Smoke would be bad enough, but this heavy fog was impregnated with macro-nanites called nanoleeches. NBC gear would provide some protection, but if you stood in the smoke long enough, the bots would burrow through. In minutes, there would be patches of discolored, itchy skin on the victim. In a few more, dozens of sizable abrasions would begin to leak blood, but worse would be what was happening inside. Nanoleeches were designed to eat through respirator gear; once in the lungs, they would tear through the soft tissues and burrow toward blood bearing vessels. There they would act as miniature pumps, sucking out blood and squirting it into the lungs in a stream a few molecules across. Multiply it by a few million, and infected persons would literally drown in their own blood. It would be a horrible way to die, and using it was forbidden by the Laws of War.

That's when a coded signal was transmitted, and the fans on top of the buildings turned on. In moments, hot air was sucked into the top of the building and pumped into the interior. Defenders hurriedly set up thin, plastic sheets over breached windows. Those in the bunkers shut the doors and sealed them with rolls of tape. The hot air traveled through the hallways and ductwork, building pressure and forcing the air already there to vacate through any hole it could. Within seconds, the bulk of it came sneezing out through the breached doors, taking the nanoclouds with it. The attackers didn't even have time to curse before the building coughed out their venomous clouds back over them. Unbondable retched, screamed, and died in pools of their own blood.

Then, small doors on the roof of every one of the residence buildings opened. Armored figures darted out, half meter tubes held awkwardly upright. Almost in unison, each one pulled the strings dangling from the bottom of their tubes, sending shards of burning light half a kilometer into the air. Once at apogee, the flares deployed parachutes to float slowly to ground, turning night into day again. Select window screens began to smoke and glow as laser weapons inside were set to rapid repeat and the triggers held down. On the ground floor, hardened defenders turned the corridors into killing fields, sweeping left and right to mow down invaders. A few unbondable tried popping ion dust grenades, but ETC weaponry wielded by *Apostles* immediately joined in to punch through the dust and kill even more attackers.

Logan jogged to the west residence block, firing his weapon from his hip. Automated sensors and physics software determined the impact point of every two-centimeter-wide shell as the gun rippled off ten bullets at a time. Men became pieces of men as whole limbs were severed by the force of the massive, fragmenting shells. He tore a breaching charge off the door and casually chucked it over his shoulder about thirty meters where the detonator shattered. An *Apostle* was already waiting to open the door for him and he went inside.

At L/V/D, the kidnappers left dozens of smoking bodies in their wake, and took one breathing one with them. They jumped into their dropship and immediately accelerated out over the studio, past the wall, and over the city. Then it angled upwards, making for orbit.

Now it was my turn.

CHAPTER 18: A SHELL OF RAGE

Sichak's voice pressed against my ear. "Sir, I have their track. They're heading for a heavy freighter in geosynchronous orbit over New California. It's about one-four-zero-zero kilometers away from our current position. They're moving fast."

"Roger. Let me know if they break off to another rendezvous. Out." I switched channels. "Doe. Launch *The Succubus*."

John Doe's voice was less than encouraging. "Aye, Captain."

Never had I ever wanted to be called Cappy, Cap, Cap'n, Caparooni, Capitan, or The Capper more in my life.

There was a jerk, a complete absence of gravity, and then a clumsy lurch as we left the docking bay of *Deadly Heaven*. I looked around at my crew strapped into their jump-seats, and I saw them staring straight ahead. Each one was dressed as always, black with silver trim, but everything was exaggerated.

Instead of bulky riot armor, or light mobile infantry armor, every member was encased in heavy assault *hard shell*s. Hulking, angular, and ominous, these were the heaviest sets in my inventory. The *hard shell*s alone weighed far more than a light suit and all of our gear. They put out an electromagnetic signature of a main battle tank. They could only move up to about thirty kilometers per hour at a motor assisted jog, faster than any man but easily overtaken by any other vehicle. They could not hide, they could not run, and they were everyone's favorite target for antitank weapons. All of this meant that using them in a protracted, mobile, land battle was tantamount to suicide, but for assaulting a ship while outnumbered, they just might do the job.

I checked the feeds from the helmet cameras of my crew, ensuring that their systems were reporting to my own, and flipped through their vitals. Their readings were all over the place, so I looked around the cabin as the ship pulled another radical turn. It appeared that they were concentrating on their jobs, but I was reminded of my first mission. The readings from their vitals confirmed that they were concentrating on the contents of their stomachs and how to keep them there. Another awkward course correction and we drifted away, turned, and made a slow line for our target. The bad thing was, I knew this was the part where it got tricky.

The Succubus bounced into the radiation trail of another craft and used it to hide the burn signature from our engines. An invisible hand slammed us to the side as the nuclear reaction engines lit off, second upon second piling onto one another as we struggled to breathe with the help of the inertial dampeners. Doe hauled on the controls, spun the dropship around and hid from our quarry behind a light freighter. The engines went dead, and the Lieutenant/Flight activated the gas steering system to adjust course as we floated by the larger craft. All of our active sensors were turned off, and our internal power consumption was dialed as low as possible. Theoretically, we should not be seen unless someone was specifically looking for us. We were like a cat tiptoeing through a crowd of giants while holding our breath, tail in our mouth. The craft made a wide arc behind the suspect freighter until we sat in its neighbor's baffles, directly behind the engines where its sensors could not see.

Sichak came over the comm. "*Momma's House* to *Dirty Girl*... your boyfriend is *en route*."

I pressed the transmit button on my forearm pad twice, producing two distinct clicks.

A few seconds later, Doe came over the intercom. "Captain, it looks like... uh... ho-*grit!*"

I linked my C^2 helmet into the *Succubus* mainframe and piped over the feed from the sensors. It looked like the ships in orbit over New California had noticed the little war happening down below. They probably also noticed the dropship rocketing up from the surface into their midst. They put two and two together and came up with: *Danger! Danger!* If there's anything merchants can sense, it's danger. And they always deal with it in the same way.

They run.

I hit the key for the intercom for the cockpit exclusively. "Focus, Lieutenant. Get us to our target."

"Captain, I don't think—"

"Say, 'Hell yeah,' Lieutenant."

"But Captain—"

There is a tone that commanders develop. It must be used sparingly, it must be practiced, and it must be honest. It must say, 'If you don't do what I tell you to do right now, I am going to shove your head so far up your ass it will pop out in another dimension.' I used it now. "Say. Hell. Yeah. Lieutenant."

"Hell yeah, Captain?"

"Now move this *fragging* boat!"

On further reflection, perhaps this did not rank amongst my ten best motivational speeches, but *The Succubus* began slipping and sliding to and fro like a crawler in an ice rink. Doe's voice was louder. "Hell yeah, Captain!"

The ship twirled. It spun. Mercenaries grabbed onto their restraint harnesses and tried to pull themselves deeper inside. "Hell *fragging* yeah, Captain!"

We came to the baffles of the target, and Doe lit up the nuclear reaction engines. "ETA thirty seconds, *Angels*. Whoahfu—"

I couldn't see the outside, so I couldn't be sure if it was a barrel roll. I also couldn't see what we avoided, but we didn't become a cloud of expanding gas, so I guess it was all okay. Tension spiked in to my spine, sending shivers from my heels to my ears, lighting a need for something raw, hot, and full of nicotine.

Doe began the countdown. "Five, four, three, two—"

The craft spun for a tenth of a second and then we were slapped toward the rear of the craft. You could hear the roar of the engines opened up to full, beating on the firewall like an angry mob of lions. Then, ominous silence.

CHUNG!

"Green light! Green light! Green light! Go! Go! Go!"

Angels slapped off their restraints and hustled to the rear of the craft as fast as they could in full battle gear. Ansef opened the same kind of belly bay we had used to fast rope down to the West Lot Station and revealed the unbroken hull of the heavy freighter. Richardson tore the breaching plate—over a meter in diameter—from its restraining straps on the wall, popped through the hole and laid it down on the hull. The magnets latched on tight. Richardson and Lopez activated the ring, and everyone waited while the internal breaching laser array carved the internal circumference.

The Key to Damocles

Archer kept up his own private mantra. "C'mon. C'mon. C'mon. C'mon."

One little red light turned green, but the other did not. Richardson did not wait another second to spin the locking ring open and yank the door wide. Walt jumped into the darkness and began cursing. "Captain, we're not in!"

My veins were suddenly awash in ice water. "What?"

"There's another *grit-licking, mud-raking, mother-fragging* hull down here!"

Thompson jumped down and took a look. "He's right. Richardson, get the breaching ring down there!"

"Can't!"

Her voice cracked like a whip. "Don't give me 'can't' soldier!"

And it was then that Richardson stated the obvious for everybody. "Lieutenant, the breaching ring is one-point-four meters wide; the hole it makes is only a one-point-three-five meter circle!"

That was when we heard the nuclear engines of the freighter start up. The vibrations of the massive pumps squirting nuclear fissionable material into the reaction chamber crept up our legs to our ears like a line of fire ants. In less than a minute, the lasers in the reaction chamber would begin heating the fissionable material, burning off the stabilizing gel and starting the nuclear reaction. If we were on the outside of the craft once it started moving on a pillar of fire...

A goddamned Trojan horse. Again, I thought about commitment. *Calm, they need calm.* I dialed for a calm voice, but I swear the words that came out were someone else's, someone smarter. "Richardson, shut the door. Unlock the magnets, move it to the side to create a new hole with an overlapping edge. Then you can lower it down through the middle of the enlarged hole."

Richardson did as he was told and a few seconds later we had a figure eight in the hull. Richardson turned the breaching plate sideways and dropped it down to King. Men followed suit one at a time. As they went, Thompson sidled up and dialed into a private frequency with me. "I never would have thought of that."

I pushed her to the hole. "When it's your team, you will."

"Doe, get this ship back to *Heaven* and do not, I repeat, do not be seen. Once there, help Pilot Sichak any way you can."

230

"Aye, sir. Give them a little 'hell yeah' of your own."

"You can bet on it." I jumped. I landed awkwardly five meters down, but at least the greatly lessened gravity ensured that there was zero chance of getting hurt. *Yet*. We were just at the edge of the range of the ship's gravity web, but we had to activate our boot magnets to get sure footing. The sound of the engines was definitely louder here, so I must have imagined the sound of the belly bay doors above closing. "Richardson! Move!"

Everyone turned on their helmet lights, and I led them inside of the metal beast, looking for a likely place to burn through. The problem was, I was no expert. We had been able to study the freighter for a few hours and pick a likely spot to cut. Now, we had no idea what make, model, or class of craft was inside the hollow shell. We had no idea where to cut to hit open space, and where would hit batteries, deep circuitry, or worse: munitions, canisters of O_2, or fuel cells. We had to run because we were short on time and long on death that was coming fast and angry. There was a deep resonance in the steel on every side as Doe lifted off and sped back toward *Deadly Heaven*. Light streamed down upon us as *The Succubus* cleared our hole and exposed the miracle of space though the figure eight.

"Captain!" I spun on my magnetized heel, the excessive inertia of the *hard shell* pulling me off balance. Archer had his lights pointed at a loading door. It was a simple, little thing. Two meters square, it had to lead to a corridor where supplies could more easily be loaded into the ship when in dock. It was an airlock with a big, wide entry.

"Richardson! Hit that *fragging* thing! Archer! Extra share." His posture said the sniper was grinning like a fiend. I would rather he helped Richardson as the big man slapped the breaching ring down and got it started. As the ring finished, flashes out in the darkness rippled on every side. The whole ship rumbled like a beast that was waking from a hard sleep and razors of starlight stabbed in as the fake outer shell was cast off of the interior craft. Worse yet, there was no O_2 on the other side of the ring, which meant we needed another double wide breach.

If the first hole took forever, the second nearly took the rest of our lives. The craft shuddered as the runaway nuclear reaction provided thrust that struggled to overcome the mass of the craft. Jagged clouds of scrap metal were slipping across us, and in a few more seconds we would be fast enough to be impaled on them. The breaching ring was tossed down and soldiers followed into an area barely large enough to contain them. Richardson had already set up the ring again and started it cutting. The ship began to haul ass as two green lights lit on the ring, saying it was ready, and there was air on the other side. There was a distinct shift in the stars outside and I barked an order. Richardson grabbed on to the ring hatch and snatched Lopez's combat harness. Lopez grabbed two more *Angels*, who in turn grabbed more. We became a human pyramid, everyone holding fast to each other. That way, none of us flew out of the holes in the outer door when the spaceship spun to its new heading. It was like being dangled by the nape of your neck over a chasm that spun into infinity. Actually, that's exactly what it was.

The ship stabilized its course, and we let go of one another. Richardson pressed a button, releasing the pressure on the other end of the hatch. Frosty air spewed out through vents on the outer edge of the plate. Then he wrenched the wheel and opened the hatch. His helmet light revealed some kind of supply room beyond, and I felt a vice on my chest release. One by one, the *Angels* hustled into the interior room. I only hoped the enemy attributed the hull breach to debris flung from the mass they had just left behind.

Once inside, our lights illuminated a massive, military style pantry. It went off in all directions, stainless steel rack after rack, loaded with chemically inert polymer cans filled with synthetic food labeled according to its texture. Other shelves held cans of flavoring, chicken a'la king, mu shu pork, bacon and beans...and rank upon rank of them stood empty. Never one to pass up intelligence, I tried to divide how long they had been here by how many cans of food were missing, figure in how many each can would feed—

The door at the far end slid open into the airless room. I hit a key which told everyone to look at me. Then I snapped out battle signs as fast as my hands would do them. *Scatter. Lights Out. Avoid Detection.*

To their credit, they moved like they had been set on fire. They dodged behind racks at our end of the room and took up firing positions over shelves of rations. Across the room, a bright light sprang to life at waist height. I turned off the blinded lowlight filters in my C² helmet and ran through the visual systems. The infrared showed a glowing, trashcan-sized interloper. I clicked a macro on the miniaturized keypad, sending words scrolling across every HUD in the room: *Hold position. Weapons hold. Await further orders.*

There was hope. This was a model 87-EDC. These things were as common as toilets onboard star craft. Everyone used them, or one of 86 previous models, because they were cheap, effective, and easy to get hold of. I had twelve of the legged models on *Deadly Heaven* myself. They were programmed and outfitted for emergency damage control, and they were very good at their jobs. The problem with them is that they were dumber than a brick outside of their area of expertise. They could fix a circuit board, fight fires, and seal breaches in seconds, but their programming was very specific and anything outside their purview tended to get overlooked. I was just hoping that a recently installed boarding gate and a dozen armed invaders were way outside its purview.

Normally, these things sounded like a pile of pots and pans riding on an electric engine with a bad case of asthma. In the airless environment, however, it seemed like a mechanical ghost trolling across the aisle toward us on rubber-tracked feet. It came to the central aisle and paused. A cloud of white ejected from its body twice, and then it paused, watching with sensors for where the mildly radioactive dust got pulled with the expelled gas. Of course, it went nowhere because the boarding hatch that had compromised the room had been closed. With nothing else to go on, the trash can moved along the floor toward the wall that faced the outer hull of the ship. I sent a quick signal to Thompson, who used her considerable sniper skills to slip silently away from the oncoming bot. She made less than no sound, but having no atmosphere helped. The bot continued obliviously until it stopped at the loading hatch, obviously staring at the boarding plate.

It vented some more. Again, no breach sucked out the dust and gas.

Then, apparently unsure of what to do when it couldn't find a breach, it did what most engineers would do: it sprayed the entire surface with sealant. The thick, gelatinous foam spewed all over the wide door from its fan-shaped nozzle. It took only a few seconds before it was done, but it waited for the foam to finish expanding and then harden into a blob of caution-tape yellow resin. Then it went back to the environmental control panel by the door. Bits of electronic code flashed invisibly between the two quantum devices. Air began to leak into the room. Slowly at first, the trickle continued to build as the EDC bot monitored the internal air pressure. Once the pressure became normalized, the bot shot out a few more spurts. It detected no air movement, so it checked off the last item off its list and transmitted its access signal. The door opened, and it rolled out, making noise like a medieval knight with a bad pollen allergy.

Everyone began to breathe again. I looked over at Ortega as we broke cover. "*EWO?* Please tell me—"

Ortega's smile was plain in his voice as he held up a small palm computer. "I trapped its wireless access passcode. We should have free run of the ship until they figure out we're here."

Score one for the good guys. And that's another reason I don't use automated doors.

I used hand signals, hoping to squeeze every second of stealth I could out of our situation. After all, it wouldn't take too long before someone on the bridge noticed communication signals being generated inside their own ship. *Standard Dual Line March. Weapons At The Ready. Weapons Free.*

Everyone stacked by the doors, Ortega in the lead with his sensor, next to Smith, with his silenced carbine. It was up to him or Archer in the back of the party to eliminate any threat before an alarm could sound. Neither of them looked comfortable with the prospect of being responsible for the team's survival. Nothing I could do about that except move on. I hit a three-letter combination and sent it to the team:

XQT

Ortega hit a button on his palm computer. It repeated the silent call of the EDC bot and the doors opened as if by magic. The *Angels* filed out into the spinal corridor of the ship. Microcomputers grabbed the incoming sound from the helmet pickups and plotted source from reflection and strength like a complex game of pool. It constantly created a map of what was on every side. The reflected sounds from the stainless-steel hallways and polymerized steel floor grates provided a picture-perfect surface for our holo-sonar units. We had a map for thirty meters in every direction that updated every time we made any noise. Now we just needed to know where we had to go.

A burst transmission slammed into my C^2 where the microcomputer unraveled and decoded it. An icon of scales appeared in the upper corner of my HUD, but it wasn't until I heard Grisham's electronic voice that I understood what it meant. "Captain, I just received a call from Mr. Lionel's lawyers. He is offering you a contract to recover one Katie Ranner, an actress with a lifetime contract with L/V/D. The payment is ten million credits alive, one million dead with no loss of genetic material to outside sources."

Dead or alive? I bet she would find that comforting.

His recording continued over my silent sarcasm. "The contract specifies a ten-minute window for acceptance."

My recorded and burst transmitted reply was short. "Triple the rewards and send the contract back. If they accept, electronically sign it and send a copy to *Haven*."

We made it to an elevator. Lopez pointed at it excitedly.

Death Trap. Move Along. I signaled. An elevator would have cameras, and would become a prison the second someone noticed us inside it. What we needed was emergency accessway: a ladder, or preferably stairs.

Again, Grisham's icon interrupted me. "Captain, your offer has been accepted."

I smirked as we continued down the hallway, a perfect covering formation *cracked* when Lopez refused to move and pointed at the elevator. The formation stuttered and nearly shattered. I stalked back toward Lopez who continued to point at the elevator like a puppy looking for a place to go wee. My left hand whipped in the air, the other busied with my rifle. *Standard Dual Line March. Move!*

He tapped the wall incessantly. He might have even hopped up and down if he wasn't wearing one hundred and thirty kilos of *fragging* armor.

MOVE!

To his credit, he kept radio silence, but move he did not. I stalked toward him, face burning, clenching armored gauntlets with the obvious intent to reach down his throat and pull out his internal organs in alphabetical order. Then I saw what he was pointing at.

There are laws, and there are rules, and there are traditions. Of the three, traditions die the hardest. Centuries ago, people died while riding elevators when a building caught fire. To remedy the situation, people began hanging signs next to elevators to tell people how to get to other escape routes in times of emergency. I had ripped them down from *Deadly Heaven* because it made no sense to tell an invader how to get anywhere on my ship. But here, against all odds, was a placard marked 'EMERGENCY EVACUATION ROUTE' in bright, red block letters. It showed a map, small arrows leading to the main up/down access way, and a logo at the bottom. It was a familiar symbol found in colonies far and wide; it was the red helm and blue planet of the Knights of Earth. In our current situation, it was like crashing through a door to an enemy bunker and finding a MENSA meeting. Like a kick in the crotch, the realization came fast and hard; we were in fact on a civilian craft.

I signaled. Translated literally, it meant: *Two Four You*. Lopez acted like I had just sucker punched him with a sack full of hammers. He should. I just doubled his pay instead of sucker punching him with a sack full of hammers. Later, it would make a convenient excuse that I didn't have a sack full of hammers, but for now I used the butt of my rifle to smash the bolts that kept the piece of plastic attached to the wall and took it with. Ortega began slapping the sensor, adjusting the knobs constantly. His hands flashed up. *Sensor feed is* — his hand fluttered like landed fish—*Wonky. Engine Interference?*

A burst transmission came from Sichak. "*Momma's House* to *Dirty Girl*, your boyfriend's climbing in the window."

The dropship from the planet had just docked to this ship. I clicked the comm twice and waved the team into motion. Forty meters later, and around one corner, we got to the stairs. The sign advised that these were emergency stairs, and an alarm would sound if it were opened. Without waiting for an order, Ortega flashed the code and the door opened *sans alarum*. After all, you wouldn't want alarms going off every time the mechanicals went out through one of these to fix something.

We progressed down the stairs, every meter tightening the tension bar on my shoulders just a bit more. They'd have at least five minutes before they could land and repressurize the bay, but at our cautious pace, we had already blown that comfortable lead. By now they'd already be unloading, and unless they were lazy, they'd have our target out of the ship, in the middle of the crossfire. I was praying hard for lazy.

Ortega looked at me and shook his head. This was an emergency stairwell, and had been built to withstand catastrophic decompression of the ship. The heavy walls were fuzzing out his sensors, and we were flying blind. At least there were no klaxons yet.

As we approached the bottom floor, deep metallic sounds began resounding through the steel of the ship. Within seconds, the expert AI pulled out the reflected engine noise seeping through the walls and floor. Our HUD told the story: Heavy Machinery and Heavy Robotic Movement. Estimate… Landing Bay Traffic.

It was even kind enough to give us direction and predicted distance.

The door at the bottom landing opened, and I remembered a little too late that between the airless pockets, heavy batteries, and electronics that infest the walls throughout any given ship, holo-sonar wasn't perfect. Sometimes it would misidentify a direction. Sometimes it would halve the distance to target. Sometimes it would double the *fragging* distance so that when the *grit*-licking doors opened, you were face-to-face with the ass-*cracking* landing bay—

—and the dozen goddamn unbondable standing in a rough circle as mechanicals took care of unburdening the dropship. I don't know if they were getting an after-action report, simply jaw jacking, divvying up duties, or making plans to perform a ballet. What mattered was that these guys were armored, and armed.

And they were looking right at us.

Adrenaline surged like a tsunami outward from my brain and cranked my internal volume to full. "ACTION! ACTION! ACTION! Advance and fire!"

The gunfight at the O.K. Corral had nine gunfighters standing less than five meters apart. For forty seconds they unloaded sixguns, shotguns, and rifles at one another at extremely close range. Six survived and three men walked away completely unscathed. Historians blame the use of black powder weapons, which made a wall of caustic smoke that obscured both sides and made targeting purely guesswork.

We were a few short of two dozen soldiers, standing fifteen meters apart, across an open bay with little to no cover between us. We had no convenient fog. At this point, it would not be skill, it would not be leadership, and it would not be luck that determined a victor; it would be brute punishment. How much could we take? How much could we give?

Orders erupted from me, spiking the feed on the mic. "Clear lanes! Clear lanes! Open fire when you have a shot! Fire at will! Fire at will!"

The first six seconds of how you assault a room full of hostiles will determine if you live or die. We had drilled it to death for weeks. Ortega tossed his sensor unit to the side on its sling as he advanced, clawing for his weapon and sidling out of the firing line of other *Angels*. Smith mirrored him, jogging left as he aimed over his weapon and opened fire. Behind them, King and Richardson advanced and broke to the side, their heavy weapons screaming songs written in lead. Our aural filters cut in, saving our ears, as our visors darkened to save our eyes from the bright plasma trails of our ETC weaponry.

Our enemies had been fighting police agencies armed with pushguns. They had fought militia armed with lasers. We were boarders, so we should be using plasma weapons. All that taken together, their first reaction was naturally to pull pins on grenades and send them twirling toward us. The ordnance exploded in ionized gas and silica dust smoke. They were designed to shatter plasma and electron packets, not to mention diffuse beams of coherent light. The steel core armor piercing rounds we were firing didn't care in the least. It was these two futile seconds that turned a defeat into an absolute slaughter.

That small pause allowed the rest of my team to enter and set up a firing line, ripping holes in the enemy position. One man, his helmet sitting dejectedly on the floor, caught a round just below his eye. His skull ruptured like a grapefruit. King's burst was right on, centering a dozen rounds on his target's chest. The ten millimeter-long electrothermal chemical rounds impacted within a split-second of one another. The first shattered the trauma plate of his chest armor. The next further crumpled the polymer/metal laminate. The third punched deep and split layers of Kevlar. Each bullet impacted less than a hand-width from the previous in line, weakening the whole and providing an opening for the last four to reach tender flesh. Organs shredded, bone shattered, blood spurted, and life fled. Two *Angels* to my right concentrated their fire on the same enemy, severing an arm and a leg on his right side. More shots collided with the mass of men, but their hard armor plates turned them to the side, or soft armor weave jumpsuits sucked up their killing kinetic energy.

Then they returned fire.

My brain hung on every moment like a lingering lost love, painting every second in colors so bright it made my heart ache. Bullets snapped by, so slowly I could almost reach out and touch them, sparking like firecrackers on the walls on every side. I could feel them pushing in, little pickpockets looking for a liter or two of blood. The heavy assault *hard shells* clicked or squealed with glee as they ricocheted away, leaving their tender charges untouched in the hail of fiery death. I had to push forward, taking my turn at the door to death before moving to the side to let Ansef come up behind. The *Angels* formed a ragged line along the wall. I took my place at their center. My left hand dropped the evacuation placard to the floor as my A2R-91 rifle came up as if willed by its own, demonic soul. "Advance and fire!"

It was like watching colonial soldiers march in a deep-seated cadence, but instead of long elegant rifles spurting smoke and giving birth to musket-balls, brutally short angular black weapons erupted with lances of monochromatic plasma fire and steel-cored lead. Beautiful light trailed on the ass end of hundreds of flying rounds. Red stains appeared on urban camouflage paintjobs. Men grabbed their chests and collapsed, others stared dumbly as limbs went numb just before the rest of the body was cut down. One attempted to flee, but was ravaged by Richardson's squad support machine gun as effectively as if he had been dropped naked in a pit of carnivores. The last man standing moved forward to draw fire from the bodies of his unit, working franticly at the action of his weapon as he sought to get his fresh box of ammunition in place.

Unbondable or not, you're a brave and loyal bastard. I took careful aim, deliberately lining up the combat scope as I tried to steady my hands, mentally preparing to let go of the moment and gently squeeze the trigger with one, smooth pull. Before I could,

The Key to Damocles

I heard the electronically muffled crash/snap of a rifle sending out a single bullet.

A shattered hole appeared in his visor.

My target collapsed and did not move again.

Ever.

Thompson lowered her rifle.

Her shoulders slumped a bit.

It was over.

We were breathing air recycled through our armor systems, so it should not have carried the weight of so much blood, screams, and death. Shouldn't have, but things never seem to work that way. Mechanicals sprang to life across the landing bay. EDC units rolled toward the doors to space and sprayed them with yellow goo to seal the hundreds of bullet holes we had created. Others went on about their business. Two massive bots, built like forklifts with heads, were noncommittally taking crates of ordnance from the wings of the dropship while their smaller cousins were hooking up lines to remove the fuel from the docked bird. I thought about what would have happened if a stray round had punctured the fuel hose and I shuddered.

"Is anybody injured?" Smith and Tsang's armor looked like it had been chewed by some mythical beast. Everyone had blunt trauma injuries where bullets had hit soft armor instead of hard plates, but no holes. Nobody's vitals were redlining or dropping off. Everyone was bruised but alive, and though spent brass rattled on the floor like a guilty conscience, that was all that mattered. "Lopez, King, secure that far doorway! Archer, spike that door open and cover our rear! Ortega, scan the dropship! Richardson, Thompson, Smith, Walt, prepare to board and sweep that craft!"

Without being told, Tsang and Ansef ran to the broken circle of bodies with their aid kits. Long, Ansef's pair, walked ahead of them with his rifle ready, waiting for one of the injured to do something stupid. I moved up next to him, and we let our eyes frisk the bodies for movement. Injured or dead, there were an awful lot of hands on weapons. Ansef found a live one and kicked his weapon away. Only then did she kneel down and get to work, popping his helmet and exposing his pale, European face. Long gave the order to be still simply by pointing his rifle between the unbondable's eyes.

Archer's cynical whine crackled over the comm. "What are you doing? We might need those medical supplies."

I felt hot blood fill my face. "You know the Laws of War, Sniper."

"But they're unbondable, Captain! We could shoot them in cold blood live on a newsfeed and nobody could—"

I felt something make a fist inside my chest. It scooped up words out of the darkest part of my soul and tossed them out of my mouth. "Archer, shut your *fragging pipe-hole* before I have Ansef wire it shut."

The sniper looked like I had slapped him, and I'm not surprised. I didn't bother to put it over a private channel and if you think a *'pipe'* refers to something made of a corn cob, then you've never heard a mercenary curse. He was correct on one hand; these were unbondable and had no legal rights whatsoever. He was wrong on the other. I may have to fight and kill them, but I did not have to sink to their level. Four enemy soldiers were alive, but none of them resisted as we disarmed them and dragged them away to be tended. Funny how a few bullet holes will take the fight out of somebody.

Meanwhile, Ortega had found one life sign on the dropship. It was our target, unconscious but stable, behind the bars of a miniature brig. This was the last bit of bright news we were going to get in that landing bay. The bad news was that the brig was locked and we didn't have the code key. The really bad news was that the bars were dense and strong, and would take at least fifteen minutes to cut each end of each bar with a vibroknife. Even worse, alarm klaxons began to sound throughout the ship as somebody finally noticed that we were here. I had Thompson shoot out the security cameras as I walked through the dropship, where I got hit with the worst news of all: there were enough disturbed jumpseats to fit thirty-odd soldiers. Fourteen bodies were on the floor, four of them breathing, and no bodies in the back of the landing craft to account for ground casualties. That left way too many unaccounted for.

At least our target was alive, but when the high-pitched screech of the vibroknife biting into the first bar failed to rouse her, I knew she had to be drugged in some capacity or another. It was great to have a hostage that wasn't panicking, but now she was dead weight to a team that was already loaded down. I wandered back out to the open bay, considering my options. Ortega tapped on the wall mounted computer station, but it became obvious that the entire area had been locked down from the bridge. We couldn't just escape on the dropship, which would normally be my first choice. We had to get to the bridge and...

I took a moment to reconfigure the bots so they would refuel the dropship. I looked down and found I was standing over our last kill of the frighteningly short battle. It had been a masterful shot; it had penetrated instead of skipping off only because it had come in perfectly flat to the front of the armored glass. My eyes found Thompson checking the team to make sure everyone was uninjured, had topped off their ammunition, and was doing their jobs. If she was anything like me, it would hit her later. I'd have to remember that.

For now, the alarms had been sounded, and our lives were ticking away with every sweep of the second hand. "Thompson! You're in charge of Team Two. Take Smith, King, and Tsang, and secure this area. Get our target out of her cage and keep the enemy from destroying this dropship; it's our ticket home. Everyone else will form up on me. We will be Team One, and we must get to the bridge to release the locks on this craft."

Archer looked left and right as everyone began to form up in their groups. He shook his head as if he were the only man in the universe left with a gram of common sense. "Uh, Captain? How exactly will we find the bridge?"

I was going to have to have a long, involved talk with Archer very soon. Questioning me in a briefing room was fine. Doing it in combat was going to get someone killed. "Weren't you paying attention? We find another *fragging* elevator. Now MOVE."

The team formed up, and we went back up the emergency access stairs. I took a second to glance at the thoroughly shattered evacuation placard, long enough to determine that the upper deck we had started on did not contain the bridge. There were seven decks, so I guessed that the third floor was the best place to look for command and control. To our amazement, when Ortega held up his palm computer and mimicked the EDC-87, the door stood aside like a loyal soldier. Then I remembered that this was a civilian craft. When it went to 'lockdown' it was to avoid panic, riot, or loss of life due to any given emergency. And in an emergency, you'd want your repair robots to be able to move, wouldn't you? This was much more like what mercenaries call 'restricted access', and really wasn't meant to turn the ship into a series of hardened pillboxes and killing fields the way we were used to. It would take extra measures from the bridge to contain us more thoroughly. That would take time. The faster we moved, the further we'd get.

I made a finger gesture that looked obscene, but meant nothing more than *'Load Armor-Piercing Ammunition.'* We loaded in turns. Half the team cleared their blue-marked magazines and grabbed red-tagged ones from their bandoliers, then the other half followed suit. Our target was safe in a controlled location; there was nothing to fear from over-penetration except lessening the property value. I learned that lesson young... worry about salvage after you survive. Spend too much time worrying about breaking the other guy's stuff, and he'll kill you with it, sure as hell.

We had made it out of the stairwell and found the placard. No bridge on this level, but I was taken aback by what I saw. There were dozens of overlarge rooms, each one clearly marked on the map: Genetics Lab A, Genetics Lab B, Computer Lab A... The ship was simply stuffed with meeting rooms, lecture halls, and science stations. This wasn't just a civilian transport; it was a science boat. Once again, I had that distorted reality feeling of someone who is doing a full on, heavily armed dynamic entry on a store full of wide-eyed children holding fluffy, stuffed animals. Hermetic seals on the doors and large signs confirmed the evacuation placard.

I ordered the team up one floor. We flashed our code and entered the fourth deck. The placard here showed the bridge as well as more genetics labs, cryogenic freezing facilities, science stations, and computer station after computer station. If the computer rooms were even moderately modern and filled as shown, then there was enough computer equipment on this bird to run a dozen research stations. It just didn't make any sense.

I pressed the team onward, wondering how long our codes would be good for. The answer was immediate. Ortega signaled, *Enemy Seen.* Then immediately followed with, *Jamming In Place, Strength is High.*

The Key to Damocles

The entire team hunkered down over their weapons as I typed a text message and burst it to Thompson to warn her of our situation. The tiny packet of information had a better chance of finding a hole in the static that blanketed us. She replied with a burst of her own, obviously corrupted by the electronic interference: Copy. Pinn-d Dpwn by enemy fi-e. EstIM-te eijht, 08, ene-y -oldlers. Holding S-Ation.

They were under fire.

As close as my team was, my comm reached them with minimal fuzz. "*Angels*, get me to that *frayyiny* bridge, now."

The next door opened, and plasma streams poured by us like horizontal drops of lava. Nobody had to be told to return fire. They didn't even need to be told how. Ortega slipped to the side and reached for his weapon. Richardson stepped into the hole he had made and began laying about with his squad support weapon like it was a fire hose. His armor blossomed with steam and fire as he became everybody's favorite target. Bullets screeched like a flock of wounded birds as they punched through steel barriers or glanced off walls and floors. They found bodies along each wall and reached in to smack the life out of anyone they touched. Corpses and pieces of corpses flew back under the constant impacts, but lines of plasma were hurled back like spears, blurring the lines of his armor and dulling the sharp edges. Then the doors slammed shut in front of us and drowned us in silence.

Three precious seconds ticked by, hopping on our nerves as smoke slipped from the barrel of Richardson's squad support weapon. I gave orders for everyone to move from in front of the door. That's when Richardson toppled over backwards and stopped moving.

CHAPTER 19: BREAKING POINT

I know what happened. There are logged communications, sensor readings, orbital satellite feeds, and even camera feeds from each soldier and news crew. I know what happened; I just didn't want to believe it. I wanted to deny it for as long as possible. Days later, I'd visit the site, and I'd see the bodies. Only then was I sure that the data didn't lie. In many ways, we are still animals, and we need to touch it and see it before we accept what made our friend more than just meat is gone.

Fifty *Angel/Apostles* used their sensor-men to verify that no lingering snipers were left behind, and then called the all clear. People poured out of their bunkers and into the streets. Faced with the devastation and loss of human life, some celebrated, some were wracked with guilt, most were just happy to be alive. The battle had been hard fought, and over two dozen people had died as a result. They had killed over ninety enemy soldiers, a feat for those outnumbered five to one, but even that takes its toll on those who haven't been trained into it as a professional soldier. It takes a toll on us too, but at least we learn to process it later.

The unbondable were in full retreat. They knew their ride off planet had abandoned them. They were moving through the city, shattering into small units and cowering inside tenements. At this point, the people of West Lot were willing to just let them go.

Tony made an impassioned speech, thanking *The Angel's Apostles*, *The Radiation Angels*, and the brave men and women who had stood up to defend the civilians hiding inside. The media covered it quietly, and then began their barrage of questions.

This was it; this was the only story on planet Persephone, and every news service was covering it. They even had camera drones flitting over New California, and they showed the fleeing unbondable as they carved a swathe of death to nowhere. They would surely be considered spies on a planet that yearned for no less than to see them dead. Some of them were heading for the spaceport. Quite a few were heading back to their command center to gather what supplies they could. Some of them were just looking for a spider-hole to jump in and pull the entrance closed afterwards. Regardless, they were on edge and burning from a resounding loss, so everything they met died. They gunned down gangs that had decided fighting for the police might erase a lifetime of random violence. They shot groups of men who patrolled their neighborhoods against looters. They shot reporters who came out to ambush them with questions. In one case, a group of startled unbondable opened fire on a pregnant woman and her two children as they came out of an abandoned store, arms full of canned goods.

A flying camera drone watched it all though telescopic cameras from three hundred meters up, and then broadcasted the feed to its masters. In seconds, the unedited footage went out over every newsfeed the company owned. Only seconds after that, they had reaped a king's ransom from the other stations to share the visual data. Five minutes after that, they showed it to Tony Lomen and asked if he had any plans to stop the massacre happening on his streets.

Bastards.

God damned bastards.

For weeks they had crucified him for daring to give people the freedom and tools they needed to defend themselves against an unseen enemy of far greater strength and resources. They had cast him as the villain, sat back as he and his people were dropped into a meat grinder, and then showed him something as awful as the dying body of two children and their young, pregnant mother. Then they asked with cocked eyebrows if he really was a hero, cameras zeroing in on his face to catch any possible gaffe.

Frag politics, *frag* public opinion, and *frag* the media. Tony had already done the impossible, and he owed nothing to anybody. But...

If you watch the recording, you can see the woman's pain slam into him, and you can see the tortured rage thrum through his arms. You can see him looking at the battle-weary police officers, the tired mercenaries, and the holes in their armor. You can see the moment where the woman performs her last act, reaching out a dying hand to touch the head of an already dead child, the other cradling her now empty belly.

You can see it reflected in his eyes. That's where the fire starts, a furnace of fury so bright it would blind satellites.

Wrinkles tightened into angry caverns filled with the winds of rage. Written across his face in letters twenty meters tall are the words: YOU WILL BE AVENGED!

He marched to the podium like a Titan of Righteous Fury. His little fireplug torso grew with each breath until he towered over the police station behind him. He opened his mouth, and his voice reverberated inside the soul of every listener. "As Acting Station Chief of West Lot Station, I am declaring a state of emergency. All West Lot police officers are being recalled to duty. I don't care where you've been the last few months. All of you. Get here. Now.

"In addition, I am putting out a call for aid and comfort from any armed militia, hospital, police organization, or mercenary company. We can't pay you, but Lord knows we need the help. Those undocumented, unbondable mercenaries that surrender will be taken into custody and be given a fair trial. The rest of the jackals will be cleared out with fire and steel. All militia members, report to your mercenary liaisons. We aren't done, yet!"

News agencies went berserk with questions that Lomen simply ignored. They began to bathe him in the standard baste of lies and innuendo, but they had overlooked a crucial point. They were not the only ones with a voice, not anymore. There were pirate stations in the audience as well. They saw with other eyes, and their faulty, finicky new sites were gaining momentum.

They had new stories of what had really happened in the days preceding The Battle of West Lot. They had tales that came from the mouths of those who had been there, and they rang true. Every conflict with the official reports from established media chipped away at mainstream credibility. More and more viewers turned away from the big stations to listen to their fellow citizens, and the information they found. Gradually, people ignored the typos, the low-resolution pictures, and amateur presentation. They had found Truth. Truth can be burned, it can be shot, it can be crushed, dismissed, or suppressed, but it cannot ever be completely destroyed. In the end, Truth is harder than diamond, more precious than gold, and it will always be sought out and rediscovered. Truth cannot be killed.

That was the first time anyone referred to Tony as a hero. It would not be the last.

The Key to Damocles

Tony gathered his leaders together with the liaison of the *Apostles*, Captain Kei O'Leary. She had been secreted in West Lot for hours, coordinating the response of her masquerading mercenaries in other buildings. Deception complete, she was free to come to the fore. They discussed their options, and talked about tactics. The O'Leary I knew would have jumped in with both feet just for the chance to hear the crackle of gunfire, but now she was in command. She had men beneath her that depended upon her for their survival, and while she had been hired by me to support and advise the police and militia of West Lot, technically her job was over. Now, she should have sat back, waited for me to return and get paid. But wrong had been done, wrong was still happening. She was measuring herself against a man she felt was still her commander, and she knew exactly what that fool would do. Everyone present then looked to the silver titan sitting with them, Master Sergeant Logan. He nodded sagely and added his voice in the assent. He had served with that fool, too. O'Leary called for the rest of the *Apostles* and ordered her soldiers to assemble for combat.

The combined forces of the defenders of West Lot left a skeleton crew of mercenaries, all of the walking wounded, and three of the oldest police officers. The rest broke into teams with areas of responsibility and got five weeks of intense urban combat instruction distilled into five minutes. Police fliers were manned and rocketed out of the station, patrolling the skies, acting both as close air support and as spotters for the ground troops.

Then the survivors of West Lot began a doomed march to root out the unbondable from New California.

CHAPTER 20: TWENTY METERS AT A TIME

Rocketing away from Planet Persephone,
Unknown Spacecraft, 04:10, 11/13/2662

As this happened, Ansef was attaching an autodoc to the hookups at the collar of Richardson's armor. The entire front side of his gear had been heavily scarred by incoming plasma fire. The plates were thick, and could turn aside dozens of direct hits, but the sheer volume of incoming fire had melted the hard armor and simply vaporized the soft ballistic cloth underneath. Blackened flesh poked through in at least five places, shallow holes the size of my fist in his muscled frame. Ansef didn't have to shake her head to let me know his condition was dire. Autodocs were a miracle of modern medicine, a tiny computer and scanner hooked up to dozens of doses of lifesaving drugs. These gray boxes had rescued millions from death on the field of battle, but it couldn't save them all.

I began organizing what to do next in my head. "EWO, bounce an active wave off of that door and find the hydraulic system inside for demolition. Is anyone else rated on Richardson's weapon?"

Nobody answered, though Archer looked like he had been slapped. "We're not going to just leave him here?"

I barely grabbed a hold of my temper by my fingertips. "Richardson is a one hundred and fifty kilo man. He's carrying twenty kilos worth of gear and he's wearing one-hundred-thirty kilos worth of armor. Just who do you think is going to be able to carry him in battle without tearing open the cauterized layer of carbon on his wounds and causing him bleed to death?"

Archer said nothing. I got up in his face, the chest plates of our armor scraping. "Who?"

Archer tried to back up, but I followed him, slamming him into the wall. My voice redlined the microphone, creating a squeal of feedback. "WHO?!"

Archer very carefully let his weapon drop on its sling and raised his hands in surrender, but I shoved forward again and screamed even louder, voice steaming with bile.

The Key to Damocles

"That's RIGHT, so until you grow a set of BALLS and lead your own *FRAGGING* team you can keep your *GRITLICKING* tongue to YOURSELF. You've done nothing but BITCH and *CRACK* my ASS since we got on this ship, and if you don't STOP, I'm going to SHOOT YOU MYSELF and LEAVE YOU HERE." Archer looked left and right, and saw nothing but tinted black helmets and body language that said he was truly on his own. "DO YOU GET ME, SOLDIER?"

He nodded slowly. I used a forearm to bounce his helmeted head off of the wall behind him. "I SAID, DO YOU GET ME?"

Archer was shaking, trembling as instincts fought with pride inside his crusty little head. He had to take a few breaths before he was able to say, "I get you, sir."

"DAMN RIGHT!" And I shoved away from him and turned back to the team. I handed my rifle and ammo pouches off to Ansef and picked up Richardson's oversized weapon. I couldn't clear a jam quickly, or aim it as efficiently as Richardson, but I could point it and pull the trigger. Lopez grabbed the boxes of 10mm/long disintegrating link ETC ammunition for the machinegun and began hanging them on my web gear. Ortega had marked the place for the demolition charges in grease pencil. Charges had been set. "Richardson's best chance is here. We draw their fire, find the bridge, and shut this entire operation down. If we do it fast, Richardson lives. We do it slow, we all die. Move back. Archer, grab Richardson"

Everyone shuffled back from the door. Archer pulled Richardson's body as slowly as you might imagine. Finally, he got out of the blast radius, and I pointed to Ortega. He signaled *Jamming Still Active*. Next was Walt. His response was *Explosives Set and Ready*. I held up one thumb.

The *Angels* rocked on their heels as the small, focused packets of explosive went off, sending the blast burrowing into the wall and crushing the mechanisms keeping the doors closed. I flicked my hands, sending Archer and Lopez up to pry the doors open by brute force. They creaked, spewed hydraulic fluid, and finally slid back on their tracks, revealing the carnage beyond.

The enemy may have taken down Richardson, but he had reached out and smacked the life out of five of them. They had been hiding in doorways, shooting over makeshift barricades, or leaning out from around corners, but his armor piercing

250

ammunition had punched through their cover like tissue paper. A quick glance and a check of vitals confirmed five dead, and judging by the blood trails, there were two more wounded out there somewhere. I signaled for *Move Out.*

We traversed the hallway, leery of the medical-style, hermetic airlock doors we passed. The signs of battle were widespread, and even at the end of the hall we found holes in the floor from Richardson's assault. Lights had been blown, door alarms whined that they no longer had any kind of seal, and I wondered if any delicate equipment beyond had been destroyed. We reached the next bulkhead door, and the *Angels* repeated the procedure of placing explosives and prying the doors open. The entire team stacked up to focus an overwhelming amount of fire through the gap as soon as it appeared. Lopez and Archer grunted and heaved; more oil squirted from ruptured engines and the panels parted with the moan of a dying sentry.

The next hall was well lit and untouched. I signaled the team forward and we passed more labs and computer rooms. Again, we reached the bulkhead without incident, planted our charges, and blew the door. I was worried, because we had enough explosives for only two more doors before we had to think of some other way to get past them, but the next hallway was clean and we moved on.

Overall, I would have preferred another ambush.

The team was relaxing, getting used to the environment and being inured to the constant threat. It was a dangerous thing. Like a man taken and dumped in a freezing stream, it was cold, but not immediately life threatening. Take the same man and put him in a hot shower long enough to begin to enjoy it, then dump him in the same stream. The shock could stop his heart.

I had to frame this just the right way because just saying 'stay alert' was the kind of thing idiots did when there was absolutely nothing to be alert of, or about. It was much better to say be alert of something, rather than give a blanket order. I was composing the admonition when the hermetic airlock to my right, Genetics lab A3.2.17, hissed and cycled.

"*CONTACT!*" The massive machinegun in my hands came up like a staff, and I lunged against Archer and Lopez, tackling them both forward and down. "MOVE! MOVE! MO—"

The bomb hidden inside the airlock antechamber exploded.

The Key to Damocles

There are generally considered to be two classifications of explosives: fast and slow. Fast explosives, like those we used to kill the door locks, were usually inside of some kind of device. They were meant to create a focused blast that reached out with the force of God's middle finger to destroy things in a localized area.

Then there were slow explosives. These burn 'slower' only in comparison to fast explosives and are usually contained in an object they are supposed to destroy. This turns the object, or casing, into hundreds of flying shards which are meant to kill.

Both kinds create a shockwave. Fast explosives focus it, and slow explosives use it to sling crap everywhere. Using small amounts of fast explosive on a spaceship isn't much of a problem. Little bang, little damage, no problem. The problem lays with using large, slow explosive devices a spaceship; they create a big shockwave of high-speed air that rushes away from the point of detonation. This concussive force has to go somewhere, and very often the sealed compartments of a spacecraft do not have enough space to absorb the explosion. That's why people don't use them on spacecraft.

That's why people *usually* don't use them on spacecraft.

The bomb inside the airlock exploded. The device itself was blown into a million bits. The hard casing cracked and became shrapnel moving at several hundred meters per second. Faster than the eye can follow, a globe of white expanded out past the fragments, slamming into every surface of the airlock. The interior walls bulged, the interior door was bent open like the lid of a tin can, the ceiling shattered and the floor dented. Every surface hit not only absorbed some of the force, but redirected it back. That meant a two-front wave came out of the half open door, the first much stronger than the second. But both wrecked havoc.

Unable to clear line of sight with the bomb, the first wave knocked Long off of her feet and got her moving. The second slammed her into the wall. Fragments came after and peppered her body. She fell and did not move.

Walt, Ansef, and Ortega were pushed over backwards and slammed into the deck. The shockwave slid along my legs, up my body, and pushed me so hard into the two underneath me that I thought we might be compacted into one person. Bits of flying metal burrowed into my boots like creatures from a horror movie, looking for any bit of flesh. My HUD cracked and began sprouting random bursts of static. Lights for twelve meters in each direction blew in showers of sparks, excited gas glowing in midair for a moment before the charge was lost and we were cloaked in shadow. Emergency lights popped on and computer screens warned that this deck was no longer sealed, with breaches between this and the one above as well as below.

That's when the bulkhead door at the far end cycled open, and a half dozen men opened fire.

They were stacked for maximum firepower, three men kneeling in front of three men standing. White streaks of plasma seared down the hallway toward our prone forms, clawing up sections of wall and decking and bursting into clouds of vaporized metallo-plastic compounds when they hit us. Once again, there we were, caught in the open without much in the way of cover, but nowhere to retreat and nowhere to run.

Ortega pushed off of the floor and emptied a magazine. Ansef rolled into the damaged airlock and began firing from cover. Walt bounced to his feet and grabbed Long, intent on dragging her under cover. She began to squirm and move, but her legs were both bent at horrible angles. He passed in front of Ortega, fouling his line of fire as more hot daggers of superheated gas nibbled at us like rats. An unlucky shot caught Walt in a thin spot of armor at the knee, and topped him over onto Ortega.

The fire intensified and became less accurate, a sure sign that these people thought they had us in the meat grinder. The bad part was they were right. I pushed off Archer and Lopez, bruises screaming even as they were born on my flesh, kicked into a clumsy forward roll to clear their bodies, got to my knees and slung up Richardson's machine gun. The weapon had been waiting, but now that it felt a hand on its grip, it loaded up all its software and came online. The pressure of my shoulder on the butt stock started the gyroscopic unit in the receiver, and set it to spinning at unbelievable speeds. Through flashes of static, I could barely make out the lit reticule of the simple sights. I muscled it unsteadily onto the group of targets and depressed the trigger.

Steel-cored lead propelled by hate and fear burned the air between my targets and me. The muzzle wanted desperately to kick off target, but it was tamed by the gyroscope spinning in its sealed, magnetic chamber. It became as the waves of the ocean, slowly climbing off target and gently washing downward back across them. All the while it thundered like a spate of psychotic lightning, twenty-five rounds leaving the firing chamber every second. Two of my enemies fell, chewed into airborne particles of meat by high velocity bullets. Ortega regained his footing behind me and opened fire, but he screamed and it stopped. Ansef ducked behind cover to reload, and all beams converged in upon me. All I could think of was Richardson falling like an axed tree.

Then, my weapon went silent.

All the while, as the world slowed down and my mouth went dry and bitter, my mind nattered to itself. *This is it, Rook. You're a dead man. This is as far as you make it.* Suddenly I was tired, and I just wanted to lay down for an eternity or two.

And another voice, the voice of my Captain, Captain Arthur, replied. If you are going to die, you stupid son of a bitch, then at least go out proudly. Go out on your feet, Soldier!

Struggling against the weight of my equipment, fighting the gyroscope inside my weapon, I stood. His voice kicked me again. *That weapon isn't going to do you much good, empty, Soldier!*

I took the machine gun off my shoulder and reached for one of the big, clunky boxes of ammunition as my thumb caressed the stud and ejected its empty counterpart. I was reminded of the unbondable's body in the shuttle bay, a nice, clean hole in his helmet. I slammed the full magazine home. The box and gun talked for half a second and the motor fed the first round. The gun opened its own chamber and slurped the chain link into its mouth like a line of pasta. I brought it back up to fire, unsure if I'd hit anything at all.

If you can't hit the *fraggers* then get closer, Rook!

My feet began to move. Slowly at first, grinding glass and bits of broken plastic beneath armored soles. I leaned forward, aching for speed, for distance. Like running in a dream, it felt like I had to push against some invisible wall to make headway, scrabbling for purchase. Beams sizzled desperately close and I felt my bladder let go.

I fired.

Chained ammunition slid through the machinegun effortlessly, launching out with deadly intent. Two men spurted blood and screamed, clutching at wounds that opened on them like the effects of an ancient curse. Of the pair that was left, the standing one fired his weapon blindly in one hand, his attention on his belt as he scrambled for a grenade. His kneeling partner caught a glancing bullet in the helmet, and he stood up on reflex from the shock, putting him in line with his partner's fire. He caught a stream of plasma between the shoulder blades and pitched forward, burning. The grenadier saw this and dropped the bomb at his feet before bolting out of sight. I took two more steps. The door at the end of the hall tried to close, only to jam on the helmet of the last dead unbondable. The grenade went off with a muffled crump, and then all went silent.

I dropped to my knees and just hurt for a minute.

I felt more than heard muted motion behind me. What I saw did not fill me with hope. Lopez and Archer were fine, though their armor had taken more than just a casual beating. Ansef was mostly untouched, but she was tending Walt's nearly severed knee. Long still writhed on the ground, one arm and both legs broken beyond immediate repair. Ortega had taken a plasma packet to his trigger hand and lost three fingers along with the magazine and grip of his weapon.

Then I realized that I couldn't hear a thing. Well, that's not true; I could hear fuzzy conversations and strange approximations of sounds. The tone was off, with odd reverberations, and a ringing that started and only got worse. My helmet's seal had been cracked, and I had absorbed some of the punishing rapport of the weaponry around me.

I shook my head to clear it, something which has never worked in the history of mankind, and managed to finally kill my HUD completely. I had to bring all of my discipline to bear just to focus for a few minutes. I sent Lopez and Archer to the pile of dead at the end of the corridor. There they pried open the doors and Archer took up guard. Lopez came back and Ansef tried to get him to help her, but I waved him toward the rear to guard our back-path and took his place as her aid.

It was very bad. Every second, my hearing improved slightly, but it became clear that we were well and truly screwed. Long did, indeed, have many broken bones. None were obviously life threatening, but she was out. Ortega was missing most of a hand and could go on with painkillers, but he'd be firing with his off-hand. Walt's knee had been turned into superheated steam, and it was only a miracle that he hadn't already died of an embolism of vaporized blood to the heart. My comm unit was down. Hell, every helmet-mounted computer device I had was down, but Ortega relayed an update from Thompson saying they had killed six unbondable, no friendly casualties, but two targets had retreated and escaped. Just that took ten minutes, since each message had to be repeated over and over to catch the whole thing through the storm of jamming being pounded into us.

This was a commander's greatest fear: moving slowly, getting torn to bits, dying by degrees. A whole command could come apart during a battle of attrition as soldiers looked around and watched themselves die twenty meters at a time with no clear sign of success.

I nodded as Ortega relayed Thompson's report and my orders back, all through clenched teeth. It was probably for the good, since I was sitting on Walt's chest and clamping my hands around his leg to immobilize it while Ansef worked. We got him stable, and she went to Long while she trusted me to administer a pre-measured amount of anesthetic to Ortega. All the while, he stared at me with sad, brown eyes. The painkillers began to take effect as I sprayed a liquid bandage onto his stumps. It dampened his discomfort, allowing him to ask, "They're going to get away with it, aren't they, Captain?"

I just barely caught what he was saying over the sound of ringing in my ears. I mulled it for a moment, then I unlocked and lifted the visor on my helmet so that he could hear my reply, which was so vile, it probably caused any Bible within earshot to spontaneously combust. It gave everyone heart to know the boss was still committed, and gave me a few seconds to come up with a real answer. "We'll take the three of you back to Richardson, and then we'll go blow open the bridge."

Ortega winced. "You're shouting, Captain. Hearing trouble?" I nodded. Without a second's pause he took off his helmet and pressed it to me. I tried to wave him off, but he pushed it to me with his good hand. "Captain, I know what's coming."

I stared at the missing fingers of his right hand and nodded.

"Come on. Take it."

I pulled it from his grasp and tried to put it on my head.

There's a little vanity that I never admitted to anyone. Because of my long, dreadlocked hair, I have to get helmets generously cut so that they'll fit the extra bulk. This one was meant to fit Ortega's buzz cut. There was only one thing to be done.

Slowly, almost with reverence, I pulled my combat knife from its boot sheath and grabbed a hold of my tightly bundled hair. Ansef watched with wide eyes as I severed the whole thing with one cut. I put the helmet on and linked it into my forearm computer. This one didn't have near the computing power or sensor systems of my C^2 helmet, but it would make blowing my brains out a lot harder. I programmed in my own personal communication frequencies and got acclimated to the smell of Ortega's sweat and halitosis.

The HUD came to life, and I adjusted the internal speakers to offset the ringing in my ears. Diagnostic software warned me that this volume could cause hearing loss, but given the situation, I ignored it. My mind was finally becoming able to crawl out of the muck and run at a normal pace. If only the others were so lucky. Ansef had finished with Long, but she was completely immobilized by spray-on casts and asleep from the intense cocktail of drugs. Walt would also have to be carried because, even with a cast, any weight on his leg would cause the hole where his knee used to be to collapse.

Ansef shook her head and dialed into a private frequency with me. "Captain, Richardson's probably pretty shocky, Walt and Long are little better. If we move them too roughly, they may not make it."

Then I got the call. It was Sichak, the transmission powered up so far everyone on this side of the solar system saw it scream by. "Captain! Your vessel is charging its hull. I repeat, your ship is charging its hull. You are preparing to enter Slipspace."

That was crazy. We hadn't been in the air an hour, and there was no way we had cleared Persephone's impressive gravity well. Trying to jump now would be a lot like suicide, but messier. There was no way to predict where the ship would pop out of Slipspace, or if it would mate with a rogue planet or star on the way there. Coming within a few million light years of a black hole would be even worse. It was the act of the insane...or desperate. I looked around, and from the body language of the group, I guessed they had all heard it, too.

A second later, Thompson came on, clear as a bell. "Captain? We found the encryption chip in one of the enemy helmets. I'm sending you the code to bypass the jamming."

And like that we bought a few seconds of peace and quiet, the code telling our systems when to talk in the microsecond pauses in the static. I had to do this fast. "Lieutenant Thompson, leave one soldier to hold down the fort and get up here. You have five minutes to recover Richardson, Ortega, Long, Ansef, and Walt. Our path won't be hard to follow. Begin moving now." Ansef looked as if she'd been slapped. I pointed at her. "That's right. You go and make sure Richardson and Long make it. Lopez, Archer, and I are going ahead to take the bridge and release the shuttle. Sichak, load all torpedo tubes with the fastest things we've got and begin giving chase at maximum speed. Prepare to fire the moment we are clear."

My orders were acknowledged all around. I brought up Lopez from the rear and called back Archer from ahead. He came, and brought two satchel charges and eight grenades scavenged from the enemy dead. Despite having enough goodies for a right pretty Christmas bash, he looked like I had just urinated on his feet. Can't say I blame him. I was betting that there were only a handful of unbondable left, and I knew that the bridge was up ahead. Between that theory and fact was a gulf of unknowns filled with jagged rocks. I stopped for a moment and readjusted the firing straps on my gun. While I did that, I took a long, hard look at Archer. "Well, Sniper, if you are going to quit on me, now is the time."

He chewed that over for perhaps three seconds. "No, sir. I can't say I like you very much. And I can't say I'd shed a tear if you were *mudraked* by a pack of rabid dogs on erectile stimulant medication, but you are my captain. I can say I've never quit on one yet."

I decided to take him at his word. I spared a second for Lopez, who gave me a thumbs up. "Ready, Captain."

I nodded. "Alright, according to the evacuation sign, the bridge is up around the next dogleg to the right or the left. You two go right, I'll go left. The area in the center should be Security.

That's where any remaining soldiers will be to hold us off. If this ship is anything like *Deadly Heaven*, it's going to take fifteen— now thirteen minutes to enter Slipspace, so that's our deadline. No matter what happens, we have to take the bridge, free up the shuttle, and get back there for launch."

Archer nodded and made a 'get on with it' motion. "And how do we do that?"

I squashed the urge to *crack* his genitals with the butt of my machinegun and instead pointed to the few remaining demolition charges on the ground. "I have a plan."

And then someone noticed or guessed we had cleared the jamming and switched the algorithm, so I had explain it face to face.

CHAPTER 21: ONE MUST LEAD, ALL OTHERS FOLLOW

Logan's internal recorder tells the whole tale. It is brutal, honest, and unmerciful. The rest can be put together from radio logs, satellite images, helmet cams, and stolen newsfeeds live from the scene. I wouldn't have bothered if it wasn't so important to me to know how it ended. I would assemble it days later to act as a cleansing agent to my soul.

On the ground, hundreds of thousands of kilometers behind us, another game of cat and mouse was playing out with Darwinian efficiency. Teams of mercenaries, police, and civilians were spreading out across New California. They were hunting dangerous game, and they thought they were prepared. Unfortunately, tempers were running high, and they hadn't thought things through.

Leaving the safety of West Lot was the worst thing they could have done, but the only guy who had the experience to tell them that was hurdling away on a ship driven by a pillar of nuclear fire. They were prepared, but no more prepared than their prey. Their enemy was more experienced at urban combat and still outnumbered them three to one. While the unbondable had lost their air cover, *Deadly Heaven* was chasing me instead of guarding them. The natives definitely knew the terrain better, but of course the off-world mercenaries were in charge. The best mercenaries listened to the militia under their control; others dismissed their input. In short, they were heading face-first into a bear-trap with big, sharp teeth and a thousand-kilogram tension spring.

Within fifteen minutes, there were fifty more dead enemy mercenaries. Despite strict and explicit orders from Lomen, the hunting parties were opening fire with the flimsiest pretenses. It was understandable; the mercs and militia had just spent the better part of the night being shot at, and they thought they were aching for payback. What they were really doing was killing the doubts and fears inside themselves by giving it to their enemy. It never worked, but they didn't know that, so they didn't arrest and contain. They shot to kill. It was more understandable for the mercs; we are not trained to do police work. Add in the facts that the mercs don't like to be shot at more than anyone else, plus they knew the unbondable had no rights under the Laws of War, gives you a recipe for a no-bag-limit mentality and a bloodbath. Because none of the unbondable expected to be taken alive anyway, they fought to the last bullet and the last man. In those fifteen minutes, two dozen whole teams of militia and police were wiped out.

O'Leary was out in the field with a double-sized squad. She had every reason to be confident; she had four mercenaries, ten policemen, ten militia, and Logan with her. She also had the liftoff site of the enemy dropship from Logan's onboard computer. She was making the same assumption I had… the liftoff site was where the home base for the unbondable had been set up. That's where she was going aboard a commandeered civilian cargo flier, but about fifty of the enemy had the same idea.

They were set up in an old, rundown school. It was a good choice with thick walls and plenty of space, blocked off and locked up months ago as one of the first casualties of the anti-tax movement. In a poor neighborhood like this one, with the lights shot out and fear of unpatrolled, riot-strewn streets, any movement at the school that was seen would be quickly ignored as somebody else's problem.

O'Leary ordered the landing a kilometer out, since the unarmored civilian flier would doubtlessly be destroyed at the first sign of incoming fire. The walk was a short one; she was using experienced point men, and was advancing her force in stages. They came under fire the moment they came within line of sight, and she expertly set up her teams in buildings across the street. A few mercenaries and Logan took back streets to circle around to the west side of the school while the stationary teams began harassing the defenders with fire. Logan and his group reached the rear untouched. They broke down the back door to an abandoned tenement and made their way through to the fourth floor set of apartments. Whether the enemy had a working sensor system and had spotted Logan's thermal bloom, or an old-fashioned pair of eyes had spotted them setting up at a window, Logan's team began taking fire almost immediately. The over-engineered, government-built tenement, with thick walls and floors that even supported a templar model cyborg, provided adequate cover but little in the way of good firing positions. O'Leary conferred with Logan, and neither of them could see an easy way forward. O'Leary immediately got on her comm and called for serious backup. That's where everything began coming apart.

The quantum radio log between Captain O'Leary and General Reeves was not hard to get, and they tell how everything began to collapse. O'Leary typed in the frequency and decryption code. "*Artificial Angel*, Actual to *Apostle*, Actual. Come in."

Reeves must have been near the radio room because he answered immediately. "*Apostle*, Actual here, I read you O'Leary."

"Reeves, I need you to play cavalry, here. We're pinned down."

"Pinned down? The newsfeeds have live shots of West Lot, and I don't see anything dangerous going on at all. Looks like your contract is up, in fact." His voice made it clear that he was moving cash numbers in mental columns.

"The contract is not over. I am no longer at West Lot. There are hundreds of unbondable roaming the city." I wasn't sure if she believed this next bit or not. "And they may circle around for a counterattack. I'm sending you my GPS coordinates. I have a mixed force of twenty-five. We are pinned down and require immediate fire support."

"Mixed force? Where are the rest of my men?"

"Our men, and they are supervising other teams. The opposition has scattered."

"Goddamn it, O'Leary!"

"Look, I'm in a jam. We're getting paid to do a job. I am the man on the ground. I say this is part of our job, so I have continued the mission. That's the *fragging* situation."

"And who authorized you to decide to continue the mission, Captain?"

"You may be General, but I ponied up half of the cash to start this team. It is as much mine as it is yours."

There was a long pause, full of grinding teeth and pulsing neck veins. This was no way to run a team, and no way for the charter members to treat one another. The cardinal rule of combat is that there must be one, one and only one, in charge. One must make the decisions; one must take the blame and the responsibility. Others help, manage details, run minutiae, but it all must begin and end with one person. If not, situations like this pop up like cobras in every field of grass. Reeves' reply just made things worse. "You're not *him*, O'Leary."

Her reply transmission was full of bile. "Well, that's true, but neither are you. He would have left a standing force at the Ortegas' and been here, chewing mud and dodging bullets with the rest of us. Now, are you going to come unjam me or am I going to have to get creative?"

Considering that when O'Leary got creative, it usually involved explosives, it was no wonder that Reeve's curse was imaginative, short, and involved impossible bodily positions.

O'Leary was unfazed. "Is that a 'yes'?"

Thirty minutes later, Reeves called out his presence and marched a squad of twenty more men onto the floor where Logan had his team. He deployed his men, came up behind the master sergeant and then dialed him on a private frequency. "This is *cracked*. Logan, I figured you to be a lot smarter than this."

Unmoved and immobile, the cyborg never turned his attention from the school bunker as he replied. "She had a legitimate concern, General Reeves. These men are now cut off from all backup. They are scared and desperate. They could do anything."

Reeves made a sound halfway between a huff and a grunt. "You've bought into *his* goddamned legend too, haven't you?"

"She was right about that, too. He would be here."

"You're full of it. The contract ended when West Lot was defended last night."

"The police would have responded to this on their own. They would have been massacred."

"So *fragging* what? Let them die; they're not *Apostles*, they're not *Angels*, they aren't even mercenaries!"

Logan left his position by the window and moved so fast it looked like he came chest to chest with the General without traversing the space in between. With a synthesized voice that seemed to come from the depths of earth he said, "General, whatever you may think, I was there last night. The police and militia fought an impossible battle with everything they had for three hours. They lost a lot of people they loved. When it appeared the city they had sworn to defend was in danger, they responded like soldiers even though the city had spit upon them for months. If that doesn't earn your respect, what does?"

Reeves' eyes narrowed, his voice hoarse and dangerous. "You're being insubordinate, Sergeant."

Logan slowly turned his back on Reeves, reminding the General that he didn't work for him; Logan worked for *him*.

Reeves cursed and cut the line to Logan. He chewed on his bile for a few minutes before getting back on the radio and sending out a short string of code words. Two missiles jumped over a line of buildings, arcing upwards like birds of prey before secondary engines kicked in and sent them screaming toward the roof of the far end of the school. They passed through the makeshift rolling door on the roof— still open from the dropship's liftoff— and found their way into the soft targets inside. The explosions rippled out within an instant of one another, tossing debris skyward, and sending red-hot shrapnel sailing through the interior walls of the north wing. It was a calculated move, meant to destroy any other craft they had powered down and waiting inside. It did kill three flyers and the ten men prepping them for launch, but it also ruptured twenty aeroline refueling tanks sitting nearby. Flame geysered out of the north wing like a demon's arterial spray. It blackened the sky and set the grass afire. Burning smoke hung in the air like bad blood, then it began to fall in liquid drops to pool and spark and eat. Within seconds, the whole north side of the building was a raging inferno.

Reeves voice was smug. "That's the way a general handles things. That's how *he* would have done it." Reeves then called his dropship again and had it climb to high position above the city, out of handheld missile range.

Soldiers in both prepared positions began sweeping the entrances in the middle and southern wing of the school, waiting for the unbondable to begin evacuating. Reticules skimmed past every opening. O'Leary gave her order. Anyone with a weapon was to be shot on sight. Anyone without a weapon would get fifty meters to put their hands up and drop to the ground.

The Key to Damocles

The Apostle's dropship, *The Bastard*, radioed in to the team, pinpointing lifesigns inside the building with their much more powerful sensor array. It appeared as if ten of the unbondable had been incinerated in the blast, but the rest were moving south through the structure, hoping to stave off death or surrender as long as possible.

The Apostles outside were content to wait, until one of the fresh arrivals broke the tense silence. "What the —?"

The General moved out into the hall towards the soldier. "What is it, Franklin?"

"I'm not sure, sir. I have movement by the third door in the southern section, but it doesn't look like an armored man. No weapon."

Immediately everyone on that side of the building looked at that door. There was, indeed a flash of movement. Then another. And then a woman broke free of the shadows and smoke, half running, half crawling out across the playground. A flurry of voices clogged the comm.

"I have a target!"

"She's not in uniform?"

"That's not a mercenary."

"Hold! Hold! Hold! Target is a civilian!"

Reeves' voice cut through the mess. "Weapons hold, confirm. Weapons hold!"

A chorus of confirmations came back.

Reeves rushed back to Logan's position and actually crawled to the window to take a look himself. "What is she doing?"

Reeve's medic in the next room piped up. "General, she looks like she's got several bruises, she hasn't had a bath in a few days, and I see some signs of malnutrition. Do you think the unbondable—?"

O'Leary was the one to reply, voice cold and deadly. "Yeah, that's exactly what happened."

The woman continued to run, and swerved between the playsets strewn across the grass like the rusted bones of a dead god. There was something on her face, beneath the terror and pain, something like hope.

A shot rang out, impossibly loud and obscene. The woman tumbled forward like a tossed rag doll. She came to a rest face

266

down in the grass and did not move. For about a minute, nothing happened, and nobody said a thing.

Franklin's eyes were best, again. "Movement!"

Another woman, better fed than the first, but no less abused, was pushed out the doorway.

Reeves cursed in a whisper. "Where are the unbondable, now?"

Logan looked over his shoulder. "They're at the windows, waiting for us to come out. I see fifteen, lots of small arms, but nothing that will reach us. I don't see the sniper, but he's using a gauss sniper rifle. It'll punch through any one here, including me."

"Then we can't go out there; it'd be suicide."

"They will keep killing civilians."

"Of course they will because they've done their research, and they think they're dealing with *him* out here. They figure he'll rush out there like an idiot and get himself killed."

"They will keep killing civilians."

Reeves ducked his head and rolled over to look up at the silver giant. "I'm sorry, Logan, but that's not my problem."

The chatter across the comm came to a screeching halt. If one listened closely, you could hear O'Leary muttering under her breath. For his part, Logan stared at the General with unblinking eyes. The cold, clinical glass dissected him, laid him bare, and somehow his blank face managed to show disgust at what was there.

"General, may I borrow some of your team's ammunition?"

Reeves shook his head a bit, taken completely off guard. "Uh, yeah Logan but—?"

The cyborg's only response was an order over the entire link. "COVERING FIRE!"

And then he completely obliterated the broken window with the casual sweep of his left arm. His massive hand gripped the upper sill, cracking the concrete as he levered himself out into open air like a man hopping a fence. Soldiers began to discharge their weapons at the enemy a split second before he hit the ground with the sound of two cars mating. The sidewalk cracked and buckled, pieces went flying outwards from the force of two tons of metal dropped twelve meters. Logan's composite frame squealed, screeched, but held. Before the debris from his landing managed to make it back to earth, the Master Sergeant had hefted his twenty-millimeter automatic cannon and rushed the enemy position alone.

O'Leary called out, "You heard the man! Let's give them something else to think about! Aim at the windows! Fire at will! Fire at will!"

Logan moved like an epileptic tsunami. Advanced metal muscles and neuron clusters fired at superhuman speeds, propelling him forward in jerks and hops over, around, and sometimes through obstacles. Left, right, forward and back, his course was more than simply erratic… it bordered on the psychotic. Every time the sniper managed to line up the crosshairs of his scope on Logan's massive chest, he bounded in a new direction. The unbondable probably cursed, grit his teeth, and brought his rifle down, down, down, trying to follow the silver giant as he fitfully charged the building. For a split second, almost too fast for him to register, the sniper had Logan centered in his scope. As the reticule swung wildly across the Master Sergeant, the unbondable took the shot. The bullet cracked by Logan at a little more than two thousand meters per second, ripping the air open as it passed.

The metal wings on Logan's head were made to look like the decorative flash on a knight's helm. If you looked closer, you could see that they moved, slowly adjusting to put the pickups at their end in just the right position, allowing him to focus in on input from dozens of sensors. He heard the two hundred gram, magnetically driven shell pass by. Other sensors measured air density, humidity, pollution index, temperature, and together they tracked the bullet's trajectory all the way back to its point of origin.

The sniper pulled back on the bolt, ejecting the kicker cap that accelerated the metal projectile into the magnetic 'barrel' of his rifle. Logan launched himself into the air, diving behind a low wall. The sniper drove the next projectile home, lifted the huge rail cannon and swept the wall, meter by meter.

Logan rolled along the dusty balding dirt, checked his inertial mapper to orient himself on the correct window, and popped up. The sniper caught sight of him just as his twenty-millimeter autocannon swung above his cover.

The soldiers, both inhuman man and human machine, fired.

CHAPTER 22: THE RAGE OF EXILES

In Transit Away from Planet Persephone,
Unknown Spacecraft 04:45, 11/13/2662

The second demolition charge went off, reverberating down the hallways like the cough of a giant. I let another spray go from the machinegun in my hands, keeping the last three defenders in the *fragging* security room. Archer's voice stabbed into my head. "We're through, we're through!"

"Drop grenades! NOW, NOW, NOW!"

A head popped around the door over the top of a light carbine. I sprinkled the doorframe around him with high-velocity steel-core bullets, and he beat a hasty retreat. I squeezed off two more bursts and began to seriously wonder if Archer and Lopez had decided to skip the action sequence and move right to the love scene in a closet somewhere. That's when the first grenade went off.

When we had come up to this section, explosives in hand, I had signaled the other two around to the left, and began creeping down the corridor to the right. In the center of these two passages was Security where there would be weapons, armor, and other security apparatus for our enemy to draw from. This office was traditionally the last, hard point for a spacecraft, and as such, it probably had some basic properties, most notably only one door, so that it could be held with a minimum of crew. Directly across the hallway from that door would be the entrance to the bridge. In the hallway, on both sides of the doors, would be pop-up barriers. They would be up now with whatever defenders were left stationed behind them. I needed to funnel them into Security, and there was only one way to do it. I had set myself up as a *fragging* target, firing down the passageway and carving chunks out of the barriers designed to stop plasma weaponry.

The defenders obligingly retreated into Security, and that's when Archer and Lopez set out cutting charges, one at a time, up on the wall. The last one had finally blasted through a power conduit, a fire suppression pipe, and the thin inner wall to Security itself. The hole wasn't impressive, barely the size of a large man's fist, but it was big enough for them to begin spitting live grenades into the room. The first one was a concussion grenade, the next one fragmentation; the effect of each inside an enclosed space would have been dramatic to say the least. But then there was a series of six, sympathetic detonations.

My armored boots thudded on the deck like ten-liter buckets full of sand as I hopped the nearly demolished barrier and peeked into the ruined wreckage of Security. Three bodies, at least I think it was three, were now the consistency of hamburger. That told me we had caught them just as they were preparing to chuck their own explosives into the hallway. The first explosion had stunned them, and someone had let go of their spoon. When you have three guys with a grenade in each hand, you only need one to screw up.

I shouldered the sliding door back into its frame and glanced around, confirming that the room was clear. While I did that, Lopez and Archer covered the way onto the bridge. I hefted the machinegun. The damn thing hadn't gotten any lighter. I dumped the half full box and loaded in a fresh one. Normally, I hate to waste ammunition, but if I couldn't get this done with the box in the weapon and one on my hip, I really should take up something safer. Say, horse ranching.

I looked around for any switch, computer or device that would open the doors to the Bridge. It was possible, this was Security, but I hadn't thought of that when I had ordered my men to use explosives. Everything was cracked, blasted, shredded, or smoldering. The good thing was that the bridge had just lost all security operations, including internal sensor systems, and the jamming was gone. But on the other hand, there was no easy way to unlock the *fragging* door. We found three good grenades on the corpses, but there was no way to focus their blast enough to do more than dent the heavy blast door across the hall. I handed them to my men and kept looking.

"Captain Rook?" A cultured voice slithered out of the public address system. "Oh, Captain Rook?"

I tongued on the external speakers to my helmet. "This is Rook."

"Oh, good. I'm afraid there's been some kind of confusion and I'd like to see if I can bring this whole affair to a...an amicable resolution." The voice was calm, cultured, educated, and... wrong.

Something just wasn't there and my primitive brain balked at it as unnatural.

I adjusted the volume up a notch more to compensate for the ringing dregs in my ears. "I'm listening."

"Um, I'm hoping that I can invite you onto the bridge and you won't, say, kill everyone you see."

My mouth moved without my brain fully engaged. "You actually want me on the bridge?"

"It would be so much easier to show some of these things than to just tell you."

"Shut down your slipdrive and we'll talk." I walked to the PA and smashed the camera with my armored fist. Then I made hand signs: *Switch to Frequency Thirteen, Decryption Routine Delta.*

Just as we switched the quantum radios to the new specs— hopefully fouling any attempt at eavesdropping— the voice came back, cuddling up to me like a mangy tomcat. "There, Captain, it is off."

"Wait one while I confirm." I exchanged weapons with Lopez and called *Deadly Heaven.* The slipdrive had been paused, not shut down. The hull was hanging at a higher quantum state, only five minutes from entering faster than light travel, but as far as I could tell, this was as good as it was going to get. My biggest problem was that this close to entering Slipspace, the quantum based comm units were barely making it through the interference from the hull. "Alright, I'm coming in."

"I will open the door for you."

A friend once told me that putting my face in the blender was going to get me killed one day. I hoped today wasn't the day he was proved right. I sent Lopez and Archer down the hallway to take up defensive positions, and the door to the bridge opened. My stomach fell away into open space as the barrel of a massive cannon poked through the crack, held inside the grip of an oversized glove of an assault *hard shell.* Apparently, I had found the unbondable commander.

His armor was similar to the one I was wearing. Granted, it was many years older, but it also lacked my rakish bullet holes, plasma burns, and shrapnel scars. I couldn't identify his weapon, but judging by the general shape and barrel, it was a plasma cannon. Not pistol, not rifle: cannon. From its size, it belonged on the front end of a spacecraft or crewed by three men with a tripod instead of hovering at the end of my nose. For a moment I thought I could crawl into the damn thing and set up camp. Guns are funny that way.

He backed up onto the bridge, and I followed slowly, taking in the bizarre scene. Dozens of scientists were hiding in here, hands shaking and white knuckled on the grips of small plasma carbines. Each one looked more terrified than the last, white lab coats discarded and clumsily replaced with emergency armor vests from the ship's stores. They looked at me like I was the grim reaper himself.

Only two men were unmoved by my presence. The first was the unbondable commander, who motioned for me to drop my carbine. The second was a finely dressed and immaculately groomed middle-aged man, the owner of the voice from the intercom.

"Captain Rook, so very good of you to join us. Welcome to *The Rage of Exiles*. I am her Captain, Malcolm Silver," he said.

I sized him up in about a second. He was a politician, perhaps an executive, maybe a lawyer. That was how he carried himself, with assured knowledge acquired through years of practice and position. He reeked of success, of money, and authority. His sharp blue eyes spoke of endless confrontation, and his soft manicured hands said his tactics were of the indirect sort. In short, he was the kind of person that most civilians find themselves wanting to trust, and the kind of man a mercenary instinctively stays away from. "I am afraid we find ourselves at loggerheads. Perhaps if you come into my office, we can resolve this to both our satisfaction?"

Loggerheads? I watch a lot of vintage pre-exile movies, so I knew what he was saying, *but who talks like that anymore?* The unbondable commander pushed his gun a little closer to me and again motioned for me to drop my weapon. Slowly, I complied, raising one arm to distract him from precisely where the carbine was being placed. As I stood back up, he motioned with his weapon again to move me toward Silver... and apparently took no notice of the gun sitting directly in the path of the automatic door.

I moved on without further intimidation, and absently thumbed the record button on my armpad. Everything I saw and heard would be captured, but a little error message told me that the quantum charge in the hull was keeping the signal from being beamed back to *Deadly Heaven*. Silver motioned behind him to the Captain's chamber off the bridge and I went. I could feel the weight of many eyes, a dozen ineffectual barrels, and one, massive, very effective muzzle on my back as I preceded him into the room.

My own Captain's chamber aboard *Deadly Heaven* had been transformed into a closet for electronic warfare equipment long before I took her over. This one, however had kept its original purpose, and was decked out with dozens of redundant displays, master control panels for the ship, a huge wooden meeting table ringed by large, plush chairs and set with service trays, boxes, as well as some paperwork. Silver swept past me like he was entertaining a king or pontiff, sliding his fingers along the lush, dark wood and appearing to marvel at its solidity. The unbondable Captain blocked the door, though he did let his cannon hang on its sling instead of pointing it at me.

"Captain, could I offer you refreshment?" He pointed to the service trays of amber-filled crystal bottles and rocks glasses, opened boxes filled with high quality cigars and even set a rat gnawing at the base of my brain by offering another filled with cigarettes. I shook my head. "Ah, well. Perhaps you would like to take off your helmet?"

I shook my head again.

Silver made a nonsense gesture as if swatting away a lethargic fly. "Very well. But not even you could have a moral objection to sitting down so that we can discuss this matter as gentlemen?"

I was about to crack wise about where he could shove his chair, but I figured there would be plenty of time to be obstinate later. I sat down opposite him, impressed that the chair only groaned a little, and crossed my arms as closely as my *hard shell* assault armor would allow.

"Captain, how much do you know about The Knights of Earth?"

"Refresh my memory."

"Of course, sir." Silver scooped a remote from the surface of the table and clicked a button, bringing one of the screens to life. It was one of those badly written, horribly acted, public-servicey kind of productions my father used to call a 'cult of three a.m.'

video. A bland announcer voice, specifically engineered from an AI to be comforting, non-threatening and somewhat hypnotic, began droning on about KoE and their mission to regain the home world of humanity. After just a few seconds, Silver muted the display. "Captain, I'm sure you know all this. What I can tell you is that what the video says is true: we simply want to go home."

"Home? Aren't you being a little dramatic?" Humanity might have sprung from Earth, the seeds of colonized space exiled as soldiers or criminals, police or radicals, protesters or undesirables, but only a few thousand a year could ever claim Earth as a home.

"Respectfully, no I am not. Earth is our home. It is where we belong. It is the spiritual center of our souls, our birthplace and the common mother to us all. It is peace in a galaxy of confrontation. We work toward our dream of Reunification." You could hear the capital R in the word like a punch. Though his face was serene, his words ran deep with conviction born of repetition. He intoned the words like a prayer, articles of faith that buoyed him in dark times.

I was beginning to believe my father was more than a little right calling the video a 'cult' film, and Silver was more than a little unhinged. "Earth doesn't share your dream," I said. "Those people are still shuttling off anyone they don't like to Mars on a pretty regular schedule, and they haven't sent out invitations to come back in from the cold."

Silver's face fell, like a child who found a Christmas bereft of toys. "No, they haven't, but I have a question: Have you ever spoken to a fresh Exile?"

I shook my head. Most Exiles were near basket cases. They were taken from a world that absolutely forbids violence and indoctrinates its population from birth to abhor even the defending of oneself against imminent attack. Children as young as thirteen have been shuttled off to Mars to live or die in the squalor of the urban wreckage that passed as cities there. Those you meet living full lives away from the red planet were rare, and they don't often want to talk about their life back on Earth.

"I have, Captain, and let me tell you the place is a paradise." Silver played with his remote, bringing new screens to life, showing scene after scene of paradise. "Renewable energies have eliminated pollution. Food programs have eliminated hunger. Think of walking the ancient structures of our forefathers, marveling at the natural wonders of the Grand Canyon or the Congo Basin. Imagine the freedom of a place where you never have to worry about some killer virus, monstrous alien species, explosive decompression, or war. Imagine the freedom…"

What he didn't mention were the robotic peace officers, ready to pounce if you stepped out of line. New laws were passed with impunity, and every individual human right was ground under the heel of the fictional rights of 'society'. Individual cultures were stamped out in order to make way for a megalithic monoculture dictated by leaders living in crystal castles far away from the masses. There were forced breeding programs for some and mandatory sterilizations for others. Freedom fed through a water bottle hooked on the side of a cage. My eyes glided back down to the wooden case of clean, white, cigarettes and my fingers twitched. "None of this really matters, Silver. You won't get any closer to Earth than the L-5 space station before the killer satellite network blasts your ships into nuclear dust. Men have tried, whole fleets have tried, and they left nothing behind except a ring of debris between the earth and her moon."

Silver's eyes flashed. "Yes! Exactly! I can see you have a keen tactical mind, Captain, and thus you can appreciate our problem, and our position in all of this."

Somewhere in the last three seconds the conversation had gone off the map, and without realizing it, I lowered my arms and leaned forward in my chair, trying in vain to find out where it went. "I'm not sure I follow you."

Silver took to his feet, pacing back and forth along the opposite side of the table. "For centuries, the Knights of Earth have studied the killer satellite array. We have dug through millions of terabytes of information on far-flung worlds, researched the dying memoirs of exiles and poured through every databank on the Mars research stations. We found that the array was… *is* called The Damocles Project. It was built by the best minds Earth had to offer in the field of high energy research, robotics, computing, and aerospace engineering. It is a magnificent accomplishment, but it was built by men, and everything built by men has a back door in it somewhere. We have found it."

Silence crashed into the room like the boot of an entry team. It sat there between us like a one-ton wild animal, chewing its cud and wondering who to tear apart first. My mind expanded out in every direction at once, sorting through possibilities that all turned into ashes in the end. I could only shake my head. "Impossible."

"Captain Rook, you are not thinking this through. Remember the Earth Unified Government ended war and then used soldiers to 'colonize' very remote star systems on shoddy star craft. Then they used the police to round up criminals and exile them to Mars. After the robotic police force was built, they exiled most of the police. At every turn, they found people willing to do their bidding to rid the planet of the stain of violence and then betrayed them." Silver lunged forward, planting his hands on the desk like the very picture of a movie lawyer bringing home a conviction. "What, do you suppose, they did to these scientists who built the largest weapon system ever devised?"

The wheels of my mind spun, screaming for traction. "They couldn't."

"They could, and they did. And thereby they gave us the keys to the back door." Silver snatched up a glass and poured himself a drink with shaking hands. "You see, these men of science knew what they were doing. They believed in their work. Still, something might go wrong; they might need a way to access space, for resources that were in short supply. They might need new genetic seeds from Mars if a plague wiped out a species. In any case, they made a way to get back to Earth past Damocles, just in case."

"How..."

Silver took a gulp of his drink and winced even as he smiled. "Like I said, we looked for the information. Some of it was found on Mars, some of it in old diaries left by the exiled scientists. The largest chunk, the most important part, was from our founder, Leonard Swanson.

"He was a junior research assistant on the project, a minor player, but an important one. Doubtless, some of the scientists that were building Damocles knew what their fate was to be. Others like Swanson did not. They were simply victims of their own specialty, cut off from their holy mother because they did what they were told. He began the Knights of Earth to get back home. Sadly, he did not live to see his dream become reality, but he set us on the path. His sacrifice," again Silver appeared to be lost in rapture, "allowed us to get this far."

Inside my helmet, there was an insistent chirp, and a message from Ansef scrolled across the top of my HUD. *Casualties worsening, must get wounded to med bay soonest.* That snapped me out of Silver's convincing illusion of safety and back to the matter at hand. I stood as my hands went to my sides, and my hands clenched and unclenched of their own accord as my blood began to race. "What does this have to do with Persephone?"

Silver held up his hands as if to ward me off and backed up to the far wall. "Captain, I told you there is a hole in Damocles. Actually, it's more of a door. Or really, a key. It is a complex mass of data that must be sent on a specific frequency in a specific order to disarm the system and allow a ship to pass."

"A data key?"

"Yes. And the scientists were sure to encode it in a way that would be near impossible to lose while it may be needed, and once Earth appeared stable, would fade away with time." He paused, dramatically. "They used an alphanumeric sequence based on their own DNA."

I placed my hands on the table, leaning in. "But the scientists are many generations dead."

Silver reached the wall with his back and leaned into it, once again at ease as if someone had flipped a switch. It made me check the exits to make sure they were clear. There was only one, and it wasn't. The unbondable Captain stared at me though tinted glass as Silver continued, "Yes, Captain. And a few hundred years ago, that would have made the DNA keys unreadable, lost forever in the genetic soup of humanity. Thankfully, we're a little more advanced now. We've robbed graves where they could be found, recovered and rebuilt genetic material from preserved samples, and even recreated family trees with meticulous detail to cross reference and eliminate the wrong strands to bring back the antique DNA sequences we need."

"You've got to be kidding."

The Key to Damocles

Silver spread his hands. "Captain, we are motivated by a higher calling, and we've had hundreds of years."

"Why here?"

"Well, there was a sequence missing. Doctor Olivia died of a heart attack before he was exiled from Earth."

"Then your key is missing a tooth. Worthless."

Silver wandered over to the corner by a computer console. "Not precisely. You see, his wife, Linda Olivia was kicked off-planet because of her protests of the treatment of the Damocles staff. We got her DNA from her corpse for a baseline."

"How does that help?"

"When she was exiled, she brought her daughter, the Scion of Olivia."

"So?"

"Several hundred years ago she, the Scion, began acting under her mother's maiden last name of Ranner, and she became an interplanetary superstar. When she died, her DNA was preserved and every few generations, her face is reincarnated, cloned, to continue working for L/V/D."

My voice was barely a whisper, but the external mike picked it up anyway. "Katie Ranner."

Silver nodded. "Katie Ranner."

"You plunged an entire planet into chaos to kidnap one woman."

Silver spread his hands as if to say, *it's not my fault.* "Captain, I doubt they would have given her over just for the asking."

"And now that you have her, you're going to unlock Earth."

"Precisely!"

I was getting agitated, but there was nothing I could do to keep it out of my voice. "Do you have any idea what happens after that?"

"We will take over administration of the planet and aid it in assimilating into the galactic community."

I glanced at the hulking unbondable in the corner to make sure he wasn't getting too jumpy as I got angrier. "Galactic community? Are you *cracked?*"

"Captain, it will be quite easy. They have only a robotic security force armed with non-lethal weaponry and a population hypersensitive to violence."

"But what after that? What happens when the Exiles across the galaxy want reparations? What happens when other people figure they have a claim on the 'mother of us all'?" And then I felt stupid because he wasn't going to destroy the killsats—

"You misunderstand, because after we put in the key to Damocles, our ships will be able to pass. It will still be there to defend against all comers. We will turn it into a new Jerusalem, a new Bethlehem, a new Mecca, and people from across the galaxy will come to see their ancestral home." His smile was greasy, self-satisfied, like a scavenger picking over the corpse of a lion.

And they'll all leave a pile of cash behind. You're looking to turn Earth into a quasi-religious theme park. It was a sure thing that almost none of humanity would be interested in going back to the spinning hunk of rock that spawned their race. It was also a sure thing that even if only one percent of trillions of humans came to Earth, KoE would soon be richer than even L/V/D.

And what would be the price paid by Earthers, culturally unable to defend themselves against the tide of abusive patrons? And there would be abusive visitors. Their forefathers had kicked our forefathers out of the only sandbox not littered with cat crap. It seems like such a stupid thing to still be bitter about three hundred years later, but there are people who would use it as a reason to pick a fight. Who was to say the people would cooperate with Silver's theme park? *Then again what choice would they have?* "Unbelievable."

"Rook, if I may be frank, the Knights have need of your skills. Not just for a few days or weeks, but as a permanent addition to the organization. We will very soon have vast resources, well, even more vast recourses. Think about it: you can go home to Earth, live in comfort, and command thousands in defense of our mother planet against any who would dare impugn her with attack."

This guy may be floating in space without a proper seal, but I considered his offer for three breaths. I had to admit, the prospect had its attractive points. Commanding thousands, lap of luxury, and who doesn't like vast resources? But then I thought about who I would have to work for. As the last breath left my body, I thought about my father. I knew what he'd say to this freak. "Silver, I want you to turn off your quantum drive, surrender your ship, and prepare to be transported back to Persephone."

The commander to my right tensed, and his hands began creeping down to the controls for his weapon. Silver looked despondent, disappointed, and resigned as he walked back over to the table and sat down opposite me. "I'm sorry, Captain. We've worked too long to even consider doing that."

My heart was already pumping faster, turbo charging my body as it prepared to fight. "Turn this ship around, Silver."

"Please, Captain, be reasonable." He leaned back slightly, and his hands disappeared beneath the table. "Your crew is mutilated, trapped, and dispersed throughout my ship. You are here alone, and no backup is coming. Do not presume to dictate to me."

"All the backup I need are the four Mark 73 torpedoes loaded and ready aboard *Deadly Heaven*. All I need to do is make a call to turn this piece of *grit* ship into a miniature *fragging* sun." And there it was. Danger: hot, wet and red, it pulsed in the room between us. The unbondable took a step forward, placing the barrel of his cannon close, too close, as in 'within reach'.

Silver was unfazed. "Then you must never make that call."

Like a cobra, my right hand lashed out and latched onto the barrel of the plasma cannon. The commander touched off a salvo of shots into the floor, setting the rug on fire and searing the paint off my armored glove. I kicked away from the table, reinforced chair rolling on its castors. I planted my feet and pulled the weapon viciously, knocking the commander off balance. My left fist shot in and slammed into the side of his helmet, rocking his head back and to the side. As he reeled, I pulled his weapon again, knocking him off balance once more. It gave me just enough time to reach in and yank the emergency release catch on his weapon harness. It came free, and I gracefully swung the huge unit up into my waiting arms. The commander fell backward, crabbing away along the floor from the smoking muzzle which was now leveled at his face.

I almost had time to say something witty when Silver shot me.

My helmet protected me from the roar of the weapon, but the bullet went fast and free, impacting just over my solar plexus in a picture-perfect kill shot. My breath whooshed out and everything seemed to slow down. I had time to watch Silver begin to scream and drop the massive pistol, coddling his wrists against his chest. I saw blood vapor erupt from the nice, clean hole in my armor and spray across the rich, wooden surface of the conference table. I staggered backward, dropped the cannon, and fell against the wall. It took forever before I slid until my body was horizontal with only my head propped up against the wall. I couldn't feel anything except an all-encompassing numbness, an emergency hum from every fiber of my being telling me something had just gone horribly wrong, but I could see everything.

I could see the commander scramble for the cannon. I could see tears creeping out of Silver's eyes as he nursed his wrist. I could see the hulking borg-rated pistol sitting on the table. I could even see the mounting bracket where the pistol had been concealed underneath the table the whole time. Thick foam from the fire suppression system shot into the burning spot on the rug, putting it out immediately, and to me it looked like water floating down in zero gravity. I had all of eternity to ride every second, but I couldn't move. I couldn't even breathe. There was a darkness collecting inside my skull, a grim reaper that passed its hands before my eyes and left shining comets behind.

Silver's voice was tarnished and cracked with pain. "I think I broke my hand."

The commander picked up his massive cannon from the floor and reattached the harness around his shoulders. His voice was a like a handful of gravel tossed in a rock tumbler. "I'm not surprised. Those things are meant for people with metal wrists. You should have fired it from the mounting bracket." *Like I told you to*, hung in the air and mixed with Silver's whimpers.

"He will have recorded the whole conversation."

The commander moved toward me. "He can't get a communication out of the ship so it's got to be stored in his battle computer, I'll-"

And then there were three quick explosions out on the bridge.

"The scientists!" Silver half whined and half screamed. "Get out there and kill those last two mercenaries!"

281

The Key to Damocles

The commander glanced at me, a rattle of submachine gun fire cut him off. Silver was near hysterical. "Erase it later! Those scientists are critical to the cause, get out there!"

The commander stepped out the door and laid down a line of fiery plasma. There was the chatter of return fire, and then the door shut. I could almost hear the deep thud of the commander's steps.

Silver limped over to the computer panels in the corner and began punching in commands. Alerts flashed across the screen as he resumed the process to enter Slipspace.

All the while, I desperately tried to hold the darkness at bay.

And tried to breathe.

CHAPTER 23: THE RAGE OF ANGELS

Silver almost crumpled against the console, the pain from his shattered wrist echoing in waves outward across his body. Tears peaked out from underneath his eyelids as he tried to breathe deeply and relax.

The voice of the unbondable commander crackled over the intercom. The fanatic had to turn it up, most assuredly to hear it over the ringing in his ears from the pistol shot. "Silver, get the internal sensors online. I need to know where these mercenaries are."

Silver's voice had lost its polish. Like a finely tuned machine knocked out of whack, it had gained an irritating whine. "Never mind them! What about the scientists?"

"That's what you said when the *Angels* landed on planet. That's what you said when they reinforced West Lot! That's what you said an hour ago when you had me evacuate the scientists instead of sending men to the landing bay! These *Angels* have *mudraked* us for the last time. I will not ignore them again!"

"The scientists, Carver!"

Leon Carver. The unbondable commander was the butcher of New Lebanon. "DEAD! They are dead! Rook put his rifle in the doorway and the damn civilian-model sliding door could not close while it was obstructed. When they heard your shot, the two men he left outside pitched in grenades and then finished the lab coat wearing monkeys off with small arms. Your scientists are dead, you *pole-smoking*, little *jacka*."

Already pale from pain, Silver's skin became blue. "Kill them."

"I'm trying to! The holo-sonar in this unit is broken. I need you to activate the backup sensor station on the bridge and—."

"KILL THEM!" Silver screamed, his hand cutting off the intercom and any chance at rebuttal.

Every proud, clean line of his clothes and proper posture told the world that, from his point of view, he was a pioneer, a visionary. In reality, he might not be one of the political leaders of his organization, but he was the one who got things done, no questions asked. Now he was clearly coming apart at the seams. Today had been filled with delicious victories and crushing disappointments. Now he needed new scientists, new ruthless mercenaries, and now a new right hand. His left hand played with his left ear, and then awkwardly with his right, trying in vain to free them from the ringing left by the thirteen-millimeter magnum pistol left forgotten on the floor. His left wrist shifted slightly, and he cradled it close again. He stared at the numbers on the screen scrolling down to Slipspace, trying to maintain his calm, and murmuring, "What else can go wrong?"

As if to answer him, a dark shadow came over his shoulder and his face impacted on the screen with all the grace of a car wreck. His head drew back and slammed forward again, and again. The hardened plastic screen held, but his nose did not. Blood exploded downward over his nice, clean suit. His head drew back and through glazed eyes he saw my helmet reflected in the dark surface. His voice held a distinctive gurgle. "I killed yo—"

"Not. Quite." My mechanized glove, entwined in his hair like a violent lover, pushed one last time and plastered his face across the screen. Fire raged inside my chest, burning like the heart of a reactor as feeling returned to my extremities. The shock was wearing off, but my limbs and my brain were only barely on speaking terms. When Silver collapsed to the floor like a boneless sack, he took me with him.

I lay there, splayed out like road kill, contemplating the line of blood that led from the wall to the console for several seconds. With any luck, the hardened armor plate beneath my skin, the source of constant annoyance and reminders of an old wound, had stopped the armor piercing round that had defeated my *hard shell*. My biological monitoring equipment said I was in 'fair' condition, which meant ambulatory, but the software was in the helmet. Ortega's helmet. It had not been calibrated to me, and so the data was largely worthless. I could be slowly bleeding from a pinpoint puncture of an artery. A clot could be making its merry way to my brain. I could be suffering from an arrhythmia of the heart that would cause it to fail if I put any strain upon it. In any case, I had two choices: I could go and find the unbondable commander and put him down like a rabid dog, or I could wait here to die.

James Daniel Ross

I don't even remember getting up, but somehow I did it. Blood splashed out of the bullet hole in my chest and left a bright red splat on the carpeting. I had to lever myself up onto the command console, steadying legs that felt like the bones had been surgically removed. That's when the blinking countdown to Slipspace caught my eye. I took a second to tap on the console. At some point, the infomercial for Knights of Earth had come back on. It nattered on in the background, and I got drawn into the presentation without even realizing it. Scenes flashed by: peaceful plains, verdant green hills, lush jungles, pictures of animals unknown outside of a zoo, except on Earth. I wondered what it would be like to walk on the soil of Earth.

And then I thought about the cost. No matter what Silver thought, even attempting to bring Earth into the greater community of colonies would be like taking something simple, stupid, and innocent and tossing it naked into the worst slum you can imagine. Earth was a slave society, but it couldn't be saved from the outside. It needed its own leaders, its own heroes, to lead the charge and heal centuries old wounds.

And what if Earth has already given birth to all the George Washingtons, Mahatma Gandhis, Charlemagnes, and Utawis? My fingers hovered over the last button, given pause by that most awful of thoughts. *What if you can't get off this ship in thirty minutes?*

I began entering commands. Thankfully, Silver was still logged in, and I was able to reset the countdown for Slipspace to thirty minutes. I changed the faster-than-light course for *The Rage of Exiles*. Alerts popped up, and I overrode them numerous times. The computer, which thought I was Silver, let me do it. I unlocked the door to the shuttle bay. I tried to reach Archer and Lopez, but no one replied. I switched *freqs*. "Rook to Thompson."

"Thompson here, Captain."

"Can you reach Archer or Lopez?"

"No, sir. There's localized jamming going on."

The commander must have a personal jamming unit installed in his armor. I paused for only a second, fingers flying like wasps over the keys. "If I am not at your position in twenty-five, that is two-five minutes, you are to open the door to the bay using frequency," I read off the numbers as I entered them into the console, "and get back to *Deadly Heaven*."

285

The Key to Damocles

"Sir?"

"Twenty-four minutes and fifty-nine seconds from now, you are in charge. Do you read?"

"Crystal, but Captain—."

"No 'buts'. Rook out."

I closed my eyes, and the galaxy rotated around me. My chest ached like I had been knifed in the sternum. Blood oozed out of my chest in a slow stream, every drop taking a little of myself with it. The darkness was like a black dwarf, pulling me in with arms of seductive steel. I felt the world fall away, slipping through the fingers of my numbed mind. Like an ice pick in the eye, a shrill warning beep sounded behind me. I glanced back to see we were twenty-five minutes away from Slipspace. I took a deep breath and marshaled as much hate as I could to keep me in the here and now. I popped a pill from my first aid kid and used a can of RealSkin™ sealant to plug the hole in my chest.

I walked to the door, and it dutifully opened, revealing the wreckage of the bridge. Blood was everywhere, and scorched pockmarks showed where the fragmentation grenades had kissed the walls and ceiling. Across from me, the main door to the bridge was caught in a continuous loop. It would open, pause, close until it hit the rifle I had laid in its path, and open again. I had worried that someone would kick it out of the way, which had not happened. I was worried they had someone who could override the safeties on the door and cause it to slam shut anyway, convince it there was an explosive decompression or something. None of that had happened, but when Carver had chased my men out into the corridor, he had stepped on it. The casing was bowed out in the center and had cracked, and the barrel was sticking up like the mast of a wallowing ship.

Now I needed a weapon. I glanced around and saw lots of low-power plasma carbines in the hands of dead scientists. I picked one up, set it to rapid fire and used it to destroy the few working computers on the bridge. The plasma entered and flashed glass, plastic and metal into gas. The gas disrupted the plasma packet, and it had the effect of a miniature detonation just inside the consoles. None of the bolts punched clear through the monitors. The damn thing, and the dozen more like it on the floor, would be useless against Carver's assault *hard shell*. I flung it into the far wall and wobbled back into the Captain's chamber.

A curse bubbled up from my stomach before dying in my throat as my eyes drew themselves behind me to the massive, borg-rated thirteen-millimeter magnum ETC pistol lying dejectedly on the floor. Normally, pistols are weapons of last resort. Then again, if I wasn't at the last resort, I was driving up to the front gate, and I could definitely smell the mai tais.

I walked over and scooped up the massive block of metal into my gloved fist. The matte surface pebbled the light like the promise of damnation, assuring me that underneath the finish was six kilos of barely contained destruction. I ejected the magazine with the sound of a giant mandible, and checked the clear plastic sides. The oversized bullets were loaded in a single stack, eight tickets to the hereafter. I realized they were eight very large bullets, but what if I had to shoot nine times?

Weapons almost always come with a spare... absently, I pulled out the drawer on the meeting table and snatched the full magazine laying there. Seventeen was a far more comforting number. The only thing that worried me now was actually pulling the trigger. Silver had already proved the recoil was violent enough to shatter a man's wrist, but what about a man inside a muscle-augmented *hard shell?* I shifted the weapon to my left hand, pointed it at the command console, and lined up the triangular sights. I pulled the trigger.

The recoil was painful, like punching a train as it sped by. The angry battle cry of a giant exited the muzzle, and only my helmet stopped it from slamming into my ears like a sledgehammer. A lance of plasma fire two meters long shot out and licked over the surface of the computer. The wad of lead encased hardened steel crashed through everything in its path until it reached the bulkhead far behind the monitor. The last working computer screen on the bridge sputtered and died. Now there was no way out, no way back. In twenty-three minutes, this ship was going to Slipspace into Persephone's star.

It's all about commitment.

I flexed my left paw into a fist again and again, satisfying myself that while there was enough of the left-over blunt energy from the recoil to numb my hand, it had not broken. The heavy, armored gloves did their job perfectly, but the gun still bucked the muzzle clear off of the target. I'd have to hold it with two hands.

I could feel the painkiller I had taken working its magic, so I ejected the partially depleted magazine, loaded in the full one, and activated my radio. "Thompson, you said there was jamming. Is Ortega able to pin down the location?"

He could, but it took longer than I wanted. His voice was heavy, slurred, as he guided me down, into the bowels of the ship. I knew I was close when static began creeping into the radio like the sound of approaching doom.

Then Thompson came back on the line. "Captain, I have the countdown marked at fifteen minutes. What do I do if it runs out and you are not back?"

"You have your orders, Lieutenant."

"But, Captain—."

The door ahead of me opened, and all communications devolved into static. I cursed and thought about backing up to clarify my order, but the sound of gunfire hit me like a spur in the ass, and I surged forward to reclaim my wayward men.

The area was two floors high, and piled with crates big enough to store a civilian passenger vehicle. The entryway was a sieve made of bullet holes, and spent casings littered the ground like rice thrown at the devil's wedding. Blast marks scarred the crates, the small ones obviously from plasma carbines, and the larger gouges could only be the work of Leon Carver, the unbondable commander, and his plasma cannon.

Every fiber of my legs began to shake, urging me to run ahead, to plunge in to find my enemy and destroy them. Adrenal glands began pumping like a fire hose, and I had to make a conscious effort to keep my feet glued to the floor. I had to wait. I had to listen. Or, more precisely, I had to let my suit listen and collect all the sound it could to build a reliable map of the room ahead. The holo-sonar was already working, drawing out the lanes in between the boxes collecting every clatter, every footstep. It was just going way too slow.

A dark shape walked from between two crates. My mind skipped the inconsequential details, all I saw was: male, light armor, plasma carbine. *Not an Angel.* I raised the heavy pistol in both hands, sighted, and fired.

There was an explosion of blood and gore as his arm was nearly separated from his body in an instant. The bullet burrowed thorough his torso like a hungry maggot, bursting from the other side and puncturing the crate behind him without slowing down at all.

The good news amounted to one enemy was down, and the massive sound wave had filled out my map of the cargo bay.

The bad news was: everybody knew I was there.

Leon Carver activated his loudspeaker and cranked the volume up until it filled up the entire room. "Silver? Goddammit, Silver? What are you doing here?"

The voice, a simple, plottable sound, was like candy to my sonar, highlighting a big red triangle marked Unknown Contact 17. The holographic sonar microcomputer fixed the positions of everyone and everything in the room to within three centimeters, and I leapt in their direction. Crates flew past me, and I closed the distance to a mere two rows when a burst from a machine gun erased the data in a single stroke. Static leaped across my HUD as crazy echoes and a hail of frequencies confused the program. A few whining booms, the telltale sound of a plasma cannon firing, blossomed into life and highlighted Carver's position. I dove around the crates between us and drew down on his back. We both touched off our weapons at the precise same instant.

The bullet from my six-kilo pistol hit the backpack-like hump of his power armor. Sparks flew, hydraulic fluid sprayed in a wide arc, and his whole frame lurched forward from the impact. I hit the floor hard on my side and began wrestling the monumental automatic up to track in on his head. Carver lunged to the side, taking cover from the threat in front of him as he spun around to face me. His voice was like rocks and glass being shaken in a bag of bees. "Dammit, Silver it's me—!"

Our eyes locked for one heartbeat.

I pulled the trigger, sending a round to tear a huge gouge out of the side of his helmet. Without wasting an instant, he ran back into the maze of containers. I levered myself up and followed, taking cover at the end of the crate-alley. I aimed around the corner and stared down the sights of the pistol. It came up, up; it centered directly on Carver's retreating back.

Archer's shrill call chilled my spine. "Captain, nine o'clock!"

The Key to Damocles

I shoved away from the wall as a line of plasma bolts stitched up the crate where I had just been. I spun to my left and pulled the trigger twice. The huge lump of metal in my hand bucked like a branded stallion, rattling the bones in my wrist despite the heavy padding and muscle augmentation of the gloves. Bullets flew on greedy tongues of flame, slamming into another unbondable's body. They made large holes going into the soldier's light armor but left the body as gruesome showers of gore as the armor piercing rounds shed their expanding sheaths, which in turn created massive exit wounds. His body jerked, fell, and lay still. I scrambled back to the crate and leveled my weapon down the artificial corridor again. I found only square shadows and rectangular patches of light. Carver was gone.

I glanced to my right, down the narrow opening in the stacks of crates, and saw Archer standing behind a makeshift barricade. He and Lopez had pulled a few inconsequential crates down to create a wall, for all the good it had done them. Several of the one-meter cubes were smoldering from small caliber plasma strikes. One was burning merrily where Carver's cannon had punched a hole clean through it.

The mere presence of flame without alarms and fire suppression response from the automated systems told me that the security station we had *fragged* was in a complete shambles. For some reason, the backup systems were offline too. It could have been because of the almost complete destruction of the bridge. I hoped whatever system failures were creeping across *The Rage of Exile*s would not affect the shuttle bay doors. "Status report."

"Pretty bad, Captain." Archer turned from my direction and pointed his carbine down the other walkway. "Lopez took a hit."

I jogged the dozen meters to their location, eyes on the nearly useless holomap, and gave them a quick once-over. Archer appeared to have taken several direct hits, but none penetrated his assault *hard shell.* Lopez was on the ground, wallowing under Richardson's machinegun and grabbing his leg as bloody steam oozed out. Carver's shot through the crate had found its mark.

Thompson chimed in. "Captain?"

"Yes, Lieutenant?" I slapped orders into my armband, clearing my HUD and sending out a clean ultrasonic pulse into the cargo bay. The map, floor to ceiling, wall to wall to wall to wall, and everything inside, was complete in less than a breath.

Carver was nowhere to be found…

Again.

Dammit!

"Sorry, you just came on a few seconds ago. The jamming has stopped." Thompson stopped short of telling me I had thirteen minutes remaining.

"Locate the jamming and give me his new position." I heaved the crates to the side with one hand and hip-checked them to the side to reach our fallen member.

"No, Captain, the jamming has stopped completely. Cut off suddenly."

I guess that's what I hit inside his hump. "Roger, we are inbound soonest, out."

Archer moved the last burning crate out of the way. "Thought you were dead."

My adrenaline was fading, and painkillers can do only so much. The bullet lodged in my subdermal armor shifted and pinched. "Be glad nobody took bets. Help me with Lopez."

"Captain, you know you have a hole in your chest?"

I gritted my teeth as the pain began inching into my body as if goaded by Archer's observation. "Yes, Archer, I'm aware of that."

We detached the machinegun carrying strap and tossed it to the side before we could manhandle Lopez into a sitting position. I signaled him to turn on his radio and began checking his vitals. His voice sounded like he was supporting a few thousand tons with his groin alone, but he was alert and lucid. "Already on, Captain."

My hands stopped, "And you're not screaming?"

"No, but I really want to, Captain."

I shook my head and went back to work, which Lopez took entirely the wrong way. I removed his helmet carefully. His short hair was plastered down, and he was sweating profusely. I checked the readout on his chest plate and saw his vitals were dropping. He was wan, pale beneath his Latin complexion. He was starting to hyperventilate when he finally said, "Just trying to make you proud of me, sir."

"Proud? Kid, I am *fragging* awestruck." I popped the autodoc out of his belt pouch and fit it to the back of his neck. "When I write your letter of commendation, I'll have to make up whole slew of synonyms for 'unbelievable badass'."

He started to say something, but the micro-bursts of drugs from the autodoc stabilized his vitals, slowed his metabolism, and pulled him into sleep. I began working on the rest of our fallen comrade's armor.

"What now?" Archer asked. "We can't carry him very fast in his armor."

"We get him out of it and to the captured dropship." I pulled open a hatch on Lopez's chest plate and punched in the override code. Armored sections began to unlock, cables unplugged, and flat motors disengaged, allowing us to pull his arms and legs free of their heavy coffins.

"We're just going to leave this stuff here? These shells are worth a million, easy." Archer began fiddling with detaching Lopez's torso plates.

"It's just equipment, it can be replaced." *Reeves and I had this exact same conversation once.* I sprayed Lopez's wound with a can of synthetic skin and then tossed it. "Give me his chest plate."

Archer finally got the last latch to let go and pulled the front plate free of Lopez's armor. He handed it to me and I busied myself stripping off mine. "This is going to be a hard run with him over my shoulders and that *hard shell* out there."

"It's worse than you think. That guy out there in the *hard shell* is Leon Carver, the Butcher of New Lebannon" Lopez's plate, the same design and the same size, clicked cleanly into place. The suit confirmed that it was now airtight.

Archer went pale. "That guy's the *fragging* Butcher? How can this get worse?"

Despite everything, something inside of me relished telling him, "In eleven minutes and five seconds, this ship is going to *slip* into the sun."

"Sun?" Archer had been moving the machine gun to the side, and it slipped though his suddenly numb hands. "We gotta run. We gotta run, right now, right *fragging* now!"

I ejected the magazine from my oversized pistol and consolidated rounds so I had one full magazine and one with only two rounds. "Wait."

"Wait? WAIT!?" Archer sat back and motioned to every side. The light machine gun was out of rounds, but casings were everywhere. Archer's ETC carbine was still smoking slightly from constant use, not that it would breech a *hard shell* anyway. "For what?"

"Drop everything you're carrying and pick him up."

"Pick him up? Captain, we have got to get the hell out of here!"

I loaded the full magazine into my weapon, checked the chamber, and hefted six kilograms of chaos in war-weary hands. I glared at Archer. "Pick. Him. Up. Now."

Archer dumped his pack, gear, and web belts, and then picked up Lopez across his shoulders. All the while, I was wishing with all my might that Ortega would magically show up with his scanner and tell me where Carver went. Somewhere out here, the unbondable commander was waiting. Perhaps he had rushed forward to the bridge with a mind to check on the status of the ship. Maybe he had run to engineering to alter the course of the ship, or finish the drive into Slipspace. That thought left me a chill, because if he could override the Captain's orders to the slipdrive, he could alter course and escape with the ship. In the great scheme of things, losing Carver would be worth a moment's regret, but if this ship got away, then Earth was doomed. There just wasn't time to go looking for Carver, and even if I got to a working console to delay the Slip, I wouldn't have Silver's log-in to authorize the changes. All we had on our side was time, unfortunately when his ran out ours ran out, too. We had to move. We had to do it now. I signaled *Move Out*.

Quickly, we advanced. I swept each corner as we moved toward the exit, eyes always on the HUD. There was no sign of Carver, but if he were sitting perfectly still and making no noise, my holo sonar wouldn't show him anyway. We hugged the left wall to minimize our exposure to our flanks, and within a minute, I was staring at the exit up ahead. I turned to Archer, sagging under the burden of his teammate even with the help of the *hard shell*. "Alright, we're going to—"

My HUD changed colors from green to yellow as a series of metallic 'tink tink tinks' sounded at the entrance. I spun and leveled my weapon, but all I saw was a small, unobtrusive cylinder. That's when the little device began to scream. It flooded

The Key to Damocles

the room with hollow frequencies, reverse signals, broad spectrum sounds, and purposefully distorted noise. It slipped past my hearing filters and jabbed at my brain. It crept along my skin and tingled at my spine. It infected my blood and made my teeth itch. Immediately, the HUD dissolved into static again. When the machinegun had fired, I had lost soft objects, like people, but this cacophony was specifically designed to turn my holographic sonar map into an unreadable mess.

I signaled *Halt!*

And waited.

Carver came in the door cautiously, trying to edge around the doorframe to find me without exposing too much of himself. As soon as I saw any chest at all, I sighted the borg pistol and pulled the trigger. The range was fifteen meters, and even the slight deviation at the barrel put the bullet off by a handful of centimeters. The armor piercing round hit a curved shoulder plate, skipped off, and wasted itself on the wall behind my enemy. The boom cleared the map for a split second, the simple sound enhancing it for a moment, and then it dissolved back into static. Rather than retreat, Carver slung himself out of the door and let loose with three quick shots from his cannon. I dove under cover as they impacted the nearby crate, wall, and floor.

"Archer, back. Back!"

And then the gravel-and-glass-bead voice ground into my ears over my own comm frequency. "You really should buy better encrypting software, Rook. This stuff is ancient, at least a year old or more."

Son of a... I popped back out and took a single shot. One handed, too fast for sights, it went wide, but Carver unleashed another salvo of white-hot plasma down the row. A few made it through the crate behind which I took cover. Two punched through and creased, but did not breach, my torso armor. Archer was already backing up when I flashed a hand signal. The manuals list it as *Retreat!* exclamation point and all, but most mercenaries simply refer to it as *Run Like Hell!*

"I'm going to get you, Rook. You *cracked* a good deal for me, here." Carver's voice hounded my heels as I ran. Boxes flew past us as we moved as fast as possible along the wall. After only a few breaths, white bolts flew past us on both sides. I grabbed Archer's left arm and pulled him down another row. I jockeyed to

294

be in front as we began taking turns at random, sure that any second I was going to run face first into Carver's weapon and he would make good on his promise. "I'm going to watch you bleed out and then burn your entire team to the ground!"

Archer stumbled and fell. There was simply no way he could keep going like this, carrying a full-grown man across his shoulders at full speed. Even with the muscle augmentation of his *hard shell,* he just couldn't—

There, ahead on the floor, was the screamer, still chugging away.

Now, why would any man unleash a device into a room to make a sonar map useless? A new holo-sonar development? Unlikely. Less likely that a criminal like Carver would get one before I even heard of it. He's outnumbered, but not outgunned. He needed to even the odds by taking away my map. Which means...

I signaled to Archer. *Prepare to Move Out. Double Time. Return to Rendezvous.* There was a beep to tell me I had ten minutes remaining until Slip.

I took careful aim on the screamer and gently squeezed the trigger.

The thing may have had some armor, but the massive round fit to breech a combat cyborg's skin blew it apart like a child's toy nonetheless. The sound of the shell casing striking the floor redrew my map and located Carver near the center of the room. I punched Archer on the arm to get his attention and gestured at the exit, then spun as another screamer was launched from Carver's *hard shell.* My map disintegrated as I exposed myself in the central walkway and began backing toward the open door. Carver poked his head out from behind a crate for just a second, and I sent a bullet downrange at him. Rather than take cover, he popped out fully and let loose with a stream of plasma from right to left at waist height. I dove for the crates on my left, rolling on my shoulder in a failed ploy to trade stability for speed. As I tumbled, my left leg flipped up too high, and a stream of plasma splattered on my shin guard. Armor vaporized underneath the assault and the protective gel inside flashed into ionized steam, disrupting the packet of superheated gas and saving me from the worst of the damage. I finished off my roll and tried to come to my feet, only to fall forward on my face as my left leg buckled.

295

The Key to Damocles

It felt like it was on fire from the knee down. It could be there was no 'like' about it, as I glanced down and saw thick, black smoke rising from my leg and foot.

There was screaming, too close, too loud, and too personal to be from over the comm. I wondered why my speakers weren't filtering the noise. Then I realized that it was coming from inside my helmet. The person screaming was me.

Carver could hear me over the open comm, and I could feel him inside his hundred plus kilo suit of armor rattling the deck plates as he rushed to finish the job he started. I rolled to the side and brought up my weapon. He was too eager to score any kind of hit, and fired as he came around the corner. Despite the directions in every in manual on the subject, he was slinging the barrel and turning his plasma weapon into a tightly focused flamethrower. A burning line of plasma raked across my stomach, heating armored components but failing to breech the heavier armor there.

I centered the sights of my pistol on his torso and, despite every manual on the subject, yanked the trigger hard. Bullet holes blossomed across his chest, at first vaguely centered, but as the punishing recoil numbed my hand the grouping became looser and looser. Five rounds flew through the smoke rising off my leg and impacted on his chest before the slide locked back empty. Five rounds burrowing through mostly random chunks of armor and flesh. Five times his body took the kinetic force of a thousand slaughterhouse's pneumatic hammers. Five times my wrist did the same.

His stream of fire faltered and died as he staggered back. I willed my finger to move, gritting my teeth and growling like a beast. I pulled and pulled, trying to get one more round out of the weapon, only to find it empty. I tried to change magazines, but as I slammed my last two rounds home into the weapon, my abused hand lost its grip and the gigantic pistol tumbled from numb fingers to the deck plates. Waves of burning pain from my leg rippled upwards and left me awash in agony. I could only stare down the barrel of Carver's cannon, waiting second after second for him to pull the trigger and erase me from existence.

And then he tottered, stumbled, and fell over backwards.

I followed suit, twitching weakly and staring at the weak florescent lights through tear-filled eyes.

The sound of my own breathing was deafening inside the helmet. The smell of my own breath made me want to gag. Primitive centers of my brain worked with my left hand and got the face shield open just before I rolled over to vomit across the floor. Thick bile and half-digested food oozed out of my mouth as my tired body tried to void itself and failed for lack of energy. The active screamer across the room punished my ears every second the helmet was open. I choked down what wouldn't come out and spit the half mouthful of leftovers weakly onto the floor before collapsing onto my back and shutting the visor again.

I tried to activate the medical unit for the *hard shell*, desperately seeking relief from the soul-searing burn that threatened to blot out my senses, but again, my fingers were stunned and throbbing from the massive recoil of the pistol, and typed only random gibberish on the forearm pad. I just sat there only able to do three things: Listen, hurt, and try to breathe.

Archer's half-whine snuck into my helmet. "Captain, I'm clear of the deck."

I opened the visor, brought the armpad up to my nose and painstakingly punched in the command to have the *hard shell* inject me with painkillers. I slammed it shut on the noise of the screamer and steeled myself to move. "You have Lopez?"

"Yes, sir."

I took three huge breaths and tried to sit up, but gravity and pain chained me where I was. "Get to the shuttle."

"Roger."

Gentle but firm, I heard Thompson's voice in my ear. "Captain?"

"Go," was all I could manage.

"Captain, I have nine minutes remaining. What is your ETA?"

Nine minutes? So soon? My helmet beeped again, making it officially nine minutes to Slipspace. Pain. Endless, throbbing pain. It pressed down on me and held me in place. Again, I tried to move. "Lieutenant, I don't think I'm going to make it."

"Captain, you have to."

And then I remembered that some genius had set this entire ship on a collision course with a sun. Agony gave way to anger, white and hot. It bubbled up in my voice like tar. "Lieutenant, my leg's in a bad way. I'm out of time. I think its best that you just go."

"We can't, Captain."

Goddammit, Thompson! Don't get sentimental. Men die in combat. Even Captains. "Lieutenant, you have your orders."

Her next words crashed into me like chunks of ice off a waterfall. "Captain, I have been trying to tell you. Orders or not, there is nobody on this shuttle that can fly it. You are the only one who is even vaguely rated."

There were no thoughts in my head, just the stinging shock of having possibly caused the death of my entire crew. "If I'm not there in seven minutes, you do the best you can."

"Roger Captain."

I got to my knees and the pain from my leg nearly caused me to black out. But after my leg calmed down, it became apparent the agony was fading, the edges dulling, but not fast enough. Worse, I wasn't going to get any real relief until I got to a medical bay. I closed my eyes to breathe, and then a torturous shock flung my eyes open. I had fallen over.

I tried to stand.

I slipped.

I tried to stand.

I fell.

I tried to stand.

My numbed hand slipped in the pool of my own vomit, and I slapped back into the floor, coaxing my burnt leg to new heights of misery. A part of me wanted to just sit there and cry.

Something dark and dangerous, equal parts stubbornness, hatred, training, and instinct grabbed the weak, wobbling part of me by the throat and pinned it to the floor of my mind. It whispered to me in a violent voice. *If you give in to this, everyone in your command is dead.*

I planted my hand on the deck with the sound of God slapping a titan.

If I give in to this, everyone in my command is dead.

I pushed. The bullet lodged in my chest pinched and burrowed a millimeter deeper. My scream echoed hollowly in the cargo hold.

If I fail, all of this will have been in vain.

My left hand brushed the massive borg pistol on the deck, and the violent part of me made me pick it up.

Persephone will burn.

I heaved myself to my good knee, trying to keep the other straight to lessen the anguished vice that held it.

More people will die.

I righted myself, squatting on my good leg as I fought against disability and distraction, trying to keep my balance and my sanity.

If I give up, no one will know why we died. Why anyone died.

I pushed with one leg. Muscles and servomotors inside the suit protested in unison as I came shakily, slowly, to a stand.

Get fragging moving, solider.

I looked out across the huge expanse of floor between me and the door. The gibbering thing broke loose and ran around my skull, shrieking in terror at the prospect of every step from here to there, and every step from there to the shuttle. A warning buzzer sounded in my helmet. The counter said seven minutes remaining until the ship Slipped.

I took a step.

The pain exploded, flaring up like an aeroline fire, engulfing my ears, blinding my eyes, erupting on my tongue with bitterness. All I could smell was my own burnt flesh. But then it lessened, it receded and in the hollowness left behind, the ringing became a voice, soft but strong. I knew it, somewhere deep in my soul, it fed an unseen hunger, balmed an old hurt, lifted me and pressed me onward. It whispered to me, *You're a hero, Rook.*

I took another step.

And another.

And another.

And each time it was louder, the voice stronger. And my soul sung in a choir with it. I reached out, leaned forward, and caught the doorframe leading into the hallway. I looked back across the handful of meters to the body of Carver. It might as well have been a grand mountain top. I had done the impossible. Now I just had to do it again.

Beep!

Six minutes.

I leaned on the doorframe, sweat dripping from my face like a heavy rain. It collected on the visor and ran like tears. I could feel the synthetic morphine rushing through me, finally pushing back the agony to tolerable levels. I let go and took two more steps, unsteadily, into the hall. *Looks like I might make it after all.*

And that's when a plasma stream passed by so close it blistered the paint on my armor. I heaved myself around clumsily and saw Carver clawing his way to his feet, blood trickling from three of the holes in his chest plate. Without thinking, I lifted the six-kilo monster in my left hand and sent a bullet his way. Off balance, shooting off-handed, I wasn't surprised to see it go wide.

Carver gained his feet as I settled down to use my last bullet. The barrel shook like a branch in the wind. He swung his plasma cannon into line. "You don't get away that easily, Rook."

An inconsequential panel's flashing lights blinked insolently in my peripheral vision. "Yes, I do, *fragger.*"

I shifted aim to the control panel for the door and squeezed the trigger.

The one thing, perhaps the only thing, the media gets right is control panels on automatic doors. They're hardwired so that if they are destroyed, they assume there's been catastrophic damage to the panel due to decompression or fire and try to shut the door to seal the compartment. They can be overridden from the bridge, however, but *The Rage of Exiles* no longer had a bridge, it had a morgue. My bullet sent plastic flying in thousands of tiny shards. Carver took aim at me and squeezed his trigger, but the plasma bolts impacted on the lightning-fast blast doors that came down between us. I heard him scream unprintable obscenities over the radio.

My response, "I hope you tan well, Carver," shut him up. Then I ordered everyone to switch frequencies and decryption routines. At least it would keep him out of the loop for a little while. I resisted the urge to check the countdown, and I wasted no time getting back on the move.

The pain medication was in full effect, but my head started to swim every time I tried to put more than just scant weight on my leg. I had to limp heavily, listing to my right.

I considered throwing the massive pistol away—it was empty after all—but the weight at the end of my arm helped balance me out. I spared a second to grab a fire extinguisher off of the wall and douse my left leg. Strangely, I felt nothing. I ditched the thing and kept moving.

Beep!

Thompson's voice was smooth but brittle. "Five minutes, Captain."

"Roger." I sounded like a corpse with a mouth full of *grit*. I firmed up my own as best I could. "In route. Begin warming up the engines if you can."

"I can't."

"Use the shuttle's comm system to call Doe. Have him walk you through it."

"Roger."

Time kept falling toward my death... quickly, too quickly. I decided to take an awful risk and use an elevator to traverse the decks between my team and me. I got in and pushed the button. There was a stream of smarmy toneless music that dissolved into static. The elevator jumped a meter up in its magnetic bottle before quickly, but gently, descending to the correct deck. My heart pounded like a jackrabbit until the door opened halfway and ground to a halt, power flickering on and off. I stepped out and began lurching down the corridor when there was a screech and crash from the direction of the elevator. I did not look back.

I had four minutes remaining.

I gimped as fast as I could, the fire from my leg and the stabbing pain in my chest combining to form a haze of screeching fog. It cocooned me in my own little world of misery, and made me blind to everything except for the path directly ahead. I pulled up short when I realized that lines began to creep toward my position on the HUD. I shook my head to focus past my discomfort and suddenly saw clearly. The lines were the holographic map of the docking bay, built hours ago when we had first captured it. I was almost there.

Another beep, and then there were only three minutes remaining.

I gained no spring to my step, but I swear to Christ, I was springing on the inside. Hope allowed me to shoulder aside the pain and cover the last hundred meters. The doors slid open obediently and for a panicked moment, I thought I was in the wrong place. I was expecting a floor littered with blood and spent casings. Instead, I labored to get myself inside a docking bay that looked like a black box.

The Key to Damocles

The nuclear engines of the unbondable's dropship were hot, burning miniscule amounts of fuel to keep the reaction chamber going. Even at low idle, they flooded the whole chamber with dangerous levels of radiation. The usual alarms were silent, but the hazard lights had popped up all along the dropship and were rotating merrily. Thick, black, rubberized tarps had automatically deployed from rolls along the ceiling to protect the walls from being contaminated, and a matching unit had drawn to cover the ceiling. The floor had been swept clean, and more sheets were drawn over the stacks of crates. Plates had been brought out from storage by the robots and laid out to protect the floor, but now the mechanical loaders stood along the wall like terracotta warriors.

The thick floor plates were spongy; I felt like I was walking through the negative of a cloud-castle dream, and I had to rely even more on the balance provided by the cartoonishly large pistol to keep me from tottering over. I hobbled to the airlock at the back of the craft when I heard the door behind me cycle closed and, an instant later, the one to my right cycle open.

Instinct sent me into a forward dive as plasma erupted from the dark opening, burning out in all directions, scoring metal and burning rubber wherever it hit. That familiar sound of a man who sounds like he gargles with razorblades clawed at my ears. "You're a cockroach, Rook."

I looked up at him, and I swear he was enough to make me believe in the walking dead. Blood dripped from three of five gunshot wounds, he was limping where a bullet had at least dislocated his hip, and perhaps had penetrated to shatter it completely. His gun swung in wobbly arcs, and his head snapped from side to side in a textbook symptom of *venom* overdose.

I managed to get to my feet and lunge on my good leg behind a stack of crates as he fired again, tracking a wild course across me twice. The unfocused plasma unleashed its heat and fury, but failed to breech my armor. *Lucky, lucky, lucky.*

He chased after me, blood high and patience short. His whispers had a monomolecular edge that shaved off brain cells. "I end you here, Rook."

I propped myself up on the rubber-covered crates and dove over them, rolling across as he unleashed another long burst. I could hear him gasping, and his voice began to bubble, telling me one of my shots had hit a lung. "You know what?" said Carver. "Despite your legend…"

I started to crawl and shrieked with pain as carbonized skin slipped free of the muscle of my shin.

"…despite the fact that people talk about you in respectful whispers…"

I grasped onto the pain like a stallion, allowing it to take me into the very primitive parts of my soul. It gave me strength enough to get to my feet and actually run five steps around the next man-sized pile of crates.

"…despite the fact that everyone follows you around and French kisses your ass…"

He followed me again, getting closer, closer taking shots every time he got a glimpse of me going around the next side.

"…you're really not that tough."

He managed to break into a run, whirling around the corner only to find my hand had clamped like a steel vice on the barrel of his weapon for the second time that day. I felt the hate start in my toes and funnel upwards, building pressure until it reached my mouth.

"No, not tough," I replied.

He tried to jerk the barrel away, but I held on for dear life for the half second before my left hand came swinging in, wielding the six-kilogram borg pistol like a caveman with a rock. The force of the blow spider-webbed his faceplate and knocked him to the ground. I let go of his weapon and reached behind me to the stack of crates. With one heave, I pulled the whole sheet down across the bastard. Like a gladiator in a net, he fumbled on the ground as I lifted my injured leg, grit my teeth, and snarled.

"But at least I'm not stupid!" And I brought my entire weight down upon the barrel of the plasma cannon.

Most weapons are made to withstand terrible conditions and continue working. While terrible conditions include dirt, cold, water and heat, it does not cover my foot. Without getting too scientific, the math went something like this: one hundred and change kilogram me plus one hundred thirty kilo suit, multiplied by strength augmentation, and weighted for armored boots, divides one plasma cannon into two pieces of worthless techno-junk.

I lost more skin than I wanted to think about.

I almost blacked out.

His wail of frustration was so worth it.

I stumbled, but managed to stay upright. My stomach churned and my head swam, but I stayed upright. I had to choke down bile, and blink twice before the world stopped doubling or tripling in front of me, but I stayed upright. Then slowly, slowly, I began to limp toward the rear airlock of the dropship.

I could hear Carver struggling with the radiation sheet. I heard his helmet bounce across the floor, but there were only one hundred thirty-two seconds left, and I had to get my team out of here.

That's of course when Carver shot me.

The pain was immense, starting at my right lat muscle and washing out. It was disturbingly familiar, an agony I hoped never to feel again. I stumbled, pitched forward, and fell. My left hand dropped the borg pistol and latched onto the handle to the airlock. I twisted clumsily, and wound up facing up and backward, legs sprawled. All I could see was Carver steadying his own thirteen-millimeter pistol and taking shot after shot.

Again, I was caught in endless spaces between seconds, watching the bullets explode from the end of his gun, going wide and slamming into the side of the dropship. His face was drawn and ashen, his bi-racial features spoiled by a deep cut, probably from flying shards of his faceplate. I watched as beads of blood dripped onto the floor. I focused in on them, finding hope in the thumb-thick glops. I stared at his eyes, and reflected the hate I saw there right back at him. Like me, his hands were protected by armored gloves. But like me, the first shot had numbed his hand. Each shot provided another shock, and his aim worsened the harder he tried to kill me. He emptied his magazine as I managed to get my legs, suddenly made of clay, beneath me. "Thompson, emergency decompress the landing bay."

He came closer, fumbling in his pouch for his spare ammunition. He dropped the magazine out of the weapon and began to stalk towards me.

"I sent you the codes from the bridge. Use them, Thompson. Emergency decompression, now," I repeated. He came closer, steps faltering but too fast, fed by God knew how much venom and hate as hot as a volcano's heart. I gripped the handle for dear life.

"Emergency decompression, now!" He was only three meters away, and he began to lift his weapon. I stood as straight as I could, and his barrel followed me up, centered in the middle of my face.

"If I'm going to hell, you're coming as my slave." Carver set the barrel against my faceplate with a sickening metallic *tink*.

I was screaming into my comm. "Goddammit, emergency decompress now! NOW! NOW! NOW!"

I saw Carver close one eye in a parody of aiming, his smile the very picture of a nightmare executioner, when a deep, resonant thud drew his attention.

My right hand grabbed his weapon and twisted. He squeezed the trigger on reflex and the shot missed my helmet by a perhaps a millimeter. But before he could even yank it out of my hands, the grinding gears and sudden hiss riveted him into place.

I made sure my speakers were on. "You get to go to hell alone, *dogfragger*."

And then I clocked him backwards with my shoulder. He left the pistol in my hands as he took three hopeless steps for the exit. There was no point, the bay was decompressing, venting its atmosphere into space. The landing bay door was opening and the human sized doors wouldn't open without the help of high explosives.

The main vehicle doors parted, and the air left with a demonic thump. I was pulled off my feet, and Carver was yanked back towards me, but both of us were too heavy, and the air supply too small, to fling us into space. His face was exposed, so his eyes immediately froze, and the air was sucked from his lungs in a violent burp, but what really killed him was the difference in pressure between his internal organs and the vacuum of outer space.

The holes in his body acted like little nozzles, and most of his blood came rocketing out into the nothingness on all sides. Streams of red were pulled apart by the cold hands of space, dissecting the blood into a horrible crimson vapor. It blossomed toward the ceiling, ruptured cells freezing in mid-flight as his desperate hands tried to plug the holes, tried to grasp at his life that even now lessened to a trickle. The gravity web beneath our feet brought the storm of ruby glitter back down even as his flailing ebbed. He fell to his knees. His shoulders slumped. His head lurched back to rail silently at the ceiling. If not for the gruesome scarlet of the flakes and the silent scream on his face, he might have been a snow globe diorama. The fine sparkling stars fell as flurries of sin and vice, collecting on the rubberized mats, melting on his still warm armor, and pooling on his shocked, frozen face.

Carver was dead.

My internal systems noticed the change in air pressure and sealed my suit. The shot to the back had destroyed electronics but not breeched the armor. It pronounced me safe, but the digital timer said differently. I cycled the airlock and lunged inside. Precious seconds were lost as it filled with air. Even more seconds escaped me as I opened the interior door and dove inside to the waiting arms of my crewmembers.

Everything became a blur as they hustled me forward. Archer ran ahead to open the doors and clear the way as I half jogged, half limped through the narrow aisles. Someone had to pry Carver's gun from my death grip and toss it into a locker. I painfully flexed that hand while the other unfastened Ortega's helmet and tossed it to someone for quick storage. Immediately, Tsang and Ansef were next to me, locking their own armored arms beneath mine and carrying me faster than I could hobble alone.

They had to abandon me at the cockpit; there simply was not room for us all. Thompson started to rise from the pilot's chair and I shoved her back down roughly with one hand. She was obviously trying to keep her cool, but her self-control was becoming worn and threadbare as she said, "I can't fly this beast, Captain."

"You're going to have to." I leaned over her, flipping switches and dials as I stated the painfully obvious. "That seat will not hold this armor and there is no time to take it off. Just grab the throttle and yoke and wait for my go ahead."

I skipped preflight, I skipped safety checks, I overrode the safeties, and in thirty seconds violated every single rule in every single flight manual in existence. I did remember to scream for everyone to strap in tight as my gloved hand closed on a handle set into the ceiling for just such a purpose. Green lights sprung into life across the console. If I had had the time, I would have sung praises to God, but as the countdown ticked past fifty-five seconds, I forwent the formality.

"Go!" The word leapt from my lips and Thompson tightened her grip on the throttle and pushed it to the stops.

The ship skidded, the ship lurched, mechanical muscles inside my glove whined as they struggled to keep me from splattering my face across the console. The dropship did not leap free of the bay of the doomed spacecraft. My eyes flew across the flashing panels and HUD for eighteen precious seconds, eliminating possibilities until they lit upon a lone flashing red light.

I punched the button, simultaneously cracking the panel and disengaging the magnetic landing gear. The ship shot from the bay as if from a cannon. There was a horrible crash and screeching sound as the top aerodynamic surfaces were sheared off by the doorway to the bay. Debris rocketed past us like confetti as we left *The Rage of Exiles* behind.

Five seconds later, *The Rage of Exiles* blipped out of existence in realspace.

Less than a second later, it reentered realspace in the super-hot gasses of the star Persephone and became heavily distorted by the gravity well.

One one-hundredth of a second later, not one molecule of the ship touched any other.

Cheers erupted behind me in the crew compartment as I slumped against the wall, bone weary and hurting everywhere. I saw Thompson sitting a little too stiffly in the pilot seat, full of something still pent up inside. I set one, mangled glove on her shoulder. "You did a spectacular job, Lieutenant."

Thompson laughed like a macaw as emotions began to erupt, hot and raw, from wherever she had bottled them. "Thank you, sir. But next time might I make a suggestion?"

"Sure."

"Perhaps more than one of us needs to be flight certified?"

"OK, but until then, I stay with the ship, you go get shot." We laughed as Tsang and Ansef came forward and plugged mini-computers into my suit's on-board doctor, trying to assess the extent to which my body was damaged. They got the readings.

They weren't laughing.

The Key to Damocles

As the adrenaline and synthetic morphine faded, echoed pain became an ear-splitting din of torment. A phantom addiction whispered the need for a cigarette in my ear as the medics began uncoupling armor joints and passing them back for other crewmembers to pack away. Ominously, they left the armor on my injured leg alone. Ansef murmured something about skin integrity as they helped me back to a seat. They leaned me back and then then flipped me over to do the same with the *fragging* hole in my back.

I glanced to the side as they shot me full of muscle relaxants and painkillers. There, strapped flat to an acceleration couch, was Richardson. With all the medical equipment piled on and around him, he looked like he was being attacked by dozens of blood sucking worms. I wondered if my cleverness would cost him his life. I wondered if Earth, or Persephone, or anyplace else, was worth his life.

It was an hour later when we had slowed enough to dock with *Deadly Heaven*. I sat in the copilot's chair and kept my hands near the controls, but with all the medication floating through my blood, I didn't dare do it myself. I talked Thompson through it, who all the while looked like she was being given a colonoscopy with a flagpole. There was a bump, a scrape, and a jerk at the end, but we made it into the bay without damage to *Heaven* or her crew.

Immediately, we made course corrections to begin the long journey back to Persephone. Most of our fuel had been burned up in the chase, so we needed to use most of the remainder to get into position for a short Slip and the long realspace flight back using gravity 'cheats' to slow down before we entered orbit. It would take time, but we didn't have the fuel to do this action-movie style.

Hours after that, the medical robot, Bugs, pronounced that my armored ribcage had saved me from death, twice. The bullets had begun to tumble, as all bullets do, once they had pierced the assault *hard shell*. As such they had turned off true, and had impacted my subdermal armor at an angle, spoiling the piercing properties of the bullet and allowing my artificial ribcage to absorb the kinetic energy. Each impact had still measured up with being hit with a lance mounted on a motorcycle. I had lots of internal bleeding, but it only took an hour of surgery and half a dozen nano-infections to get me out of danger and feeling human again. I'd still need an expert's help replacing my ribcage, though.

I slept for a good long while.

I awoke in the recovery room and called Thompson down for a quick situation report. Most of the other *Angels* were fine. We'd have to get Walt a replacement leg, but at least Long was already up and about, albeit in three separate casts. Ortega would have to replace a few fingers, and he could probably make do with universal donor cloned replacements. Lopez was still in surgery, but he should be doing fine soon. I told her to feed the crew, get them to pack their equipment, and then let them get some sleep. She actually saluted before leaving in something of a hurry. I couldn't blame her; next to me in the recovery room lay Richardson. He had not improved markedly for being in surgery or medbay. His vitals were still touch-and-go.

That was when I started going through the electronic reports with Grisham's help. The first thing I did was check on any communications from Logan, Reeves or O'Leary. It would be days before we reached Persephone, and days more before I could piece together precisely what happened, but that was the moment when I found out my friend had died.

I checked to make sure I was alone before I put by face in my hands and silently cried.

CHAPTER 24: WE ALL FALL DOWN

Planet Persephone,
New California, Rochester Burroughs, 06:25, 11/13/2662

His name is Master Sergeant Thomas Logan. He is a cyborg. His body is a one hundred- and seventy-five-year-old design. It is made of high-tensile polymers, ceramic and titanium laminates. He weighs two tons and can lift almost three and he is impervious to nearly all man-portable small arms. His life expectancy on the modern field of battle is only about three minutes.

Survival was dependent on milliseconds, millimeters, and fractions of a degree.

The gauss slug cracked above his head, moving many times the speed of sound. His sensor vanes were plotting bullet trajectory and speed, measuring the sound density and echoes, drawing a bright green line in his subconscious all the way from point of impact to point of origin. Microcomputers flooded his neural network with impulses, forcing them to work harder and faster, and the world slowed down and sharpened into crystal clarity. Information was fed to him by hundreds of separate units inside his CPU, telling him everything from the relative humidity to the grain weight and velocity of the hardened tungsten spike that just barely missed his head.

He wanted to stop. He wanted to go home. He didn't want to try because he might fail. He might die. It wasn't the dying though. It was the failing. If he failed dozens of civilians, prisoners would burn to death.

He popped up and spun, thirty kilo assault cannon swinging into line with the sniper. He 'strained' his heart frequency monitor, and caught the barest hint of the sniper's life signs inside the darkened window. He aligned his sights and fired as the sniper's scope found him. Two triggers snapped, and once fired, the bullets could not be recalled by any power in the universe.

The sniper's slug was faster, and it screamed through the air with deadly intent, smashing into the front of Logan's cannon. Steel parted like butter as it splintered the hand guard and barrel. Plastic and metal went flying as it continued to traverse forward and down, snapping two fingers off of his left hand before exiting and tumbling into his shin. The projectile hit perfectly flat against the heavy laminate armor plating and ricocheted off, leaving a fist-sized dent and sending a head-sized crater worth of dirt up from its grave. Had it hit straight on, it would have torn his high-tech foot clean off.

As fast as the sniper's slug was, however, Logan had already fired and a burst of three rounds were burning the air toward his position. One impacted the wall, obliterating brick and causing it to tumble as it slammed into the enemy. The spinning round impacted the kneeling unbondable in the right leg and the round, barely slowed by the bone and muscle it found, severed the foot completely. The next also hit the wall, passing through the aluminum windowsill and spinning a quarter turn before striking the unbondable's chest. Instantly, his light armor failed. It passed through him like a flying rock, gathering flesh before it and exiting his back as a cloud of gore with a jacketed lead core. He was already dead before the third came through the window and smacked against his helmet, creating a small hole in, small hole out, and an explosion of brains within. His heart stopped, all signals clipped like a thread on a loom. In a very real way, Logan felt him die. He dropped the mangled cannon, bolted for the darkened school doorway, and growled out over the radio, "Sniper down! Repeat, sniper down!"

"Continue firing at the windows." Reeves rolled to cover and stood up to shield himself with the edge of the window as Logan disappeared inside the school. "Logan, pull back and we'll regroup!"

"Negative, General. There is no time." Logan had to duck to get inside, his massive body blotting out the daylight, sensors automatically shifting from normal to a whole spectrum of visual and nonvisual inputs. They fed him information in dyslexic gulps: fifteen humans in the classroom to the right, one weapon inside, primed... thirteen humans ahead, fifteen energy weapons primed. Logan was sitting smack dab in the middle of a shooting gallery. Heads popped out from around doorjambs along the hall, glowing in his thermographic sight like training targets.

The unbondable to Logan's right exposed himself and leveled his rifle. Almost faster than the cyborg could think, his arm lashed out, his gorilla-sized hand closing around the foregrip of the enemy's plasma rifle, and the hand positioned to hold it steady. Logan's eighth eye glanced over, saw the soldier, saw his screaming face through his visor, and saw the line of terrified, dirty women cringing behind him.

A horribly cold fire lit inside the *Angel* as they cowered, a rage that burned and built. It strained at his sanity and filled the ghost of his heart to bursting with terrible, awful things. Logan squeezed until bone and steel mated like demonic lovers. Then he pulled. Hard.

Logan's ears filtered frequencies and adjusted for distortion. He heard the unbondable cry like a schoolchild and heard the wet tearing sound of muscle and tendon ripping apart as he collected the gun and the arm from the disgraced soldier. Screams exploded from everywhere, filling the hallway with confusion as he tossed the weapon and limb out the front door behind him. Logan made one transmission. "I have contact with the enemy."

Logan's comm was literally inside his head and linked into his thoughts, so there was no extraneous outside noise, but sometimes there are whispers in the transmission as the mental line between transmitted signals and private thought were blurred. The underlying whisper hoped for a quick death, a good death.

Then rifles came around doorjambs up ahead and the hallway erupted into packets of superheated matter and beams of coherent light. Another whisper inside his head hissed, *I have to get the prisoners out. It has to be now.*

Logan reached out to his right and closed a metal hand over the last in a row of lockers along the wall. It took only a brief tug to make them come loose, and he pulled them from their moorings like a row of chain link fence, creating a wall across the hallway. As one hand pushed them forward, the other, half-missing, hand did the same with the lockers on the opposite wall. He pressed forward and hunkered down behind, reinforcing the light metal with his body. The light metal lockers shattered the plasma packets but paid a terrible price for the momentary protection. The paint immediately caught fire, sending up clouds of choking black smoke. The lasers, however, passed through as if the barrier was not there, shattering on his heavily armored skin like a violent rain of light. The women would have no such protection. There was nothing for it. Soon an unbondable would palm a grenade and toss it over the barrier and then...

He turned up the volume on his external speakers to full and screamed, internal translator chip transposing words into Spanish, "Run! ¡*Dirigido ahora*! Run now! ¡*Quédese bajo*! Stay low! ¡*Muévase*! ¡*Ahora*!"

There was a pause that seemed to last forever, then unkempt, abused bodies began pouring out of the classroom. Logan leaned to his right, using his gargantuan artificial chest to provide solid cover for the refugees as metal burned and lasers pierced lockers like icepicks. He almost forgot to mentally flip off the translator and make another radio broadcast. "General, Hold your fire! Civilians exiting the building. Civilians exiting building!"

"We have them, Logan. A *fast mover is* coming in to provide cover," Reeves called back.

Immediately, *The Bastard* did a low pass flyover of the target school, jamming pods screaming, thermographically-active smoke canisters spilling from the bottom like burning hail. These nodule-covered cans hit the soil, sparking and belching, and quickly bounced to a stop. They threw up a wall of smoke, providing visual cover for the women who bolted for distant alleys with the street sense of those born to the slums.

Another three women dodged into the hall and out the front door as the locker barricade began to truly disintegrate, superheated metal tearing along dotted lines made from incoming coherent light and packets of energy. Logan's sensors detected the last civilian leaving the room and running out the door, but then she stopped.

Come on lady, run. She hovered there, at the edge of safety, caught between freedom and hellfire as second after second ticked by. *Run, damn you.* Then she came back in, ducked low as random shots pierced the barrier more and more often. *What are you...?*

She had to scream to be heard over the incoming fire. "Soldier!"

Logan tried to shift position to provide her cover with his body. Whatever she wanted, this was not the time for thank-you's or heroic speeches. "Run!"

She jerked, and almost bolted, a very human response that couldn't reach her feet. *"¿Entiende usted?* Do you understand? *¡Más presos arriba!'*

More prisoners. Logan had to turn, had to look, and behind him saw a woman: dirty, bruised, and abused. Her lips were split from careless punches and hair matted from days without washing. She had been held, she had been jailed, she had been reduced to less than nothing by those who had held her. But her eyes... her eyes could lift mountains; they were the eyes of a goddess. Despite everything, she had not broken. They looked remarkably like *his* eyes.

Words erupted from deep inside his robotic chest, born of fire and the pieces and parts of him that were still human. They carried the weight and power of a rockslide, a promise so strong that the collapse of a star could not break it. *"¡Los salvaré!* Go!"

The volume of fire increased and, as fast as he was, even a cyborg cannot catch light. As smart as he was, he couldn't outwit physics. As powerful as he was, he couldn't intimidate packets of plasma. The woman turned as part of the locker wall gave way, her back instantly blackened, her rags burst into flames, and she pitched forward.

Just like that, she was gone.

In his soul was a great respect for the nameless woman who even now burned like a satanic candle. As flames licked at her body, burning with the smell of fat, flesh and hair, something unthinkable and apocalyptic took root inside of him. Injustice piled on injustice, fear upon fear, anger cannibalizing anger until it built into something rare, terrible, and terrifyingly familiar.

Two-millimeter wide beams of light deflected from Logan's skin like hot hail as he shifted his massive feet. He gathered his legs as the sheet metal corpses of lockers began to run like wax in his titanium laminate hands. Flat motors bunched with high-performance whines, and a growl of servos bunched up past their stopping point as his brain asked for ever more power out of his robotic coffin of a body. The incoming weapons fire paused, an intake of breath as rifles were reloaded and barrels allowed to cool. It was a scarce second of serenity until the lockers tore with the screeching wail of dying children. Paint smoked and burned, throwing up a roiling curtain of clouds as molten steel sagged. A rogue wind parted the acidic black fog and revealed a titan, made not of armor and motors and plastic, but a two-ton man made solely of vengeance.

He launched over the fires like an animal, sounds indescribable by a human mouth roaring from his speakers. One unbondable leaned from cover and raised his weapon when the Master Sergeant's hand closed over his helmet. Time seemed to slow as he looked directly into the silver palm, which trembled and squeezed. Logan strained as warnings went off across his body: *incoming fire detected, internal temperature at serious levels, load stress tolerance exceeded in right hand unit.* The unbondable mercenary fumbled with the release straps as the visor starred and cracked. The buckle slipped through his fingers. Logan's fingers nearly met as the helmet collapsed on his enemy's head like an eggshell.

Another shooter came around a corner down the hallway, and Logan picked up his last victim around the chest and slung himself to the side. His arm came up and over his head, putting his entire bodyweight behind the corpse. In an instant, every electronic muscle convulsed, and over two tons worth of lifting potential focused on a single man's weight. Dead arms snapped as the body accelerated to bone-crushing speeds, hurled in a short arc limited not by strength, but torque. Logan's metal bones screamed electronic warnings as his synthetic spine wrenched violently, accelerating the hundred kilo corpse to seventy-five kilometers per hour. It traveled only five meters before smashing into the body of his teammate. Light armor is meant to protect against bullets, blades, and energy. The weight of one man crashing into the other flung both back, snapping the target's neck with the force of a car wreck. Of those that remained, three ran for their lives, six cowered under cover, two opened fire, one pulled the pin on a grenade. Logan decided the one with the grenade would be the first to die.

Logan leapt on the unbondable like a two-ton lion. He snatched the hand holding the grenade, ripped it from his body, and tossed the whole thing after the three fleeing renegades. The following explosion was accompanied by a flash that highlighted the cyborg's next victim's screaming face in his chest plate. Logan swept him off his feet and gripped his ankles together in one hand. He fired at the Sergeant's metal face, blinding eye number seven before he could get a proper grip on the struggling mercenary and sling him around like a flail. Two more unbondables came around their cover, and Logan beat them to death with their comrade.

Blood went everywhere, limbs becoming detached and tumbling through the air. Blood poured over his armor, finding cracks and working deep inside like fuel for a demonic engine. Each death did not quench the terrible wrath that erupted there, it only caused it to grow larger, fiercer. Logan's perceptions stuttered, fluttered, as synthetic adrenaline and electronic stimulants crashed into his gray matter. A warning whispered in his ear: *Caution, Hard Drive Recording Corruption / Emotional Overload Imminent.*

But he did not stop, could not stop, not until they were all dead.

"Logan? Logan?" Words began to intrude on Logan's private abattoir. They brought him back from the edge of sanity, if only just barely. Reeves' voice was not designed to calm, and he wasn't Logan's favorite person right now. "Goddammit, Logan, I can *fragging* see you like a *fragging* supernova on our instruments, so you're not *fragging* dead."

A head popped around the doorjamb of the main entrance. The templar model cyborg turned toward it like a spooked beast and it went away.

"What is it?" Reeves voice growled over the comm. "What?"

Reeves charged forward and pulled his subordinate back, only then did he look himself. The General tried to take a quick peek that stuttered into a full, long look as he shook his head in disbelief. His eyes first fell on the guttering body of what was obviously one of the hostages. Beyond it, however, the neglected school had been transformed into a madman's dream of gore. Body parts were everywhere, and blood splattered every wall and much of the ceiling. Juices pooled and ran along the floor, springing from strewn body parts and piles of entrails. Men and pieces of men had been pulled apart and tossed aside. As he watched, Logan sent an unbondable tumbling through the doorway to his right. The disgraced mercenary flew through the air like a rag doll, impacting the wall with a collection of sickening pops and cracks. It must have been surreal, like living through a scene from a horror movie.

Reeves switched frequencies and called again. "Logan?"

The Key to Damocles

Logan had to bend over almost double to get through the classroom door into the hallway. His silver skin smoldered with scorch marks, his hands dripped with blood. It must have been like watching a demon being born. One of the *Apostles* ducked back outside to be ill. The rest edged in behind their General, knowing they shouldn't point their weapons at the Master Sergeant, even as their instincts told them this is precisely what they should do.

"Logan, wait."

"General, we have no time. There are still some women trapped upstairs. I'm going to try and reach them." Logan turned away and began marching up the hallway. It burned him that Reeves was here to escort him out when he had a job yet to do. Agitation blinded him to sensor feeds, years of training, and common sense. Even his camera eyes began experiencing data overflow as his brain focused on only the very center of the image. In humans it is called 'tunnel vision'.

Reeves' voice became honestly angry, urgent. "Goddammit, Logan!"

Logan bit off an angry retort as he entered a 'T' intersection and an alert screamed in his head like a nail in his temple. It came too slow, too late. The two-ton cyborg was knocked off his feet by a three-kilogram, explosive warhead. It detonated on his right side, and he was blown through the opposite wall. Debris cascaded down upon him, and he flattened dusty tables and chairs beneath his bulk. The beast inside him yelped and went silent. Logan took an instant inventory of his body and saw that three eyes were out, his right arm was working on backup servos and he had a minor hydraulic leak in his right leg. The sane part of him was awake enough to comment, *anti-personnel rocket. Lucky.*

He tossed a chunk of concrete off of his chest and clawed through the cloud of dust to take cover at the edge of the templar-shaped hole in the wall. His sensors came alive and felt Reeves set up his team to fire down the spur hallway at the unbondables trying to reload their rocket launcher. The enemy took cover in classrooms as the *Apostles* put up a withering wall of fire. Logan dodged out into the hall again and took position next to Reeves. Surprisingly, the General was in the lead, his automatic weapon chattering a deadly song. He spared a second to sneer at the Sergeant.

"We're here to help, you self-righteous bastard. Now pay attention to your *gritlicking* sensors. You can't save anyone if you're dead." Reeves' meat eyes met Logan's glass lenses. An apology flashed between them, first one way, and Logan bowed his head to send it back to him. Reeves smiled like a Norse god as he reloaded. "Get upstairs. We'll hold them here."

Logan pulled himself up, the film of rage clearing from his perceptions. Data started flooding in as he sought his spiritual center with slippery hands. *I've always prided myself in being above any moment, but it's been harder and harder since...* Logan throttled the thought into silence as sensor inputs suddenly brought the world into startling clarity. One of Reeves' team tossed a grenade and called for cover. Everyone ducked back as it rattled the building, and the cyborg took the second delay in the firefight to continue down the hallway toward the stairs. The sounds of battle faded as he sprinted through the concrete tunnels.

Reeves had been right, and wrong, all at the same time. The purpose of the soldier is to defend people. With guns, with bombs, with their body, with their life; it is the purpose of the just to shield the helpless. Women, helpless women, had been dying in front of them and Reeves had chosen to do nothing because it was expedient, easy, cheap. *Wrong.*

And what did I do? Logan had charged ahead, his emotions breaking free and dragging him along like a pack of rabid dogs. He had ignored protocol, training, the chain of command, positively everything except exacting vengeance. *Not vengeance, was I looking for...?* Was he trying to make up for past failures with future victories? A fool's errand, digging a twenty-meter hole to make up for not finding gold in the first ten meters. Eventually, all you have is an extremely deep grave. Logan knew, knew down to his metal bones, there was something severely broken inside his mind, but he had always managed to control it up until now. He was losing his grip on sanity, and just thinking about it was like having a cold dagger nicking the base of his spine.

The women... I have to focus on the women. Logan reached the stairs and began bounding up them eight to a stride, heavy metal feet cracking the fake marble tile. He listened with his internal heart frequency monitor, and found a group of living people on the third floor. Air quality sensors began chattering alerts at him, telling him that the air was becoming more and more poisonous, filled with smoke from various plastics, oils, and chemicals. He 'listened' to his sensors, and they said that the ambient temperature was beginning to rise alarmingly. He skidded to a stop on the second floor and looked long and hard at the thick, metal fire doors to the main hallway. The tiny window was black with roiling smoke beyond and the door glowed in his thermographic vision. He flipped his internal comm to transmit. "General, you have to evacuate. The second floor is filling up with smoke. I don't know what the fire in the north wing has found, but it's feeding on it and growing exponentially."

Reeves came back to him almost immediately. "Roger, get the women and get out. We're almost done with this lot down here."

Old memories, old seminars, old training flooded back into his head, a dream of a life he once had. Logan scrambled up the next set of stairs as he guesstimated the number of burnables and debris inside the school, the fire-resistant nature of the building, estimated airflow, and fuel sources from the unbondables. The numismatics program grabbed all the numbers from the front of his head and crunched them in a microprocessor. It popped out something impossible; it said that the fire should have died out ten minutes ago.

At the top of the stairs he paused, tried to capture a sense of calm, and opened the door to the hallway. He crept out as quietly as possible, which was not very; he was built to take on tanks in hand-to-hand combat, not for infiltration. He registered several enemy soldiers who had clustered in the room two doors up and on the right; probably trading fire with O'Leary right now. Further down there was another group of signals, not moving, no energy weapons active.

I could just go for the prisoners, but then the unbondable would be free to interfere with the rescue. Logan crept down the hall slowly, wondering if rage or wisdom made him stop in front of his chosen door. He doubled up and dove through a classroom door made to fit standard people, shoulders taking out huge chunks out of the frame on either side. His mass and momentum carried him a full seven meters and into the far wall. He rolled over debris, flattening tables strewn with extra weapons and spare ammunition. The first gunman caught the shards of the door square in the chest and went sprawling. The other two managed to turn before he swatted the next, crushing his chest and sending him out the window. Door-boy sprayed the cyborg with a burst of laser fire from the floor, so Logan stomped on him like a bug, flattening his chest and killing him instantly. The last one actually threw his gun out the window and held his arms high in the air.

Logan and his prisoner stood there for infinite seconds, clots of blood falling from nooks in Logan's metal skin and fear stinking up the room. The unbondable began to quiver, to shake all over. He tried as hard as he could to stand still. Urine dribbled down his leg.

For a moment, a long moment, Logan thought about simply snatching his enemy's head from his shoulders and moving on.

And then, as the beast in his soul began to growl happily, he thought about it again.

He did not have time for this. "Disarm Strip."

Slowly, the unbondable began to comply. His helmet was first, then his chest plate. It revealed not a devil, not a demon, just a guy... a frightened, youngish guy at that. He probably wasn't much past twenty and now there was no conceivable way he would live to see thirty. Logan felt a stirring of sorrow until he remembered the burning corpse of the woman downstairs. He decided to feel sorry for her instead. The Master Sergeant hit the radio and told O'Leary, "Prisoner coming out."

"Where is he coming out—?" Logan gave the wall at the bottom of the windowsill a few swift kicks, sending concrete chunks sailing out into the playground. She giggled. "Never mind."

The prisoner loosened his pistol belt and let the holster, magazines and grenades fall to the floor. "They're going to kill me."

Logan reached forward and caught both of his wrists in one metal hand. "Yes. They will."

Tears began streaming down his face. "What will I do?"

"Make peace with God." Logan swung him out of the window and knelt down, lowering him as far as possible toward the

The Key to Damocles

ground before letting go. The unbondable still fell five meters, and it looked like he twisted his ankle when he landed.

O'Leary snorted over the comm. "Yeah, talk to the invisible guy in the clouds; that'll help when they hang you."

Logan ignored her aside, as he stared down at the doomed man who grabbed his ankle and rolled around in pain. "Do you have him?"

Her sneer came in crystal clear, one could almost feel her setting her sights over the prisoner's chest. She could have shot him right that second, but it would have disappointed *him*, so all she did was watch. "Oh, he is all mine now, Master Sergeant. Go get those girls."

Logan turned to leave and ground to a complete stop. In the corner, normal eyes would see a liquid heat radiator. Large, clunky, metallic, it seemed utterly normal. A perceptive man would notice the paint beginning to bubble around the pipe that emerged from the floor, but it took no special talent for the ridged metal fixture to draw Logan's attention. To his eyes, tuned into a wider spectrum of radiation, the radiator glowed like a sun. Knowledge, old skills almost forgotten, began spinning through his head. All pretense of stealth discarded, he rushed out of the room and ran down the hall, his feet cracking tiles as he activated his comm. "O'Leary?"

"Yes, Master Sergeant?"

"I need a layout of the school, the fire's current position and the specifications on the liquid heat radiator system."

"What?" She sounded annoyed. His request was probably distracting her from watching the unbondable crawl.

"I need schematics, specifications on the heating system, and the fire's current position." Logan reached the door with fifteen life signs beyond it. No weapons powered up. He kicked in the door and levered himself inside. In the classroom were fifteen women in a cage made of faux wrought iron fence, probably stolen from one of the buildings in the surrounding area, and several cots along the walls. The women screamed behind bars of iron, cowering in the corner. Dirty, unkempt, abused, they stared at their savior with abject horror.

He crossed the room, grabbed the gate, and pulled. Soldered, wrapped wire joints gave way with the sound of gunshots. The entire front of the cage came off and smashed into the floor with a shuddering clang.

"*Señoras, soy de los Ángeles de Radiación, debo rescatarle aquí.* Come with me and stay close." They sat there for a moment, staring at him and trying to blink him out of existence. Four meters tall, covered in blood, leaking hydraulic fluid from various joints, he probably wasn't what they expected from a white knight. Then, one of them came forward, slowly. She paused at where the front wall of the cage had been, then she took one step more. Like a shattered dam, the women suddenly flooded out into the main room. One or two stopped to salvage cots along the wall, but most clumped up right next to the Sergeant, holding onto one another and shuddering.

Logan spared one look into the corner, and again the radiator was hot, too hot. Standard air temperature in a government building was almost universally about twenty-two degrees Celsius. The air temperature on the first floor had been twenty-nine degrees. Up on the third floor, it was closer to forty-three and climbing fast. He had assumed it was from the fire, but maybe it wasn't in the way he had assumed. The radiators were far hotter than this, passing one hundred degrees on their surface and going higher, much higher by the second. As they walked out into the hallway, the white paint was starting to bubble and blacken.

"O'Leary?"

"Yeah, yeah, Sergeant, I'm trying to find someone that knows."

"Lomen has a tame hacker; have him look it up."

"It's more complicated than that. Most of the computers that have the information you want have been turned off, blacked out. It's not just about getting the information, it's about finding a place that has it."

"Roger. Look, it's getting hot in here, can I get a pickup on the roof?" Logan and his group reached the staircase, but it was quickly filling with smoke. "Wait, there is too much smoke, we need something to filter the smoke."

One of the women rushed in and began hacking immediately. Logan pulled her back out and closed the door. He looked left and right but didn't see any signs, "*¿Baños?*"

As one, they pointed at one particular door. He took them down there and pushed open the lavatory. He gave them terse instructions, and they began ripping strips of cloth from their tattered clothing and turned on the water. "O'Leary, where's my extraction?"

"*The Bastard* is coming in on your order. He's going to touch down on the far side of the roof. He can be there in thirty seconds."

Finally, some good news. "Roger."

A chorus of cries echoed from inside the bathroom.

Logan glanced in and saw the water was gushing out even with the slightest turn of the tap. It came out not so much as water, but as water combined with steam. Suddenly everything came into focus. *It's not about the fire, it's about the aeroline.* "General, you have got to evacuate, now."

Reeves voice was strong, confident. "We're on our way out. What's wrong?"

"It's the aeroline, General. I think it has accelerated the fire in unforeseen ways."

"Um, what does that mean?"

"It's just a gut call, General."

"That's enough for me. Take whoever you have and get them the *frag* out."

"Roger." Logan collected the fabric swatches went into a bathroom stall. He knocked the lid off of the fill tank and saw that the water was steaming, but not scalding. He plunged the handful of rags inside and handed them out as they jogged back to the stairs. "*Puesto éstos sobre sus caras.*"

They took the rags and placed them over their faces.

He moved into the hall and double-timed it up the stairs. The rag-masks weren't perfect, and there was a lot of coughing and stumbling. Plus, the hottest air and thickest smoke had collected at the top of the staircase. The women fell behind as the cyborg called upon his abused body again, building a running start on the security door to the roof. He collided at top speed, the door, hinges, and sections of wall gave way with a crack and scream. He stumbled onto the roof, followed by thick clouds of roiling smoke and a blast of hot air. The women came next. "Logan to *Bastard*, I am ready for—."

And there he was, engines idling right where he was supposed to be. The tired, dirty women found new energy as they piled into the flier. Logan had to pick some of them up and set them into the open sliding-doorway. The last one held onto him tightly.

"Please."

"Miss, you have to get on board." He could have broken her grip with the least effort, but it seemed wrong to force this woman, who had been forced so much, so often, so recently.

"Por favor. Hay mujeres todavía abajo."

"We already saved them, they're safe already."

"No, mujeres en el hospital."

Prisoners in the infirmary. There are some things that Logan had lost when he traded in his body for metal. One of them is the sinking feeling in the pit of his stomach. *Am I brave because I'm brave, or am I brave because there's no meat body to tell me not to be?* "*¿Dónde está el hospital?*"

"Tercer suelo, ala del sur, hacia el este." Microcomputers whispered to Logan, third floor, south wing, north east side.

"I'll go get them." Logan pulled her hands from around his neck, then called the pilot of *The Bastard* and told him to lift off and circle. His feet crunched on the gravel roof as he bounded back toward the smoking mouth of a doorway. "General, I'm going back inside."

Reeves reply was expected. "What? Are you *fragging* nuts?"

"There are women still in the infirmary. They're on the third floor so they might still be alive. I've got to try."

The Bastard lifted off just as there was an explosion on the north wing's first floor. It blew out all the windows and shook the school to its foundations. Smoke rocketed into the sky, turning early morning into the darkest night. Reeves voice was instantly on the comm. "What the *fragging* hell was that?"

"If we're lucky, it was an ammunition cache going up, but if I'm right, the radiator uses a stable liquid polymer compound to carry heat to the whole school. The storage bay for it is probably next to the gym where the aeroline fire was. The aeroline is superheating the polymer and the pressure is building in the heating system. The pressure valves must have fused. That was the first rupture." Logan leapt from the upper floor to the lower, heedless of the damage to himself or the school. "When the polymer comes out it's heated to near plasma. When it hits oxygen, it explodes."

"But it's supposed to be a heating element. You're telling me it burns?"

"If you get anything hot enough, and then give it oxygen, it will burn."

"So, the entire school has turned into a bomb?"

"That's about right." Logan burst into the third floor and had to switch his holographic map. The entire hall was filled up with smoke, not the camera-friendly haze of the mindscreen theaters, but the thick, heavy rotted custard of reality. "If we're lucky, the system is old fashioned and linked, and that relieved the pressure. If not, we have at least two more explosions to look forward to. Maybe more if every floor and every wing has their own heating reservoir."

"One day you're going to have to tell me how you know all of this."

"I was a firefighter, once."

"What!? When?"

"At least one body ago, General." Temperatures had rocketed still further, and anyone exposed to the air unprotected would severely damage his or her lungs. Logan ran on, hoping and dreading... the heart frequency monitor inside his skull picking up signs of—

Life.

"General, I have them. There are—" *Eleven? Oh God, eleven.* Logan opened the door to the infirmary and struggled inside before slamming it behind him. Indeed, there were fifteen bodies in various states from barely conscious to dead. The unbondable were surely looking to make a slaving run out of their time on Persephone, using the women while it was convenient and all but ignoring those who were severely damaged or fell ill.

Reeves was in his ear again. "Logan?"

On a good day, Logan can carry ten men, if they had the wherewithal to grab onto him and he was wearing a harness. These women were malnourished and thin, but none of them could be trusted to grab onto his back, which meant he would have to stack them in his arms. Through the door, up the stairs, he'd only have room for six without those on top crushing those on the bottom. Six, if they were lucky. "There are too many, General. There are eleven live women here. I can only get six; I can't carry them all."

There was a definite pause. "Sergeant, grab the six worst cases and head to the roof."

"Worst cases?"

Reeves voice went off like a pipe bomb. "I've given you a lot of leeway today, Sergeant. It *fragging* ends now, you sanctimonious *gritlicker*! Obey my order!"

Logan took the verbal slap and stood a little straighter. "Yes, sir."

Reeves heard the change in the tone of voice. "Move!"

It took only a second to rip the plastic ties that held each woman to her respective cot. Logan found a pile of blankets and a few jugs of water for an office-style cooler. He popped off the tops and poured them over the lot, soaking them down. As gently as he could be, he took each woman in turn and wrapped them in the cold, dripping blankets. He gathered up the six like a bundle of sleeping kittens, limp and awkward. Those left behind were not wholly coherent, but still they cried, begged, to be taken along. Logan thought about them burning to death, left here to suffocate in their beds.

Tina...Elizabeth... Guilt hit him like a rogue comet, shredding his concentration. Mechanical limbs quivered as they mistook old memories as new input, unsure of what commands to obey. Logan reached back into his mind and shut the door on his past. He had to focus, had to be here, now. He needed clarity or five dead would be eleven dead.

He tightened his grip incrementally on the limp bodies in his arms and opened the door. Smoke belched into the infirmary, filling up the topmost meter of ceiling with choking plastic, paint, and metal residue. He squeezed out and shut the door reflexively behind him. He wondered if he was doing them a favor or not, prolonging the inevitable, as he raced again to the roof. That mechanical eyes could not cry was another crime against his salvaged humanity.

He burst out of the hot coils of liquid darkness. Screaming in from the south, *The Bastard* touched down lightly, engines sitting at high revolutions to keep most of the weight off of the roof. Logan closed the distance as fast as he dared and laid the women onto the roof. *The Bastard's* copilot came back to the door, clipping on a safety belt as he leaned out to accept the barely conscious forms, one at a time. News minidrones, little more than flying cameras the size of a golf ball, began sweeping in from everywhere, documenting the tragedy for the edification of the human race.

In the north wing, the vats of aeroline had burned themselves out, leaving behind levels of heat the human mind can barely comprehend. Concrete had spawled and cracked, the aluminum rolling roof the unbondables had installed had sagged and melted, eventually catching fire. This was just one more component of the burning pool that covered the floor beneath the half-melted steel vats containing the liquid polymer for the heating system. The fire continued to raise the temperature of the vats, causing the liquid inside to move through the connected pipes on convection currents alone. As with all matter, when heated, it expanded. It continued to grow as energy was imparted to it until it reached the limits of the pipes that contained it. Then it ceased being a heating system and became a bomb.

The polymer liquid was flashing between plastic steam and plasma inside the pipes when the radiators finally ruptured. It immediately turned the air into an unbreathable, superheated, plastic fog. More importantly, it dispersed through the air, putting plenty of oxygen atoms between the plastic. There were numerous and sundry small fires throughout the school. All the cloud of gas needed to ignite was one.

The second floor of the north wing detonated like a fuel air bomb. Glass rocketed out with the same effect as an antipersonnel mine, and burning plastic vapor settled over everything, turning the entire first floor instantly into an unrecoverable blaze.

Logan staggered, nearly stepping on one of the prisoners. *The Bastard* started to wobble and scrape across the gravel. The pilot gunned the engines, leaping off the roof and away from danger. Again, smoke blotted out the sky, and this time did not clear. It was like working at twilight. All Logan could think of were the women at his feet and those left behind to burn to death.

"Logan to *Bastard*. I need you back down here."

The reply was instant. "Negative, Logan. The situation is too unstable."

"*Bastard*, I have more women to load up."

"Not my problem, get them to a secure—."

Reeves broke into the transmission. "Reeves to *Bastard*, get down to the roof."

"General—."

"Shut your damn mouth and get down to the *motherfragging* roof. We have civilians and *Apostles* that need extraction before this whole place goes up."

And Apostles?

The Bastard swooped in without further comment as Logan turned back toward the door to the roof. Helmets sealed against the increasing smoke, women wrapped in wet blankets and slung over shoulders, Reeve's team appeared, one by one, carrying those Logan had left behind.

Thank you, Reeves.

Logan could hear the pilot's teeth meet as words wriggled between them. "Roger, General."

The Bastard moved close and hovered above the deck. Aeroline engine exhaust seared across the roof, and the cyborg had to load the last three women from his feet at one time, lest they burst into flames. There was another explosion, this one rocking the surface underfoot. *The Bastard* lunged away from the rising clouds of black smoke and the running *Angel's Apostles* tumbled to the roof.

Logan's hungry feet bit into the gravel of the roof, tearing large gouges as he launched himself like a massive metal primate across the distance to the first fallen soldier. He landed with a resounding crash, electronic joints squealing in protest. He scooped the two tiny humans into his arms and sprinted back to the edge. *The Bastard* grudgingly wafted closer, directional nozzles spraying erratically as the thermal plume of the fire roiled the air all around it.

Logan's sensor input was coming from everywhere. With eyes far beyond human, he could see the air currents flowing up on thermal wings, buffeting the craft like angry demons. He saw the winds push the craft, and the engines slew to and fro, sometimes leaving the loading door clear, sometimes cutting it off from the outside world with a column of aeroline flame.

Logan whispered to the *Apostle* as he stacked the two people together in his arms. "Hold on to her tight."

The Key to Damocles

The soldier grabbed on tight and wrapped his legs around her.

"Hold it steady!" Logan growled.

The pilot's answer was immediate. "What do you think I'm trying to—?"

At that exact moment, Logan saw the hole coming, and computers embedded deeply into wetware took over. Faster than a heartbeat, electronic hardware measured the two bodies in his arms to within a milligram, calculated drag, and gravitational coefficient. They fixated on the target, and whispered trajectory to his muscles. Then he heaved the bundle in his arms.

They flew into the wall of smoke, heading for the converged exhaust of the two engines. They hung in the air for endless moments, unseen and unsupported. Then the rising tide of hot air shook *The Bastard*, engines swiveled to compensate…and then *The Apostle* and his charge landed inside the craft. The copilot shoved them roughly away from the open door and into the relative safety of the flier's belly.

The next *Apostle* skidded to a stop at Logan's side, woman slung over his shoulder.

"Wrap yourself around her." *The Apostle* did as he was told and then the Sergeant gathered them up.

Less than a second later, another pair thumped onto the floor of *The Bastard*. A few seconds later, another pair. The last mercenary almost fell as he all but collapsed under the weight of his oversized burden. His voice was forced past gasps. "The… General's… right… behind… me."

The woman immediately began kicking and screaming, trying to get away in a blind panic. With hands that could shatter stone, Logan grabbed ahold of her and pulled her back to the edge of the roof. She continued to scream and twist as Logan stowed her beneath his left arm. His right hand then hoisted the *Apostle* by his web belt. Logan leaned close to him, as if whispering. "Make a ball."

The *Apostle* curled into a fetal ball and Logan heaved him across the fifteen-meter gap, putting him neatly through the door. Logan then hoisted the hostage, who was still flailing like mad. Nothing he said could calm her, all she would say was, " ¡No volaré! ¡No volaré!"

Logan grabbed her by one arm and one leg and lobbed her at *The Bastard*. She landed on the edge, legs dangling over empty space until the copilot, and other *Apostles* grabbed her and dragged her inside. Logan glanced across the roof, only to discover he was still alone. "General?"

"Coming, Logan."

Another explosion rocked the building, the entire west wing disappearing in smoke and fire. "General, give me your location I will—."

"Get on the flier, Logan."

"I can't leave you, General."

"Get on the flier."

"No."

"Christ Almighty, Logan! For once you are going to obey my order as if it came from *him*!"

There were three seconds of silence between them. "Understood, General."

Logan turned and radioed *The Bastard*. "Two tons coming aboard on the port side. Pilot, make room."

There was a flurry of activity inside the door as the sergeant jogged back from the edge. The Pilot gave all clear, and Logan sprinted for the edge. He leapt into the air, trajectory marked in glowing lines across his eyes. The flier listed in the thermal tides as if drunk as Logan brought his legs up to his chest and tucked in his arms. Logan flew through the loading doors, skidding against the far wall as the entire craft lunged toward the hard earth. The Pilot yanked on the control yoke, pulling the whole craft out of its dive and back above the roof level of the school just as General Reeves broke out of the stairwell and ran across the building.

"Down! Down!" Logan picked himself up and stepped over to the open doorway.

The pilot's voice whipped out across the comm. "Master Sergeant! I need a warning if you are going to move around the cabin. You weigh enough to alter the center of—."

Logan shouldered aside his tirade with an order of his own as the remaining fingers of his left hand clamped on the doorframe to secure himself in position. "Get lower! I'm going to lean out to get him!"

The Key to Damocles

And Reeves was running for his life, an unmoving bundle of rags in his arms. Logan's meat body would have strained to see detail, but his cyborg body interpreted this urge and kicked in all kinds of sensor gear. It was immediately obvious what had held him up; the woman's life signs were extremely weak. A small autodoc was clamped around her neck like a collar, stabilizing her enough for transport. Worse, Reeves' vitals were all over the place. Carrying extra weight from good food and better booze, his heart was edging into dangerous areas. He was trying to simultaneously dump his gear using quick release tabs, run full tilt, and carry the woman. The best thing that could be said was that his cybernetic legs would not falter or feel fatigue.

Explosions rocked the first floor of the east wing, casting up an undulating wall of black heat. The flier jerked up and away from the roof. The cyborg's titanium feet slid a few centimeters, and his left finger and thumb dug deeper into the armored body of the flier. The flier's sensors cut through the blinding cloud like a broadsword, reading General Reeves on the roof, the raging fire and building explosions below him. Logan's own equipment slipped between the folds of dark matter like a scalpel, reading the poor woman's artificially stabilized life signs and Reeves' hammering heart. He could read the ragged gasping of the General's lungs, measure the flow of blood through his organs, see the electrons powering his legs as they pushed harder and faster than any meat could match.

"We've got to get closer!"

"Not if we want to stay in the air!"

Five meters to the edge.

The Sergeant reached out, causing the flier to lurch again and come closer to the school. "Closer!"

Three meters to the edge. "Negative, Sergeant!"

Logan's sniper mangled hand gripped tighter, tighter, deforming the doorway as hydraulic fluid squirted from the masticated steel stumps. "General?"

One meter. No answer. Logan leaned out further.

The second floor heating system failed and the superheated vaporized plastic detonated.

The Bastard leapt seven meters further away from the roof, dropping three meters. "General!"

Reeves leapt into the sky, wounded woman clutched tightly.

332

James Daniel Ross

The third and final floor of the east wing exploded.

CHAPTER 25:
IT'S JUST A JOB

In orbit around Planet Persephone,
Deadly Heaven, 28:10, 11/20/2662

I talked to the screen holding Tony's worn face, unable to give my words force or warmth. I felt like a hollow shell, and my voice echoed my pain. "I can understand your position, Tony. There isn't a government in existence that can run with no cash. At the same time, you can't level taxes on people that have no visible signs of supporting themselves. You have to give them the confidence to settle down and begin engaging in commerce again. That's going to take cash, which some of them have, and security, which they don't feel they have at all."

Tony took a swig from a fruit juice container. I hoped that there was just fruit juice in it. "So how do I give them security?"

"Just keep doing what you're doing. You'll be fine."

"Thanks, Todd." Tony looked like was going to break the connection, then he said, "How are you holding up?"

There really was no answer to that. A long-forgotten teenager inside of me coughed up his stock answer. "Fine."

"Yeah, sure. Come and see me when you get a spare minute, will you?"

I nodded, and he cut the connection.

I rewound the sensor data of the flier. I hit play. I watched it again.

Lieutenant Thompson came in, and she stood silently by while it played out. I paused it at the end, and she put a few data chips down in front of me. I opened a virtual port and the chips gave up their data to my laptop. I scanned the reports and mail. *Apostles* were transferring up to *Deadly Heaven* soon so we could go down to L/V/D and drop off Miss Ranner. At this point, we needed the extra manpower.

Everyone who needed it was recovering down on the surface in a nice civilian hospital near the Ortega compound. Our two medics and two of our able-bodied *Angels* went as well to stand guard, leaving little more than our pilot, Thompson, and myself onboard. I electronically signed the few bits that required it, authorizing drafts from *Deadly Heaven*'s virtual vault to pay for medical treatment. The rest was really all trash, including yet another cease-and-desist-and-we-will-arrest-you-soon from

The Key to Damocles

PISs, so I set them to the side and turned back to the wall screen.

I rewound the sensor data of the flier. I hit play. I watched it again.

The first floor disintegrated in flame.

Thompson took one step toward the door before asking, "How long are you going to torture yourself, Captain?"

My voice was low, dangerous, alien even to my own ears. "Not your place, Lieutenant."

The second floor went up.

"It's got to be someone's place, Captain." I said nothing as Reeves leapt into the sky. "Very well, Captain. It is very late. Perhaps you could watch in your cabin?" and she left.

The third floor exploded.

Death: quick, hard, and merciless.

I rewound the sensor data of the flier. I hit play. I watched it again.

But she was right. I was in the main briefing room. When the *Apostles* started showing up, I would have a constant stream of people moving by the door. By sheer weight of probability and psychology, someone was going to stop by and say something stupid.

I shut off the wallscreen and shut down my laptop.

I limped in a haze through *Deadly Heaven*, the familiar walls giving no comfort. Opening and closing each door in an endless ritual made the halls seem more like a tomb than a safe haven. Even the sound of my cane was horrible and hollow on the metal grate floors. It seemed like the images of death reflected from every portal and every shining surface, following me in a cloud stinking of guilt. Finally, I reached my cabin, threw off my shirt and pants, and lay down on the cot while wearing only my underwear.

And I lay there.

And I stared into the darkness.

I could see it.

I could see it still.

The last sane voice in my head whispered, *Don't watch it again*.

I hit the 'on' switch, put the laptop on my chest, and fed the sensor feed onto the wall display. I hit play. I watched it again.

The second floor went up. Logan leaned out to catch Reeves, further and further, a sick parody of the Sistine Chapel. Death: quick, hard, and merciless. There was a knock at the door, and then it opened without waiting for an answer. I rewound the sensor data. I hit play. I watched it again.

O'Leary walked in, not timidly, but her saunter definitely spayed. The *Apostles* must have arrived, but I hadn't expected her to come with them. She sat down on the edge of my high-walled cot, the scent of gun oil mixing with vanilla, sandalwood, and her.

"Get out."

O'Leary gently laid a hand on my shoulder. "No, I don't think so."

I dialed in the voice of a wounded animal, a voice that said, *I am dangerous.* "Get out, Corporal."

O'Leary didn't quite giggle. "I'm a Captain now, Rook. You can't order me to pick my nose, much less leave."

"My cabin."

"My friend."

"HE WAS MY FRIEND, TOO!" I grabbed the computer, sat up, and flung it into the far wall. The hardened casing, built especially for mercenary needs, stubbornly refused to break. It just sat there, casing dented, screen flickering, my nightmare replaying over and over.

I felt her arms snake from behind me, pressing me close to her. Hate exploded like a red fog against the back of my eyes. I grabbed her thumb and twisted. Her free hand hammered into the base of my skull, blinding me for a second and making me let go of her hand. I spun, fast and angry, leading with an elbow aimed for where her head should be. She lay down, causing me to miss badly, and lifted one firm leg to knee me in the face. A tooth loosened, swelling already started, and stars clouded my vision as I grabbed the offending leg and twisted viciously. We fell off the cot and rolled around on the deck. She gouged at my eyes. I palmed her throat. She clubbed my ear. I slammed her in the solar plexus.

At some point the door burst open.

Thompson came in, pistol at the ready. "Captain!?"

From her position on the floor, O'Leary swept the Lieutenant's legs from beneath her. She slapped my head and bounced it against the wall and then landed a left hook on Thompson's chin.

"Get OUT!" I was still getting to my feet as O'Leary grabbed Thompson's gun and tossed both her and her pistol into the hallway. "We are GRIEVING!"

And she slammed the door.

I grabbed O'Leary from behind, and she crushed my instep beneath her boot. I roared as she turned and began a series of incredibly fast, powerful blows against my midsection. A normal man would be staggered, but my armored plate shrugged the brunt of the punishment to the side though the barely closed bullet holes burned like hell. I fastened my hands around her upper arms and heaved her into the shelf, sending books on tactics and horse training flying. Her head bounced, and her eyes seemed to lose focus until her boot lashed out and hit the raw patch of barely healed shin.

Blackness swirled in, and I went to my knees. She hit me in the face once… and twice… and I caught the third blow and pulled, slamming her into the floor and all but collapsing on top of her. She struggled. We grappled. At some point we stopped fighting and started hugging.

I started crying.

And over her shoulder, the bastard laptop continued to loop. Her voice slipped into my ear, breathless and tender. "He wasn't your responsibility anymore. He chose his own path."

"He was an asshole, a braggart, and a greedy manipulator, but he was also a General." I watched Reeves leap, Logan's arms outstretched. He arced high, high enough. He leapt far, far enough. It should have been far enough, dammit. It should have been far enough. Reeves arced into the air, and started to fall short. He made a split-second decision. He pulled up his legs and placed them against the woman in his arms…

…and kicked.

O'Leary cupped the base of my skull in her hand and pulled me closer. "He lived as your student…" His cybernetic legs imparted extra momentum to his charge, momentum robbed from his own mortal shell. "…but he died your equal." Logan's hand closed around the woman's out flung arm. "You taught him how to do the right thing."

Logan and I watched Reeves fall to his death, again. My voice could barely crawl past my throat. "It got him killed."

"Sometimes that happens. You taught me that. Love is not a shield, friendship no armor. There is nothing you can do but train, and hope, and work as a team…" The data began to loop again as O'Leary pulled away to look me in the eye. "I'm your equal, too."

I nodded gravely. *So, how long before you die?*

She leaned over and closed the top of the laptop, cutting off the feed and blanking the wallscreen. Then she kissed me. I kissed her. And then she consumed me… all of me.

It was animal, and ephemeral. Even with my multitude of hurts were drowned out by the symphony of her touch. Her passion was like a brushfire, scorching across me and burning all the broken parts away, leaving only the living flesh of my soul, raw, pink, and tender. It wasn't about Reeves, it wasn't about us, it was about both she and I sharing what we needed with each other to face another day with the pain. We fell asleep, limbs intertwined.

Some animal part of me sensed that she was awake, and that snapped me out of sleep long before she even considered moving. I ran a calloused hand down her athletic frame, relishing the hint of female softness even as I traced over dozens of ugly seams. She shifted her head to look at me, her Asian eyes filled with more warmth than I can ever remember her expressing in her life. The light dusting of freckles made her look very young in the dim light.

A cloud of emotions started to well up inside me, and I began to say something when she clapped a hand over my mouth. "Ugh, morning breath."

Crammed into the tiny bed, our limbs were tangled together like branches after a storm. It took several careful moments to unwind ourselves from one another. She stood and stretched, ugly scars and beautiful curves doing a dance in the low light. She reached over my desk, between two reproductions of cowboy movie posters, and adjusted the lamp up a few notches before turning and staring down at me with her hands on her hips.

"Rook, before you say anything, don't. You've always had a real bad case of white knight syndrome and if you say something now, it's going to be something stupid and I'm going to hit you... more." She busied herself with gathering her uniform and placing it on the desk as she continued. "I'm not some star-struck waif. I'm not a desperate street urchin. You do not owe me anything, and you sure as hell don't own me. I'm not even a subordinate anymore. I am a... I am the Captain of *The Angel's Apostles*. I knew what I was doing and I wanted to do it. I never understood what your aversion to sex was, but it was clear that you needed it badly, so I gave it to you."

I levered myself off of the cot to my feet, careful of my many tender spots. I was so close to her in the tiny cabin I could smell the old sweat on her and could feel the heat coming off of her skin. I opened my mouth but she barreled right over me. "You don't take direction well, do you? Well, let me spell this out. We are not going to get married. I am not going to have a child. We both have clean medical records and we are both consenting adults. We are not falling in love—"

I reached in and took hold of her and kissed her. My day, already starting obscenely late, got a little later. This time it was tender and slow, soft and gentle. When it was done, we lay in each other's arms relishing the scent of love and the all-encompassing warmth of two bodies. My right leg was trapped beneath her and fell completely asleep before I shifted to cradle her even more closely. I whispered in her ear, "Thank you... Captain."

O'Leary jerked for a second, then relaxed, laying her head on my wide brown chest. "Well, at least it wasn't stupid. You're welcome, Captain."

We used my personal shower to clean up, using far more than my fair allotment of hot water. We toweled off and dressed in our respective clothes. "When do you want me to gather my men?"

"That's a good question." I smiled a bit and pulled out the room's only chair, a dubious stool that attached to the wall underneath the desk. I sat down and started lacing up my boots, wincing as the barely healed skin on my right leg protested.

O'Leary backed up to the cabin door, a frown forming on her lips and her eyes narrowing. "Why are you smiling?"

I shrugged as I pulled on a dark green T-shirt and then a black sweater. "I feel better."

Her gathering anger evaporated, but it was replaced by something uncomfortable and new. She looked out of her depth, as if she were in a play where the script had suddenly changed. "Good. That's good. I'm going to go check on the *Apostles*. Give me some advanced notice before we drop. None of this all-hands-to-the-dropship-immediately *grit*."

I stood and stretched, the dents in my cybernetic chest plate creaking and cramping the muscles around them. *I'm going to have to get that fixed soon*. "Sure, O'Leary, no problem."

And she stood there for a few more seconds for no apparent reason. "Alright."

I reached out for her and took her in my arms. She felt tense, uncomfortable, almost desperate when she hugged me back. "Thank you, Kei."

"Don't mention it." She seemed back on her normal footing when she pulled away long before I was done. "Seriously, don't mention it. Having a new crew looking at you like you're some kind of hotshot playboy probably won't instill a lot of morale."

I wasn't sure where she was going with this, but I was beginning to believe that she was actively trying to spoil the mood. "Thanks for the advice. I'm going to go check on our passenger and then go get some chow. I'll probably look to drop down to the planet in an hour or so."

"Very well. Oh, and I liked your hair better long." She left in a hurry.

I sat down, and my shoulders sagged. I was never able to get a good handle on O'Leary. I know she often had sex with members of the crew, or at a gypsy ship, after a mission. It was how she came to terms with things, and as long as nothing got too serious, I was happy to turn a blind eye to it. I had suspected she would have liked to add me to her list of conquests, but now that it had happened, she seemed dazed, withdrawn, unsure. To say I could fathom even the simplest of female minds was absurd, let alone someone as complex as O'Leary. I knew this had opened up a whole new level of intricacy to our relationship, and I could also feel a warm, hungry spot in my heart for her. I could not say it was love, but it felt like a piece of her was there, now, and would reside there forever. She would say it was old fashioned nonsense, of course, but it was still there.

I shoved it out of my mind as I opened a drawer and took out several pills. I swallowed them dry, hoping that they would do their jobs and reduce my healing time and stop my burns and abrasions from itching or becoming infected. I walked to the medical bay and checked in with Bugs, the medical bot, and he immediately informed me Katie Ranner's life signs were perfectly stable. The unbondables had given her a king-sized dose of time release sedatives, ensuring she would be asleep and pliable for whatever medical tests had to be done for three whole days. It was dangerous, but not unheard of in kidnapping cases. I had done the exact same thing to the captured unbondable in Brig B, in fact. It seemed fitting, anyway.

She had been awake in Brig A for several days now. Her only company, and only contact was with Grisham, as per my orders. I could trust any of the *Angels* with my life, but even I would not put one of them alone in a room with a woman whose every hair follicle held DNA worth millions to the right buyer. *That is approximately where trust crosses over into torture.*

I had Bugs reset the tooth O'Leary had loosened the previous night, reset the synthetic skin on my shin, and make sure she hadn't cracked any bones. With a nominally clean bill of health, I left. All of the halls were deserted except the mechanicals of the crew as I made my way to the very heart of the ship, furthest away from all the sensitive areas, to the brig.

Forget what you see in the mindscreen theaters; if humanity could make unbreakable doors made of light, they'd have them plating the outside of their ships five thousand deep to keep it safe in combat. Jail cells have changed very little in a millennium, and they can be counted on to have bars: heavy, thick and made of stuff even Logan cannot scratch.

I heard her long before I saw her, chatting amicably with Grisham, who was giving his integrated personality a long-overdue workout. They were discussing high performance fliers of all things as I walked down the line of cells and stood in front of hers.

James Daniel Ross

She was like a goddess. Forget what you know about beauty and just imagine the perfect girl next door. Despite the large numbers of African extraction actors in L/V/D's stables, Ranner held her own as a golden-haired European beauty just this side of attainable. Her eyes were so green they could have been cut of emeralds, and her body was only enhanced by womanly curves instead of weighed down.

I found myself trusting her implicitly. Since I had seen her, and previous clones of her, in feminine hero roles since I was a toddler, that was no surprise. I grabbed that intimate openness and strangled it. No matter what I felt, I did not know this woman. I cleared my throat.

They stopped talking immediately, and Katie fixed me with those big, green eyes. Even the *Radiation Angels* overall she wore imparted no strength or power upon her. I could almost feel the butterflies flitting around inside of her and sense the urgent fear in the way she clasped her hands. She was an actress and an exceptional one at that, trained to it from birth. I reminded myself that I had no idea what she was really feeling, only what she wanted me to think she felt, or something like that.

"Miss Katie Ranner?"

She glanced from me to Grisham, but her companion stood as silent as a piece of furniture and gave no obvious help. She stood up, thrusting her chest out like a woman on trial for her life. "Yes."

I made a 'sit down' motion. "No need for that, Miss Ranner. My name is Captain Todd Rook. I run *The Radiation Angels*. You are aboard our ship *Deadly Heaven* and we are now in orbit around Persephone. As I'm sure Grisham has told you, we rescued you from your kidnappers under contract from L/V/D, and are set to return you to the surface as soon as we clear one thing up."

Like O'Leary only minutes before, she seemed a little confused. "If you all are the good guys, why haven't any of you come to see me in the last three days?"

I unconsciously went to parade rest, clasping my hands behind me. "Four. Actually, it has been seven days but you were asleep for some of it. I do apologize if your company was a little lacking, but we have to return you to L/V/D with zero loss of DNA."

"Did you have to keep me prisoner?"

Oh, boy. "L/V/D contract specified we should return you intact, unharmed, and with the most limited possibility of you being cloned. I had Grisham bring your meals and keep you company. When we drop onto the planet, we are going to bundle up everything you have worn, slept on, or had significant contact with since you arrived. Grisham has been recording all of your movements, and will supervise the cleaning of this cell when you go. All of that will be downloaded to your employers as verification. You were meant to be protected, not a prisoner. I am sorry for any inconvenience; it's all a part of zero loss."

"Ah, I see. Will you return me to L/V/D now?"

"As long as that's where you want to go."

She started, as if I had slapped her. "Excuse me?"

"I have a contract to return you to your employer. If you decide you do not want to go back, I will not force you. So, I am here to ask... do you want to go back to L/V/D?"

I held my breath because this is where things could go off the tracks very quickly. Her eyes narrowed, and darted back and forth across the room. "Why are you asking me this?"

I had only the honest answer to give her. "I am not in the kidnapping business, ma'am."

She looked truly terrified, adrift in a sea with no land in sight. It was as if the very concept of having this choice, let alone the choice itself, was too big for her to comprehend. "Yes... yes I will go back. L/V/D has been very good to me."

I straightened up and gave her a little bow. "Of course, Miss Ranner. I wouldn't have asked except—"

She gave me a slightly imperious wave. "No, no, no, I appreciate it. Thank you, Captain."

"We will be dropping within the hour. If you have not eaten, I suggest you do not. Landings in a military craft can be somewhat rough. Good day."

I finally started to breathe again. I figured she'd go back to her golden fishbowl if given the chance, but there's always the slim possibility that she wanted to leave, and would jump at the chance to live as a 'normal' person. Of course, she would have even less chance of survival than those poor refugees that fled Persephone over the last months, but she had no way to know that. I made my way off to the mess hall. Apparently, Thompson had chatted with some of the *Apostles* about what had happened on *The Rage of Exiles*. They used to look at me like an urban legend; now I was more in the realm of demigod.

Dammit.

I ate in a military fashion. It goes something like this: grab plate, fill plate, grab fork, begin eating, stop eating when plate is empty. It takes about ninety seconds. The twenty or so mercenaries saw this and took the cue. Some grabbed a little extra chow, others started packing up the abbreviated personal effects they had brought with them. By the time I left, all the decks of cards, electronic games, and portable musical wingdings had been stored. I touched one of the intercom panels in the hallway, and speakers all over the ship warbled out a synthetic boson's whistle. My voice came next. "Good to have you aboard, *Apostles*. Thank you for the assist. *Apostles* prepare for drop in thirty minutes. *Apostle* Actual, I need six of yours to Brig B for prisoner transfer to dropship. All mechanicals to their stations. Refuel and check of *Apostle* dropship to commence in fifteen minutes. *Angels* to your stations. Mechanical Request: one environmental suit to Brig A. Repeat: one environmental suit to Brig A. That is all."

The computer aboard *Deadly Heaven* routed my last order to one of the servant robots who grabbed an environmental suit from a locker full of them and delivered it to Ranner. I imagine Grisham had to help her get into it even as another two robots came in to collect all of the cloth she had touched during her stay, along with the toiletries we had provided for her. Finally, as the last seals were set, and she began breathing her own recycled air, more drones entered the cell and began cleansing everything with high temperature chemicals. I arrived moments later, dressed in light combat armor and carrying a satchel with my laptop in it.

We made our way to the docking bay and piled into *The Bastard*. I paused a second and stared at the deformed edge of the doorway where Logan had grabbed for dear life. I took a seat at the front of the craft and waited for the sickening lurch of takeoff and freefall.

Glancing back, all the *Apostles* looked strapped in and ready even as Grisham and Ranner came aboard. O'Leary walked up and down the rows, making sure everyone was indeed in their place, and even taking a moment to cuff one or two of the more jubilant members of her team. The rest arrived moments later, whirring bots carrying stretchers upon which the unbondable prisoners from *The Rage of Exiles* were restrained. These were strapped down, bot and all, in the cargo section. The doors closed and a slight pressure on my ears let me know we were about to go.

I took a deep breath inside my helmet as the magnetic gear unclamped from the deck and microbursts of compressed air moved us out into open space. It was disorienting and lonely because usually at this time, I was busy giving orders, checking lists, updating files, doing the things officers do. Now O'Leary glided up near me and took the seat across the aisle. She strapped in, checking her C^2 armpad and obviously responding to voices over the comm only she could hear.

I leaned back as the nuclear reaction drives cut in and pushed us toward Persephone. I began going over all the problems I had solved and all the threads left hanging. I had this feeling I was almost done, and at the same time my troubles were just beginning. I craned my head around and looked at the distorted patch of doorway metal again. I wanted to reach over and take O'Leary's hand.

I didn't.

BOOK THREE:

THE POWER OF THE PEOPLE

CHAPTER 26: SHIFTING SANDS

The Bastard touched down at L/V/D upon a landing pad that looked more like a Roman amphitheater. *Apostles* stood as one as soon as we settled and began trooping out the rear hatch onto the tarmac. I grabbed my cane, shouldered my laptop case, and queued up to exit the craft when a hard, heavy lump landed in my lap. O'Leary was at my side, one hand holding a rifle over her shoulder like a witch's broom and the other perched on her shapely hip. "You look naked without one."

I unwound the belt to expose the holster and black polymer laser pistol inside. "Thanks, I—"

O'Leary had jerked to alertness, all femininity cast aside as she punched keys on her forearm command pad. I stood and, with practiced ease, flipped the belt around my waist, buckled it, and secured the leg restraint. O'Leary made a few arm gestures as she gave orders I could not hear. Finally, she tuned me in to the situation. "We've got a problem, Captain. There's all the makings of an ambush outside."

I activated my C^2 as she piped me the feed from the *Apostles* that were already outside. She was right. I picked my cane back up and motioned for her to continue. Armed and motivated mercenaries shuffled out again, a few stacked at the loading gate while the rest encircled the dropship. Ranner, dressed in her bulky environmental suit, tried to stagger to her feet but O'Leary pushed her back into her seat.

"You're not paid for yet." Then she tensed. "Get ready, Captain, the reception is hot."

I passed Ranner and made a 'be still' motion as we filed out of the craft into a sunlit morning festooned with rifles. Men were stationed everywhere, dressed in flat black armored gear common to police departments the universe over. More worrisome were their Pritchett high frequency laser carbines, all of which were pointing at us.

O'Leary looked like a cat dropped in a dog pound. The *Apostles* were nervously fingering the plasma rifles slung on their shoulders. All it was going to take was one wrong move, one tense finger, and this landing pad was going to turn into a slaughterhouse. The only bright spot was that it wouldn't be *Angels* or *Apostles* lying dead on the tarmac. We were wearing heavier armor, carrying more powerful weapons, and backed up by *The Bastard's* semi-smart anti-vehicular weaponry. We could easily survive ten seconds of fire from these people, and in return render this entire area a smoking ruin. That would make me all warm and fuzzy. If destroying this landing pad and all those in it were the point of the exercise; it wasn't. Now, I just needed to find out why the reception was so hostile before I had to kill a lot of defunct Agents.

Why are they waiting on the tarmac, announcing their presence? Something nettled at me as faux soldiers moved from one bit of cover to another, trying to keep all the *Apostles* in sight. *Why are their guns drawn before we exit the dropship?* I was looking left, and right, seeing an ambush, looking right into its face, feeling the exposed fangs and smelling its breath, but something was wrong. *This is not what an ambush feels like.*

Lionel was always amicable in our dealings, and I hadn't even breathed a word of betrayal toward him. He wasn't a soldier, a mercenary, or even a police officer. He was a business man, and business men like crisp, clean transactions. They booked services and paid for them. They expected to pay for them. This is the way businesses work, and it makes them safer to work for than governments, by and large. Add to this the fact that Lionel knew about me; more specifically, he knew what a relatively small team of men under my control could do to someone I do not like, and there's no way he'd try a bait-and-switch like this.

It was theoretically possible the Knights of Earth had contacts on Persephone. In fact, it was likely. Now that their ship was atomized nuclear gas and their mercenary team fragmented, the wise course would be to lay low, not force a bloody confrontation. Both of which meant either this was part of a plot so complex I couldn't wrap my mind around it, or a tactic so stupid it didn't even enter as a possibility into my mind. I was betting the latter.

I brought up my forearm pad slowly and touched a few buttons. In less than a second, my comm unit was hooked up to Grisham and, using him as a relay station, I made a covert call to Opus Lionel. At the same time, one of the federal/planetary Agents stalked forward in a passable imitation of a combat crouch, his weapon leveled at my chest. He stopped just out of reach and pointed at me like the specter of death itself. He spoke in perfect English. "Drop your weapons."

I muted my conversation with Lionel's secretary and turned on my helmet's loudspeaker. "Not a chance."

The officer started, and shook his head as if the problem was with his hearing. "I said, drop your weapons."

I shrugged and crossed my arms, looking around and addressing no one in particular said, "This guy isn't understanding me. Can someone tell me how to say 'go to hell' in Spanish?"

I tongued the toggle to turn off the loudspeaker and reactivated my comm as O'Leary rattled off a string of Spanish curses so vile some of the Agents actually flinched. I suppose you could translate it as 'go to hell' once it had been seasoned by a cargo hauler, a drunk sailor, and a cranky mercenary. It hit the Agents like a physical force, and their stances became rigid, alert, angry. The lead Agent lurched as if he wanted to lunge at O'Leary—an act sure to be his last—but his discipline held, and he only pointed at me and then to the ground. "You are under arrest by the authority of the Planetary Government of Persephone. Put down your weapons, get on the ground, and interlock your fingers behind your head!"

I was getting nowhere with the secretary, so I made a final plea over the comm and broke contact, switching back to my loudspeaker. "Alright everyone, get back aboard."

Immediately, *Apostles* began double timing it back onto *The Bastard.*

The Agent backed off a few steps, sighting down his Pritchett. "No! You are forbidden from leaving! You are under arrest!"

There is this thing that happens when people in positions in power are in power too long. They begin to believe that having power is the natural state in which they dwell. They believe it is something they innately possess, instead of something that is gifted to them by people under their control. When they are defied, their reaction follows a very reliable sequence: first disbelief, then shock, then anger, then violence. If I could get O'Leary's mercenaries aboard before the last stage hit, we would be fine. If not, this was about to get ugly. Very ugly.

The Key to Damocles

He didn't believe I was serious when I gave the hand signal to depart. He was shocked when the ranks peeled from around *The Bastard* and the first mercenaries double timed it up the ramp. He began to shake in fury as the last *Apostle* quick stepped up the ramp, and O'Leary and I started up afterwards. I should have guessed I was too late.

I opened a channel to Grisham to reconnect my earlier call and try to hammer all this out when I felt this raw, greasy heat erupt at the small of my back. In the blink of an eye, I went from annoyed curiosity to painful realization. *That asshole just shot me!*

Everything around me screeched into slow motion as I started to fall, cane splaying from numb fingers as my whole spine throbbed. I saw the few mercs at the top of the ramp point, scramble, and try to get their weapons out.

And there she was. O'Leary stepped directly in front of me, spun like a dancer dressed in razor blades, and grabbed the back of my armor. With the grace and power of a seaborne storm, she spun her rifle off of her shoulder with one hand, using the shoulder strap to sling it up as she grabbed the pistol grip. Like a scene from one of Lionel's movies, she dragged me into *The Bastard* and at the same time lay down a withering storm of plasma packets, all the while shouting her orders for emergency takeoff over the comm. Rough hands grabbed me under my arms and pulled me the rest of the way into the dropship, almost flipping me over as the ramp assembly started to close. O'Leary was still at the opening, sending out one superheated packet after another. Two more *Apostles* came to join her, but they did not quite block out the body of the lead Agent on the tarmac. What was left of his head smoked in the morning sun, ruptured by a well-placed hit from a plasma rifle. It had been one of O'Leary's shots, of that I was certain.

The *Apostles* pulled me into the belly of the craft, laid down one of the acceleration seats into an approximation of a cot, and flopped me face down upon it. The medic wasted no time using a vibroknife to strip off my armor and examine the hit. He barely managed to get the blade put away before the craft lurched into the air. He grabbed onto the seat for dear life as the craft slewed to the left and right, I heard chaff thump from the launchers along with at least three active electronic canisters. About the only good thing was I couldn't hear the cannons lighting off. *Maybe this damage could still be contained.*

O'Leary chuckled as she sat down in the seat next to my improvised cot and strapped in. "Was that how it was supposed to go?"

I felt my temper slip loose its bonds as my adrenaline faded and pain washed over me. "What the hell are you so happy about?"

"Three things." She put her weapon on safe and strapped it to the back of the seat in front of her. "First, it looks like you only have second degree burns from the laser hit. Given a few hours with some dermal regenerators, you'll be fine. Second, I memorized an entire section of <u>Starting Barroom Brawls, Spanish Edition</u> and it finally came in useful. Thirdly, I got to save a real, live, living legend."

"Eat *grit.*"

"Look grateful." O'Leary pretended to pout as she punched me in the shoulder, sending nauseating waves across my back. No doubt she thought this was funny as hell.

The Bastard leveled out and the medic went back to work, spraying my lower back with a topical anesthetic that immediately muted the pain, then followed with a dermal regenerator, and finally a layer of synthetic skin. In less than a minute, I was able to get up, rearrange my shredded clothing, adjust the seat, and sit like a normal person. Medicine in a can at its finest.

Even as my body became whole, heavy thoughts broke free and slid around inside my head, breaking fragile preconceptions that made my life simple. O'Leary had shot a man in the face, and it didn't bother her in the least, but it had been my brilliant idea to trip the Agent up as he threw his weight around. This is one of the many reasons why not only should soldiers never try to be cops, police should never try to be soldiers. My only comfort was kowtowing to assholes on a power trip led to very bad places. I had no need to repeat my experience with Special Planetary Agent in Charge *grithead* Gil Carlos.

What would make them think they should, or that they could, arrest me? And then I remembered Gil Carlos, and his attempt. And then the three-times-a-day cease-and-desist letters, not from local police agencies, but specifically from *Servicios de la*

Investigación Planetarios. I had shoved them aside as the price of doing business, playing in someone else's sandbox as it were. But what if what I thought of as background noise was, in fact, something else altogether? Even if it was simple posturing before, an officer of the law had died. It was sure to become something more now.

The broken ideas inside my mind began shifting, falling together in strange new shapes, creating disturbing thoughts, when my forearm pad began beeping with an incoming call. I shoved my helmet back on as *The Bastard* began descending toward West Lot. I signaled Grisham to begin recording the call and answered.

It was Lionel, and he looked like a politician who got caught with two fistfuls of bribes and a dozen naked concubines while on live TV. "Captain Rook? I am getting very disturbing reports right now."

I tried being tactful. "To be honest, I really could have used you on that tarmac, Mr. Lionel."

"I was perfectly willing to come, but then I had security bust into my office with loaded weapons, throw me to the floor, and hold me there until you took off. They were convinced that you were here to level L/V/D."

Sure they were. Not the least problem with that theory was that I was already inside the anti-aircraft bubble, and if I had wanted to level the place, I could have. "You can't believe that, Lionel."

"Captain, Captain, Captain, I don't know what happened but I must ask you if you have any intention of returning my employee."

You play the innocent very well, Opus. Is it authentic? "That's odd, Mr. Lionel. I was wondering if you had any intention of paying my men for getting shot at. This was neither an easy, nor a clean, recovery."

And that stopped him cold. "Captain Rook, I don't know what you're implying, but I went through quite a bit of trouble to prepare your payment as requested. Now I have reports that you murdered a planetary Agent on the tarmac and opened fire on dozens more."

"Mr. Lionel, why were there dozens of Agents there in the first place? You know what? Just open up a *fragging* data funnel."

Though unaccustomed to taking orders, he did what he was told. I piped data from *The Bastard's* records, every mercenary helmet cam unit, and more importantly Grisham's sensor gear, to his computer. "That's what happened. Look it over. Make a decision. Make it quickly, because I will not be able to maintain Katie Ranner's zero loss indefinitely."

Opus ground his teeth together. "Is that a threat?"

I sighed, weariness creeping over me. "No, it is simply a law of physics. Her oxygen runs out of that environmental suit in about ten hours. After that, she will have to come out to breathe. From that point, she'll be leaving little traces of herself wherever she goes."

There were three seconds of absolute silence on the comm line. "Is this real?"

He must have been going over the records I sent, which was a good sign. "I have the burn pattern to prove it, but I suppose if there is anyone who can spot fake recordings, it's the people you have working for you at L/V/D. Now there are just two questions. One, could I have faked it in a little under ten minutes? And two, can your people analyze it in less than ten hours?"

Lionel looked confused, angry, and hurt. But above all, he was afraid. I was inclined to believe him, but if he was telling the truth, he had good reason to be afraid. "So where do we go from here?"

"You, and I mean you yourself, gets onto an unarmed flier with zero, and I mean absolutely no, planetary agents. You will bring the full and complete payment for our services in cash. I do not care what denomination of bills. When you are onboard and in the air, you will call me and I will give you a place to land. We will be waiting. We will be armed. I give you my personal assurances that you will be given safe passage and be allowed to leave with Miss Ranner as soon as our business is completed."

"This seems a little extreme, Captain Rook. Getting that much cash alone—"

I allowed a little heat creep into my voice. "I was just shot, Mr. Lionel. Extreme is not only reasonable, it is warranted at the moment."

"It will take more time—"

The Key to Damocles

I cut him off again. "Lionel, I can defend police stations, assault starships, rescue actors, and end revolutions. I cannot stop time."

I cut the transmission and gave O'Leary directions, who then passed them to the pilot. I used my C^2 to contact Ranner's spacesuit and download her vital stats. She had ten hours, twenty-eight minutes and thirty-nine seconds of oxygen left.

Seven minutes later we were at West Lot.

CHAPTER 27: BLEEDING

We landed three blocks away from the police station, and everyone but the flight crew disembarked. O'Leary and her men were still riding high on adrenaline and ready for a fight. The streets were all but lawless. There were an unknown number of unbondables hiding in dark corners across the megacity, and I had a shredded back plate as well as second degree burns. I could not blame them.

They came down the ramp with rifles out, sweeping their designated areas of responsibility. O'Leary strode into the middle of them, seeing to her unit as her *EWO* point man assembled his sensor unit. I watched, entranced, as she moved like a warrior goddess from man to man. She slapped the helmet of one, snapping at him to pay attention. She adjusted the aim of another, telling him gently that the alley was far more dangerous than the balcony. The *EWO* signaled all clear as O'Leary grabbed a man's finger and almost snapped it off as she told him in no uncertain terms to keep it off his trigger unless discharging his weapon. Sometimes she was harsh, nearly cruel, and at others gentle and encouraging. At all times, she was certain, proud, and unafraid.

She was a Captain of a mercenary company.

She was perfect.

Did I really teach you that?

O'Leary signaled for us to move out, and I put a guiding hand on Ranner in her spacesuit, Grisham and the stretcher carriers whirring close behind. All directions from then on were given with hand signals, no idle chatter. The mercs strained on every side like dogs eager to get out of a thunderstorm, but between me and my cane, the unbondables asleep on the bots, and Ranner's bulky getup, progress was slowed to a crawl. The movie star was the only person in the unit who didn't realize there could be death waiting behind any given window or doorway. After the assault, the enemy had slithered into the shadows and lurked like fanged serpents all across New California. My eyes swept over every likely spot as I limped along.

The Key to Damocles

Ranner broke the silence first. "The revolution really chewed this place up."

I stopped looking at the buildings as things to be used as bunkers, or quickly turned into rubble. I stopped identifying places which could hide ambushes or store caches. I had to shake my head to clear random bits of defensive and assault plans in order to actually look at the buildings. Dirt splashed along the brickwork like mold on an orange. In many places, the supports sagged. Paint flaked from façades like a patient with a horrible skin disease. Plastic shingles littered the dark nooks and crannies of the street, nestling in blankets of old trash. "Ma'am, this is how this place always looks. The damaged areas are up ahead."

From behind her faceplate, I watched Ranner give me a sideways glace that very clearly said, *I don't believe you*. And it wasn't until we reached west lot proper that she stopped.

The police station was blackened along the top where the fliers had crashed into the roof. The blast damage from the earlier car bomb had not been repaired and nothing remained of the lampposts, bus stop, or other city scenery along the streets. Other buildings were not so lucky. Holes and pockmarks blossomed like poisonous flowers across the hardened tenements and buildings on all sides. In some places, chunks of wall were missing where explosives had found their final resting place. The short wall around the police station and tenements had been expanded with new debris, including the semi-fresh bodies of downed fliers. The only remnants of the attackers had baked into black spots across roads, sidewalks and scrubby lawns. That was not all that had changed since I had last walked these streets, not by a long shot.

Ranner gasped at the many starving, listless, and wounded in the streets. The sun was just rising, but already it cast its angry eyes to the blacktop. People were pitching tents wherever they could drive stakes, police walking among them to direct where things could and could not be placed. They wound up in neat, orderly rows that quickly collapsed into a riot of baggage, trash, and weary humanity.

Across the street, safely cordoned off from the ugly glares of the refugees, were a knot of twenty-five protestors. They all carried signs praising *El Toro*, and they all looked way too well fed to be native to this area. Five police officers, who probably had a laundry list of better things to do, were standing guard. From the way the protestors were heckling and throwing trash at the cops, I don't think they realized the police were there to protect the protestors more than confine them.

O'Leary pressed onward, tightening up her group, then giving orders for arms to be placed on safe and shouldered. We crested the waves of misery at a snail's pace, quietly and cautiously. All the greatest hits were here: starvation, desperation, anger, and fear. They were on every side, pulling at us with a gravity well all their own.

Ranner turned to me and made a theatrically large gesture at the press of tents. "Captain, who are these people?"

I took my time chewing on the question, unsure of exactly what she meant. I mean, the answer was obvious, but if you didn't know to start with, being told was unlikely to be enlightening. Still, ignoring her would be rude. "These are refugees of New California, Miss Ranner."

I tried to leave it at that, but she pressed on. "Why isn't someone doing something to help them?"

We broke free of the crush of tents and emerged at the police station proper. Tony was already out front, wearing the smile of a man in constant pain. I pointed at him and said, "Someone is. He's doing his best and he's doing it alone, so please be polite to him."

I took off my helmet and gimped up the front staircase and ahead of the *Apostles*, extending a hand that was taken warmly. Tony actually blinked back tears and visibly considered giving me a crushing hug before inviting us inside. "It's good to see you, Todd, though I didn't think you'd come quite so soon after landing."

We passed the booking desk, and I relished the quickly dropping temperatures as the air conditioning fought with the day's heat. Sometime soon Tony would have to fix those front doors. At the moment though, what really bothered me was the passing people staring at me like I was a ghost. "I'm afraid it isn't on the best of terms. I'm kind of on the run. Again."

"Really?" Tony looked at me askance. "From what I gathered, you were getting ready for payday."

The Key to Damocles

My scalp tingled and my ears perked up as I forced casualness into my voice. "Oh? From whom?"

Tony chuckled and made a placating gesture. "I wouldn't be a very good cop if I couldn't ask an oblique question, would I?"

"I guess not." I nodded. A passer-by came forward and took my hand. He shook it vigorously and left without a word. "Tony, I'm afraid I have to beg you for the use of your medical bay again."

Lomen stopped in his tracks and looked me up and down, then scanned the Apostles. "You hurt?"

"Yes, but not for that. I just need a place for..." I let my voice trail off as I glanced back at Ranner, still inside her heavy environmental suit.

Tony cleared his throat. "The medical station is full right now, but I'm sure we can set you up with something."

Within two minutes, he had someone on the radio, and after exhausting all his options at getting a room alone, put us up in the old police chief's lair at the top of the station. I sent the *Apostles* up with Ranner and Grisham, waiting for an empty elevator with Tony. As soon as the doors closed on the team, Tony turned to me, his eyes guarded. "So, you want to tell me what's going on?"

Our elevator opened, and we walked inside. I waited, and waited... and waited. Tony stared at me with quickly dwindling patience until finally the doors shut. He opened his mouth to say something when I answered, "I completed a contract for L/V/D. When we attempted to drop off our payload, we were met with Agents. Lots of Agents. With guns."

Tony motioned to the small of my back. "And I thought this was some kind of fashion statement."

"Very funny. A millimeter less armor and I'd be paralyzed or worse."

"You said Agents. What kind?"

"Planetary."

My deep brown eyes bored into his frosty blue. I watched color drain from his face and his pupils shrink to pinpricks. "Rook, if L/V/D wants you dead, there is nothing anyone in this city can do to save you. They are the, and I mean the, only power left in New California."

The doors opened with a metallic tone. "I'm pretty sure L/V/D doesn't want me dead. *Servicios de la Investigación Planetarios* does."

He chewed on that as we walked down the short hallway to the chief's office. Two *Apostles* stood vigilant guard outside. "That makes no sense, Todd. Why would they want you dead? What in the hell did you steal for L/V/D?"

"Not steal—" One of guards opened the door and we went inside I motioned toward the faceless, oversized, sexless white EVM suit in the corner flanked by two more mercenaries, "— recover. Captain Tony Lomen, may I present Miss Katie Ranner?"

He stopped breathing altogether for at least ten seconds.

It has been a long time since I have met someone that has left me tongue tied and clumsy. I guess maybe it has to do with being the private god of war for a team of mercenaries. Perhaps it comes from looking over rifle sights and taking human life. Maybe it's because all the stars I really enjoy died centuries ago. Whatever the reason, I stood impatiently by as Tony shook Ranner's hand and went through the motions of introduction.

I finally decided to set my laptop up at the oversized wooden desk. I flipped the unit on and logged in. In seconds, I had contacted Logan and gotten real-time updates on everyone's condition. Most of the *Angels* were at least somewhat stable though Richardson was still touch-and-go as the doctors waited to see if the rejectionless cybernetic replacements I had ordered installed would indeed be rejectionless. Aside from their needs, the entire rest of the team was tired as hell. Four were right now on their way to *Deadly Heaven* to trade places with Thompson. They would hold the spacecraft, and she would be my proxy in Mezzo-Americana. The only trouble now was that John Doe was way over his flight limit for the day, and the team members were all wiped from the stress of dealing with wounded and standing guard all day. Logan could take up some slack, but would it be enough? *If someone made a move against us now...*

Tony finished worshipping Ranner and came over to me. There really wasn't a lot of space to speak privately, but to his credit he tried.

"Uh, Todd? What's with the spacesuit? Is she contagious?" I patiently explained zero-loss to him, and he seemed to pick up on it immediately. On the other hand, he seemed less than impressed by my growing list of troubles, including the ten-hour time limit and manpower issues. "Sounds bad, but I'm on the other side of both problems. Did you see those people out in the street?"

I nodded. "I saw. It's good people feel safe enough to be outside. It's a good sign, Tony."

"That's not what's going on." With a little hop, he managed to settle his fireplug of an ass on the desk, one foot dangling in midair. "I didn't know it, but there were already dozens of free-floating cameras from local news crews in the area during the assault. There were another dozen hand-helds amongst the civilians. Everything that went on during or since has been televised live on the quantum net. Most of the pirate newscaster websites have crashed multiple times because of bandwidth overload. Ever since the assault—people have taken to calling it 'The Battle of West Lot'—refugees have been pouring in. Word is going out this place is safe, and it seems like the entire population of New California is pouring in here. There are thirty thousand people out there now. More are coming in from the spaceport and out of rat holes all across the city. Tomorrow it could be a hundred thousand. The day after, a million."

I leaned back in the obscenely comfortable chair and steepled my fingers in front of my face. "And you're running out of living space, food, bathrooms—."

"And police, clothes, blankets, medications of all kinds." Tony clasped his hands in front of him, and I watched his European skin flush pink and then white and red as he applied pressure. "People are camping on the street. The heat wave has no end in sight, the city aquifers are dangerously low from the lack of rain and soon they are going to dry out. I need help, Todd."

And there it is. I sighed. Many times, I've been on some God-forsaken rock with a pocketful of freshly paid credits when someone looks at me and says that they need, and you can hear the weight of the word, help. The problem was even as rich as I was, I could not simply throw money at Tony. It seems like an easy solution, and for a while it is, but if the things it buys are free to those that need them, soon they have no value. Worse, it robs the people of their self-determination. They learn not to depend on themselves, and instead wait for some fickle twist of fate to deliver them. Charity has its place, but too much is even worse than none at all.

I thought about the gangsters at the Cathlist church. With that much money all at one place at one time, it means someone, or rather many somones, are going to try to lop off some while nobody's looking. I saw Ranner listening intently from across the room, and I heaved a sigh. "I can give you money."

Tony leaned over me, breathing shallowly. "How much?"

"Not enough, Tony."

"But—" I shot him a dangerous look.

"And it's a one-time thing. No more. Ever." *This is how friends are lost over money.* "And that's what you'll tell everyone."

His color started to rise. "But—"

I shot out of my chair, back protesting a bit through the medication. "Captain Lomen, can I speak with you outside?"

Tony started to flush, but he bit his lip and nodded mutely. We left without further a word spoken until we entered an abandoned office *cum* bedroom down the hall. Then I turned to him as gently as I could manage. "I will give you money, and if you're smart, you'll use some of it for food and the rest to fund the security forces."

"Todd, these people have nothing; you can't turn your back on them."

I drew myself up to my full height, newly minted skin on my shin screaming when stretched. I stared down my nose at him, watching thunderheads across my face reflected in his blue grey eyes. "Get a hold of yourself, man! You've given these people everything they need: self-reliance, self-determination, and self-respect. With those three things, they can gather together and move mountains. Without them, they will never go anywhere and New California will become one, massive ghetto. These people do not need to be given. They need to earn, they need to be led, and they need to believe."

"They can't do any of that on empty stomachs, Todd."

I nodded. "I will get food. It will be cold, but it will be filling and it will keep them alive. Everything else is up to you."

At that, all color drained from his face. He started to sweat. "So, what happens when it runs out?"

"What happens when the media finds out I am solely supporting you and your refugees? How long before someone starts wondering if I've bought myself a little slice of Persephone on the cheap? Do you want to live the rest of your life with everyone thinking you're on the take?"

"I can live with that."

I pointed out the window, my voice louder than I wanted. "Can they?"

The window had been blackened for the assault, but he seemed to look through it, to the milling throngs of hungry people outside. "How can I do it?"

"You already know."

Tony seemed to age a decade in front of me right then as he buried his face in his hands. "Do I?"

"If you can lead one, you can lead one million."

The captain inside of him seemed to wake, lending steel to his spine as he took a deep breath. "Well, I guess we'll find out."

I reached out and took his shoulder, hoping the gesture was one of camaraderie and not condescension. "Stop thinking of them as outside of you. Stop looking at the world as your people and the general population. You are more than a policeman now. You are a leader, and those people are as much a resource as a liability. If they won't feed themselves, find a way to make them. If they won't go find blankets, set someone to go do it. If there aren't enough cops then, for Christ's sakes, get a man to train twenty, and then twenty more and twenty more. Make your own solutions, Tony! If I'm right, then sometime soon one of these *gritheads* from the old government is going to show up and try to take control. If your people are too weak because their leader won't lead, then he will snatch them up from underneath you."

Tony looked like I had thrown him a life preserver. "Maybe that would be for the best."

I quelled the urge to punch him. Twice. Hard. "Yes, because that worked out so well for them when the going got rough."

He swallowed and then he nodded, his jaw grinding into a more stubborn gear. He began breathing harder, stoking the fires inside of himself. "When does the battle end, Rook?"

"I'm sorry, Tony, but it doesn't. Life is only fair when you force it to be. You're a lawman. You should know that." I opened the door to the hallway and my MercTool chirped. I took it out and read the message scrolling across it.

Tony looked down at the dark stain on my pants leg that was beginning to drip down my boot and onto the floor. "You're bleeding."

I pushed the MercTool back into my pocket and nodded. "All the time."

Richardson had died on the operating table.

CHAPTER 28: THE POWER OF THE PEOPLE

I sent back an acknowledging message to Logan at the hospital and then left Tony, O'Leary and Ranner, everyone, inside of West Lot proper. I limped down the stairs, relishing the pain in my leg as I broke free of the police station and submerged myself in the mass of anonymous humanity beyond.

Unrestricted by helmet, rifle, and armor, I felt naked and free as I weighed the loss of one of my team. Lonely, broken eyes drank me in as I limped among the tents. People too weak to stand barely lifted their heads to watch me pass. But vacant looks soon became purposeful stares. Refugees began shifting to watch me pass. Word of my appearance outran me and before long people were coming over from a few rows over, and then from the surrounding buildings. They watched me like a silent parade, row upon row of unwashed, haggard faces. My hackles raised and my palm itched for the grip of my pistol as the camp began to come alive around me.

An ancient Latin-extraction man, stooped and weathered, stepped out of the line and met me face to face. His bushy mustache bristled, and his eyes were like sharp pieces of obsidian beneath heavy brows. I came to a jerky stop half a step away. He straightened, vertebrae by painful vertebrae, until he looked me in the eye. I met his gaze as an equal, unflinching.

His English came out as a wheezy gasp shredded by the years behind him. "Do people thank you very often for the work you do, mercenary?"

I shook my head, pointedly aware that I was surrounded and my leg was not going to take me very far, very fast. "Not often."

"That is a shame, *señor*." He stuck out his hand. "*Muchas Gracias*."

I looked down at it, dumbstruck for a moment. I grasped it gently, afraid my heavily muscled hand would snap his wrist with the least amount of effort. "You are welcome, sir."

And I looked around at all the people, their faces glowing as if I were a legend made real for their benefit. The bubble collapsed, and they came pressing in, touching me, patting my back, shaking my hand. I greeted and smiled and blinked back tears as the people rushed in to be the next to be near me.

In the life of a mercenary, I have experienced many things. Only twice before have I seen an outpouring of gratitude this uncompromising, this honest, this pure. I have never seen it from people this hungry, hot, and poor. Even the cameras that appeared at the edge of my vision could not detract from this moment, the unadulterated exhilaration of being *loved* by everyone in sight.

A man tripped, and it took a few seconds before he could get back to his feet. Two women shoved each other less than good-naturedly, each wanting to be the next to sprinkle me with affection. I was like a savior to them, an icon of safety, a symbol of food, shelter, and stability. I was what they needed, especially when I was not. They knew my name, and they thought they knew me. God save me, I didn't have the strength to tell them any different.

But then things became oppressive. The bubble continued to collapse, and my personal space evaporated. A woman hugged me tightly and kissed me deeply, setting the crowd to cheering. The mob pressed in further as those in the back wanted their five minutes in the presence of their hero. The crowd began to shove, to shift. I was carried on the tide of bodies. The venom dream struck me again, masses of icy corpses dragging me to my doom, and I shivered despite the heat. I looked across the two hundred meters at the front of West Lot, and suddenly I realized that I could not get back there even if I wanted to.

Suddenly, a piercing alarm sounded, and an officer came out of nowhere. Accustomed to obeying authority, the crowd parted instantly.

The uniformed policeman came right up to me and saluted. I returned it smartly as he said in heavily accented English, "Excuse me, sir, there is an update waiting for you inside."

I nodded. "Lead on."

The crowd moved aside for us, but I could not make any kind of grand exit. My leg was still stabbing at me, dripping blood in spits and spatters. I had to lean on the officer because my leg would not hold me. The crowd saw this and...*cheered?* Yes, they were cheering as I waved goodbye to them. Perhaps my wound made me more human, more real to them. Regardless, I walked back into a storm of activity and all thoughts of the people were swept aside.

The police officer leaned over to me as we moved up the steps. "Sir, I understand you are a mercenary and all, but realize you are something of a celebrity now. Enough rabid fans in one place at one time, and they could trample you with their love."

I stared at the officer with wide eyes, taking in his words with a measure of horror. I nodded a thank you to him, and patted him on the shoulder. I had to file that away. I had to remember a week ago these people would have happily spit on me and burned my corpse after hanging me from a light pole. In another week, they might be willing to do the same again. Between now and then, it was a real possibility that they would smother me with adoration.

O'Leary was in the lobby, lining up her men and giving orders over her helmet radio and command forearm pad. I stood to the side as a civilian medic came over and, after gesturing for permission, began to work on my leg. O'Leary got to me soon enough.

"I'm sorry, Captain, but there's a situation at the Ortega complex. I have to get back there ASAP."

"Situation?"

O'Leary motioned her men into motion. "I've got planetary Agents disembarking within one kilometer of the compound on three sides."

I looked at the blank faceplate of her helmet, but I knew what she was thinking. Neither of us believed in coincidence. Enemy troops—and militarized police definitely fit the definition—surrounding a friendly stronghold required attention. It was her responsibility. She had to be there. Now.

"I left Ranner with two police officers upstairs." I saluted her and she returned it quickly. "Good luck, Captain Rook."

"And you, Captain O'Leary."

And then she was gone, her squad running through the tent alleys as *The Bastard* touched down in a clear spot down the street. The medic finished applying synthetic skin to my shin and thought for a second about cautioning me to take more care. Evidently, the look on my face stopped him. I don't blame him;

the look on my face at that moment could have bored holes in plate steel.

Why? Why? It made a twisted kind of sense to try to capture me at L/V/D. If Lionel was to be believed, he wasn't giving the orders, which meant it was probably someone in the government or planetary police. The only reason they'd want to skin me alive is simple; I had shown them up. I had stopped a revolution which had sent them packing. There I was in their territory, and I should have been fairly easy to surround and capture. Had I been a little less confident of a man, that's precisely what would have happened. But now they were extending themselves outside of their zone of safety. They were taking on heavily armed, motivated mercenaries with police grade equipment. It would be lambs to the slaughter. Political cartoons to the contrary, one does not rise to the upper echelons of government service by being a complete and total idiot.

Then my MercTool chirped.

I yanked it out of my pocket and read the message from Logan scrolling across. Without thought to my leg, I bolted to the stairwell and ran up at a full sprint. Agony blossomed across me as I pushed myself, floor after floor, until I burst into the old chief's office and vaulted over the desk and into the too-comfy chair.

The policemen snapped to attention, then drew their pistols and looked back into the hallway as I turned on the wallscreens. The dozing laptop came to life, and I typed orders to Logan almost as fast as I could think, brown fingers blurring as the newsfeeds brought me the truth of his words. Planetary police had surrounded the hospital in Mezzo-Americana.

My orders were simple. 'Master Sergeant, get yourself and all ambulatory to a choke-point. They reach our wounded over your dead bodies. Clear?'

His reply was immediate. 'Crystal, sir. It has been a pleasure, Captain.'

I read that last bit again, because Logan was telling me I had told him to die in the line of duty, and he fully expected to. A growl escaped from between my teeth.

I piped the feed to O'Leary's command channel, and she gifted me back a LIDAR map showing three fliers lifting off from L/V/D and heading toward West Lot in a combat formation. A message from her accompanied the pictures. '*Apostle*, Actual to *Angel*, Actual. Should I turn around?'

I sent back four words. 'Do your duty, Captain.'

I motioned to one of the officers and he tossed me his radio. "Tony?"

"Yes, Rook?"

"Get everyone inside. Now."

There was a definite pause. "Should I be worried?"

"Yes. Get them inside. Now. We have incoming in five minutes, tops."

Alarms began to blare from every speaker. "What should we do?"

I felt ice water flood my veins, and a supernatural calm descended upon me. "Keep your people under cover. I will handle this." I stood and began to make my way toward the door much more slowly than I came in.

"You'll handle this? What is *this*?"

"Three fliers. Planetary police. They're coming for me."

"They're coming for you, your backup just left, and you're going to fend them off with your mechanized lawyer?"

I glanced over at Grisham. I motioned for him to come along. "That's about right."

"So, you're about to tell me he's actually a rampaging expert ninja-bot in disguise?"

"He is?" I glanced at Grisham who managed to look discomfited by the whole idea. "That'll bring my odds of survival way up."

Tony had the makings of a royal fit starting on the other end of the radio. "I am not leaving you to the wolves, Rook."

"You don't have any choice. You have a higher duty, and these Agents will kill anyone they have to in order to get to me."

"Why?"

"I wish I knew." I sighed. "It's been an honor, Tony. Stay under cover. Just do me a favor and make sure Ranner gets back home."

His reply sounded small, defeated. "Will do."

I tossed the radio to the cop and saluted smartly. I waved goodbye to Ranner with more cheer than I actually felt and then thought about going back to the desk for my helmet and pistol.

The Key to Damocles

Frag it. I'm not going to fight my way out of this one, and if one shot to the head wasn't going to do it, I bet they were willing to make as many as it takes. I walked out the door and into the elevator, Grisham in tow. I hit the button for the basement.

"Grisham?" The bot looked at me. "Please record."

Unable to ignore the programming dictums of his integrated personality, the mechanized man clasped his hands and leaned forward. "Ready, Captain."

"My name is Todd Michael Rook, Captain of *The Radiation Angels*. Being of sound mind and body..." It was short, sweet, and to the point. By the time the doors opened, I was done. "Store that in your secure onboard data vault until approached by Logan, Thompson, or O'Leary."

"Yes, sir."

The tunnels down here were of the type found in government buildings the universe over: cold, dank, and unfinished. We were only twenty steps from the morgue, and I walked in without knocking. Nobody was on duty, which suited me fine. It took just a second to locate the computer that told me which freezer I needed. I limped over to the wall, opened the small door, and pulled out the long, heavy tray upon which sat a greasy, black bag.

I couldn't give my trembling hands time to betray me, couldn't give the harsh chemical smell time to turn my stomach. Above all, I could not let my heart fail. I unzipped the bag and stared into the dead and fire-mutilated face of General Leoff Reeves.

I don't know how long I sat there, marveling at how death had changed my friend, thieving away the warmth and light within him. Now he was just meat. I knew it as well as the first caveman or ground-breaking scientist... there was nothing left of him inside, but here I was, all the same. Whirring quietly, Grisham brought over a stainless-steel stool and set it down behind me. I thanked him absently and sat down. All of a sudden, a lonely voice filled up the cold metal room. It was mine.

"I am going to miss you, you bastard." The whole building rumbled, the telltale of three fliers busting ass overhead at mach-something. I frowned as I took a last look at his face, shuddering inside as I saw how his neck was completely the wrong shape. "You made me proud. Now it's my turn...See you soon."

372

I zipped up his bag and gently shoved the tray home. I shut the door, relishing the feel of the cold metal, relishing the feel of anything in these last moments, really. I stared at my reflection and saw the naked fear behind my eyes. I murmured, "What does it matter how a man falls down?"

And I realized that Grisham was looking at me, almost expectantly. I waved him off. "You had better stay here. It would be a shame to lose my will to a stray shot."

"I understand, sir, but my data vault is inside a hardened polycarbinite laminate case. It could withstand re-entry from orbit, if need be. Seeing as that is so, I would really rather stand next to you for a little while longer."

"They are likely to shoot first and capture me second. Why in hell do you want to be in the middle of that? You still have some self-preservation software running, right?"

Grisham affixed me with a somber stare from his fake face. He seemed to consider, which is a stupid idea since his brain will do fourteen million computations a second, then he bowed a bit. "When the falling is all that's left, sir?"

"You have been raiding my movie vault, haven't you?"

Grisham managed to shrug and look embarrassed. "It is part of my programming to integrate myself into your crew."

This is stupid, order him to stay here and be done with it, he's got too much vital... Aw *frag* it all to hell. I smiled a bit despite myself. "All right, come on then."

We exited the morgue, rode the elevator, and got caught in the clot of people desperately trying to come inside. Everyone had heard the klaxons, which thankfully had been turned off, and was desperate to escape whatever kind of attack was coming. I pushed against the crowd, Grisham in my wake, and saluted the officers who were desperately trying to keep the crowd from trampling one another to death. They looked scared, which probably meant they had a good grasp of what was about to happen.

I squeezed out the front door and cut to the side, pulling free of the crowd trying to funnel into the station. An old woman was pushed in the wrong direction and fell at my feet. I stopped to pick her up and press her into the confused arms of a vaguely familiar young man still in line. "Watch her."

The Key to Damocles

He had the physique of a dancer, and the proud face of some kind of professional functionary. After another look, I was pretty sure this was one of the congregation members from the Ninth Street Cathlist church. Despite his health, youth, and faith, he pushed her away as he frowned and glanced around, looking for danger from any quarter. "She's not mine... Captain."

My hand shot out and gathered the front of his shirt in one scarred ball of flesh. I yanked him out of line and brought him up until our noses touched, my heartbeat as clear in my ears as a church bell. "Do not tell me she is not 'yours', pal! You belong to each other, all of you! You work together from now forward, or you all starve in this little crumbling *grit-hole*." And I threw him back into the crowd, all of them awestruck at the display. I stepped back and addressed them all, voice harsh and final. "You have to look after each other. All of you. You think this is bad now? Just wait. The less effort you all put into survival as a group, the faster you'll all circle the *fragging* drain!"

The man did not turn red and take a swing at me; he did not scream and yell. He, like rest of the crowd, looked cowed and embarrassed. They pushed a little softer, they whimpered a little less. I reached out and gathered the old woman gently into my arms and pushed her toward the dancer. The young man took up the woman and acted as a buffer amidst the press of bodies, murmuring something to her I could not hear.

I turned away and marched out into the tent town, painfully aware of the streams of people on all sides. The situation at West Lot station was repeated everywhere. Everyone was trying to get inside, fast. The streams were pooling at the entrances, chokepoints that could turn into killing fields for gunfire or feet at the flick of a switch. Community leaders were herding them as best they could, police and newly minted militia keeping the pace steady and breaking up fights born of panic. Not surprisingly, the bussed-in protestors had fled at the first sign of trouble.

Alone, I limped by the final rows of tents that stood like pall bearers on either side. I saw a makeshift table, where some of the refugees were playing a card game to pass the time. Single cigarettes and whole packs sat as a pot in the middle, and I snagged one of the plastic wrapped bundles in passing. It wasn't like I was going to die of cancer now. I began slapping the pack against my opposite palm, packing the tobacco tightly to keep it from burning too fast. My feet crossed from the ruined grounds and sidewalk of West Lot onto the trash strewn streets. War-scarred buildings loomed on every side as I walked to the middle of the intersection, the rhythmic slap—slap—slap of the pack of smokes the only sound to disturb me until the roar of jet wash obliterated everything else.

One of the fliers swooped in like a bird of prey, executing a presentable combat landing some twenty meters down the road as the other two circled menacingly less than three hundred meters up. The flier on the ground immediately trained in on me with a full broadside of ship mounted cannons as I tore the plastic off of the cigarette pack and flipped open the lid. Everything waited with bated breath as they ran their sensor gear over me to make sure there wasn't a suitcase nuke shoved up my ass or some such. I slipped out a cigarette and perched it between my lips as I took out my MercTool and activated the mini-blowtorch. The ramp slapped down and planetary Agents, dressed in black and toting their heaviest guns, disgorged like vomit from a dog. I brought the blowtorch up, careful not to burn my face on the white hot plasma flame, and almost touched the end of the tube in my mouth when I was given pause.

I'd started smoking as an act of rebellion when I was sixteen. My habit managed to survive my father, my mother, and dozens of friends who rode me mercilessly about it. I finally had to give it up in basic training because suddenly I had to push my body to its limits on a daily basis in order to keep up. I had ignored cravings for ten years, cravings my psychiatrists said were nothing more than a transfer of discontent, or oral fixations, or something similar. My last cigarette had left me coughing and raw, but still the urge remained. Here, now, faced with the end, I realized that this simply was not who I was anymore.

It was too bad. Puffing carelessly on a cigarette as they came at me with rifles aimed would have summed up how I felt about this entire ordeal quite succinctly. I snapped the MercTool off and put the cigarette back in the pack. With a casual toss, I sent the pack spinning back into the field of tents behind me.

The men fanned out in an arc ahead of me, ten meters away—spitting distance for any kind of rifle—and waited patiently as a last member of their team left the safety of the grounded flier.

The Key to Damocles

A nondescript Latin extraction man came down the ramp and walked along the dirty street. His suit was freshly pressed, his gait had a whiff of military and lot of authority, and there was the distinct bulge of a full holster at his waist. I shifted my weight so it was all on my good leg and perched my hands on my hips. He clearly wanted this to look good for whatever cameras he had running and there was no point in me playing the part of the cowering criminal.

He paused at the line of his men and sized me up, which was probably pretty smart. His scans would have told him that I was unarmed, accompanied by what was very clearly not a combat model robot, and that alone would have made me a little skittish. When a man comes loaded for bear, he clearly wants to bargain at least and fight at most. When a man shows up to a hostile meeting without armor, helmet, or weapon of any kind, it is good to be wary. At the same time, however, it would be interesting to see how the newsfeeds treated him for his overabundance of caution.

After a second or two he triumphantly stepped forward until we were less than four meters apart. It was brave; I could have crossed the space between us in less than a second and killed him with my bare hands if I were healthy, and if there weren't a dozen armed men pointing guns at me. *If, dammit.* As it was, I crossed my arms and tried to exude impatience. Finally, he smiled. "Well, Mister Rook. It looks like the game is over. I have you now."

And all of a sudden there was a rockslide in my brain, thousands of tons of detritus sloughing away and exposing bare facts beneath. This man was not here because of some troublemaker running around on his planet. He was not here for the *Angels*, or even the leader of the *Angels*. This man was here because of *me*. I struggled to maintain an indifferent demeanor. "Do you?"

His eyes narrowed and he glanced left and right behind me. "Yes, it would seem so."

"Really, well, that's quite an impressive feat, Mister…?"

"Director. Director Saracho."

"Ah, yes, I have a lot of panicked orders from you, Director."

His jaw worked back and forth, grinding his teeth into stubs. "I bet you do."

"I also have a few of your Agents."

He smiled again, sure of his hand and eyeing the pot before him greedily. Unfortunately, the pot was me. "Well, we will have them back soon."

He motioned an Agent to his right to come forward and take custody of me, but I stalled him with a raised hand. *Interesting, even now you are all terrified of me.* "There is only one thing I don't get, Director."

Saracho cast a withering glare at his subordinate. "And what is that, Mister Rook?"

"Why are you so frightened of little old me?"

Beneath his Latin complexion, he went green and then grey. His pupils shrunk to pinpricks and his breath became shallow. "I am not afraid of you, Rook."

Ah, Director, you are a liar.

Confidence welled up within him again, and he began to flush. "And even if I were, it hardly matters now. You will not pain me again. Arrest him."

The Agent took another step forward but halted and raised his weapon, pointing over my shoulder. I caught soft footfalls from behind me broken by the tattletale crunch of trash beneath soles. I turned my head slightly and caught my breath as Father Gallego, leader of the Ninth Street Cathlist Church, walked to stand abreast of me.

Still stooped and gray, yet possessing of some indefinable internal youth, he managed to move like a man of the cloth should: humble, nonviolent, non-confrontational, but possessing the might of a man devoid of fear. Right now, I was wishing for a little fear; he was standing in a free-fire zone, and I didn't want an old man's blood on my hands.

He smiled and made the sign of the cross to bless the gathered troopers. "God bless you and keep you, officers. Is there anything I can do to help you?"

The director growled and flushed a little deeper red. "*Padre*, you must leave here immediately."

Gallego clasped his hands behind his back. "No, no I don't think I do, my son."

Saracho rolled his eyes and motioned his pawn forward again. "Just arrest them both."

The Key to Damocles

I held up my hand again in front of the peon again and growled deep in my throat, stabbing him with a look lovingly crafted to stare down dictators and tyrants. The soldier backed up a step. I wasn't going to start a firefight *sans* firearm in the middle of a populated area like this to save my own skin, but I was going to be damned if they were taking the *Padre* just for standing up for me.

Gallego cleared his throat and spoke with a mix of certainty and humility I could never have mastered. "With all due respect, this man is no criminal. I and my flock are in his debt. You will not take him today."

Saracho slapped the trooper in the back of the head, and gave a terse order in Spanish.

And then more footfalls distracted the half ring of riflemen again. Grisham whirred and moved out of the way so she could stand at my other shoulder. Short, plump, still bearing a bloodstained eye and the slowly fading signs of abuse, she looked like a colossus right now. Dressed in ill-fitting coveralls, Miss Anita Cody walked forward. I spared a second to look over my shoulders and saw that the people had stopped filtering into the buildings and were coming back into the *fragging* street. *Goddamnit Tony, get those people out of here before*—!

"You cannot have him." Her voice was clear, bright, full of a power I couldn't describe. She did not voice an opinion. She wasn't quoting scripture. She was stating a fact of life, a law of physics: immutable and unbendable.

Like his men, Saracho ran through disbelief, then shock, then anger, but he did it in less than a second. "Run along *little girl*—"

She took a half step in front of me and planted her feet shoulder width apart and jutted out her chin in total defiance. "You cannot have him."

One of the riflemen sighted in on her, smack dab square in the chest. *Oh God.* I raised my arms and sidled around her, into his field of fire. Saracho smiled. "Can we dispense with this *farsa*, then? Are you coming along quietly?"

"No, he is—" Cody tried to get around me, but I moved to keep her behind.

I glanced back at her. "They will kill you, Anita."

Inside her eyes, I saw the hidden storehouse of screaming fear ready to break loose at any second. Behind the walls of iron will she had built, all the hurt, the pain, and the terror of violence was still there. She knew the dangers already when she said, "They might, but they will not take you."

And another voice called out from behind me, full of forced cheer. "Of course they're not!"

Tony came trundling in on his short, stubby legs, twenty-four policemen trailing behind. All of them were in dress uniforms. All of them were armed with rifles, real rifles, with scars where the *Radiation Angels* insignia had been removed. He interposed himself between the row of black clad Agents and me, his very presence pushing them back like a gale force wind. "Director Saracho? Tony Lomen, acting station Chief of West Lot."

The Director crossed his arms and pulled one of his soldier lackeys back even with him. "Chief, can I expect you to comply with the law and remove these people so I can take this felon into my custody?"

"That's the funny thing." Tony feigned consideration as he ran his fingers through his closely cropped field of gray beard. "You see, you almost have it all: you have the fliers, you have the uniforms, you have the badges, and you have the guns. What you don't have... is the jurisdiction."

Saracho nearly had a fit, his voice reaching into tenor as he spat, "Juris-DIC-tion?"

"Yep, jurisdiction... legal pull, mojo, power, clout, authority. You need it, and you don't have it."

Saracho began to quiver as a storm of noise began to build behind me. He had to shout to be heard clearly, but he would have shouted regardless. "I am an Agent of the planetary government!"

"Which dissolved some months back." The sounds of the mob got closer, threatening to drown out the conversation with the growl of thousands of angry tongues. Tony raised his voice so that he could be heard over the crowd building like angry thunderheads amongst the tents. "Which is a shame since we really could have used you... well... any time before now, really. Once you left us to rot, your authority ended. Your government dissolved. You aren't the director of a dead dog's dick right now... sir."

The crowd heard, and reacted. The survivors of The Battle of West Lot pushed to the fore, leavened with police and new leaders flush with indignity at their abandonment. They became calm, quiet, possessing of a single hive mind controlled by their stumpy leader who even now faced down the director like a titan before a firestorm of the gods.

The Agents, like most police, are drilled and drilled in force management in order to stay alive. Never go one-on-one, always call for backup, never get surrounded, never be outnumbered. One by one, these rules fell by the wayside. They shifted from one foot the next and even lowered their rifles, abandoning force resolution for conflict resolution since their small group would never be able to scatter an armed crowd of this size. The presence of police officers— in their mind, brothers in arms— further clouded the issue.

But the director's fury built, mimicking Carlos, the subordinate I was now certain he had personally sent to kidnap and torture me. In his mind, his authority on this planet was absolute; anything else was fictitious, a fantasy meant to humiliate him. He could not see the situation on the ground had greatly changed. He pointed an arm at me like a death sentence from a Roman emperor. His voice screeched, "Take him into custody!"

A thousand rifles, pistols, and carbines slung out from underneath light clothing... cloaks, thin robes, and shawls meant to keep off the sun. The entire crowd behind me seemed to become a massive Lovecraftian monster bristling with guns. The sound of them priming all at once was enough to get the hair on the back of my neck to stand at attention. Tony chuckled and hitched at his belt. His next words started friendly enough but gathered the momentum of rage as he continued.

"No, that isn't going to happen." In the long seconds of quiet that followed, safeties snapped off like thunder. Tony chuckled, his expression sinister. "Now, if you please, I'd like for you to take your fancy Agents and your fancy suit, get aboard your fancy flier, and get your fancy ass the hell out of West Lot before I arrest you for impersonating an officer of the law!"

Saracho lunged forward, but three of his men dove and restrained him. They pulled him back as a bloody flush rose to his cheeks. His short hair bristled as he began to scream in Spanish. I wasn't sure exactly what he was saying, but I was willing to bet he had read the Spanish edition of <u>Starting</u> <u>Barroom Brawls,</u> too. Maybe he had ghostwritten it.

Though they were cuffed, pushed, and punched by the director at least once, the whole squad clustered around him and ensured any shot would have to pass through their bodies before reaching their boss. They were better men than he deserved.

Then I noticed Saracho wasn't looking at Tony. He wasn't even cursing at the crowd. All of his rage, all of his attention, all of his venom was centered on little old me.

His eyes narrowed, saying very clearly, *I will get you.*

I bobbed my chin at him once, sharply. *I'll be waiting for you.*

And he just went crazy again. Tony got on his radio and made a call completely swallowed by Saracho's snit. In less than thirty seconds, half a dozen police fliers were screaming overhead, keeping an obvious watch over the heavier troop carriers Saracho had brought.

Then, without a shot being fired, and without a coherent order given, the Planetary Agents began wrestling their director toward their landing craft. The tension spiked once again as Saracho unholstered his pistol, only to have it wrested away by one of his guards. This drove him to even greater levels of fury. The Agents took a hold of his limbs and carried him up the loading ramp. It closed at a snail's pace as the engines spooled up, melting the asphalt beneath the craft. There was a jerk, a lurch, and the flier leapt into the air, propelled by the riot of cheers on the ground.

Weapons were placed on safe and shouldered as a roar of animal victory exploded behind me. The crowd dissolved into an impromptu celebration, clapping, hooting, kissing, and dancing. The people of West Lot had faced down the wolves at their doors and had done it with no shots fired. If you had to do it, that was the best way, bar none.

Though I doubt they understood it too well themselves, I did. Last week they had proven they could defend their homes from armed men; this week they had stuck a sharp stick in the eye of fake authority. They were developing a sense of self, a sense of pride, of unity. They were feeling the birth of their political will.

Gallego was lost in joyful, tearful prayer. Tony looked like a new father as he strutted across the place where Saracho had minutes before stood. Anita jumped up and hugged me tightly around the neck. She kissed me, face wet with tears as she whispered in my ear, "See? You are a hero."

I felt my throat fill up suddenly. "That's funny. I was thinking the same thing about you, Miss Cody."

Tony turned to the crowd and motioned to one of his officers, who handed him a megaphone that looked like nothing so much as a ping-pong paddle. Tony held it up to his mouth, his voice captured by the miniaturized electronics and turned into the rolling thunder of a god. He cleared his throat, took a deep breath and barked, "*¿quiénes son usted?*"

The question took the crowd by surprise. People just now sifting out of the surrounding buildings looked at one another, wondering what they had missed. A tense hush fell over the crowd, all eyes, on the short, graying leader that now asked a question they didn't understand. Who was he talking to? What did he mean? Grisham moved up next to me and handed me an ear bud from a compartment in his chest. I placed it into my ear, expecting another dire report, but instead I heard Tony's words, in his own voice, remixed and translated into English. I nodded my thanks to Grisham.

Lomen took another deep breath. "Who are you?"

The crowd again looked amongst themselves, each one searching the face of the others for the answer.

He shook his head, face falling as he asked again, "Who are you?"

Gallego's voice, clear and resonant, called from the front row. "We are West Lot."

Without skipping a beat, Tony stabbed his finger at someone behind the priest and asked, "Who are you?"

The man there swallowed with some difficulty, and said. "We are West Lot?"

"Who are you?"

Anita was next, her voice joyful and proud. "We are West Lot!"

"Who are you?"

A few people answered at once, saying in a stumbling unison. "We are West Lot."

"WHO ARE YOU?"

And the people answered in one voice, a sound that rattled the sky and shook the ground. "WE ARE WEST LOT."

Tony pumped his arm in victory and the crowd cheered again. Only after minutes of celebration did he raise the amplifier back to his face. "West Lot, you did it! You lived through the worst the terrorists could throw at you. Abandoned, separated, alone, and without hope… yet still you survived. They frightened you, burned you, lied to you, and still you lived."

The crowd became very quiet, remembering the long months of hunger, pain, and terror. Tears began to fall from thousands of eyes as families held each other closely. Slowly, slowly, those without families began to comfort one another. Strangers no longer, these people were united under a common name, a common bond of blood and pain. They looked upon Lomen with an air of holiness, embracing him as he finally took them as his own children… their victories to be his, their pain to be shared in his very soul. "But we banded together, didn't we? You saw them assemble outside our walls and threaten us with death, but you stood strong! You blunted their knives, turned aside their guns. You faced them with honor and courage. Because of that, I am proud."

The crowd cheered again, shining with sound brighter than any sun. Tony took the time to clear his throat and dab at his grey eyes. If it were anyone else, I would have said it was for the cameras. "But you did much more than face them. You beat them!"

The crowd erupted again. Tony began to feel out his pacing, taste the words on his tongue and weigh the emotions of his heart. "And now our old *masters—*" a word he spit out "—come sauntering back with handcuffs and guns, telling us we must listen, we must submit, we must give up one of our own—"

A crescendo of denials exploded from the people of West Lot, sounding like nothing so much as the growl of Fenris.

"—and again you stood strong. I was here, the *padre* was here, but it was you, it was West Lot that told them: 'Go Home! Crawl back into your hole! You are not needed or wanted here!' And when they rattled the chains they believe you should wear, WHAT WAS YOUR ANSWER?"

The crowd defiantly raised voices, fists, knives, and guns into the air.

The Key to Damocles

"YES! Yes, that's what you told them. And you know what that means?" The crowd hushed, leaning forward, perched on the edge of his every word and waiting for the next. "You are free!"

It built like a wind, sweeping aside all the hurt and doubt, a wordless cry that bonded them even more tightly into a whole. It lasted for long minutes, washing over the assembled congregation. Tony looked at me and smiled, tired and frightened. I gave him a thumbs up, and he nodded. He had faced his greatest fear and come out the other side a stronger man.

We both knew what came next, but he did not falter from it. He trusted the people who looked toward him for leadership, and they trusted him in return. He raised his hand and the crushing voices subsided. "But there is much left to do. We are gathering more people, day by day. More and more people hear about what we are building here, and they come to find food, friends, freedom, and safety. They, too, are our brothers and sisters. They, too, are our people. They bring with them their hopes and dreams, their fears and wounds. They will need food for their bellies and shelter against the harsh sun; but even more, they will need guidance and fellowship."

And then Tony stalled, his voice catching in his throat. I leaned forward with everyone else in the crowd, waiting, waiting. *Go on, go on.* Finally, he sighed and set his face in the very picture of a stalwart patriarch.

"We have outgrown this place." The crowd's reaction was immediate and unhappy. Tony waved them to silence. "WHO ARE YOU?"

The response shook the glass in every pane for a mile around. "WE ARE WEST LOT!"

"Then what are these buildings? If you are West Lot, then what is this place, except where we set our feet? If we were not here, what significance would it have?" Tony pointed in every direction. "LOOK! Look at the lines of dirty tents on every side of you. Breathe in the smell of unwashed bodies and pots of shit. Is this how our brothers and sisters should live?"

A scattering of 'No's answered him.

"West Lot, I tell you that this place has served us well, but it is time to move on. We cannot survive as a commune. We will fall to disease and starvation. We will fall upon one another in revolution as dictatorships war with one another. We have to

384

strive to regain our civilization before circumstances devour us whole. We must find places to live, clean out our stores, and reconstitute our police forces. We must hold elections. We have to believe in one another, for it is the only way we will survive. Make no mistake, we have told the vultures to go away once, but we will have to do it again." He breathed deeply, lungs rattling with emotion. "They came once with guns; next time they will come with food, and then with money. They will seek to buy us, to seduce us. They will offer us whatever we desperately need in order to fit their chains around our necks again. And as soon as that happens, we will be disarmed, declawed, silenced, and ignored again... until the next time this happens. Then we will be abandoned again!"

In the long pause that followed the crowd was deathly silent.

"So, we can grow and adapt, we can grow and starve... or we can submit." The silence turned cold, unwelcoming, and seemed to stretch forever. Finally, as the weight of dark thoughts lowered onto individual shoulders and turned to lead, a short Latin-extraction man emerged from the crowd, torn and dirty clothes marking him as some kind of office worker. His hands were clamped around a rifle scavenged from the corpse of an unnamed unbondable. He stood five paces from Lomen, executed a clumsy about-face, and faced the crowd proudly. Then he raised the rifle above his head.

The crowd cheered in agreement.

More were joining the office worker, more was going on, but my MercTool beeped again, scrolling bad news across the little red screen. I bounced a comm signal through Grisham to my laptop, confirming the terse words with Logan. The crowd cheered as I limped forward next to Tony and leaned in to whisper a few, quick words. He looked me dead in the eye and nodded. He brought the megaphone back up.

"West Lot! The vulture Saracho has struck again. Even now, he menaces those that stood with you at The Battle." There was no need to clarify which one. "What say you?"

A crashing storm of silence cut every voice short, but as the assembled people of West Lot looked at me, they raised rifles into the air.

Tony turned back to me. "West Lot stands ready. What do you need, Captain Rook?"

The Key to Damocles

And for a second, I could not see the multitude in front of me for the tears blurring my eyes. Then, between one breath and the next, I came up with a plan. I looked deeply into Tony's eyes because it all hinged on him.

CHAPTER 29: HIPPOCRATES, JUDAS, AND LEONIDAS

Richardson was screaming in pain, and I was clawing for a weapon that turned to fog in my hands. I called his name, balling my hands into fists as burning plasma fell from heaven like the tears of damned angels. The fire was raining down from the unblinking eyes of news cameras. Inside of every black lens, inverted ghosts of *El Toro* pontificated like despotic gods. His words congealed like bloody lard and fell, blazing as they made reentry. Fat, burning globs struck the city around me, cracking concrete and setting smoke weeping toward the heavens.

I scrambled for the side of the blasted street and snatched up a pointed aluminum rod. I cocked my hand back and took aim at the center of the closest camera when thousands of fliers surged into the sky, blocking my shot and drowning out the world with words of thunder.

A shout got my attention, and I saw planetary Agents crawling out of every dank sewer, dark alley, and scorched crater. Saracho, made of clay like a B movie abomination, was at their lead. He wielded a massive chain like a lasso, twirling it above his head with the sound of sleigh bells. He swung it at my face, and I saw the chain links were handcuffs clasped together end upon end. It struck the side of my face and blood spurted in thick, heavy drops.

I shifted my aim to him and threw.

Cold, hard, metallic hands the size of dinner plates grabbed me and pressed me down. I started to scream until a calm voice made of magma and stone enveloped me.

It said, "Captain."

I woke up.

Logan let go of me as soon as my eyes found focus on his bare metal face. He stood back respectfully, ignoring the tears boiling out of my eyes and snot dripping out of my nose. About one half of a percent of the population has this reaction to Kezitine, a popular anesthetic. Doctors loved using it to put people under because it was so safe; it was more or less everywhere. I'd rather take a little liver damage thank you very much, but nobody ever asked. I grabbed a handful of blanket and cleaned myself up. As I pressed the wads of thin cloth to my face I managed to snuffle out, "Where is my Lieutenant, Logan?"

"She is on her—"

Thompson came in, uniform rumpled, dark rings under her eyes set off by the ashy texture of her face. She stood at some semblance of attention and saluted. I pulled myself up on the bed and began tracing over my torso, feeling the tender spots where my skin had been sewn shut. "Report, Lieutenant."

She braced herself before continuing. "Long is out of surgery but will require time before her bionic legs sync up with her brain. Walt is out of surgery, but his replacement knee is acting quirky. He needs lots of physical therapy. I think it is safe to say that both of them are out of action for at least a week; a month would be better. And of course…"

"Richardson is dead," I finished. "How about everyone else?"

"Ortega got a replacement hand graft, and it's going to be a few days before it can be used. Between surgery and nanite infections knitting tissue together, everyone else is whole, but I can't say healthy. We've all been beat and battered. The *Angels* are tired, Captain."

"I understand, Lieutenant. I just need a little bit more."

"Captain, I don't—"

I cut her off. "Tell me about the situation on the ground, Thompson."

She closed her eyes as she condensed the last few hours into as few words as possible. "After the initial push, the Master Sergeant secured a few weapons from the enemy, and we managed hold the hospital. Station Chief Lomen managed to diffuse the situation in the street. We have twenty militia members downstairs flying police colors and guarding the entrances. The local chief is a real by-the-book, law-and-order type. Lomen was able to argue to the local police that they were breaking the law by helping Saracho. They took it to a judge and then an hour later to a court, disputing the jurisdiction of the Planetary Agents and securing an injunction. The Planetary Agents cannot work in Mezzo-Americana until the court case is decided. PISs is apparently using some of the old-guard politicians as their lawyers and not having too much success."

"Any circling vultures?"

She shook her head. "Sichak is keeping an eye on every flier with a PISs transponder. None of them have even come near this city except to go to the court building."

I smiled inside at that. *Saracho must be ready to swallow his own tongue in frustration.* "And whose idea was it to give up our arms and ordnance?"

This is the bit Thompson had been waiting for. She answered without hesitation. "It was mine, Captain."

"Was anyone hurt or killed during the Agent's attack?"

She didn't have to ask if I counted wounded Agents, of which there were plenty. Logan had gone in alone against the first wave, disabling or dismembering Agents and securing their weaponry. "No, sir."

"Then you get a *bye* on this one. We are in a war zone, and we must be armed to do our jobs. There are the Laws of War and the words out of my mouth. No other rules, no other laws, no other traditions should mean anything to you. If I ask you to, I expect you to ignore the laws of physics. Your men are your highest priority. All other considerations be damned. Never give up your weapons unless you are surrendering."

"Richardson needed medical care, sir."

"And getting it to him as fast as possible nearly got you all killed." *And he died anyway*, I didn't say. That part wasn't her fault; it was mine. I asked what time it was and cursed at the answer. "If you have no other choice, next time just agree to their terms and then smuggle weapons in anyway. Now, any word from L/V/D?"

"They will arrive in thirty minutes. We are going to do the exchange on the rooftop emergency pad."

"They're cutting it real fine. Any protest from the hospital?"

"I didn't think to ask."

The Key to Damocles

I smiled. "Now that's what I like to hear. Is Grisham still with Ranner?"

"Yes, sir. He's still there and still recording everything."

I started to get out of bed, wincing at the twinges from across my newly repaired chest. "Excellent. Go get three *Angels* and Ranner. Get to the top floor. Have Ortega disable the emergency exit alarm but don't go onto the roof. I'll send Logan along shortly."

She nodded, saluted, and left, taking all sound with her. I just settled back, eyes closed, and tried to focus past the drugs and pain. The urgency of the moment kept clawing at me, and I could only relax for a few seconds before I levered myself off of the hospital bed and onto the ice-cold floor. I tossed off the never-stays-closed-in-the-back hospital shift and stood nude in front of the full-length mirror inside the closet.

My whole body is a map of past battles: old scars, old burns, old memories written in blood. The largest by far was the newly reopened and closed seam that went from under one armpit, down and across my belly, and then up underneath the other. It was angry and purple underneath my dark brown skin. I flexed, and I hissed as the motion provoked a searing pain. The burned skin on my shin had finally gotten the time it needed to set and fuse to my natural dermis. Only now I noticed that the fake skin patch the hospital had used was tinted to match a Latin complexion and not my own. By far the most noticeable was the huge, twisted crater where the massive anti-borg bullet had pierced my chest. The *hard shell* could not have stopped it, nor could my armored chest cage have done any better. Both together managed to save my life. *Just barely*.

Logan shifted from one titanium laminate foot to another, something I had never known him to do before. "What's on your mind, Logan?"

"Nothing, sir."

I reached into the closet and grabbed my pants. "It wasn't your fault, Sergeant."

Logan began clicking like an out of tune flier, robotic muscles reacting to human stimuli and trying to shudder. "Captain—."

"Oh, no. None of that, asshole." I pulled on my clothes, piece by piece, pleased to see someone had managed to replace the tattered uniform I had been wearing and even supplied a set of

390

armor from *The Cherub* or *The Succubus*. "You led; he followed. It should have been the other way around, but it wasn't. He did follow and that's all that matters. Maybe he should not have. Maybe he was right and you should have let those women burn, but I don't believe it and neither do you. He made the decision, and he alone. You can question that, or his decision, but you do not get to steal it from him. That lessens the kind of man he was, and robs him of the nobility of what he did."

Logan nodded, somewhat grudgingly.

I pulled on my shirt, my heart surging at the unit patch emblazoned in day-glow green on the chest. When I faced Logan, I did it as his Captain. "I wish many decisions had been made differently while I was off planet, but considering what happened, you all did some good work. There are lots of women who are alive and free today because of what you did. Stop punishing yourself."

The door opened, and a fifty-ish doctor came in. He looked at me like I was some kind of caveman and at Logan like he was the devil himself. Then he adopted a stuffy, superior air.

Okay, I admit it; I rolled my eyes at him. "Sergeant, go join up with Thompson. I will be there shortly."

Logan nodded and shuffled out of the door, having to turn sideways and crouch to get through the human-sized portal. Again, I wondered what was bothering the giant. It wasn't just Reeves' death because it had started at the church. I had to make time to talk to him.

The doctor cleared his throat. "If you are completely done gathering wool and getting dressed, perhaps you can get undressed so I can examine you."

It was not a question, nor was it delivered with anything but contempt. I denied the urge to choke him with my bare hands, even just a little bit.

I took off the shirt and sat on the bed, expertly lifting my arm so he could get a good look at the seam on that side. The doctor leaned over with a pair of odd glasses on, peering through the computer enhanced display of the lenses at his handiwork. He cleared his throat again. "I suppose you think you're some kind of hero?"

I raised my other arm as he moved to that side, wincing again as it pulled the freshly patched skin taut, but I did not answer.

He poked one or two places, and then continued. "Must be easy, solving all of your problems with guns."

I breathed in deep a second before he asked me to, which earned me an annoyed glance rather than a 'thank you'. He kept poking, concentrating now on the bullet holes. "Disagree with someone, just blow their head off. No need to negotiate! Kids in a church, kidnappers in a school, policemen in a hospital... all of these problems can be solved with lasers, bullets, and grenades. Must be very easy to be you."

My pulse felt like machinegun fire. Hot, wet words filled my mouth, forcing me to swallow hard. The doctor crossed the room, opened a cabinet with his thumbprint and got a can. He returned and used the spray anesthetic to dose my chest wounds liberally. "I argued strenuously against admitting your people, but apparently your bank account is rather large."

He turned away and went back to the medical supply unit, turning in his anesthetic and grabbing a can of dermal regenerating macro-nanites and a can of spray-on skin. He turned around and administered them professionally, pausing to examine a few sections of skin more closely, all the while keeping up his monologue. His voice was becoming stronger, more assured as he came to realize I wasn't going to hit him. "But I wonder at which point my Hippocratic oath requires me not to treat someone like you. I mean, I have to save lives. At what point does saving the life of someone like you cost the lives of hundreds, if not thousands, of others? I wonder if I should recommend you be placed in mandatory psychiatric care. Looks to me like you qualify, if anyone does."

He glanced into my eyes and flinched at what he saw. He beat a hasty retreat to the case and returned his medical gear. I began getting into my shirt.

I took a deep breath, feeling around for my center. I found it and pulled it close, letting the tension and anger flow around me. I felt it all swirl out of my feet as I went to the cabinet and retrieved the rest of my property. Just as I was certain I was past his nettling, he decided one last try. "I suppose you think you're pretty tough, don't you?"

"I was just thinking about how brave you are, sir." I faced away from him as I swung a combat vest on over my shirt, amazed at how calm my voice was. "I mean, there's an entire megacity burning to the waterline, and here you are in a nice, well-lit hospital, able to complain as much as you want about how they manage to survive."

His eyes narrowed. "Now look here—"

I dropped a bag onto the bed and began filling the pockets of the vest with various bits of equipment. I could hear scorn seeping into my words. "There are people suffering from malnutrition, dysentery, lack of prescription meds, as well as numerous battle wounds from defending their homes against criminals. But here you are, bravely holding down the home front."

He barely looked human anymore as he puckered and said, "You son of a—"

"So my question is, really, are you so pissed off at me because you hate what I do, or just jealous because you're so cowardly you won't see it yourself?"

His volume escalated, turning his voice into a shrill cry as his face. "I am a doctor, and you will show me some respect!"

"You've been paid, and paid well, for your work. And since you did your job for money instead of out of any humanitarian impulse, I'd say I owe you the same gratitude I'd owe a prostitute."

I shut the door behind me as all blood drained from his face. The corridors around me were packed with tense hospital staff, each one carefully avoiding my eyes as I looked everywhere for a map, directory, or a simple *fragging* arrow telling me where to go. I heard the doctor explode out of the hospital room about the same instant I found a sign for the stairs. I got to the door I needed when I felt a hand clamp down on my shoulder with surprising strength and spin me around. I saw the fist coming a mile away, and it was something akin to child's play to move my head to the side and allow him to slam his fist into the fire door behind me.

Everything in the hallway stopped as my doctor howled in rage and pain, cradling his hand close to his body and bending over double. I grabbed him in full view of a dozen nurses and guided him the five short steps to a set of chairs along the wall. I sat him down roughly and the positioned myself directly in front of him. When he did not look up, I got closer, and then closer. I stuck my crotch at the end of his nose, forcing him to sit up and

393

look at me. A nurse arrived and began tending his hand when I leaned down very close to him.

Somewhere in the last thirty seconds, he had realized the depth of his mistake. It took visible effort for him not to cower as the intense pain from his broken hand sapped his will. I leaned down close to him and he flinched.

I may have spoken in a whisper, but other than the odd interruption from the PA system, the dead silence in the corridor let my words carry to anyone who wanted to listen. "I don't know what your problem is, Doc. I don't know if you hate what I do because you hate what I do, or if you hate yourself for not being man enough to stand up and do it yourself."

I searched his eyes for comprehension, understanding or respect. All I found was fear and loathing. I sneered and performed an about face. He raised a hand to ward off a blow that was never started as I walked across the hall and into the stairwell. I began jogging upward.

My MercTool beeped as I passed Lopez on the stairs, keeping guard on Grisham and Ranner. I flashed him a smile and a punch to the shoulder. "How's the leg?"

He nodded at me and smiled. "Doing fine, Captain."

"Good to hear. If it starts hurting, let the medics know." I continued past him and hit the panic bar, opening the door to the roof. I glanced at the screen on the MercTool. 'L/V/D Incoming' and then stowed it away again.

This had to be done just right because avoiding a fight had more to do with theater than tactics. I jogged out to meet the four *Angels* that weren't on guard duty over the wounded, or wounded themselves. Thompson turned to me with an armload: fresh C^2 helmet, a rifle, spare battery packs, and my command laptop in its case. I accepted them.

The L/V/D ship was a speck on the horizon. I glanced around and was reasonably pleased with how she had dispersed the *Angels* across the rooftop. She looked to me for approval and I gave her a terse nod and thumbs-up.

The craft came in, guided by expert hands. It landed with the rear doors facing me and I could hear every asshole on the roof pucker so hard they became singularities. As the doors opened and began to clamshell away from the ramp, we were either about to be paid, or about to be shot at again.

Thankfully, for once, things went in my favor.

The doors finally opened, and Opus Lionel, CEO of L/V/D studios stood with three functionaries, each bearing two Trauma-Shoxx™ suitcases. There were several bodyguards inside the ship, but their weapons were holstered under clothes, and they had the rough and tumble feel of personal protection consultants, read as bodyguards, rather than the spit and polish fascism of the PISs(y) Agents.

Lionel strode down the ramp with an air of frustrated majesty, silken suit ruffling in the jet wash from his personal flier. He smiled, his white teeth glowing against his burnished black skin, but the quality was strained. "Captain, I—"

I was tired, I was cranky, and I had just spent two hundred grand to have my subdermal chest-plate replaced with a bonus lecture from an idiot. I was in no mood to shout pleasantries. "Have your flier cut its engines!"

If Lionel looked a little perturbed as he gave the order, his bodyguards looked like a team of cats dropped into a wolf enclosure. Hands began straying toward their concealed pistols as the aeroline engines spooled down. The *Angels* did not point their weapons at the guards, but they did raise the barrels from the roof in a clear warning. Oblivious, Lionel came down the ramp with his functionaries, his steps efficient and forceful. He stopped at the end of the ramp as I moved forward to meet him. Neither of us offered a hand in greeting.

Pride stood like a wall between us. I had shown him that he was not master of his own kingdom, and he could not forgive me for that. I was still miffed when my ass was in a sling, he had acted like a civilian instead of a mercenary. *Nobody said it was a fair universe*.

There were a few heartbeats where everything could go sour in a hurry, and then Lionel sighed audibly. "I assume you have my movie star, Captain Rook?"

I signaled for Lopez to bring Ranner and Grisham up onto the pad. I mimicked him, crisp businesslike. "You have my cash, Mr. Lionel?"

His aristocratic African features twisted a bit, and he waved his flunkies forward. They sat the Trauma-Shoxx™ suitcases on the flier pad and punched in the code. Lopez and his charges came onto the roof as the cases popped open and displayed a veritable sea of cash... Three hundred thousand, one hundred credit slips. I looked down for a moment and then cast a glance back at Grisham. Immediately, he activated a small device in his chest which sent out a signal to the cash. The nanites imbedded in the nylon slips aligned on him and whispered back their serial numbers, confirming total, veracity, and location. He sent a text message across my HUD to that effect.

I motioned to Ranner, who came forward timidly. Her footsteps gained strength and confidence the closer she got to her boss. As she walked up the ramp, she flung herself into Lionel's arms, and he embraced her warmly. I motioned to three *Angels* to come collect the cash as Lionel cracked the seal on her vacc suit helmet to expose her golden blonde curls. As the three *Angels* retired to the stairwell, an L/V/D functionary came forward and pressed a reader to the back of Ranner's neck. She jumped a bit, but Lionel held her tightly until the little box let off a triple beep. The assistant nodded, and immediately Lionel was all smiles again, cooing as he passed his employee deep inside the flier and into the arms of his personal guard.

He turned and opened his mouth, but I forestalled him with an upturned hand. "You can keep the vacc suit and read the personal computer log. There have been no breaches since she was put inside, and the suit has not been opened. If you give me a quantum signal address, I can have my lawyer pump over his personal inviolate logs to further prove zero loss has been maintained."

We exchanged the information quickly, and Lionel collected his functionaries. Technically, our business transaction was over, but I still had something eating at me. There were too many unanswered questions. They were walking up the ramp when I called out, stopping them in their tracks. "Did you have your men look at that sensor feed we gave you?"

Lionel stopped. He turned back toward me slowly, eyes narrowed and nostrils flared. I swallowed my damn pride and walked up the ramp into the belly of his flier. "The ambush at the landing pad, did you confirm the recordings?"

Lionel's eyes widened, and veins on his neck and forehead pulsed dangerously. I took the chance and removed my helmet so I could look him directly in the eyes. What he wanted everyone to see was raw fury, barely contained. What I saw beneath it was fear. I was barely surprised when he said, "The footage went missing, Captain."

My stomach tightened into a knot of acid. I have found that if you discover one plus one plus one equaling sixteen, your math is off. If it happens over and over, you are not seeing a number hidden somewhere in the equation. If I were right about what was coming next, I was going to march the severely undermanned *Angels* into a nuclear furnace. *Again*.

I closed my eyes and took a deep breath. "Do you know what a palace coup is, Opus?"

His eyes told me he knew very well.

CHAPTER 30: A CAMERA IS A WEAPON

Gathered in the Chief's office of West Lot Station, the small group of us stared into the eyes of *El Toro*.

O'Leary cursed and kicked over a chair. Thompson was quieter about it. She stood at the window fuming as Tony chuckled like a man who found out all the scary noises in his attic was a family of vermin having intercourse. "*Jimmy* me with my pants on."

Lionel's stony face on the split screen gave away nothing of his feelings, but I bet he was leaning more toward O'Leary's reaction than Lomen's.

Bernal, one of the judges of West Lot, leaned forward and stared at the information scrolling slowly across the wall screen. "But this man has a clean background. Nothing more than a few citations for disturbing the peace during various protests."

I nodded. "That's what made him perfect."

The judge looked particularly un-judicial in his dirty, ripped clothes, but everything at West Lot was becoming threadbare these days. His pencil-thin, snow-white moustache bristled in indignation. "So how is it nobody could find information on this man, and yet here he is, sitting in your list of employees?"

Lionel flinched. "Judge Bernal, remember he did nothing more than a few bit parts for my company, hardly a major player. And you have to agree that my people are not law enforcement—"

Bernal crossed his arms and leaned back in his chair, dark clouds gathering on his face. "I understand that, but somebody had to see him, had to recognize him. I'm wondering why no one ever alerted the police."

I paused the information on the screen, mentally tagging specific dates in his resume. "Oh, I'm sure people did. Then they were contacted and told it was a false alarm. I mean, who would respond to sightings of *El Toro*?"

The Key to Damocles

Bernal looked askance at me. "Servicios de la Investigación Planetarios."

I nodded. "Precisely."

O'Leary got it. Lomen got it. Lionel got it, and it was causing him to sweat profusely. Bernal was still nonplussed. "You are accusing a highly decorated government official of sponsoring a terrorist, a very serious charge. Do you have any evidence?"

I bit back on my opinions since in my perfect world, the burden of proof should be the same for president, dog catcher, or homeless guy. I also think the punishment should be the same for politicians, military, police, movie stars, or regular citizens. It never works that way, but it's sound in theory. "Nope. But luckily I'm not a police officer."

Lionel looked like a man in an inferno suddenly tossed a fire extinguisher, but Bernal's mood became positively black. "If we are discussing the assassination of a public official—"

And that is my problem with working inside any given system. As long as everyone plays by the rules, any system will work. It's when someone breaks the system, and then demands you still play by its rules that things go wrong.

"Assassination won't solve anything, Your Honor. On the other hand, if you want to send your militia against another superiorly equipped, better trained enemy, I can hardly stop you." Not impressed by my forced misunderstanding, the judge made a harrumph deep in his chest. I sighed. "I can get evidence. All it will require is first going after the one man who has already provided us with numerous confessions on live broadcast." Everyone, as if on cue, turned back to the wallscreen and looked at *El Toro*. "He will give up Saracho in seconds; guaranteed."

Thompson shook her head. "But showing his corpse is not going to help settle down Persephone. We need something more of a confession. Something powerful, irrefutable, and preferably live."

I nodded. "I think I can remove him from play and ruin him as a martyr at the same time."

Lionel and Richardson spoke as one, "You can't torture him."

I sighed. "Actually, I can. He is a non-uniformed officer inside of a war zone, giving orders to troops that violate the Laws of War. But I'm not talking about torture."

Lomen leaned forward in his chair. "How will you find him?"

O'Leary answered for me, "Saracho will show us."

Lionel spoke first. "Captain, I have invited these people into my home in good faith. You can't make this public. There would be riots. There would be murders. There would be military action against me and my employees—"

"It won't happen."

"Rook—"

"Lionel, you are going to have to trust me on this. You will dodge all the crap that's about to hit the fans. It won't be painless, but I think we can guide you through it."

"Rook—"

"But you need to do precisely what I say."

"Rook—"

"Lionel, I can help you, but only if you trust me."

He stared at his screen, trying to delve into my eyes as he weighed his massive empire, an empire that would surely be cut into ribbons and distributed to everyone on the planet if I betrayed him. It took long seconds before he nodded.

I glanced back at *El Toro*. His name was there, his real name, but I refused to read it. It would not tell me why he had betrayed his people. It would not give me insight into his next move. All it could do was personify him, humanize him, and I did not want that happening inside my skull. In three days, I would murder him, and it would be easier to do to an icon than a man.

Bernal was still not convinced. "So how do you plan to do all this?"

"By using the weapon we've been ignoring all this time. The one *El Toro* has been beating us over the head with. We will use his allies to lead us to him, and use his followers as the teeth of a trap,"

"I still don't understand."

So, I told him the plan.

He shook his head. "That's going to take a miracle."

I drew myself up to my full height. "I think I have one more in me."

O'Leary drew her gun, charged it with a snap, and holstered it, giggling.

I can see why he was so skeptical, but if I was right, then it should all fall into place. The trick is to know what happens if 'X' happens…and then make 'X' a reality. I'd just need to make sure

The Key to Damocles

Saracho was playing chess while I played army. As long as he moved when he should, it would be fine.

The next morning, three things happened in quick succession. From the outside, they looked completely unrelated. I knew better; it was my plan, after all.

First, Tony called a press conference. Not only did the established media types flood the streets with every camera they could spare, dozens of the now wildly popular pirate casters, as well as dozens more startup newsies, showed up for the show. They were not disappointed.

Tony announced that the people of West Lot had received an anonymous donation of ten million credits, in cash. The money was going to buy food for the refugees, and fund their move to their new home: The Persephone Planetary Justice Center. Both bits of information caused an explosion of questions, which he answered as quickly, and politely as he could.

Within hours, a cadre of police officers flew to the Justice Center with Tony's tame hacker. He burned the security locks on the main building with minimal effort, and the police began sweeping the interior rooms to make sure it was truly empty.

Thirty stories tall, with a footprint that covered four city blocks, the Justice Center was a combination of senate, courthouse, police station, and jail. Set in the heart of New California, it had everything Tony needed: food, emergency supplies, hardened defenses, an independent power grid, medicine, operating rooms, and, if they were lucky, some armor and weapons for both the prison guards and the governmental bodyguards who used to work there. More importantly, it had ample toilet, as well as bathing facilities and plenty of space. It was a perfect fortress acting as one of four seats of power for the planet, and only something as simple as a tax boycott could have caused it to fall.

Moving tens of thousands of people across the city was an event of epic proportions. Luckily, Tony had the good sense to ask for my advice. While I had never done it personally, I did know the basic theory, and he had taken copious notes the night before. This created something closely resembling the mating of a circus and a mosh pit. The press showed up at dawn to watch the proceedings, but I waited for hours. It would take time for the constant stream of commentary to grow monotone, for the coverage to begin repeating. There were no riots, though there were a few shoving matches, so by midmorning you could simply record half an hour of news and just loop the coverage.

It was after the first repeat, about the time people thought about changing the channel, that I ordered *The Radiation Angels* to make a lot of noise.

John Doe came screaming over the city like a cannon shot. *The Succubus*, heavy with a cargo pod on one side and *The Cherub* on the other, blew over streets full of people, causing something of a panic until they saw the wings, sword and trefoil emblazoned on each wing.

It picked a conveniently cordoned off area to settle to earth, but then the engines did not shut down, they simply sat at idle, rotated to point upwards to hold the craft firmly to the ground. This created a blue-white halo around the craft and was standard procedure for a combat L&D, load up and dust off. The fact that it looked cool as hell was just a bonus; it insured everyone was watching the craft as *The Radiation Angels* came piling out of the police station like their asses were on fire.

They triple-timed down the steps like death incarnate, weapons in hand but pointed at the sky, armor gleaming and boots thumping like the heart of a running giant. The people of West Lot still cheered as they went, deluging them with love even as they broke into a run for our dropship. Police fanned out to hold the crowd back, and when I came out, I pointed at a few newsies who had slipped through to make sure they were as far away from me as possible as Tony jogged up. He brushed at his badge, meaning that there were at least two behind me within earshot as he came close and yelled over the sound of jet wash. "*Que pasa*, Rook?"

"Cordon off that *motherfragger*!" Sometimes I get lucky, and this was one of them. A reporter had broken the police line behind Tony and come forward, microphone raised, to ask questions. Tony called over an officer and had the reporter dragged away, which was guaranteed to draw the attention of every journalist in the area, including the few behind me. I, too, had to yell over the engine noise. "I have a lead on *El Toro*. We are going to find him, detain him, and question him at length. We should have him in custody in less than thirty hours."

Tony slapped my arm and nodded gravely. "*Via con dios*, you crazy son of a bitch."

I smiled at him and shook his hand. "It's been an honor."

"Same here."

And then I broke into a run for *The Succubus*. I popped my helmet onto my head and turned once on the ramp to look upon our improvised tarmac as it closed. Indeed, there had been four reporters, one official and three pirates, within earshot as Tony and I had talked. From the wide eyed looks they were giving each other, they had heard everything.

The ramp secured, I dove into a chair and the motors on the engines whined as they reoriented downward. Doe's tinny voice came over the comm with a passable imitation of military decorum. "Orders, Captain?"

A toothy grin crept into my voice. "Hell Yeah, Flight."

"Hell Yeah, Captain?"

"Affirmative." And for sixty seconds, I couldn't see, I couldn't breathe, all I could do was hang on to the five-point harness and pray. It probably looked impressive from the ground, though. That was what was important.

"Doe, dial it back and get us to *Heaven*."

"Eye-firmative, Capitan."

The Succubus leveled out, and I unbuckled and made my way forward to the cockpit. I got there with a minimum of fuss and turned one of the screens to the news channel. It took approximately thirty more seconds before six of the news stations were talking about *The Radiation Angels*. The image was shaky as the hull ionized, but the BREAKING NEWS icons came through clear as a bell. Seconds of flipping through channels, tickertape news updates and splash pages told the whole story. Within five minutes, everyone on Persephone would know *The Radiation Angels* were hunting *El Toro*.

I chuckled to myself. In ancient history, an Earther named Benjamin Franklin once said, "Three may keep a secret if two are dead."

There is a corollary rule for the media. It goes something like, 'One reporter will keep a secret, but two will race with it to get the headline.' Like a mob, the anonymity of the crowd gives cover, allowing the press to do the most horrible things in the name of 'the public good, the single most popular reason all the worst things are ever done.

All power can be abused be it political, economic, or military... violent or nonviolent. All of it can become a way to silence opposition. Cameras can be a weapon. Just because no guns come into play doesn't make it any more right. Demonization and dehumanization kill just as assuredly as bullets.

Nobody who wields power is immune from that trap, but while the media guards against the government, only the citizens can keep watch over the media. The moment they stop questioning their news, they give up their freedoms, and have shirked their duties to their fellow man. I was just happy I had found a way to use that abuse of power to my advantage for once. One thing was for certain. Somewhere on planet at least two sphincters clenched so tightly they could get stuck that way.

At least I hoped they would.

CHAPTER 31: ENDGAME

We docked with *Deadly Heaven,* and as we transferred off *The Succubus*, the few *Apostles* left aboard climbed into their shuttle and departed. I let the *Angels* stow their equipment, but told them to be in uniform in the briefing room in thirty minutes. They skittered off to carry out my orders as I stopped by my room and took a quick shower.

The hot water sluiced the stale sweat from my body and the random thoughts from my head, at least most of the random thoughts. The last time I had used this tiny cubicle I had shared it with O'Leary. Images of her supple form rippled behind my eyes—

You are going to have a lot of dead soldiers if you don't focus, asshole.

I shook my head to clear it, irritated at the missing weight from my hastily trimmed hair. I began mentally flipping through the loadout we would need for this mission. I was considering what explosives we would need as I toweled off. By the time I had zipped up my flight suit and swept the data chips from my drawer into my hand, I had a decent idea of what we would be wearing, carrying, and carting down onto planet. It was a good thing, too. There were only ten minutes remaining.

I walked toward the briefing room, habitually stretching, testing the fresh seams along my torso and wincing slightly. I dug out a Willpowerless™ container and swallowed one of the little blue pills raw. I paused at the open door to the briefing room, and stood rooted to the spot for three long breaths. There, sitting on his specially reinforced, oversized metal stool, was Logan. He shook his head slowly, flexing the freshly repaired fingers, totally fixated on his own hand.

Down on Persephone, at the space port, he had been able to find a competent repair ship and most of the worst of his hurts had been excised and replaced. His was an old cybernetic body and finding exact parts was becoming more and more of a challenge. The repair shop had thus repaired the missing structures of his left hand but had been unable to manufacture the laminate armored skin to go over it. The raw metal appendages looked like spider webs of steel and elfin girders, filled with twenty-seventh century clockworks. All alone, up close and personal with man's attempt to rewrite God's work in titanium, polymer, and ceramic, I might be tempted to sit and marvel. Even Logan might be ready to watch the fake muscles move and spin for a moment, but he sat there like a child, flexing and shaking, shifting uncomfortably over and over. In all my years in *The Radiation Angels*, I have never seen him fidget once.

Worse, I have never seen him start, ever. The man had several million credits worth of sensor systems linked into his brain at all times; he should sense anyone long before they enter a given room. Yet he jerked as I said, "I guess it's time we had that talk."

Faceless and proud, little more than a brain buried in two tons of metal, Logan managed to look embarrassed. I shut the door and keyed in my code to lock it. I walked to the altar and dropped the chips onto it, then I took the seat next to him. I laced my fingers and I waited.

Seconds died lingering deaths between us, elongating minutes like pounds of gold drawn into endless monofilament threads. When he finally spoke, the weight of silence bore down upon us with deadly finality.

"I can't stop." I glanced at him, but his head was pointed clearly at the floor between his feet. The sound of whirring motors and creaking metal was clear as tension sought to treat his mechanical body as one of flesh and bone. His hands were clasped as if to keep them from shaking, and the aerials at either side of his head trembled slightly. The silence built between us again, storing up kinetic energy inside of him until it had to burst forth. "I spent six months wandering around, trying to find something, anything to be. I spent time on planets that had not seen war in three centuries. I spent four weeks trying to be a Federal Agent on a planet in the middle of a civil war. I took a job as a bodyguard to a rich man's grown son. I even tried being a firefighter again." I got the feeling that he would have sighed if he had possessed lungs. "But I everything I tried, I failed. I was looking for this place; I was looking for this ship. I wanted to be in a place I could be proud of, doing a job that mattered.

"All the stories tell about people who change the world in huge, sweeping strokes. They all say the universe revolves around massive conspiracies and huge plots. I'm simple. I just want to help one person at a time. I want to stand in the middle of the road and protect those behind me. I want to be able to reach into hell's heart and pull out my team mates. I want bad men with bad intentions to shudder to think it's me watching over their sleeping prey. I want to feel like when I shut off for the night a few more people are alive than otherwise.

"But nothing I tried made a bit of difference, and everything I tried failed. Then Ortega found me, and we found you, and all of a sudden I'm back where I belong, with rules I understand, and still I can't seem to make anything work right. From the gang member at the church, to the flier crashing into the roof, to Reeves... I just don't know if I'm any good at this anymore."

There it was. Master Sergeant Tom Logan had doubt. Had I not heard it with my own ears, I never would have believed it. I stood up, causing him to come to attention in his seat. Of course I had planned on placing a hand on his shoulder, but even seated he towered over me. I took a deep breath. "Sergeant, if you follow me one last time, I can prove you wrong."

Electronic eyes fluttered and focused on me, boring into me. "Are you sure, Captain?"

"We will make it happen, Logan."

He seemed to swell up before me, muscles growling like the heart of a lion. His entire posture changed, and just like that, the old Logan was back. Though I gave him a rakish smile, inside I was dumbfounded, near trembling. I turned away from him and went to unlock the door. When I turned back, Logan seemed to have taken my words like laws of nature, and he was sitting relaxed, composed, and utterly still.

That this man, this giant, who had belonged to *The Radiation Angels* much longer than me, a man my predecessor had trusted so implicitly, a man who had trained me from the moment I set foot on *Deadly Heaven*, believed in me so completely was nothing short of terrifying. I busied myself, telling the altar to read the data on the chips. As I went through the mechanical task, I reigned in my emotions and shoved them in a closet in the back of my head. I could not show doubt in front of him. It would be the deepest kind of betrayal.

Minutes later, *Angels* began filing in, some wiping their hands free of grease and chemicals, others freshly washed and dressed, all of them wolfing down food as if it were the last they would ever see. I felt a twinge of guilt at this since they had been going full-tilt for days, or recuperating from injuries, or standing guard over those recovering. They were tired and drawn, but I needed them now, and it was almost over; it was almost all over.

They had been in this room several times since I had hired them weeks ago and had become attached to certain seats. Thompson was in the front, casting a steely eye for unacceptable levels of horseplay. Medic Tsang and Ansef were on the far right, growing a little closer with each whispered word and obviously on track for some kind of romance. Archer stared at the ceiling, sure that he was going to be bored out of his mind. Lopez and King were playing some kind of childish game where they hit one another, the way all men do when they forget they are being watched. Walt, leg immobilized in a cast and moving awkwardly on his cane, settled into his seat painfully, his perpetually sad eyes never leaving the empty chairs of Richardson and Long.

"Alright *Angels*, settle down." Everything stopped as if a plug had been pulled, and they turned to focus on me as I walked to the podium. "This is going to be a less than stellar briefing. So far, we don't know the terrain, though I can say for sure we are looking for a near deserted urban environment. There's going to be nearly no chance of civilians in the crossfire. Our enemy's capabilities are also a question mark, but I believe there will be few, and they will be beneath even police grade training."

Archer's studiously blank face was betrayed a sneer that snuck out on his words. "So, what can you tell us, Captain?"

"Our target." I punched a button, bringing *El Toro's* face up on the wallscreen. "I can tell you he pretends to be motivated. I can tell you he pretends to be professional. I can tell you he is, in fact, none of these things. He is a fraud with no military experience at all."

I punched another key, and *El Toro's* file, taken from L/V/D databanks, printed next to his disembodied head.

Tsang cursed in Chinese and then slapped his hands over his eyes. "An actor? The *gritlicker* who *mudraked* this entire planet is an actor?"

I shook my head. "No, he didn't. The unbondable *mudraked* the planet. He just took credit for it and fed the discontent of the people. He's a puppet, a mouthpiece."

Archer crossed his arms and propped his feet on the chair in front of and below him. "So who's pulling the strings?"

"We will know that shortly. Currently, the mission is to locate *El Toro*, eliminate all resistance, and capture him alive."

King flexed his impressive muscles as if trying to split his jumpsuit. "Alive will be problematic."

I affixed him with my best *I-am-not-gritting-you* face. "Alive, *HWO*. I will not tolerate stray bullets, failed escape attempts, accidental discharges, or overzealous restraints. We will take him into custody alive at all costs."

Archer snorted. "Even over our dead bodies?"

I nodded, my temper slipping its reins. "Especially yours, sniper. Besides, how much trouble do you think an actor is going to be?"

"Why won't this actor be seriously armed?" Archer sneered.

"Because, Archer, if you build a puppet, it is unwise to give it the ability to cut its own strings. Not only has our enemy given him a powerful voice and a powerful face, he has obviously set up a way for *El Toro* to collect funds to start his government. That's why he hasn't skipped planet yet." I ticked off my points. "He has the image for leadership, he has the audience, he has the money. What doesn't he have?"

Logan nodded sagely. "Guns."

I pointed at the cyborg. "Exactly. Without guns the police, and the military when they get back, would be able to oppose his *coup*. He needs a security force. I doubt he has one, yet, since he hasn't done any recruiting at all."

"How are we going to find out where he is, Captain?"

"That's the easy answer—"

Sichak's voice seemed to come from everywhere at once. "Captain, message from *Lightwave Cyanide*, Actual."

"Put it through."

And there was Janchea, on the screen, looking a little too pleased with himself. "I've got the movement you were looking for."

"Can you pipe it to me?"

"You got my payment?" I linked the altar to the bridge and piped out instructions to the electronic vault aboard *Deadly Heaven*. In less than a second, his computer and mine shook hands, sent the encrypted data, and broke contact. My fifty grand

The Key to Damocles

became his, just like that. He smiled and winked, just as pleased at my money as my need for him. "I am sending the data stream to your navigational computers."

"Thank you, Janchea."

"Well, when you sell the movie rights, make sure someone dashing plays me."

I couldn't help laughing. "It's a deal. *Radiation Angels* Actual, out."

But my mirth was short lived. In seconds, I had piped the feed onto the screen over the altar and chills marched up and down my spine. My stomach turned as I watched my mental loadout blown to hell as I read the intentions of my enemy off of the air traffic control feed.

Thompson leaned forward, desperate to get out of her chair and take a closer look. "What are we seeing Captain?"

You son of a bitch. "A murder."

We all watched as three large fliers formed a traditional combat wedge and flew north out of New California. All vehicles, especially fliers, have transponders. These low power broadcasts act as an IFF, Identify Friend or Foe, and make it possible for traffic controllers to monitor the situation throughout a planet, allow police to tag reckless operators, and guarantee any flier is registered for operation. These three were running with their transponders silent. There are only three groups of people who rig their units with an off switch: mercenaries, criminals, and police. The reason is the same... so the enemy can't see you coming. If we had tried using *Deadly Heaven's* own systems, it was very likely we would have missed them completely. In fact, the spaceport was the only place on planet with sensors sensitive and powerful enough to note the craft without transponders without alerting them with a combat level blast of detection radiation. This was a simple necessity for the port to do it all the time to stop smuggling of illicit goods from on or off planet, and in this case, it had worked in our favor.

There they were, running full-out north by northwest. Their objective was obvious. All one had to do was draw a line and do a little math to figure out they would get to *El Toro* in ninety-five minutes. The presence of three heavy fliers, moving in military formation, so close to the ground and silent, meant only one thing; our mission had changed. I spun on my crew, eyes ablaze.

412

"All pairs to the armory, now! Everyone on the 'wounded' list get to the bridge and put yourselves at the service of Pilot Sichak."

Without question or hesitation, the whole team bolted for the exit. Only Walt stood to the side, slightly downcast, as the healthy members of *The Radiation Angels* plowed by. I brought up the rear, and took a second to put a hand on his shoulder. No mercenary liked to be left behind.

"I wish I could come with you, Captain."

"Well, Walt, you get your wish. I need you to get to the armory as well."

He looked like I had just slapped him. He gestured at his leg. "Captain, I am not ready for combat—."

"You won't need to be. You were trained in stabilized firing systems?" He nodded. "Then draw out a set of light armor. You are going to be with Doe in *The Succubus*. He's going to need a gunner."

He went ashen underneath his light brown complexion. If there is anything that scares a mercenary, it is ship-to-ship combat. On the ground, one is ultimately dependent on oneself. On a ship, you are constantly at the mercy of a pilot, computers, missiles, chaff, and electronic countermeasures. It feels like giving up a level of control over one's destiny.

Considering how many bullets I had caught so far during this *frag*-filled *piñata*, my empathy for him had serious limits. I grabbed his shoulder more tightly and steered him out the door. "Come on soldier, we are short on time."

I modified the equipment of each *Angel* in my head and from memory, punching authorizations into the armory computer as fast as my fingers would fly. Deep inside the rows of benches and cabinets, weapon lockers unlocked and plates lit up with the names of my soldiers. Deeper still, a huge rotating carousel cycled through suits of armor floating limply above the ground on reinforced hangers. The *Angels* moved from station to station, pulling equipment, weapons and armor, preparing for battle inside and out.

I had finally finished assigning equipment in a record four minutes and thirty seconds when Logan appeared out of the shadows, his approach masked by the cacophony of loadout. In his hands, he held a coffin-shaped tube. I cursed as I saw the blinking red lights across the display on the side.

The Key to Damocles

He set it down less than gently. "The medical unit is on the fritz. It refuses to hold an airtight seal, which is good since the oxygen recycler's missing the infuser and anyone we put in here is going to suffocate."

I groaned. "And let me guess, that's our last one."

"Yes, Captain."

I remembered the last time we needed one of these stasis tubes. I had made a mental note to get the damn thing replaced. Of course, then I got chased across the universe, shot at and then retired... *Excuses, excuses.* I tried to focus. "All right, get a set of medium armor, including helmet— actually get him a set of that Galaxon Mobile Suit pieces of *grit.* He'll have trouble running, but it will have to do."

Logan nodded and disappeared which gave me time to get into my own armor. I began strapping web belts full of equipment on when Ortega wove past the last few *Angels* leaving the armory and stood at attention just at the edge of my peripheral vision. I tried very hard not to sigh. "Yes, *EWO?*"

Ortega remained at attention and clenched his jaw. "I am still listed on the wounded roster, Captain."

I finished lacing up my boots and strapped the armored plate across my shin. "I know that, Ortega."

"I need to go with you, Captain."

"Ortega, they just replaced half of your hand less than sixty hours ago, and it takes at least one hundred and twenty hours in order for the macro-nanites to seal the old growth to the graft. That hand could pull itself apart under the right stress."

"Captain, they are bringing three ships worth of Agents. That's at least six sniper pairs. They will have an engagement range of two thousand meters. Logan's systems will only clearly, one hundred percent, verify a human target at one thousand, tops, and I'm the only qualified *EWO* you have." Ortega puffed out his chest. "I can handle it, Captain."

I picked up my helmet off of the arming bench and handed it to Ortega, who obediently took it in his good hand. I turned away from him and bent over. "Are you sure about that?"

"Absolutely, Cap—" I snatched up my rifle and tossed it at him. Before he could think, he brought up his empty hand.

A commander can save himself a lot of trouble by setting an impossible test for a subordinate, to illustrate his point. The only

414

thing that can go wrong is the said subordinate can actually pass the test.

Slightly swollen, two different skin tones clearly separated by a nasty seam, his hand worked flawlessly all the same. It closed around the forearm guard and held the weapon steady away from his body. His pupils shrunk to pinpricks, his breathing became shallow and rapid, and he swayed on his feet. But he did not drop the *fragging* rifle.

Grit. I tapped on my forearm pad, unlocking his armor, sensor unit, and weapons. Then I took my helmet and weapon from him. "All right, get suited up, *EWO*. You have ten minutes."

I left him in the armory, staring at his hand as he flexed it. He reminded me eerily of Logan. The men needed rest, soon. I wish it could be now, but we had to get down to Persephone immediately or else all would be lost. I called Grisham and had him report to the dropship. I would definitely need him.

I had believed Saracho would send a small force of his best men to protect *El Toro* from my threats. He had not done that. He had, in fact, sent three shuttles worth of Agents to *El Toro*. It was way too many soldiers to hope of keeping it a secret, which meant he did not want to keep it a secret. Saracho sent three shuttles worth of men to kill *El Toro*, not save him.

Ten minutes later we were in freefall.

CHAPTER 32: THE ENEMY OF MY ENEMY IS MY CANNON FODDER

The Succubus screamed through Persephone's atmosphere just twenty minutes ahead of Saracho's assassins. The craft was aimed like a bullet, pointing at the heart of one of the largest cities man has ever built. It was fifty kilometers wide at its widest point. It contained every imaginable style of architecture, every possible sized building. Certain areas had standard air traffic lanes, others were equipped with ancient roads with painted lines. But nothing could disguise the layers of dust and dirt that covered every surface. The sheer size only accentuated the lack of fliers or crawlers. There were no lights and no pedestrians. There weren't even any bodies. Even the animals were kept away with high frequency noise and electric fences. It just seemed to go on forever and ever, a glutted polyglot of architecture completely devoid of life. This was Flat Town Monroe, and if you've ever seen a mind screen movie set in recent history, you have seen it.

We detected electricity usage at three different guard stations that dotted the ring around the city, and there were thousands of media stations as well as environmental units running on residual power, but there was one building pulling way too much to be empty. I routed a call to Lionel through Grisham. In seconds, the confused moviemaker agreed to order his security troops to keep their heads low. I cut the line and ordered Doe toward our target.

Doe began to lose a lot of the swagger out of his voice the moment he realized how little space there was between the monolithic towers of the flat town. The whole craft slewed from side to side as he navigated along the streets, staying low to avoid detection. "The only place to land on ground level is three blocks away from our target, and it is coming up fast."

Dropship too big for urban work, dammit. I opened up my comm. "Make for that spot, Flight. Ground Team Two make ready!"

The Key to Damocles

A few seconds later, Thompson came online with, "Ready, Captain!"

"Doe, plant Team Two!"

Everyone was thrown forward as *The Succubus* lurched to a stop in midair. Doe pushed the collective down and hit the pavement harder than I would have liked, but the shotgun sounds of catches disengaging was comforting at least. Doe's voice came over the intercom. "Team Two planted, catches away, proceeding to target."

And then we were off, rocketing off of the tarmac a ton lighter than before, leaving behind a disposable cargo pod that immediately blew open and disgorged Team Two. *The Succubus* fought for altitude, blowing past buildings as it made sharp turns in an ever shrinking spiral until we crested the high-rise. "Ground Team One make ready!"

Again, the dropship fell to the roof. "Planting Team One!"

The remaining *Angels* slapped the latches on their five-point harnesses and bolted for the exit. We piled out onto the roof and away from *The Succubus*, allowing Walt and Doe to get in the air almost immediately. Ground Team One hustled over to the roof access door as the obscenely hot jet wash crested and broke across us. Logan reached out with one mighty hand and buried his fingers into the metal fire door. His muscles whined only for a second before the door came away; lock and hinges shredded like paper.

"Go! Go! Go!" I pointed at the opening like an idiot, as if there were any doubt as to where my men were to advance. We broke onto the steps, and Team One immediately divided into two assigned Pairs that leapfrogged one another, each covering a stairwell in turn as the others moved on. Ortega made a signal, and I called a halt.

It took three long minutes for him to put his sensor unit together. I used the time to expand my map and watch Thompson and Team Two. She moved them into select locations, and her training as a sniper served her well. The two pairs were set up with she and Archer ready to do some damage and then evacuate past King's automatic gauss weapon. If all went as expected, they'd be abandoning position before contact was made, but if not...

Ortega signaled his readiness, and we lit out again. It only took a minute before the *EWO* made our first transmission of the operation. "Targets on floor twenty-five... eight life signs. Multiple high yield electronic signatures... could be computers, media equipment, or weapons."

Please be media equipment. "Rook to Team One— *El Toro* must be taken alive. This is an absolute priority."

A host of affirmatives came over my radio by way of answer. And we continued downward, floor after floor. The minutes ticked by at a maddening pace. All my thoughts centered on the idea this would be easiest if we got away before the Agents arrived. *So, naturally, that sonofabitch had to pick the middle floor of the fragging building. There must be some nun-killing moron with a winning lottery ticket living on a tropical beach, leeching off all my good karma.*

Floor twenty-five could not come soon enough.

Logan was first again, putting his entire weight behind one, titanium laminate hand that crumpled the fire door like an accordion from top to bottom. The team sped past him, moving up to the next corner before he hunkered down and squeezed through the hole made for a man half his size.

The building looked under construction, with bare walls, naked floors, and unfurnished rooms on all sides. These we ignored, led by Ortega's divination of the finicky sensor signals deeper into the building. As if someone had flipped a switch, suddenly there was carpeting and paint, wallpaper and light fixtures. These rooms must have been used to stage a recording at one time, and I had the annoying feeling I had been here before. A bass beat began filtering through my feet and in through my gloves. The volume ramped up the closer to our quarry we went.

As we stacked up at the door, men moved by silent hand signals even though the music from inside was clearly deafening within. Doe came over the radio. "Captain, I have three positive sensor locks. They are painting me and threatening to fire."

Goddammit. I should not have had to say, "Then light them up. Engage all electronic warfare expert computers. Get Walt on one set of guns and let the computer handle the rest. Open fire when they get into range. Do not hesitate; these people are under

orders to kill us all. If *The Succubus* dies, we all die. Rook Out."
And I pointed at the door.

Logan gave it a kick that sent it flying, and the whole world
sounded flat and tinny as my helmet's aural filters kicked in to
blanket out the thundering music. *Angels* piled into the
boardroom beyond in a flood, spreading out to cover different
areas of the room with command precision. There was a lot of
shouting, a couple of screams, and then...

"Don't! Don't! Don't!"

...and a single gunshot to my right. I glanced over at a college
aged man, unkempt and slovenly, curled up over the ten-
millimeter hole in his sternum. A laser rifle dropped from his
lifeless hands, thumping on the carpet as his body followed.
Lopez followed him down with the smoking barrel of his gun.

"Miguel, MIGUEL!" A woman sprinted to the fallen man. She
cradled him in her arms, but it was clear he was already dead.
"*¡Usted idiotas! ¡Esto es un puntal! ¡Un PUNTAL! Esto no trabaja.
Miguel!*"

Even with my scant knowledge of Spanish, I knew the word
'prop' and what it meant to an actor. I had no doubt that Lopez
understood every word. I checked the rest of the team, each of
whom had more cooperative people in their line of fire. They
leveled their weapons, speaking in a language that needed no
translator, but as I went from face to face, our target was not
here. *Dammit.* I took one aimed shot at the radio and blew it to
smithereens. Silence descended upon the room like the shadow
of death.

Ansef moved to the body and checked it briefly before
shaking her head sadly. I turned to Ortega, who was throwing a
softball-sized camera into the corner and linking its feed to
Grisham aboard the *Succubus*. We had to cover our asses since
all it would take to brand these traitors civilians in some legal
systems was twelve very stupid people.

I opened my mouth, but before I could ask, an intense,
athletic man came sprinting out of the far door, hands raised,
face as sallow as his Latin complexion would allow. Logan
called out, "Freeze!" at his highest volume, and that seemed to
do the job. The man skidded to a halt, given arrest by the gaze of
multiple gun barrels, so fast that he fell onto his ass in an
attempt to scuttle away using his buttocks as feet. I walked right

up to him, putting myself between his legs and staring down at him behind my mirrored visor. Up close, without makeup and without his camera, he looked so young, so lost.

I took a deep breath and tongued the helmet toggle to turn on my external speakers. "*El Toro?*"

He looked up at me with eyes the size of saucers and managed to nod dumbly.

The *Angels* advanced and took control of the prisoners. In seconds, we had them on the carpet and bound with disposable restraints. Tears began rolling out of their eyes as if on cue. Their leader began to shake, but didn't dare even try to hug his arms close to stop it. I leaned down to get face to face with the legendary rebel leader of Persephone, and his lower lip trembled. It was amazing to me that the man who forty percent of the planet said should be in charge of everything would turn out to be so… weak. He sat here, in the eye of the firestorm for months, untouched by the chaos he had helped foment. It had just barely brushed him, and he was a slobbering mess. I had the sudden need to stomp a mud hole in his ass.

I buried it. Barely. "Saracho has sent Agents to kill you. We are here to evacuate you immediately." Logan walked up and slung a large duffel from his shoulder onto the floor next to our target. I continued, "Put that on. Now." *Toro* stared at the bundle, and then at his comrades, who even now were cuffed face-down on the carpet. The girl on my left continued to wail over Miguel. I dialed in my command voice. "If you don't get in that armor in three minutes, I will have my Sergeant break every bone in your body and pour you into it."

He began to do as he was told, incorrectly. I threw my hands up in the air and motioned to Logan. *Toro* nearly wet himself when the Master Sergeant took hold of him. After only a few seconds did he realize Logan was dressing him like a novice tailor, fitting on the large, padded armored suit with less-than-expert motions. *Then again, it's not like Logan wears a lot of armored suits.*

Sichak interrupted me as I was building a good head of steam. "Captain, I have fast movers coming off planet. IFFs say they are planetary police forces. They are ordering me to stand down and prepare to be boarded. Your orders?"

I switched frequencies to speak only to him. "Kill them."

"Captain?!"

I took a firm grip on the reigns to my temper. Most people are taught police means people like Lomen. Their whole lives trained to obey police orders unquestioningly. The police are your friends, police will make you safe. By the numbers, they were right. Police officers do one of the hardest jobs in the universe. They deserve respect. Perhaps it's because of an adult life in the anarchy of deep space, or growing up on a planet where the law has mutated into something carcinogenic, but I have seen what corrupt officials can do to a world they are supposed to protect. They were worse than a plague. These were such men.

"They are coming to kill you and take control of *Deadly Heaven.*" I took a deep breath, trying to stay calm. "Target the ships and fire now before they get you into their range."

"Roger, Captain. Opening fire, now."

Silence followed, broken only by a rain of tears. I took the time to look over the room. It had been refurnished with lots of sleeping bags, inflatable furniture, fake guns, custom uniforms, crates of military rations, recording and transmitting equipment. They had everything they needed here to play their little game of revolution.

Lopez, Ortega, and Ansef moved *Tord*'s crew over to one wall where they could be watched easily. I found myself standing next to Miguel, who was staring at the ceiling with a face frozen in perpetual shock. I picked up his weapon and easily confirmed that it was, indeed a prop. I tossed it in the corner.

The wailing girl began to scream again. "Murderers! You killed him! He was defenseless!"

I shook my head. "He pointed a weapon at an armed man and got shot, and that's my *soldier's* fault?"

Lopez's vitals were all over the place. I moved to him and patted his shoulder, trying to let him know he had done the right thing. At the same time, I felt hatred begin as a warning rumble deep inside my chest. It was as if these young punks had no idea the damage that their pirate broadcasts had caused. *What if...?* And then I saw it, a massive stand-alone viewscreen. It looked like it had been part of the L/V/D dressing for this room, but it had been rigged with a small portable power unit as well as a movie reader and no less than three gaming systems. On a whim, I turned it on. A news broadcast splashed across the screen. *They knew.*

And just like that, the death warrant of every revolutionary in this room was signed.

Toro finished struggling into his suit, looking like nothing so much as a man wearing three sets of heavy winter clothing. I had bought the sets on a whim when I saw the magnificent defensive statistics, but wearing one was like trying to move in sand. We had never used them until now. Still, he seemed to find his courage inside the ungainly armored suit. Surprisingly his English was excellent. "Are you from Saracho?"

"No, Saracho is the one trying to kill you right now."

He shook his head like a child told the truth about Santa Claus. "No. Saracho wouldn't try to kill me."

Outside there was an explosion quickly followed by the crackling thunder of a plasma pulse cannon discharging. *The Succubus* had entered combat. *El Toro* started. "What was that?"

"That was the man who is not trying to kill you opening fire on your ride out of this fifty-story coffin." In the deafening silence that followed, Saracho came on the news channel. Speaking calmly, professionally, even elegantly, he let Persephone know that he had just dispatched a task force to apprehend the vicious terrorist *El Toro.* I swiveled my head to look directly at the actor-turned-revolutionary. "So, are you coming?"

He took two clumsy steps for the door before Logan caught him by the collar and hauled him back. The Sergeant leaned in close to our mark. "Perhaps you should wait for the Captain?"

I signaled to my crew and we started to file out when one of the other prisoners spoke up. "Hey, what about us?"

I glanced back, moved by mercy for just a moment. *I will have mercy on your victims.* I lied easily. "Saracho wants *El Toro.* You should be safe. Get downstairs and out to the fence around the flat town. Follow it in any direction, and you'll get to a security station."

The crying woman screamed again, "What about our hands, you monsters?"

Monsters? Oh, in that case you have convinced me. "You can run without hands."

She gave me a withering glare. "I won't follow you anywhere, baby-killer."

I shrugged and followed my team. Fine, stay here. The restraints should dissolve in ten thousand years or so. I hit my comm unit. "Doe? Status?"

"Busy, Captain. We have engaged the enemy. Splashed one flier, but the others managed to set down. Now we're playing cat and mouse. Only I'm not used to being a cat, and the mice have rabies. Pickup of any kind is impossible."

My temper finally got the better of me for a second. "Your ship is much more heavily armored and armed! Your electronics and ECM gear is top notch! KILL THEM ALL, DOE! That is an order!"

His brittle tone said it all. "Captain, yelling at me is not going to help. We downed one, but these guys are experts. They're out-flying me at every turn, tearing *The Succubus* apart. They've been trained in dogfights."

More training than just a few hours on a simulator, I felt him not say.

"Doe if you don't win, they aren't taking you to jail. They're going to kill you and Walt both."

There was a two second delay as he digested this. Suddenly, this wasn't a game for Flight/Lieutenant John Doe, anymore. "Affirmative, Captain."

It felt like someone had dumped ice water down my back. Without Doe, we couldn't get out of here. If any enemy fliers were in the air at all, there was no way he could pick us up. I took one deep breath and dialed for a calm voice. "Goddammit, Doe, what are you good at?"

"Captain?"

I let a little steel creep into my voice. "What are you good at?"

His answer was full of bile. "Racing, Captain."

A stray thought blindsided me, popping out of my mouth before I could stop it. "Then why in the *frag* are you dog fighting?"

There was a pause on the other end of the radio, a pause that sounded like a smile being born. When he spoke, he sounded like a madman jacked up on Venom and Methamphetamines. "Hell yeah, Captain."

And somewhere over Monroe, I heard afterburners kick on.

I hurried to catch up. I reached the rest of the team on the landing and pointed downward. If Archer had been here, he would have groaned. As it was, they only thought about it loudly.

424

Ortega signaled all clear, and we began taking the stairs two to four at a time, desperately seeking ground level as Logan picked *El Toro* up and carried him along. The constant discharge of anti-ship weaponry reached my ears even in the stairwell. The impacts churned the sky into a cloudless tempest, a hurricane of steel and broken glass as buildings acted as cover for flying gods of war. We got to ground floor as fresh small arms fire erupted a few blocks to the south. Six, basso shots echoed off the walls and then there was the high-pitched whine of capacitors discharging and the snapping of superheated concrete from laser hits.

Sichak's voice whispered guiltily in my ear. "Captain, the enemy ships have been… eliminated."

"Roger." *At least orbit is clear.* I kept Team One in the dressed foyer and brought up a HUD map of the city. I chose a suitable pickup spot five blocks to the north. Then I focused back on the area around the *Angels* as Thompson began moving herself and her sniper team to the next building in line. Things looked much worse than I had anticipated. I called Thompson for a report.

"Enemy strength estimated ninety, that is nine-zero. We have opened fire and are falling back, but as soon as they find their balls, they're going to overrun us, Captain. They have some heavy weapons. They definitely upgraded their gear somewhere."

They outnumbered us eight to one. I watched them swarm like insects on the streets around my Lieutenant's position. Even my ace-in-the-hole, Logan, was now at risk. In fact, now the question was not whether we could win, but whether I should abandon those out in the field to save the lives of those here with me. I took three, deep breaths, grabbing my panic by the throat and murdering it silently.

"Thompson, backup is en route. Continue to harass and evade." She responded with an affirmative. I turned to my *EWO*. "Ortega, can you keep this *fragger* moving?" *With your bum hand*, I didn't say.

He nodded grimly, obviously delighted to have someone who had caused his family so much trouble within reach. "I can, but Captain, you are going to need me."

And he was right. *Dammit.* "Fine. Ansef, get bull-boy to the top floor. The roof is now our evacuation point." I turned to the others. "Everyone else is with me. We're going to go slow up the men from PISs."

Logan nodded slowly and readied his massive plasma cannon. Lopez and Ortega both mimicked him. Wordlessly, we set southward.

CHAPTER 33: FEAR NOT THE HORNS OF THE BULL

War... war never changes.

You can move the pieces, you can alter the board, but war is always the same. Men fight. Men die. The smartest, the fastest, the best equipped, and the luckiest survive. Four or four million, the principle is the same. I should know; war is what I do. It's what I'm good at.

God help them all.

Saracho's Agents were, above all, policemen. Forget the military gear, buzzcuts, and combat boots. We were dealing with cops. Cops are great at their jobs: preserving life, law, and order. When forced into a high intensity armed confrontation, they have specific rules they obey, rules governed by their training.

Police officers attack with overwhelming numbers. They are trained to set up a mobile base where they can contain and analyze an enemy before attack. It is this kind of siege-style combat at which they excel and they train at it constantly. No mercenary company in the universe can do it better than the SWAT team of a megacity. What they are not trained for is mobile ground combat.

Thompson and Archer had already opened fire, sending six heavy shells into the massed group of Agents. The sniper rounds breached armor and sent men sprawling like rag dolls as the two *Angels* retreated down to the first floor and across an alleyway guarded by King. They ran away through an alley a full block before swinging around the front side of the building. In the meantime, the policemen had spread out to cordon off the building from which they had first fired. A hefty officer took out a basketball-sized drone and set it on the ground as he put the voice control unit in his ear.

The lightweight *snitch* was a joy in the city. With an AI, near-expert software pack and dozens of sensors, it had the ability to act both *EWO* and combat control center for every Agent in the field. After calibrating the robot, he started up the motor and extended the dual set of rotors. The rotors spun up to speed and the drone leapt into the air, taking stock of the current battlefield and whispering secrets back to its masters like a wizard's homunculus. These units were great: high tech, useful, sexy as hell, they cost an arm and a leg though they were slightly slow and not at all nimble. All this made it almost a shame when Archer turned it into a hail of high velocity debris with one, well-placed shot. A perfectly foreseeable event, but a shame.

Thompson added two more, killing the drone operator outright, and maiming the arm of the Agent beside him. Again, the policemen took cover. Again, Thompson moved her team back one city block using side doors and back alleys. This time, however, the Agents rallied much faster, and moved with more authority upon Thompson's position.

I had really hoped for cowed, but they appeared to be a more motivated, more disciplined force than I gave them credit for. That was good for Saracho, bad for me. They advanced in a wave, and had enough sense or sensor equipment to figure out where Thompson was going next.

"Careful, Thompson, evacuate that location, they're moving up too fast."

Her voice was harried, breathless. "Roger."

The Succubus blasted overhead, no more than five stories off the ground. It took a corner tight, so tight that all of Team One save Logan dove behind cover. At the last instant, Doe redirected his jets down at full thrust, turned the craft on its wing, and planed across the surface of the building, melting glass like wax and painting the façade black with soot. Two smaller fliers, emblazoned with the PISs logo, careened after him, leaving only echoes of their chase behind.

I tuned into Team Two again. "Thompson, move faster!"

Her reply was curt, matter of fact. "No map, Captain."

And she was right. We had no internal maps for these buildings, and that had to slow her down. I brought my team closer, skirting around the edge of buildings across the street from her. She exited the glass and steel tower and plunged across the alley into another just like it. King shouldered open the door and Team Two blew inside without waiting to take shots at the Agents.

The enemy was simply too close. Thirty soldiers had rushed into the office building after Team Two, twenty more were split into two groups to cut off all escape. That left a command group of about forty along the street, taking cover behind planted fake street dressing and looking tactical. They were used to focusing on a building to the exclusion of all else, cordoning it off, locking it down. It gave my team precious minutes to catch up.

They were like surgeons with a scalpel, lopping off power, water, lights, food, and warmth. They would make the besieged dependent on the good graces of the Agents. They would control the terrain and pacing of the conflict, and thus be able to win. Too bad they had never fought in a war zone where there is no such thing as front and rear. Someone had to harass them, split their attention. Someone had to teach them that ground combat had no real 'front' or 'rear'.

The Succubus tore a hole in the air above our heads again, slicing down the main boulevard before banking hard to the east and disappearing just ahead of a salvo of rockets. They impacted an empty high-rise apartment building in a staccato cry of dying gods. To a man, our enemies turned to watch the explosion, and then the PISs fliers following close behind. Telling Logan to hang back, Ortega, Lopez, and I used those seconds to get close. Really close.

Here, twenty yards away, it became painfully easy to spot the few beefy policemen carrying gargantuan launchers. I couldn't identify exactly what they were, but they definitely were not standard police issue.

Their first clue to our presence was a small, metal discus grenade whizzing into the midst of one cluster. It was followed closely by a second, a third, and then three more, followed by yet three more after that. Little black imps made of fire and smoke sprung to life, flinging ragged shards of metal in all directions. The Agents dove to the pavement, but only eleven were unable to get back up. We opened fire from positions of cover, trying to cause as much damage as we could.

The first man on his feet was a hulking brute, nearly bursting out of his armor as he wrestled to his shoulder a massive, box-festooned tube. I sent out a quick burst of automatic fire that caught him in the chest. He crumpled, but one of his compatriots ran forward and grabbed the weapon. My next salvo missed completely as he shouldered the launcher and pulled the trigger.

It's funny what one can do when one sees a blast of white exhaust propel what amounts to a ten-kilogram, self-guided, explosive bullet at one's face.

In less than a second, I clamped my left hand around Lopez's shoulder and tossed him to the ground. Next, I shouldered Ortega into the alleyway, doing little more than knocking him over and landing on top of him. Somewhere in there, I even managed to urinate on myself.

The missile—made for seeking out fliers, tanks, and cyborgs—bypassed us as simply beneath its notice. Luckily, Logan had taken cover moments before and the damn thing flew for several city blocks before it hit a building it could not avoid and detonated.

So, five of the men from PISs had weapons that were absolutely useless for attacking Ortega, Lopez, and me, but would turn Logan into a fireball in an instant. The presence of anti-borg weaponry changed our odds drastically; I hoped not fatally.

We popped off the ground as if on springs, and the three of us leapfrogged to the corner of the building and cover. The Agents that had sought to surround Team Two came back from around the building, and at least half of the group that had followed her inside came back out to deal with us. This was good for Thompson, but bad for me. We had yanked the tiger's tail, and instead of just a retaliatory swipe, had gotten the whole damn kitty.

Coherent streams of light sliced at our armor like angry shivs while our bullets scraped at them like talons of hot steel. I changed my magazine and brought two more officers down by shooting through their flimsy, faux bits of cover. There was a moment of peace as we made it to the safety of the corner, but then I felt my bile rise. Ortega picked up the clearly broken pieces of his sensor unit, crushed when I had thrown him to the concrete, and shook his head. Now we were flying blind. Lopez yelled and jerked back from the edge of cover, working his shoulder where he had been hit. It moved, which meant he was OK for now, but sooner than later we'd be cut to pieces.

Things were falling apart before my eyes. "Thompson, forget harassment. Get back to the back door of that place and meet us at" I scrolled across my HUD map and marked the street, "THIS point. To all *Angels*: Get to the rally point and we'll fight our way out of here. Pop smoke; cut sling load and GO!"

At that order, every *Angel* produced a blade of some kind, cut off their lower pack, consisting of whatever survival gear that did not shoot, explode, see, or hear, and let it drop to the ground. As that happened, I palmed a smoke grenade and tossed it around the corner and then blew an entire magazine blindly into the street, hoping to keep them guessing and crawling toward our position. Lopez popped another smoke grenade while Ortega set down an auto-claymore and set the timer. The dead little block seemed to wake up, extend small feet, and point itself at the corner, waiting for a victim.

We took off at a run, Logan leaving potholes in his wake that even a blind man could follow. Worse, we couldn't go in a straight line. If any of those maniacs with a missile launcher got a bead on Logan, he'd die first, and shrapnel would kill the rest of us microseconds later. We cut through the next building just as someone rounded the corner behind us and the auto-claymore went off.

Inside the dusty but finely-appointed office space, Logan took two giant steps and then cut right, straight through the sheetrock wall. Aluminum and plastic bracers went flying, clouds of choking dust tried to clog our air intakes, and wires sizzled as they crossed and tripped breakers all across the complex. We followed in his wake.

Thompson called in my ear. "Captain, They've got us pinned!"

Without even being told, the Master Sergeant turned left, back onto the main boulevard. He actually began running faster, out pacing us as he slammed through wall after wall, trusting his holo sonar to tell the difference between flimsy internal walls and solid structural support. He erupted out of the building in a shower of glass, cannon firing before his feet ever reached concrete.

Plasma packets the size of footballs belched from Logan's cannon, sounding like the hollow, laughing thunder of an insane ghost. Inside the manmade canyons of the deserted city, the battle echoed like nothing so much as the end of days. The

The Key to Damocles

Agents' armor, made to stand up to small arms, vaporized with hissing screams. Men died in agony as internal organs turned black and fried inside of ribcages. Leg bones superheated and exploded as entire muscle groups charred into carbon. One head was turned into a bonfire by a direct hit. Those who saw this, fled. Those who did not, died.

The rest of us came out onto the street, but we only had to fire a handful of rounds to eliminate the few Logan had not yet burned. Ortega had gained a new scorch on his breastplate from a shot which had failed to penetrate. A burning sensation in my left calf told me I had caught a stray shot as well.

I glanced down the alley across the street, and saw Team Two finishing their own firefight; they surely would have lost if we had not taken this group out. I slipped channels to include the entire team now that we were nearly together. "Thompson, we are behind you. Get to the main street."

They turned and bolted, King lobbing a grenade behind them to keep the remaining Agent's heads firmly in the sand. It was then Logan caught my attention and pointed at his feet. "Captain…"

I looked down and saw the corpse between us did not carry a gun, but a compact camera in its hand. The logo of one of the major networks was clearly emblazoned on the side, even though the operator was clearly wearing PISs issued armor. I looked up at the metal giant, his posture very clearly mirroring what I thought. *Oh, Grit.*

They had brought a damned news crew. *Is everyone on this planet fragging stupid?* Dead civilians always complicated everything, and the media was going to crucify us for sure.

Thirty meters behind Logan, Agents erupted from around the building, the man in the lead carrying one of the huge launchers. I raised my rifle and fired, round after round spitting from the barrel. The cyborg spun on his heel and raised his weapon just as the telltale smoke of the kicker charge pushed a missile out of the tube.

Almost faster than the human eye could follow, the two-ton cyborg twisted his body and vaulted into the glass wall of the fake offices. The missile followed like an obedient dog, smashing into the building to intercept his path. The warhead did not travel far enough to arm, so it did not detonate, but the crumpled body spewed rocket fuel across four offices and turned them into an instant inferno.

Team One began peppering the advancing Agents with fire, but it was only when Team Two emerged from the alley and King let loose with his gauss machinegun that their forward push disintegrated. Three-millimeter steel darts cracked armor like eggshells, and sliced deeply into flesh when they started to tumble. We retreated after Logan like rabbits diving into a hole, hoping the quickly spreading fire behind us would hold off the hounds for a few seconds more. Logan picked himself up and I pointed north. The Master Sergeant led the way with all the grace of a freight train.

I gave a few hand signals, sending Ortega to pop his last smoke behind us as Lopez dropped his auto-claymore to more fully cover our exit. We broke from the inferno-to-be and hustled across the street to a parking garage. All pretense of stealth thrown to the wind, we continued at a run for two blocks, coming almost all the way back to *El Toro's* broadcasting station. We had made a six-block circuit, and wound up right back here, separated from our goal by an overgrown city park. We took a moment to breathe as another series of explosions rocked the flat city's sky. Logan looked at me, and suddenly everyone was looking at me. Hunkered down behind some shallow hills, they stared at me, desperately needing something.

They were all battered, covered in light strikes and deeper burned cuts. Thompson had caught a bolt in the shoulder which was causing obvious pain, and Lopez was doing little better. Ortega's chest was still smoking, and I found myself hoping his medical equipment wasn't giving me false vitals. King seemed untouched, but I saw with horror that he had run though all but one magazine in his gun, and one more on his belt. Above, we could hear the distant hell of Doe and Walt fighting for their lives. To top it all off, my leg was starting to stab at me and cramp up from the burn that had obviously breached my armor. Between ourselves and relative safety was an awful lot of ground. They were looking to me because things were bad, real bad.

"Dammit, everybody, you look tired. They're only policemen for christsakes." They laughed. It wasn't nice laughter; it was grim, it was macabre, but it was there. "Alright *Angels*, they outnumber us, and to a certain extent, they outgun us. But now we have a fortress, and we don't even have to defend it. We just need to keep them off balance, make them fear us enough to slow them down long enough for Doe to finish up and pick us up. I think I've had just enough of this particular party. Let's get to the roof and get the hell out of here."

I tuned out everyone else and called up Doe. "Doe, how long before you can extract us?"

"Ten minutes, tops."

"Roger." *Hope you're right, Doe.*

I rallied the troops and we took off at a run northward. The large, open park had gone somewhat wild. The once pristine lake was brown and fetid. The trees had dozens of bastard children hanging at their feet. There was even a large walkway that made some kind of Irish design in the rolling hills, leaving a large clear spot for *The Succubus* to land. Excellent for a pick up, but not worth *grit* as a defensible position. First, we'd have to cut, smash or blow up enough trees for a landing pad. There would be no second because we'd be overrun long before Doe managed to eliminate his pursuers. The *Angels* would have to bypass the lazy option and climb fifty stories to get picked up. To confirm my worst fears, Logan looked over at me and flashed up five fingers. 500 meters, is what he meant. The enemy was closing in.

I looked left and right and shrugged. *There's no choice.*

He nodded. *Looks like our only option.* I pointed at the entrance. "Everyone inside–"

Then, behind us there was the rapport of a missile being fired. Without waiting another second, Logan sprinted back into the park, and the rest of us took off for the office spire. The missile arced upward gracefully, far above the highest building, before some unseen command urged it to nose down. With eyes far beyond human, it found Logan in the copse of trees. It dove like a hawk upon its prey.

Logan watched it in turn, synapses firing three times human normal, chemical and cybernetic engines pushing faster and faster against the wall of mortality. His computers crunched numbers at fantastic speeds, calculating the intercept path. The missile flashed down like a streak, and Logan reached behind him and grabbed the bole of a large oak with one, silvery arm. He braced himself and waited for an eternity of machine language. The guidance system told the engine their target was less than a second away. It primed the warhead. Logan jumped.

We managed to make the stairs at the base of the building when the missile detonated. Air was compressed so densely it formed a globe of white. Flame and light came next, leaves incinerated in an instant as shrapnel churned the ground like an impatient beast. Finally, splinters of wood were flung in every direction, they came cascading down in a charred snowfall.

We raced up to the front doors of the spike and Ortega gained entrance simply by putting a burst through the glass doors and walking through. The inside was what you would expect of a modern high rise million-credit-per-month office building. We took up firing positions in the foyer, and I used the optical enhancements in my helmet to zoom in on the blasted wreckage at the edge of the park. Smoke still obscured everything, leaves and slivers smoldering as they fell to earth like the tears of a dying angel.

I breathed in once.

Twice.

Logan?

Out of the fog, the giant limped. A vice around my chest released, and I gulped in a double lungful of air. I could see from his ungainly walk that he was severely damaged. Damaged, but alive.

"Archer. Thompson. Take up firing positions at the top of the stairs and fire at will! Missile launchers will have first priority. I want my Master Sergeant back, dammit." They hastened to obey as I turned to the others. "Lopez, prepare as many half-kilogram explosive charges as you can. Tsang, collect all remaining grenades and auto-claymores. Ansef, start upstairs with the luggage. Ortega, get your cameras ready. King, find a *fragging* map or something; I need to know where all the staircases are."

People split up to go do their jobs as a series of massive explosions came from across the city. Then the snipers began sending lead downrange. I was going to call Doe for a report when I got a call from Opus Lionel.

He looked ashen, sweaty, with dark circles that turned his brown skin purple beneath his eyes. "Captain Rook? The rest of them just left here in a hurry. There's little more than a token force remaining."

The Key to Damocles

I was glancing out of the front doors to check on Logan's progress, changing focus to watch my HUD as the other *Angels'* holo-sonar began filling out the map of this place. "Can your men take the rest?"

He nodded, but not confidently. "And I've got the press release ready."

"And the video?" He nodded. "Release that, now. And pray to God nobody traces it back to us."

His flesh was positively bloodless now, more like a wet burlap sack pulled tight over his sunken face. He made some weak noises. Whatever the general consensus of this man, he was definitely not made in a Machiavellian mold. I might have laughed if he wasn't pissing me off so badly. "Lionel!"

The president of L/V/D jumped a little on his side of the screen. As the snipers fired faster and faster outside the doors, I enunciated clearly, "Get. It. Done. Now!"

And he clicked off. A conga line of curses sizzled in my head like a fuse on my temper. *He better get it done, or we are all dead.* Lionel might be losing his nerve, and that was terrifying. All he would really have to do to come out of this fine was sit back and do nothing. If he figured that out, it would be very good for Saracho and excruciatingly bad for me. I was already heartily tired of everything being bad for me, dammit.

Archer called out, "One mag!" as Ortega ran by, slapping pencil-sized cameras up to watch the doors, elevators, and stairs. Logan shuffled in through the doors, his right leg an absolute mess all the way up to his chest. The force of the missile had ripped the armor plates clean off and destroyed whole sections of servos. He was making do with his leg locked into position, but even I could tell parts of his frame, his metal skeleton, were tweaked out of line. Even as extensive as the damage was, he was mobile, and I was grateful.

I coughed to get the huskiness out of my voice and dialed up a jocular tone. "Dammit, Logan, you look like hell."

He shrugged. "I'd say I look pretty good for a man who was hit by an antitank missile, sir."

I scoffed. "It hit the tree. Crybaby."

"I apologize, sir. I will attempt to keep my bellyaching to myself."

Archer called over the comm. "Out!" meaning he was out of ammo. Thompson called, "One mag!" a second later.

I ramped up my 'God of War' voice. "Hold fire! King, are there elevators?"

"Roger, sir!"

"Maximum load?"

There was a second or two of confusion, then, "Fifteen hundred kilos, Captain."

I fixed Logan with my best I-grit-you-not glare. "Well, so much for the easy route. Can you make it up the stairs, Master Sergeant?"

"Yes, Captain, just not very quickly." I looked behind them at the thirty policemen doing their best to leap frog across the park. I opened my comm to all *Angels*. "Thompson, save those last ten rounds. Everyone upstairs, now! Everyone, double-time it to the roof. MOVE, MOVE, MOVE! Not you three: Ortega, Tsang, King, Get over here."

There were two sets of stairs and four elevators. Even splitting all of the *Angels* into groups of two, there were simply too many entrances to try to hold. We had to retreat upwards, which wasn't horrible since in order to get picked up, we'd have to get to the roof anyway. Our biggest problem was Logan, or rather his leg. There was no way he could hoof it up fifty stories as fast as the rest of us, and I had hoped he would be racing ahead, carrying the slowest of us. It may sound cruel, but he'd be an anchor weighing us down unless we could slow up the Agents. Thankfully, I had five minutes, a half-completed map of this level, and about ten kilos of explosives. I looked into the eyes of my men and smiled like a hungry wolf.

It was time to ready a warm reception.

Four minutes and thirty-five seconds later, forty Agents arrived outside *El Toro's* revolutionary compound, such as it was.

I couldn't believe my luck. They wasted ten minutes cordoning off the building, sealing all the exits. In another five, they had their entry team ready to storm the lobby. Overall, a quarter of an hour is a fantastic response time for setting up a siege and getting ready to deploy. Unfortunately for them, it was what I had expected them to do, and all they had done was give me more time to run, plan, and prepare.

The first team consisted of eighteen men, easily outnumbering us three to one. They burst into the lobby with professional zeal, each man covering a preset angle so that there was always a gun pointing in every direction. They found the whole first level deserted, but still they were cautious.

Tiny cameras watched them enter from fixed positions around the lobby thorough fish-eye lenses. They spread out, following the deep score marks on the fake marble floor made when Logan had dragged his *cracked* leg. They came right up to the door, and their leader signaled to the man behind him, who brought up a flexible probe. He sneaked it under the doorframe, and was staring face to face with an auto-claymore. The book-sized unit woke up at the movement, looked quizzically at the probe, and determined it was insufficient reason to detonate. So, it just sat there like a dog wired up with explosives, waiting for the correct signal to do its job.

The Agents went to the other three staircases and found the trap had been repeated. Outside, another group launched the same kind of snitch Thompson had destroyed earlier. Within seconds, it had read the building and told them we were stopped on the fifteenth floor.

I had wanted to push farther, but there simply was no point. Running upstairs is nobody's idea of fun, and if I wanted my team to be good for anything, I had to give them breaks as we sprinted upwards. The only exception was Logan, who moved the slowest, but at least his metal body did not fatigue. I sent him ahead to get some distance as my counterpart downstairs gathered his team far away from the anti-personnel bomb and called outside for some backup. A bomb specialist ran into the lobby to look at the bomb and come up with a plan. This gave me twelve more minutes.

At that moment, a video press release hit all of the major, and most of the minor, news agencies. Released to 'in the know' front groups such as *weloveeltoro*.org and *eltoroparasiempre.org*, it was quickly shuffled to their media

438

shills who aired it without further thought. A shadowy figure, *El Toro*, announced a massive rally in New California tonight at midnight. He was finally coming out of hiding and required the support of his people to start a new era for Persephone. The speech dripped with revolutionary zeal. The voice, the syntax, the mannerisms were perfect. It would have fooled me. Of course, having a pool of the best actors, technicians, and effects men on the planet probably helped Opus out a lot.

We were passing floor number twenty when I got a call from Doe. His voice had completely changed. He sounded like a man in his element. Hard pumping music almost drowned out his words. "One flier down, one to go, but I have reports from *Lightwave Cyanide* that two more fliers are coming. ETA sixty minutes."

Those were the Agents that lifted off from L/V/D. With any luck, we would be long gone by the time they get here. I breathed a little more easily. "Roger."

Downstairs, a rifleman put a magazine-worth of focus gasses thorough the door at ankle height, striking the auto-claymore over and over. The trap had sustained huge amounts of damage, and was no longer functional. But it took him seven minutes to set up the flexible fabric blast shield and determine that one hundred percent.

That entire time we were running, taking stairs two at a time, when two things became clear: I had been skipping physical training way too often over the last year, and *El Toro* had never had any at all. By floor twenty-one, we were carrying him upstairs, and his bulky armor was not making the job any easier. If I didn't need him to keep an appointment, I'd have ditched him here without a second thought. We were all grateful when we caught up to Logan.

El Toro chose that moment to puff himself up inside his bulky armor and step up to me. "Excuse me, you seem to be in charge here, and I need to know—"

I grabbed him by the front of his armor, a white puffball affair I had regretted buying the moment we took delivery. I slung him around and pushed him into Logan, who could easily handle the weight. "Keep control of this luggage, would you?"

El Toro started to protest, but one look from the Master Sergeant silenced him. Logan scooped him up like an infant into his good arm and continued upward leaving the rest of us to sit down, huffing and puffing, hoping we were making better time than I expected.

Outside, the snitch kept watch over our position, whispering to its masters. The lobby now had only a token force of two men as the other sixteen stormed up the stairs at breakneck speeds. For our part, levels thirty-five through forty looked like there had never been any kind of filming done here. These levels were naked inside, with nothing but raw pillars, electrical lines, and exposed concrete. Thompson grabbed my arm and pointed out one tinted window at the snitch hovering three hundred meters away.

I nodded. "Take it." ·

She immediately shouldered her rifle and held her breath. "Fire in the hole."

The Agents on the street below, getting bored at hiding behind debris and looking tactical, jumped as the snitch disintegrated in midair. The operator probably swore at himself, but then a ripple went through the group. Now they didn't know where we were. Thompson went to the broken window and aimed almost straight down. She pulled the trigger slowly, concentrating on each shot, hoping the pounding of her heart wouldn't throw off her aim too badly. One round shattered on the asphalt road below, bringing everyone's attention to that single spot. The second took an Agent through the helmet, sprawling him out like a rag doll.

All those on the street tried to hunker down behind cover, but two more shots, and one more wounded officer destroyed any confidence they had in their position. Without orders and without any real thought, the Agents on the street ran into the office tower. Thompson took shot after shot, raining steel jacketed lead down onto the retreating bodies below. The bolt on her weapon locked open, she immediately dumped the magazine and she reached for another. Long before the empty one reached the streets below, her hand had flitted from pouch to pouch, confirming she was out of ammunition.

I reached forward and took her elbow. "Come on, Lieutenant. We have to get to the roof."

She slung the long rifle on the custom rig, holding the barrel up off the ground. Everyone else had moved upwards, giving us a few seconds alone. "What's the plan, Captain?"

"You are in charge of Logan, Tsang, and *Toro*. Get them to the roof and onto the *Succubus*.

"And you?"

"I get to make sure you have time to do your job." And then I heard the telltale whine of capacitors and the buzz of four massive magnetic bottles being generated. *They can't be that stupid.* "Thompson, get your people upstairs! Everyone else! Get to the elevators!"

We raced around the corner to the bank of four elevators. *They can't be that stupid. They can't be that stupid. They can't be that stupid.* I shouted directions like a spoiled brat on Christmas morning. One by one, we pushed tools, knives, and in once case, a stencil, into the unlocking ports in the doors. Thinking they were being serviced, the elevator doors loyally opened and the carriages slowed.

Thirty stories below, the Agents in the elevators felt a jerk as the elevators automatically began coming to a stop. One of them had the presence of mind to open up the display panel and see the error that was displayed:

Maintenance hatch open.

Automatic carriage stop.

Please remain calm.

"They're trying to stop us from going up," one of the Agents said as he activated his barely encrypted radio. "Don't worry, we can get Marco to override from the lobby."

These were men, armed men, on a planet in the midst of a revolution. They had opened fire on a mercenary force in what could be considered a war zone. That removed them from any kind of protected class of civilian. It made them combatants. Combatants always take the stairs. The Agent only fully understood this when the first grenade thumped onto the top of the carriage. The explosions echoed after us as we ran after Thompson's group. One hideous shriek and far away crash told us one of the magnetic elevators had failed completely. We hit the stairs like starving men running to a banquet.

I cued a transmission to Doe. His reply was immediate. "On my way boss."

The Key to Damocles

Then an icon representing Grisham blinked twice. "Captain, I have video I have to show you."

Normally, I would have said something witty about waiting for a proper time, like when I was sitting safe and sound in a *gritlicking* dropship, sipping coffee and checking my electronic messages, perhaps that night while I was having dinner with a few close friends, or even when I got to the next *fragging* place where I could sit down for three goddammed minutes instead of running up endless stairs with an army of *mudraking* government fascists on my heels. As it was, all I could do was gasp, which he took as assent.

In front of my face, the little ball-shaped camera we had set up in *El Toro's* office space had been running all this time. It looked like almost all of his lackeys had evacuated as I had suggested, but the wailing bitch was still there, crying over the cold body of Miguel. A tall, lanky man knelt beside her, whispering words of comfort I could not make out. The scene of misery was broken as four Agents burst into the room. The response was immediate; she began screaming at them in the same way she had abused me. As one, they raised their weapons and depressed their triggers. What they left of her resembled an overcooked meat product. Her companion tried to run, but he was cut down just the same. Less than a second later, the Agents began focusing on the transmission and recording equipment in the room. The last thing I saw was one of them aiming at our little remote.

On the heels of this transmission came the synthetic bass of Logan. "Captain, they are two floors below you and moving fast."

I opened my mike to the entire team. "*Angels*, PISs Agents are unbondable. I repeat: the Agents are unbondable."

With the murder of the unarmed, restrained civilians, they had firmly placed themselves outside of the law. They wouldn't even blink at doing whatever it took to get to us. We pushed ourselves even faster, desperate for escape. I pulled ahead of Archer, who appeared to be struggling, when the wall ahead of us blossomed with four black, flaming flowers. Archer cried out and splayed down face first onto the stairs.

I spun, shouldering my rifle and poured a mag into the idiot standing in the open landing behind us. His laser rifle tumbled from numb hands, and one of the other Agents yanked him behind cover. I dumped my magazine, loaded another and grabbed Archer by the armor plate at the scruff of his neck. His right buttock had sustained a direct hit, and was smoking badly. I managed to lunge up two more stairs, carrying his nearly dead weight before I had to put another burst down at the first head to pop around the corner. "King? Lopez? Somebody? NOW?!"

A chorus answered me, but there was no time to listen. I had to send two more bursts behind us before I could yank Archer up two more steps. My attempt overbalanced me, and I sprawled next to my sniper.

The last staircase was made in a wholly different mold from all the others. Below were access stairs like you'd find anywhere: small, cramped, and Spartan. The access to the roof was a grand gallery, with recesses in the walls large enough to house a machine gun crew. In fact, they were probably built to house film crews. Apparently, this was a dramatic point in the building, likely to be used over and over. I imagine it was great for that purpose, but it was a horrible place to try to hold against assault.

An Agent came around the corner, and I dumped the rest of my ammunition into his chest. Two men from PISs, one high, one low, leaned around the corner as I desperately tried to find my damn magazine, put it in the damn rifle and kill the damn Agents before they shot me.

I was not going to make it.

The world through my HUD distorted as a beam of coherent light melted the armored glass of my visor. Pain blossomed underneath my left eye and skittered across my cheek as I instinctively flinched away. Smoke swirled across my sight as I looked back down the stairs. I know it is impossible, but I swear I saw the flash of the ionizing laser that flashes the microsecond before the main laser lights up. That's when the staircase erupted into thunder.

King had come, and his gauss machine gun filled the landing below with death. Concrete cracked like china, and men sprawled as lifeless dolls. Archer and I could only keep our heads down. There was a half second pause as he moved to give us room to stand. Two more hurricane winds full of metal blasted beside us as Lopez and I yanked Archer up to relative safety. He, like Thompson, had been issued a machine pistol, but it fell from his hands as he screamed in pain. I slung my rifle and picked it up thoughtlessly as we got him onto the next landing.

Without being told, Lopez hunkered down and pulled Archer to his shoulders in a fireman's carry. I started to protest when Lopez shook his head fiercely. "He carried me last time; it's my turn."

And just like that, I knew I had a whole, functioning team again. They had alloyed in the furnace of war, becoming stronger as a unit than any of them as a group. They were truly my soldiers... *Radiation Angels.* I clapped him on the arm to send him on his way.

King joined me, dumping his half-full magazine and loading his last full one into the weapon's well. Then Doe's voice came like an answer from God. "Party's over, people. I am at the roof; the time to evac is now, everybody out of the pool."

King shrugged. "Permission to get the *frag* out of here before he finds another way to say hurry up, Captain?"

"Granted." I smiled, and while I could smell the burnt skin on my face, I couldn't feel anything except for dull pain deep in the bone. For the record, that's bad. I smiled anyway. "Everyone, get onboard the *Succubus.*"

King sent another short burst downstairs, and we ran up the last flight three steps at a time. We reached the roof, and even through my helmet I could feel the angry howl of our drophip's engines. Figures made tiny by comparison, the rest of the *Angels* were piling onto the ship through the wide fast-loading doors in the side.

Logan stood beside the ship, uncharacteristically tense. "Captain?"

"What the *frag* are you doing? Get on that ship, Master Sergeant."

"But, Captain—"

King and I spun at the door, peppering the landing below to keep heads down. "Master Sergeant, your leg has been *mudraked.* It's going to take you thirty seconds to hobble aboard. We will just jump aboard once everyone is clear."

"I can't leave you, Captain."

"Logan, get in that goddamned ship."

There were three seconds of silence between us. "Understood, Captain."

Logan turned and radioed *The Succubus*. "Two tons coming aboard on the port side, Pilot. Make room."

I had to spin back to the door and spend the rest of the magazine in insurance. I dropped the empty pistol and pulled out my rifle. "King, time to go."

"No arguments, Captain."

We sprinted for the dropship as Logan finally managed to struggle inside. We were almost there when a few, stray blasts slapped the roof around us. I ordered King to keep running, and I turned and dumped an entire magazine, leaning into the rifle to control recoil. The A2R-91 drew little circles across the doorway, snapping into the darkness with deadly intent. I reloaded and began running for *The Succubus*, hoping that in a second or two Doe could use the ships weapons to cover the door.

Doe screamed over the comm. "I've got incoming! Abort! Abort!"

What the...? The engines of *The Succubus* revved and the ship leapt off the roof, Logan bodily hauling King into the ship. In the distance, a small dot was getting larger with every second. My HUD focused in and automatically zoomed in to focus the PISs flier. Ship weapons, the smallest of which dwarfed anything carried by the team, lit up. In between the dot and my dropship, dark clouds exploded in midair, marking the end of a dozen incoming missiles. *The Succubus* dove between the buildings and out of sight, decoy rockets flying in all directions, seeking to lead enemy fire astray.

More beams of coherent light struck the building around me, and I dove behind a large air-conditioning unit. *I hope that this thing is real instead of some kind of prop.*

A second later, beams began punching through the cheap sheet metal as if it wasn't there. I swore viciously inside my head and leaned out to direct fire back at the bastards coming out onto the roof. One burst caught an Agent in the leg and he went down, howling. I shifted fire as he fell over, sending two more Agents diving for the rocky roof.

Below us, incoming fire from the enemy flier impacted on the building, rocking the entire structure. I was thrown from my feet. I could hear constant chatter over the comm, but it became vague, unimportant as my enemies regained their feet. I came to my knees and lined up my sights on an Agent. Without mercy or hesitation, I swept a line of bullets across him.

The Succubus popped above the roof and unleashed a storm of fire, indirect smart missiles arcing up on a deadly path.

I burned another magazine at my enemies and rolled from one piece of scenery to another. Fire followed me as an exultant triple explosion came from off in the distance. The first was from Doe's missiles hitting the ship, the second from the aeroline tanks going up, and the third from the ammunition. At any second, Doe would bring the *Succubus* around and—

I emptied out my rifle and reached down for another magazine. My hand found one empty mag pouch, and another... and another. My voice was strangely hollow as I activated my comm. "Rifle out."

All chatter died on the channel as I pulled out my laser pistol, made sure the chamber was charged, and flipped it to fully automatic. I leaned out and let a dozen shots off. Even those that connected with my target simply bounced off the PISs enhanced issue armor. I ducked back behind my flimsy cover as fresh holes appeared all across it. I dove to the ground and reloaded, painfully aware I only had two spare mags for my damn laser pistol. They were getting closer.

Forget what you see in the mind screen theaters. One man with a pistol taking on four police officers armed with rifles ends only one way. I scrambled at my nearly empty belt for a grenade, a magazine...any handy miracle would be nice. All I came up with was my MercTool. *Well, it's almost big enough...*

I stole a glance and then tossed the MercTool in a high arc, letting everyone see it glint in the sunlight. Men, expecting a grenade, dove for cover as I ran, feet clawing for distance. My ruse bought me thirty meters before they opened fire again, twenty-nine more than I had any right to hope for. Flares of fire and superheated material snapped at my heels. I dove to the turf, skidding to a halt behind another piece of fake scenery. The sound of the cracking light-smashed stone and concrete got louder and louder, the shots homing in on me without pause.

The roof beneath me began to rumble. Then it bucked, tossing me upward to flail in the air like a cat on a trampoline before I slammed back down. I floundered to my knees and took aim over the metal box but found my enemies replaced with wide smoking craters. *The Succubus* had come back for me.

Unfortunately, a massive amount of firepower had been poured into the top of this abused office building. Made for looks and longevity, no architect could have foreseen it would be hit with weapons meant to crack bunkers and tanks. I stood and ran at my dropship as flames erupted from the roof, turbulent air forcing Doe to take his ship out into open air. I could hear Logan over the comm. "Get lower! I'm going to lean out to get him!"

I was running for my life, every step screaming for perseverence as my hands worked to dump rifle and belts.

Logan's metal and glass eyes would have caught every detail, stripping me bare second by second. My vitals were all over the place. I hit the emergency release for my pack.

Five meters to the edge.

I wrenched my helmet off and tossed it aside. Every gram I shed let me go just a little bit faster, just a little faster.

The Sergeant reached out, causing the dropship to lurch again and come closer to the roof of the office. "We've got to get closer!"

Three meters to the edge.

Logan could read the ragged gasping of my lungs, measure the flow of blood through my organs. He could even detect the flares of chemical pain from the burn in my calf that was slowing me down.

"Captain!" he cried.

One meter.

I did not have the breath to answer.

Logan leaned out further.

Fires converged on the upper floors, weakening supports. Gravity raised her patient hands to the top of the building and pulled. The whole north side began to fall away.

I leapt.

One heartbeat.

A dark cloud erupted behind me.

Two heartbeats.

I stared into Logan's metal eyes.

Three...

The Key to Damocles

Logan's metal hand snapped out like a cobra, grabbing my wrist with the power of a vise causing the good kind of agony. He heaved me inside *The Succubus* and we took to the sky.

I was safe, at least for now, as we left the inferno of *El Toro's* revolution behind. Believe it or not, this was my plan working flawlessly.

Even as Tsang and Ansef picked me up off the deck, coming quickly to the consensus that my arm was now out of its socket, other things were happening.

Over the tops of a mountain range, the scattered inhabitants looked upwards, marveling at the storm of shooting stars blanketing the sky. They looked on with wonder, never guessing that this was the wreckage of the PISs dropships that had attacked *Deadly Heaven* hours before.

At L/V/D, ill-trained and ill-prepared security officers overwhelmed the few PISs Agents left behind. They were soon transferred to the prison of the Justice Center.

This went unnoticed since all the news reports could talk about was *El Toro* and his announcement. The rally was only hours away, and people were coming from all over the planet, filling New California's massive sports stadium. Forty thousand true believers had packed the stands so far. They waited impatiently, hoping their god would come and accept them, mark them as special, lead them into a world of milk and honey.

Back in New California, hundreds of refugees were in the Center, exploring new sections as the hacker opened more locks and liberated more security codes from the computers. One set of codes reached across the solar system, whispering to computers there, ordering them into action. Reality stuttered, and then millions of tons of men and metal were suddenly closer.

The Persephone fleet had been called home.

CHAPTER 34: FEAR NOT THE FIST OF THE TYRANT

The Succubus rumbled like a living thing, engines gulping aeroline as we headed southwest. After a half an hour dogfight, we were desperately short on fuel, and we were on our way to the closest megacity, Cruz de Coronado.

In the belly of the mechanical beast, I sat with a mirror and headset, checking up on the team as I considered the deep burn on my cheek. Luckily, it had hit at an angle, creating a shallow burn underneath my left eye. Forget the fashionable wounds you get in the movies, it was a streak of ugly carbon. The skin was angry and red at the edges of the wound, beginning to feel savaged even through the painkillers. Ignoring Tsang's advice, I poked a finger at the center of the slash. Agony blazed around the edges, but the center was black and dead, without any feeling whatsoever.

Archer lay face first on a seat folded down into a stretcher, the anesthetics giving him a fine, floaty demeanor. He giggled at me. "Well, Captain, it looks like you need to learn to keep your head down."

I glanced down at his wounded ass cheek, freshly bandaged. "I could say the same about you."

That one even got a laugh from Logan who was still looking back to me every few seconds to make sure I was really onboard. I stood as the dropship began its gentle descent. Holding onto rails set into the ceiling for just such a purpose, I made my way to the cabin. I paused to lightly punch Logan on the arm. I would have had to use construction equipment for him to actually feel it, but it was the thought that counted. I made it to the co-pilot's chair without difficulty, but once there I flopped down like I had run a marathon.

I did a triple check of the instrument panel and ran the fuel-consumption-to-kilometers-remaining formula twice before I was satisfied we weren't going to fall out of the sky. It was a close thing, though.

The Key to Damocles

Doe shifted in his seat twice before he cleared his throat. "I am sorry, Captain." I didn't have time to ask him for what. "That last flier probably had auxiliary fuel tanks. He had to go to afterburner all the way from New California. He must have been running on fumes when he got to us. I was so focused on the fliers in front of me… I just should have kept an eye out for something like that. Sorry, Captain."

"Doe, the *Succubus* is in one piece and everyone's alive. That was your mission and you did it. In fact, you're turning into a hell of a combat pilot. Besides, thinking one step ahead of the opposition isn't your job," *It's my job*, "but I'm proud of you for trying."

I stood up and hobbled out of the cabin, the pain from my burnt calf killing my chuckle at how Doe inflated over my praise. I walked past the assembled *Angels* gathered together at the front of the craft. Their faces were hardened, each one aware enough to know how close we came to failure, each one smart enough to know this wasn't over. Still, it was eleven hours until midnight local time and hopefully it would be a long, boring wait. They needed something to distract them from the danger. I had to lift their spirits.

I walked back to the front of the craft, pressed buttons on my command armpad and linked my headset into the ship's intercom. I clicked my mic twice to get everyone's attention. "*Angels.*"

And then everyone was looking to me. They had tired eyes. Most were wearing wounds, but it was their expressions of grim determination that rocked me back on my heels. I had asked, and demanded and begged for more and more from these people I hardly knew. They had responded like machines, giving more than I had any right to expect. Richardson had given his all. Even now, they were looking at me expectantly, ready to make my next orders reality.

The realization was humbling. It took the strength from my legs and I had to sit on the arm of one of the acceleration seats. *How can you people believe in me so much?* Tsang left Archer and began hustling up the aisle toward me, but I stopped him with an upraised hand.

"I'm fine, get back to Archer." I took a deep breath to steady myself, gathering up my mental armor from inside my soul. I put it on inside my head, becoming the Captain they needed, the man they deserved. "*Angels*, I have been running this team for six years. I have served in it as a scout, moved to a corporal, a lieutenant, first lieutenant, and Captain. I have led hundreds of soldiers into battle. You, each and every one of you, can name yourselves as among the finest I have ever seen. You should be proud." I gave it a half beat before saying, "Except you, Archer... you lead with your ass."

This got a laugh out of everyone, even Archer. The levity was good; it helped ease their fear and let them forget their troubles, if only for a moment. "I am sorry to say we are not done. I know it's been hard. I know it's been long. All I can say is, thank you." I took a deep breath, seeing some eyes glisten, watching others burn with an inner fire. I felt my resolve harden in the face of their belief, and an honest smile crept onto my face. "Well, not exactly all. Thanks to your hard work, and Richardson's sacrifice, we were able to get Katie Ranner back to her employers. Completing that L/V/D contract has netted every *Angel* a half-million credit bonus."

I had more to say, but they were too busy cheering. Eventually, I just looked at Logan and cocked my head to the side. *Can you get these people squared away?*

He motioned me off. *I'll take care of it, Captain*, he wasn't saying.

I shook several hands and clapped shoulders as I walked down the length of *The Succubus*. Made to seat seventy in the main cabin, soon I was leaving most of the *Angels* behind. The sound of their celebration seemed to fade too fast. I passed row upon row of empty seats, ghosts of the past looking at me with expectant faces. They all said the same thing... *don't screw this up*. I left the light of their presence behind as I came to the rear of the craft. I opened the door opposite from the armory and walked in.

Thompson came to attention, but I made an annoyed wave that told her to cut it out. Still wearing her helmet, she was able to ask privately, "Did you mean it, Captain?"

But I had to answer publicly. "Lieutenant, you can do many things as a commander, but lying about payday is not among them. The cash is in the vault aboard *Deadly Heaven*. We can hand it out when we get back." And I cast a withering glance at our audience. "Go and see to the men. I have business here."

El Toro took his head out of his hands and glanced up at me, his face completely empty. Thompson saluted and exited, leaving me alone with our luggage. Grisham stood in the corner like a statue; the tiny table and swing-out stools were the only other furnishings. I worked myself around the claustrophobic space to the head of the table and kicked out my stool. I seated myself and activated the computer set into the surface of the table. I set the polarization on the screen so he couldn't read it and typed furiously, bringing up files I would need and sending the 'record' order to Grisham.

El Toro shifted in his seat, less brave outside of his bulky armored cocoon. Even so, the jerk couldn't keep his mouth shut. "This doesn't look like a prison."

I rolled my eyes. "It's my prep room, sir."

Trust me when I say that of all skills in any military force, the most universal is learning to call someone 'sir' who does not deserve it. It helps to turn it into something of a curse.

He glanced about, soon coming to the realization that there was only one exit. "So, um," he glanced at the nametag on my armor, "Mr. Rook. I think I understand you are not going to kill me..."

And the worst thing was he was thinking of escaping the room, and hadn't thought about how he was going to get out of the dropship without a parachute. *Idiot.* "No, I am not going to kill you, sir."

That got him breathing normally again. He closed his eyes and let the stress of the day melt away completely. I wondered briefly if he was some kind of sociopath. He heard he was safe, and all was right with the world. He didn't spare a single thought for his friends, teammates, or whatever they were, back at his tower. "Do you mind if I could get something to drink?"

I thought about the conversation between Tony and me, specifically the one involving tossing a criminal out over a city at high speed and watching him smear across the landscape. I looked up at *El Toro* and weighed the damage to Persephone and my soul against the satisfaction of watching it happen. In the end, I settled for the mental image. I needed him alive for the next part to work. I finished marshalling my files and sat back to take fresh stock of the man. "You have an appointment with your people, *Toro.*"

He looked confused for a moment. "My name is—"

I don't care. "Saracho has tried to kill you. He will try again. You need to plan your next move if you are going to have any chance at survival."

His gears started spinning as he shifted to a less dominant position. "Um, Mr. Rook, I appreciate the effort you went through and all, but all I've seen so far is the police shooting at your people."

I hit a key. Above and behind me, a screen flashed to life. His eyes flicked from my face and drank in the vision of two of his friends being turned into charred steaming lumps by Saracho's men. His eyes widened with horror and his Latin coloring became faded. Again, I was struck by how hollow, how fragile, how small, this man was in person.

He got up and started to pace, getting no more than four steps before turning and retracing his steps. "Those *hijos de hembras* at L/V/D set this up. They sent Saracho."

I closed my eyes, feeling my way forward, picking words as gingerly as poisoned shards of glass. "Why would L/V/D want you dead?"

He slammed his fist into the table, gritting his teeth. "Because I buck the system! Because I stand for what's right, what is decent."

I steepled my fingers in front of my face, chaining my temper to the altar of my will. "Setting bombs is decent?"

What he said next almost blew my self-control to hell. "We didn't set any of the bombs." He continued, smiling like one of the boys sharing a sleazy joke. "We never did anything illegal. Saracho's men did that."

Was Saracho in league with the Knights of Earth? I worked the idea like a child's puzzle, pulling and pushing at the pieces but it simply did not fit. "He set the bombs? Did he tell you when it was happening?"

Toro shook his head, his smile dying as his brow contracted. "No. The bombings started before he found me."

"He came to you?"

He nodded, swelling further with pride. "I had been running a pirate network site for years, lambasting L/V/D for discrimination against Latinos. They look down upon us, forcing us into slave roles in the industry, never properly casting us in the roles we deserve."

He might have said 'we', but he meant 'the roles *I* deserve'. Finally, the truth was beginning to emerge. "So, it is your opinion that L/V/D doesn't have the right to hire whoever they want to make their movies? They have to hire who you want?"

And immediately I knew I had let too much truth seep into my voice. *Toro* looked at me askance, eyes narrowed. He was an idiot, but a cunning one all the same. "Why are you helping me? I saw on the newsfeeds you worked for L/V/D."

I shrugged. "I am a mercenary, a free agent, and I work for whoever pays. I am hoping once you take office as leader of this planet you will need some muscle to help you stay there."

Blinded once again by grandiose dreams, *Toro* nodded forcefully. "Oh, you are right, Rook. Now that Saracho is out of the picture, I will need bodyguards to form the core of the planetary government."

Oh, God, Grisham, tell me you are getting this. "So, Saracho was your muscle man?"

He nodded. "That was the whole deal, I become the next leader of a free Persephone, and he gets to keep playing cops and robbers. It was genius, really."

Gotcha. I locked down the computer so it couldn't be used and stood. Just being in the same room as this idiot made me feel dirty, and I had all I needed from him. "Well, wait here and relax. I'll have some refreshments brought to you. You have a rally at midnight, so you'd better prepare what you are going to tell them, sir."

I hustled Grisham out ahead of me as *Toro* rushed to catch up with the conversation. "A rally? At midnight? What?"

I stopped at the doorway and turned to him. "You need to take power immediately, before Saracho makes his own bid for the hearts of the people."

"He has the screen presence of a worm, he cannot stand against me." *Toro* seemed to swell so large he filled the room. He adapted the straight backed posture of a king. "How many will be there?"

I shrugged. "Thousands."

Far from being cowed, his eyes lit up with religious zeal. "This will be my finest moment."

I almost choked on my own bile. "You might want to get some sleep. If you need a pad to help you work on your speech just hit the blue button on the intercom."

He waved at me, dismissing me from my own ready room. I shut the door and locked it from the outside. If anything, my hatred of the revolutionary had grown. I had just spent ten minutes locked alone with him, and even after being shown two of his coworkers reduced to ash, not once did he ask about the rest of his team from his hideout. I comforted myself with the idea that I was going to murder him, just not with my own two hands.

We landed, refueled, took off, landed, grabbed food from a terrified man at an Asian food joint, took off, landed, took on coffee, took off... Every few hundred kilometers, *El Toro* wanted something else: coffee, fresh fruit, martinis, Thai food. He had accepted the role of leader of the world/superstar completely, and was anxious to flex his newfound influence. Unfortunately, I had to give in to his petty demands left and right in order to keep him happy. Finally, we made it to New California where we landed at the space port and bunkered.

I was able to impose upon *Toro* that my men had to get some sleep if they were going to be any use in defending him. He 'graciously allowed' us to sack time with a manner which earned him venomous looks from every one of the *Angels*. We ate MREs and slept in shifts on seats folded flat. It really wasn't enough, or of high quality, but after hours of dodging gunfire and bowing to *Toro's* every whim, it was a desperately needed respite.

I got four hours sleep before running off onto the tarmac. I needed some specialized weapons for tonight, and the spaceport *cum* brothel, flea market, and arms bazaar was the place to try to find them. I even got bulk price on some ammunition. I found just what I was looking for, which made me nervous. I never get what I want that easily. We managed to strip, test, and reassemble the weapons long before we had to go, but I was on the comm the rest of the night, making sure everyone else in the chain was doing their jobs. They were, but of course that's when the bad news I had been expecting showed up.

The Key to Damocles

First off, while Saracho had not marshaled forces to assault us at the spaceport, *Lightwave Cyanide* Actual had noticed our entry, and had probably seen the far off battle at Monroe. He had added one and one and come up with one hundred fifty thousand. One hundred fifty thousand credits more for our parking fee or he was going to boot us out.

I tried to shrug it off. I had the money, after all, and it was a good move for Janchea since the chances of an armed battle in a place he was responsible for defending were much higher with us here. Still, it felt like something of a betrayal, even if it wasn't.

Right after that, Logan came back to *The Succubus*, having recovered full use of his damaged leg, even if it looked only half-done. While the local cybermechanic had managed to fix several leaky hoses, untweaked the frame of the leg, and replaced half a dozen broken motors, he had nothing that would act as armored plating. Until it was repaired, Logan would be vulnerable to small arms fire to his delicate innards, especially his power supply and central computers exposed in his abdomen.

We didn't even have suits of armor anywhere near big enough to fit him. I wouldn't ask any of the other *Angels* to go into battle naked, so I couldn't risk his life in that way. I was so used to being able to call upon his massive potential for destruction, I felt very small without it.

I forced it out of my mind with further work, downloading the schematics of the Gigadome from the newly rebooted computers in the Justice Center. I exchanged a few terse notes with Lomen, who had just had another confrontation with Saracho as the latter tried to take the Center from the former. Despite my foul mood, I chuckled at that. My freshly re-requisitioned MercTool began chirping like a cicada on methamphetamines and steroids, with a bullhorn crammed up its ass. I shoved my doubts into the back of my head and turned the damn alarm off.

When I'm feeling especially scared, vulnerable, and cranky, I always find the best therapy is abusing some *jacka* that surely deserves it. I kicked *Toro* awake, brought him out of the ready room, and got him strapped into a flight seat. He began firing off questions I wholly ignored. It was easy, since the interior of the *Succubus* was pretty chaotic. Everyone squeezed back into their sweaty, stinking armor. Fresh ammunition, as well as brand new rifles and pistols, were drawn from the abbreviated armory. The team was stiff, sore, in some cases injured, and only half rested. Luckily, they were brave, professional, and had their minds fixed firmly on their half million bonus. They wrestled their equipment on, strapped themselves in, and steeled themselves for the things to come.

I finished suiting myself and made my way back to the rear of the craft and found *El Toro*. Still shaking off sleep and dishevelment, all he could do was ply a stencil to a small pocketbook computer Ansef had given him. I hoped she had enough sense to blank it of anything important first. He was so focused he didn't even notice me until I tossed a heavy armored jacket and balaclava into his lap. "Put these on or we'll be mobbed before we can get to the dome."

For the first time in hours, *Toro*'s eyes registered fear. "Mobbed?"

Idiot, don't make him think about that. I scowled down at him. "Put them on. Flight time is less than ten minutes, and we'll have you to your final location in thirty, sir."

It was time to kill a legend.

CHAPTER 35: FEAR THE WRATH OF THE ANGELS

Planet Persephone,
The Gigadome, 29:21, 11/21/2662

Finally, finally, I got to give Doe the 'go' order. We cleared preflight in record time, and I was quite sure that Doe 'forgot' to get permission from flight control before the dropship leapt from the tarmac like a giant bird of prey.

We didn't see any PISs(y) fliers, but the closer we came to the Gigadome, the less we saw of the streets below. Instead, we saw thousands upon thousands of people flooding the streets. Behind my eyes, I was seeing the Battle of West Lot, unbondable flooding in from all directions, but these crowds were distinctly different. These had brought lights, and vehicles. I was willing to bet this was the only part of New California which had more than four working fliers at one place at one time. I was shocked as they swarmed like gnats, and Doe had to ascend to half a kilometer to get out of traffic.

As we got closer to the Gigadome, the streets got wider, but even more packed with people. Each blended into the next, creating a single undulating entity that crammed into every available space. Zooming in with the ship's cameras, I saw the faces were universally young. They had brought streamers, banners, signs, and music players. Every one extolled their love and support for *El Toro*.

This wasn't a political movement, it was a counterculture party. Some were shooting modified flare guns into the air, powdering the sky with confetti and glitter. Fireworks were in abundance. Bonfires were everywhere, and I was sure they were going to start the city burning any minute. Live performers were becoming more and more common, working for love of their art and expression of political dissent. They were having such a good time I almost felt bad about what was going to happen next. Almost, but not quite. I wondered how many more this charlatan would leave as burnt cinders if given the chance.

The Key to Damocles

We came down over an abandoned office building, the roof thankfully bare of revolutionary partygoers. Doe scanned the structure and fed the numbers into the mainframe. *The Succubus* determined it would hold her weight, if just barely. The landing was so smooth, we had barely noticed it happening until Doe called out the all clear. Everyone prepared to go and I gave out assignments.

I checked in with Walt, who was currently manning guns, Ansef, who was in charge of Archer, and Archer himself, in charge of sitting on his burnt ass. Logan was not happy about being tasked with guarding the flight crew, but with his private parts all exposed to gunfire, he did what he was told.

Grisham came up as I braced *El Toro*, and took a long sixty seconds to print out a three-hundred page document. I looked over the bullet points that normally changed, careful not to touch the memory plastic portions of the documents. I glanced up at *Toro*. "As a mercenary team, we are not allowed to work without contracts or for free. I need you to sign this."

And, predictably, he balked. "Rook, I don't have any money."

I took a deep breath, pretending I was speaking to a child to keep myself calm. "Check your pockets."

He did, and pulled out a crisp, new, one-hundred credit plasticized note. I went down the contract, expertly initialing where I was supposed to, finishing it up with a signature, thumbprint, and a dab of saliva for a DNA signature. I gave it to him to do the same. He tried to read it, his manner becoming less and less sure as he flipped back and forth. "What does this mean?"

"It is a standard personal protection contract. In effect you are hiring us to keep you alive."

He looked at me askance. "For how long?"

I ran my tongue over my teeth impatiently as Thompson handed me my helmet. "Just until you get onto stage and begin to give your speech. After that, you can retain the services of anyone you would like. We're not looking to make a puppet out of you, sir."

He smiled. "Excellent, Rook. I can see you going far inside my government."

I shoved my helmet on my head in lieu of doing something rude, violent, or both, to the smiling *jacka*. I settled for saying, "Your speech is in twenty minutes, sir."

Of all things, it was really the 'sir' that got him moving, jarring him from the paranoid fantasy back into his power fantasy. He mimicked my signing, and finally we were ready to go. He chuckled as he handed me my own credit note. "Nice trick."

I pocketed the note. I grabbed my brand-new rifle from Thompson and took *Toro* by the nape of the neck. "Let's go."

Ortega, Lopez, Tsang, King, and I disembarked, luggage in tow. We crossed the roof, cracked open the lock on the door and disappeared into the building. *The Succubus* took off, and I clicked on my radio. "See you, soon."

Doe came back, his voice tight. "We'll be waiting, Actual. Good luck."

And luck we'd need in spades. We had less than two blocks to traverse, but it was covered with people who actively loathed us. We could not pause; we could not falter. We had to keep moving or we'd sink into the sea of people and drown in their hatred.

We hit the main staircase and began taking them two at a time. Immediately, *Toro* began complaining. *Why did we have to take the stairs? Why were we moving so quickly?* By the third floor he realized he wasn't going to get any answer, which just made him whine louder. *Why did we have to rush past his people? Shouldn't he arrive with some pomp and circumstance? Wouldn't it make a great scene to arrive on the shoulders of his people?* By the second floor, we were meeting the clandestine lovers and surreptitious drug users who had been looking for a private area. We blew past them in a tsunami of black armor and loaded guns, weapons never quite pointing at them, but keeping them covered with black faceplates. Some cried out, others stared stupidly, but in every case, we were past them before they knew what happened. It was an element of surprise we had to keep as long as possible.

We hit the front lobby of the abandoned office building, insurance I noted absently, and *El Toro* decided to take a small break and reestablish the pecking order. I grabbed him roughly and threw him bodily toward the door. He cast me a look made of fire and steel, but it shattered on his face as we burst out the front. As suddenly as if we had abandoned ship, we were in the hot, stinking surf of people. They were on all sides as we formed a diamond with our bodies: King at the front, Ortega in the rear and *Toro* safe in the center. I'm a big guy, but King was far bigger, and he plowed into the crowd with his impressive shoulders. Men and women were thrown to the side as he created a path for us to use, and we never slowed to less than a jog as the Heavy Weapons Officer found bubbles of emptiness as the cliques congealed in their designated areas. We were making good time, and the sudden appearance of armed men was enough of a shock to make sure anyone who was paying attention scrambled out of the way. It wouldn't last, it couldn't last. It didn't.

El Toro tripped on the curb and fell on his face. It slowed us down for just a second as Ortega wrestled him to his feet. It was only a moment, but it was in the middle of an empty space at the edge of the parking lot for the Gigadome. People were everywhere, camped out in tents and family-sized fliers, with trashcans acting as campfires, and alcohol flowing freely. They were obviously from better off cities on Persephone, considering the amount of food and resources they were displaying in an almost carefree manner. It was little more than a tailgate party, but as everyone looked in our direction, the mood of the night crashed against us, twisting like tons of metal into something dangerous and ugly.

We got *Toro* up and moving, but people were already turning and pointing at us. Like a surfer consumed by a wave, we had failed to outrun our element of surprise.

We had to move, now. "Go! Go! GO!"

King changed tactics as the groups of drunk protestors began to jeer. He steered us toward holes in the mass, and we went from a forced jog to something more approximating a run. We might have made good time, too, if *El Toro* hadn't started wheezing and holding onto his ribcage. For a man in such fine outward shape, he had the endurance of a candy bar. I grabbed one arm, Tsang grabbed the other, and we half lifted, half dragged, him onward.

These people had suckled at the teat of the established media of Persephone. There they had learned of *El Toro's* greatness, had been told that the *Angels* were devils, and had been told they were smarter, more informed, better, than anyone who disagreed with them. They had succumbed to the seduction of the propaganda so thoroughly that reality had no bearing on their lives anymore. And if you think I'm being harsh, first consider that they were thinking of taking on armed men with no modern weapons whatsoever. Perhaps they believed their righteousness would save them.

What I couldn't figure out is this... if I was the man they believed me to be, I'd kill them all without blinking. If I wasn't, they shouldn't be attacking. Perhaps they believed my evil nature would cause me to falter. In either case, they showed they had been turned into an artificially intelligent elite, full of someone else's ideas and opinions which had transcended political speech and become a religion. I was the Satan of that particular faith.

A few of the younger, healthier males strung themselves in our path, locking arms and shouting insults. My man took no notice but instead crashed though the line trying to block our way.

As we blew through this first human obstacle, we knew the timer had been set on the crowd. One man grabbed a prepackaged burger food product and hurled it at us, striking King in the middle of his chest. Things quickly got worse.

Inspired, the crowd turned the sky into a hail of food. We ran on, rolling over, under, and through anything in our path. As we ran, word of our disruption spread like an explosion. It enveloped this entire side of the building and turned the sea of people into a frothing, tempest-tossed mob. I could only hope we would get to the building and under cover before—

A canned good slammed into Tsang, staggering him even though his armor protected him from much more than a bruise. Still, it had stepped up the engagement, and within moments cans, bottles and rocks were hurling toward us.

I gritted my teeth and gave the order I had hoped to avoid. "Pushers free, pushers free! Fire at will."

Each member of the team was carrying a brand-new Pl/Ep-R11 Plasma rifle with an integrated pushgun slung underneath the barrel. They're bulky and heavy and normally I'm not one for issuing combination weapons of this type, but at the moment, it allowed us to defend ourselves without using deadly force. Deadly force was always a tricky thing because if we killed a few of these people, it might scatter the crowd. It might also spur them to charge. If they did that, none of us would survive. One thing you could always bet on… while some people did not fear death, everyone feared pain.

King flipped his weapon off 'safe' to 'push' and took aim. A man had been racing forward with a protest sign mounted on a metal pipe held like a club, intent on counting coup or something stupidly similar. King caught this particular village idiot in the crotch, crumpling the man like a paper tiger. We blew past the felled foe like the wind. We were no more than a hundred meters from the doors to the backstage areas of the Gigadome, but unfortunately, rather than giving the protesters reason to back off, our attack had incensed them more.

Two more men ran forward with makeshift weapons, and I felled both of them with high-density electron packets. Tsang did the same on the opposite side, and Lopez hit a woman in the sternum who had been brandishing a kitchen knife. Unfortunately, we had to drop the gasping *Toro* to accomplish this, and our progress slowed to a crawl. The crowd, once angry and indignant, became furious.

A man with a hastily-made Molotov cocktail in a high-proof liquor bottle charged forward. Lopez saw him first, but he and King fired at the same time, blowing him off his feet. The bottle fell and smashed, deluging the poor sod's feet in burning liquid. He began to scream as his comrades looked on in shock. Then they turned on us, more cautious but more determined to make us pay. It was as if they thought the burns on their fellow revolutionary were more our fault than his own.

We made the door in the chaos that followed, and Ortega took out his lock-cracking box and set it on the access console. I shoved *Toro* against the building, set King right on top of him to act as a human shield, and the other three of us formed a semicircle around them, weapons trained. The promise of imminent injury had no effect whatsoever on the crowd. They continued to stalk forward, waiting only so long as it took to begin arming themselves. Broken bottles, impromptu clubs, and utility knives were everywhere. It was like being in one of those movies where the dead come to life for love of brains. In fact, it was precisely like that since I've never seen a group of people more in need of brains in my life.

I had one more trick to scare the natives. I clicked on my comm again. "*Angels*, switch to plasma, warning shots on three: one, two—"

Three round bursts of blue-white fire burned over their heads like fireworks. The whining sizzle silenced them like gunshots, and they stopped in their tracks as the prospect of death cracked through their devout haze. In the cold pause that followed, the purr of our rifles' capacitors was deafening.

Come on Ortega, come on...

The bubble burst, and they all began screaming. It was as if promising to visit light speed death upon them were in some manner against the rules. It was as if they felt they were so right, so pure, we should have laid down and died like good little fascists, and anything less was simply cheating. They promised us infamy. They said they would see us tried and convicted. They promised eternal resistance. They said they would come for us and our families in the night. They promised us death. But at least they did it from a respectful distance.

I comforted myself with three things. One, since these people, like the media, demonized armed resistance, my men were the only ones with modern weaponry. Two, since I had only threatened death in self-defense, only fired in self-defense, and had never threatened their children, they were closer to tyrants than I. Three, the console underneath Ortega's electronic lock pick just gave a pleasant musical tone that translated from machine language into 'be gentle, stud'. Ortega yanked open the door. King put *Toro* through it seconds later, and we poured through like water down the drain. I was the last out of the lot, and I slammed the door just as the people charged.

The door closed. The lock engaged. Though they beat against the door with the fury and dignity of an epileptic hurricane, we were safe. Well, relatively safe. This was a back room to the stadium, clearly made for loading and unloading heavy scenery for concerts. Everything was bare concrete, covered with dust from months of disuse. Somewhere above us were a quarter of a million more people just like those outside.

If they found us... I checked the time on my HUD. "Five minutes."

Tsang began tearing off *Toro's* borrowed jacket and balaclava. The medic used the mask to wipe off the worst of the condiments left from the hail of food upon the revolutionary's pants as he shivered and gasped.

"Killed us… they almost killed us."

I sighed. "They hate my men, *Toro*. They see us as the enemy."

True to form, *Toro's* focus was never far beyond his own nose. "They tried to kill *me*!"

I grabbed his face and made him look at me. "They didn't know it was you. They love you. You can control them, can't you?"

And he took my question and rolled it around inside his head. I was amazed it didn't get lost in the dusty corners. Still, as the familiar fire lit behind his eyes and he slapped my hand away, I couldn't help but be relieved as he reentered his delusion of godhood. "Yes, yes I can."

I turned to my men, pointing at them in turn. "Ortega, Tsang… PA system working ASAP. Find a microphone. Lopez, King… secure a route to the stage. Move now."

And they scuttled off to do my bidding, leaving me alone with *El Toro*. Minutes ticked away as my men did their jobs, and as *Toro* regained his breath, he regained his confidence. He took out the pocket computer and went over his notes, but this failed to keep him busy. Soon, he was preening in a mirror that someone had hung over a sink. He visibly considered asking me for a brush, but settled for finger-combing his hair instead. He fussed over his full, Latin moustache, and fretted over the ghosts of thrown food staining his pants.

I sat down and considered all the angles, relishing the silence that came as the mob outside gave up trying to knock down the door. The quiet seemed to eat at *Toro*, though, making him aware of every echo off the bare concrete walls. He cleared his throat, shuffled his feet, hummed, anything to keep the stillness at bay.

"I have to say, Rook, I am impressed with your men. I'm not particularly thrilled with their tactics, though." He looked at me expectantly, but I did not answer. "I mean, guns? Really, positively stone age." And uncomfortable tranquility fell upon us again. He continued talking, filling the void with what he loved most. "I mean, the age of the gun has passed. Even you can see that. I am about to be coroneted Rook. Forget the politicians, forget the military, I am about to take control of this planet with only the power of my voice.

"Do you know why I'm able to do this? Do you know how I can become leader of the world?" And the stillness settled in again, unbearable and mighty it forced him to continue. "Because people have been inundated with movies for centuries, it has become its own culture… its own religion. Movies have become reality.

"Everyone knows how to spot the bad guy, and everyone feels better when they know who he is. If you know how to paint someone as a hero, people will accept him as a hero. If you paint him as a villain, he will be the devil in their eyes. It's a question of tint, of brushstrokes. If you make a mural everyone can understand, you can change the very landscape to match it." *Toro* turned to me, focused on only me as he waxed pedantic. "If you can sublimate the movie culture and recreate it: a look, a moment, a scene lovingly crafted and lovingly remembered. If you can replicate that feeling for someone going through their humdrum life, you can capture them, make them believe anything you want them to believe. Because they believe they have become their fantasy. It is what they truly want! They know their part, and will step into it without ever even noticing. They will be my army.

"The true power is not guns; it is belief! That is the most powerful thing." He stared at me with wide eyes and clenched teeth, willing me to answer, to agree, to be moved by his powerful words. I simply sat, hands folded, head bowed as if I had not heard. He frowned. "Perhaps you can't understand. That's fine. Some people are just made to obey. Only the greatest can lead from the heart."

I stared at him, wondering at what point, and what event, had broken this man so completely inside. It has never been the gun, or speech, nor any liberty, thought, or thing. It has always, for good or ill, been the hand that holds it, the mouth that speaks it, the mind that abuses it. Evil is done by men, and men alone bear the blame.

Just then Tsang reappeared with a wireless mic. He busied himself affixing it to *Toro's* lapel as he spoke to me clandestinely over his helmet radio. "Ortega is in the booth. He will activate the stadium replay cameras when *Toro* goes on stage. He cross-wired the feed into the advertising screens on the outside of the stadium. They'll all be entranced."

The Key to Damocles

I clicked over to talk to include Ortega. "Cut feed to the southern screens. I want them blank. If you can kill the lights there, do it. Get everything ready for his appearance."

Ortega gave me a quick 'roger' as Lopez came back into the room. He nodded at me, "We found a clear route, right to the back of the stage. It's all locked off so we'll need Ortega to crack the locks."

I shook my head as the grinding sounds of shifting machinery rumbled on every side. "We'll blow it. Ortega's in the control room—"

El Toro pushed out his chest and strutted up to me, putting his face close to my faceplate. "Excuse me, is something going on?"

The noises continued, filling the small space like the angry thunder of an approaching storm. I took a deep breath to steady myself, and flipped out my tongue to turn on the external speakers. "It is time for your speech, sir."

He smiled, nodded, and clapped me on the shoulder. I stared into his eyes as his grimace woke angry impulses inside of me. What it came down to is I would never know why *El Toro* was so small inside. He was nothing but a shell, a tool to be wielded by those much more cunning than himself. It was sad, but in the end it didn't matter. He had risen far enough to be dangerous, and he was now little more than a bomb to be defused, or a rabid animal that needed to be put down. I couldn't do it myself, but thankfully I didn't have to.

All around us, the noises stopped. Just outside this door a stage had assembled itself from the Gigadome machinery. It was prepped and ready; it only required one thing more.

I checked with Ortega to make sure our luggage's mic was working, then ordered Lopez to take care of the door. He pulled out a vibro-knife and cut the lock. I turned off the lights, leaving the barest flicker of safety bulbs going, turning us all into wraiths backstage. Within seconds, the high-pitched squeal of severing metal stopped, and Lopez stepped back, motioning *Toro* through. The revolutionary looked through to the darkened stage. He was given pause by the sound of a quarter million voices, blending together like the crash of a surf. It rose and fell, pregnant with anticipation. His eyes were alight with fear. I couldn't let him falter now.

"Our contract is fulfilled." I motioned outside. "Your army awaits."

Those words lit the fires behind his eyes, and he nodded solemnly. Lights speared him from all sides, highlighting him for his unseen audience. Immediately, my helmet cut out the external feed as the applause sought to deafen us. It was as if suddenly he knew who he was supposed to be, where he was supposed to be, and what his next line was. He strode out proudly, certain of his place in the universe.

El Toro spread his arms like a triumphant Christ, soaking in the adulation of his fans. His face was caught between orgasm and rapture.

I shut the door. "Do it."

King came forward with a pocket plasma torch. *Toro* began speaking as he touched the first corner. By the time the crowd cheered again, we had melted enough of the frame to seal him outside.

We had announced *Toro's* public appearance hours ago, and with good reason. Dozens of news crews had flown in, staking out prime locations where their cameras could gaze upon their presumptive king. I noted with amusement that every one of them had hired mercenary teams that created protective bubbles around the expensive commentators and equipment. And it proved necessary, as the already filled stands packed even more tightly with people ready to hear the words of *Toro*.

From the moment he came out onto the stage, there was a clamor the likes of which any politician would sell off a child to obtain. It slammed against the walls and reverberated in the hearts of the crowd, resonating back and forth, feeding on itself like a runaway nuclear reaction. On stage, *Toro* raised his arms in triumph, and the people responded with even greater fervor. He smiled, and waved, and eventually patted at his audience to move them to silence. Then he opened his mouth, and the crowd responded with respectful quiet. They bent to his will wholeheartedly.

Backstage, we were running like hell, hoping our luck would hold. Three minutes later, we were downstairs again, at the exterior door. Ortega joined us less than a minute later, and let us know it was safe.

The Key to Damocles

We opened the south-facing portal onto a vision of purgatory: tents, food, radios, parties, and fires abandoned to the whim of the moment. The lights were out, turning it into a hellish field of glowing red flames and abandoned camps. *El Toro's* voice echoed everywhere, carried by the still desert sky to every corner of the lot. We exited quietly and double-timed it to a clear section of street.

Behind us, the other three faces of the Gigadome were awash with protestors. Hours before, someone with a flier and a thick chain had pulled down the metal gates guarding the entrances. Now human rivers crammed into the gates, and up the ramps, and into a building that was likely already filled to bursting. The official numbers said this building could hold a quarter of a million. Even if they were standing room only on the playing field, it was not going to be enough by a long shot. While a fraction were willing to sit in the cold desert night and watch on the Olympic pool-sized viewscreens, most were not. They were desperate to get in, to be in the presence of their messiah, and tempers worn thin by adrenaline and alcohol were beginning to rub together fast enough to burn.

"Wow, now this is what I call a plan working flawlessly."

That was Tsang, and he was right.

"Don't jinx us, Tsang."

That was Thompson, and so was she.

We were at the edge of the lot, and between the dead monitors on this side, and the blacked out lights, everyone had abandoned this place completely. I shook my head and activated my comm. "Doe, I don't suppose we need to go all the way to the evac point. This area is secure, why don't you come down and pick us up?"

"And see, Captain, that's how it starts. First, you stop taking the stairs, then you start eating fatty foods, next you're going to be complaining about how your ass looks in your armor." The team chuckled on the open frequency.

"Doe, I can pilot *The Succubus* just fine on my own. I could leave you here." The words were harsh, but my tone was not. The team had done a fine job, and deserved a little leeway.

Thankfully, he understood, and I could count the teeth smiling in his reply. "Sorry, Cap."

The Succubus zoomed in gracefully, setting a few tents on fire as it flattened others under its belly. Pity, that. We clambered aboard and the very instant the last belt was buckled, we leapt off into the night. My crew cheered. Before us, the sky opened up into beautiful starlight, welcoming us on our way to the Justice Center. Ahead, we saw the telltale signs of storm clouds gathering just inside the ring of mountains around New California. Behind us a drama was taking a hard right turn into a horror movie.

Whatever his faults, *Toro* was a magnificent speaker. He began humbly, quietly, testing the waters as he thanked everyone for giving him the opportunity to lead them. He drew them in, gave them power even as he set himself up as their head. He made everything quiet, almost poignant, as he looked back at the road of bodies he had walked on to get to this point. Then, he became firm, telling them that everything, everything, was wrong. L/V/D kept them in slums while raking in eighty percent of the wealth on Persephone. The crowd became angry, and he mirrored them, acting as their external voice. He did not stop at matching their outrage; he fed it, using words and exposing thoughts they would not themselves. He ripped away their need for conscience, for moderation, for peace.

He extolled the need for action, but what he meant was violence. There were thousands of comforts denied these people because of the color of their skin, and they had a right to take what had been denied them: jobs, money, luxury, position. He never mentioned just how these things would be taken, nor who they would be taken from, nor that many times it would be taken from people of the same color. All that mattered was the people felt slighted, and he validated every petty grievance without qualifier.

He was out in the open, exposed and vulnerable. He needed protection, and not just food-chucking protestors. He needed an army, and he was recruiting full throttle. He was whipping them into a frenzy, hoping for them to commit to him in the deepest parts of their hearts. If he had silent vows, guilt and duty would keep his soldiers around once this party was over. But to do that he had to transcend political party, he had to blow past rally, and leave protest far behind. He had to manufacture a religious experience. He was well on his way, and he definitely had the skill to do it.

It was amazing to watch, like a lonely conductor with an orchestra of half a million. He would raise their ire, and keep them there, hungry and hateful, until they were nearly exhausted. Then he'd give them permission to breathe, letting them down slowly as he made more reasoned arguments and plans for the future. Then he'd ramp up the volume again, bringing them millimeters from a full-blown riot before letting them down and then doing it all again. They loved him. They needed him. Therein lay his destruction.

It started in the back, where people were still pressing to get in. They could hear *El Toro* on the PA, but every masterful turn of phrase reminded them they were not in his presence yet. They quickly came to the conclusion those inside the dome proper had already had their turn in the 'good spots'. They felt slighted and had just been told it was their right to take what was denied them. They began to shuffle and then push. Those in the 'good spots' felt they had gotten to the Gigadome early and deserved the spots they had picked out. The conflict began at the back of the crowd. Fueled by stupidity, alcohol, and heated but empty words, it did not stay there. People shuffled, packed so tightly that any jostle was felt three bodies over. Irritation burst into full-fledged anger, and those who were shouldered aside returned the favor in kind. Pushes became punches that slid through the crowd like a shockwave.

El Toro continued with words wearing golden-thorned crowns, bringing his audience's blood to the surface. He urged their ire higher, and higher, whipping them like a coachman who had not noticed his reins had long since broken. By the time the sound of chaos reached him, his personal exultation stuttered, and he brought a hand to shield his eyes from the stage lights, but it was far too late. Cameras watched with unblinking eyes as the crowd transformed into a mob, churning with violence. In seconds, it overtook the entire field making it look like a tempest of flesh and blood.

El Toro walked to the edge of the stage as the angry storm broke over the arena field. His face constricted, enraged at the loss of momentum. I could see it, written there as plain as day... *this is not the part you are supposed to play.* He began yelling, an angry prophet chastising the people he had just led to the promised land. Even with his voice enhanced a thousand times over the stadium audio systems, only a scant few stopped fighting. And even then the mob had a momentum of its own, and in seconds those who stopped fighting were brought back into the melee or ground underfoot.

Worse yet, those in the stadium seating above the field saw the utter chaos below and began to panic. *What would happen*, they thought, *if those angry people came up here*? They began making for the exits, but of course, people were still trying to get in. The colossal press of bodies acted like a river swelled with rain, currents crashed against each other and began to heat up.

El Toro's face contorted into something demonic as he began to scream at his wayward disciples. He jumped from the stage and physically separated two fighters. They looked properly chastised as he did it again and again, yelling and screaming, getting deeper and deeper in the crowd. He yanked a cane out of the hand of a fashionable young man who had wielded it like a club, and likewise used it to beat two more combatants into submission. It was as if he was going to conquer the entire mob single handed. The news crews held their breath, wondering in excited tones if he might succeed. I began to wonder myself.

But the revolutionary never paused to look behind him to where eddies of peace he had created once again flared into battle. He just got further and further into the crowd, laying about this way and that with the steel-tipped cane. He caught an unsuspecting woman across the eyes, and she lashed out blindly, short knife clenched in a white-knuckled hand.

In a movie, everyone in the stadium would seem to come awake at that second. Dramatic music would ramp up as the brave revolutionary leader clutched stoically at the knife in his chest. A close, personal supporting actor would dash forward to try to save his life and only be able to hear his last words. The mob would find sanity, and would stand aghast at the senseless waste of their only hope. They would each resolve to carry on the brave revolutionary leader's work into the future. Text overlays of still frame shots would detail what happened to all the supporting staff and bit players. Credits would roll.

In reality, *El Toro* had abandoned everyone who actually cared about him back in Monroe. He had no support, no crowd control. He had engineered a storm and then waded in as if his personal belief in his own supremacy would shield him. In truth, *Toro* had lived by chaos, and he died by chaos.

The knife caught him across the throat, releasing a wide arterial spray into the crowd. The scent of blood drove the fight to even more desperate levels. Blood meant death in the primitive parts of everyone's mind, and everyone was suddenly capable of killing to survive. Far above, the horrified screams of blood-drenched people finally caused those in the upper levels to stampede toward the exits. Fights broke out at the top floors, but as their bulk joined the flow from lower tiers, people were trampled.

Toro, totally abandoned and alone in the center of the riot he had created, thrashed, choked, collapsed, and died. The cameras watched, unblinking, and so did I.

The *Angels* arrived at the Justice Center, every one of us more than a little grateful for a real landing pad for once. We walked off *The Succubus* to smiling faces and holstered weapons. The police there welcomed us as brothers, and we were able to stake out space in the bomb shelter in the basement. We were able to shit, shower, shave, eat, and bed down for the night. At least, my men did.

I found a little office off the beaten path and tuned the computer to the newsfeeds. I sat there, listening to the news crews go on and on about the death of their icon. They were already reminiscing about him in sickly sweet tones. I could already tell it wouldn't work. The quantum web sites that had followed every announcement and rumor with tittering expectation were deathly quiet. I was willing to bet they would be down within a week. If someone else had killed him, anyone else really, these sites could hold him up as a noble sacrifice in the name of justice. He was a martyr to nobody but his own followers. The ripples of guilt would fragment the trendy groups that had formed around him. His death would cauterize the wound his life had caused.

At least most of it.

That was my plan and, on the surface, it had worked flawlessly.

Dawn was breaking when the information I had been waiting for finally showed up on the newsfeeds. They were bold numbers, reported quickly out of some lip service to journalistic integrity and then never mentioned again. Of the estimated one and a half million, there were eighty thousand injured... *which meant anything from split lips to heat exhaustion...* four thousand were seriously injured... *which meant broken bones to heart failure to coma...* and because the Gigadome was so far from any working emergency services, police, or hospitals, there were one thousand, eight hundred dead... *trampled, stabbed, choked, whatever...* and twenty-seven of them were children.

Should I have let *El Toro* continue? The most frightening thing was that his plan might just have worked, and I would have handed over generations of children to monster despots like him. *This planet needs stability; he would have robbed it of even the chance of coming under any kind of sane rule.* And though it was true, and even though nobody in their right mind would bring children to a political rally of this kind in the middle of the night. *Hey, twenty-seven dead children because I was clever, watch me rationalize why it's not really my fault!*

I buried my head in my hands.

I may not have lined them up and pulled the trigger, I may not have spoken the words that riled the crowd... but sure as shit, I had made the nail that failed the kingdom. I set the rally. I picked the place in the middle of nowhere so the law-leery protestors would show up. Twenty-seven children died, and I had a hand in it. I would never be punished; I would never be caught. Even if it ever came up, I had a fully-signed and declared contract with a principal for bodyguard work that expired half an hour before the deaths occurred. I was bulletproof. Despite that, maybe because of it, I cried for a while.

That is the sad fact of war. Innocence is no armor. Once a battle is joined, only one thing is certain... people will suffer. Sometimes the only thing you can do is finish it as fast as possible; end the suffering as soon as you can. That is the horrible secret of mass combat... a conscience is both the biggest necessity and the biggest liability. Sure as hell, the moment you quail in the face of that suffering, the biggest bastard will win every battle. He will surround his military bases with churches, and strap living children to the front of his tanks. And when you are forced to strike anyway, he will paint you as the villain.

The Key to Damocles

War is not so horrible because of the heroic things we do, but because of the necessary things we force ourselves to do. I knew it, but it was no comfort. Every single particle of culpability still ate at me like a cancer, hollowing out my center. It was a long time before I got up and crept downstairs to find my bunk. By the time I woke up, I had a gauntlet from Saracho waiting for me in my computer inbox.

CHAPTER 36: LOCK AND LOAD

Saracho had just watched my little trick and had decided to try and pull an encore performance, with me playing *El Toro*. My jaw clenched; my hands tightened into fists. His 'invitation', worded much more like an order, was to some kind of debate on the newsfeeds to defend my good name. I have no idea if he expected this to work, or if he just wanted to point at my refusal to come as evidence of guilt. The rules were simple: neutral ground, on camera, sidearm only, come alone. I was sure Saracho was going to break every one of them if given the chance, which was fine. So was I. In either case, I refused to answer and just made plans to be at the debate at the correct date and time.

I was absolutely, positively sure this was an ambush. In fact, it was so obvious even the newscasters were already considering it loudly on camera. They were already pushing the interview with Saracho as the coming of the next great king of Persephone, which means they saw the writing on the wall and decided to back a winner. He already had the only qualifications the media cared about: he hated Lomen and me.

What I needed was a plan. The pressure, hate and pain congealed in the back of my head, crystallizing into just the thing I needed. I dressed and stormed out of the bunker, but it took nearly fifteen minutes to find a pirate newscaster.

His name was Alberto Alberez, and he ran newsfeed.AlAl.persephone. He wasn't a big name yet, but he had some genuine insights on his site. He was friendly to Lomen, but not so friendly toward the *Angels*. Given the circumstances, that might be best overall.

It took ten minutes to make my pitch to him. He wasn't thrilled with some of the details, but he was positively drooling over the information I was handing him. He was even less happy when I summoned Logan to act as a massive silver shadow for him.

"What's he for?" he asked dubiously.

"He's there to keep you from getting a nine-millimeter migraine," I replied, not looking up as my fingers danced across my laptop.

Somewhere else in the compound, Tony was typing back, 'Yes, the emergency announcement system will interrupt normal newsfeed transmissions. Why do you ask?'

Alberez's voice took on a much higher pitch when he asked, "A what?"

I sighed and typed, 'Tell you in a bit. I'll need access to that system tonight.' and shoved away the computer. "Look, you have the opportunity to do the right thing for your planet. Just realize that 'right' rarely means 'safe'. People will kill to keep this stuff under wraps. It's going to cause an uproar like you have never seen. People are going to call you a liar. The established media outlets are certainly going to try to assassinate your character. Others are just going to try to assassinate you. And if, IF, anyone thanks you for telling the truth, it will be a long, long time from now."

All thoughts of journalistic prizes and public accolades fled from his mind. He was wondering if he would become one of the long list of journalists from various planets who have told the truth, and spent the rest of their lives on the run because of it. On the run, at best. Everyone is motivated by ideals they hold deep in their hearts, even if the ideal is simply that of their own supremacy or entitlement. The ideal of Alberez was Truth. I could see his mind working behind his eyes, and the thought of shrinking from his self-appointed duty was painful.

Finally, he looked up at Logan. "I won't broadcast anything I cannot verify."

"Absolutely. I will arrange for a terminal in the evidence processing center be made available to you for analysis. Please let me know anything you intend to exclude." I turned to Logan, saying more for the reporter's benefit than the sergeant's. "You are responsible for keeping him alive and getting him wherever he needs to be."

Logan drew himself up to his full four meters in height, hefted his comically large plasma cannon and saluted, more for the reporter's benefit than mine.

Outside, deep, black clouds raced at us from every direction. They carried spears of lighting and beat shields of thunder. On my screen, Tony's words appeared. 'It's all yours.'

I smiled viciously. I had one more score to settle on this spinning ball of dirt. Then I could go home.

CHAPTER 37: DOMINOES

The rainy season had finally arrived.

Dark skies cracked open with all the grace of a bombing run. Fat, angry raindrops slapped into the earth, sending up puffs of dust before spreading out and turning every surface into a slick, muddy mess. I marshaled my allies in a great wave, pushed by the storms that raged across the sky. It was time for this to end.

The fortress we approached was not one of steel and stone, but of mirrors and prisms. It was a palace of appearance, of lies and innuendo, but no more difficult to take for all that. Channel 311 was a building that vaulted up from the dirty streets at its feet, clawing at the sky with mirror-plated arrogance. Security men, police hired from the thousands who were out of work, patrolled the street like rats protecting the corpse of a felled knight. Without other work, heavy with responsibility for hungry mouths, they accepted the job that was to be had, and they did it, but sullenly. They carried guns. They watched the skies. They checked IDs. What they did not watch, what they were not told to watch, lay beneath their feet. There, dark shadows moved with a purpose bordering on madness.

The steam tunnels, like dank and forgotten dragon caves, were filled with the cables and pipes that kept the city's heart beating. Stealthy forms came in waves, small teams with detailed plans and hand lights. They also carried guns. They worked out of belief, out of hope. They did so like angels marching at the orders of the Almighty.

I hoped I was worthy. *I had better be.*

Far above, in the sanctimonious halls of wealth and privilege, the cue cards were drawn up, artists applied makeup, and some technicians leveled sound feeds as others prepared graphics and cameras. They worked professionally but bereft of joy. They gave the men in the corners furtive glances, eyes lingering on gunmetal flashes and golden badges. Everywhere the workers went, PISs Agents guarded the doorways, guns drawn in an unspoken threat.

Saracho sat sourly on the stage, tapping his foot as the time drew near. Enrique Martinez, a man with a dazzling smile, full beard, and a part in his hair you could grow crops in, was alone in his oblivious heaven. He was memorizing talking points, practicing his smile and getting ready for the news piece that would enshrine him in Persephone's history and make him the favorite of the world's next great leader. The men in the programming booths, however, could not fail to notice that two dour Agents stood nearby. Nobody had any doubt about the script for the next hour.

Far below, quiet men gathered in secluded spots in the steam tunnels and unlimbered heavy packs. Explosive-laden disks were pulled forth with the greatest of care and mated to the walls with all the solemn rigidity of a religious ritual.

Just then, the sound stage became a flurry of activity. The lights dimmed and then came back up. Cameras moved in like a pack of jackals. "Welcome to the Channel 311 Action News Center! My name is Enrique Martinez. Tonight, we have law versus anarchy on a very special 311 Action News."

I watched on a wallscreen, like millions of others, as Saracho took to the stage. Anywhere or anytime else, Martinez's questions would be laughably banal. At the bottom of the screen, the popularity and instant polling data, once churlish and low, began creeping upward. He recited Saracho's record, fawned over an old 'battle wound' story, and tossed him bone after bone to make the director of PISs look as good as possible. The polls continued to rise, giving Saracho hope and heart. He waxed pedantic about stability, safety, law, and order. He spoke of pride of their shared culture, about bravery and honor. He was a good tyrant, coaxing hope from a frightened and tired population. His numbers crept into the 'electable' range and I felt bile churn in my stomach. *You hired a speechwriter or two, you bastard.*

I sat back and shut my eyes, ignoring the visuals and concentrating only on what was said. I locked clips of sound into my brain, memorizing them for later dissection. Slowly, little indicators on my laptop screen flashed, showing team after team was in position and ready for the night's business. Just in time, too, since the audience believed the show was coming to a close.

"And I understand that you even invited the so called 'Captain' Rook of *The Radiation Angels* to this program, but he refused."

I began punching numbers as Saracho slouched back casually, clearly going for the 'everyman' posture. "Not only did he not show up, he couldn't even gather up the courage to call and say he wouldn't be here." He chuckled. "But I'm sure we'll be seeing each other really soon."

Yes, we will. My typing sent signals to the Channel 311 Action News office that were received and immediately answered. I turned on the visual transmission. Tittering voices pawed at my coattails. I waved dismissively and thumbed my screen over and over to authorize form after form: permission for use of my voice, my image, an indemnity against defamation, and a waiver of slander. As the forms flashed by, mimicking the lightning outside, there was a flurry of activity on the screen.

Martinez's voice betrayed his glee as he said, "Wait... Mr. Director, I think we have a special treat for our audience. I have Todd Rook of *The Radiation Angels* on a live feed."

Saracho shed all pretense of relaxation, lunging forward like a dog on a leash. His eyes filled with an insane light; his smile would not have been out of place on a skull. The single word he spoke contained equal parts lust and hate. "Rook."

I would love to get this guy into a game of poker. I smiled at him the way you smile at a rabid dog in a cage. "Mr. Director."

The view on the screen changed, becoming a large box for Martinez, and two smaller ones for Saracho and me. Even with him on top of me, the head boxes put us on visually equal footing. I could tell he hated it already.

Martinez, on the other hand, was thrilled. With the two of us so eager to fight, he could become the focus of the program as we bled. The ratings bar resized itself as the ratings quickly tripled. Every problem of Persephone was on the screen for all to see: idolized corruption, idealized media, and a panting audience for it all.

Martinez began, "Well Mr. Rook thank you very much for joining—"

But Saracho still thought he was in charge. "I see you didn't come in person, Rook."

"Well, that's because you trusted me to play the hero, but right now I'm too busy being a Captain."

Martinez opened his mouth, but Saracho's eyes narrowed dangerously and he barked, "Explain."

The Key to Damocles

I leaned back in the tiny office space, shrugging with forced nonchalance. "Well, you see, my job is to defeat my enemies. That's what I'm doing."

"Your job is murder, Rook."

"That's funny, because someone else told me that recently."

Martinez managed a word in edgewise. "Who was that?"

"Special Planetary Agent Gil Carlos. In fact, we had a fascinating conversation. I have a recording of that conversation if you'd like."

Martinez spoke again. "Uh... well, yes."

A computer-generated wire frame scene filled the screen, green cords made of vital signs on a black background. The sound was muffled, making everyone who watched lean forward and view closely.

> The standing wire frame man could not clearly project Old Fart's age, but it was clear he was speaking. "Well, well, well, Rook. It looks like you're not quite as clever as reported."
>
> *I was clearly in the chair.* "Good afternoon, Agent...?"
>
> "I am Special Planetary Agent Gil Carlos, boy. From *Servicios de la Investigación Planetarios.*"
>
> "Planetary Investigation Services. The men from piss are here. I am all a-quiver."
>
> Suddenly, the wire frame representing my vitals went crazy. Static tore up and down the lines like lightning. The sound of my screams was inhuman, and even I winced at the memory of it.
>
> The audio became less important, and the scene began skipping forward, as shown by the time/date stamp in the corner. He hit me again. Again. Again. My suffering was given visual substance to the audience, causing the polls along the bottom of the screen to gasp and stagger.

Martinez gasped and fumbled for a moment before he remembered he was live. "What was that?"

"That was Saracho's Agent torturing me."

Carlos ground his teeth but kept his composure for once. "It's a lie! That recording is a complete fabrication."

I faked a light tone, but my eyes promised him payback with interest. "Well, there's an imbedded authentication from Alberto Alberez, but everyone is welcome to download the recording off his newsfeed and check it for themselves."

"You son of a—"

"And of course Captain Lomen still has Carlos in custody." Saracho's mouth worked, but nothing came out, so I continued. "It's amazing how things change, Saracho. I mean, I have just spent the last hour listening to how brave and honorable you are."

"-Now you listen to me—"

"But I'm wondering where in the hell you were when the people of Persephone needed you?"

"You son of a bitch, how dare you question my integrity! It was anarchy out there!"

"Yes, it was, and I was out there in the middle of it."

Saracho slumped back in his chair, sneering as he made a dismissive wave. "Brave man surrounded by cyborgs and pulse cannons."

"Very true, but what about Captain Lomen and his men? Did they have cyborgs? Did they have cannons? Or were they out there doing your work for you while you were busy hiding."

"That back-stabbing glory hound?"

It was my turn to lose my temper, words coming fast and hot in my mouth. "Back-stabbing? Lomen? You're the only one here who has ordered his men to fire on the back of a retreating, unarmed foe."

Saracho jumped to his feet, "You are a LIAR!"

"Am I?" I pushed a button.

A shot of me flashed on the screen, taken from the helmet cam of one of the Apostles. I made it three steps up the ramp before the Agents opened fire on me.

"Stop that!" But Saracho wasn't talking to me. He was on his feet, his fist filled with Martinez's tie and shirt. The Director was yanking the commentator to his feet on live feed. His poll numbers were starting to wobble. "STOP showing them his LIES!"

"What, like this?" I hit another button.

> The screen showed security officers in L/V/D uniforms blindsiding the five Agents Saracho had left behind at the movie house last night. The security agents piled on the Agents like a sports team, but one Agent managed to draw his sidearm and leave two security men dead on the floor.

"Because that is the recording of L/V/D tossing your men out of their compound, something you were only able to do once you sent fifty men to murder your partner. You had taken over the place and were running it like your own little country. You have a nasty habit of using people until they'll do nearly anything to be rid of you. Eventually even *El Toro*."

"CUT IT! CUT THE FEED! CUT THIS BASTARD'S FEED!"

My box blanked; the feed was cut. The silence on screen was absolute as Saracho grasped at composure with sweaty, slippery fingers. Back in *The Succubus'* tiny briefing room, my fingers flew.

I began sending messages to Alberto Alberez. In front of me, Saracho desperately tried to slog through the shit pile he had created to some moral high ground. "I will not let this program become the propaganda arm of a two-bit group of space-faring thugs."

The seconds ticked by, thunderous in their silence, as Martinez ran a hand through his hair and tried to compose himself. "Well, we have run over our allotted time, and we have, uh, lost Mr. Rook."

Connection was made, transmission rerouted, and authentication protocols cleared. A green light appeared on my screen, and I spoke, my voice booming over the speakers in the studio and over the airwaves. "Oh, you haven't lost me at all. In fact, I have followed all of this from the beginning."

Saracho spun in every direction, clearly expecting me to have materialized in the flesh. "Shut him off!"

I continued as if he didn't exist. "In fact, that's why you tried so hard to kill me. Every time a mercenary company takes a contract on planet, friendly law enforcement agencies get notified. You had read my file, and you didn't like what you saw there."

"Shut him OFF!"

"You knew I'd start putting pieces together. It was your greatest fear. In fact, when capturing me with Carlos didn't work, and shooting me in the back didn't work, when you tried to take me into custody yourself and failed." I hit a button.

A brief glimpse of the wall of people from West Lot pointing guns at the pitifully few Agents dragging Saracho away.

I could hear thunder rumble like an angry god just outside the hull. "That was when you decided to abandon your plan, wasn't it?"

Saracho reached to his waist and pulled out his sleek, black pistol and shoved it right against Martinez's face. "SHUT! HIM! OFF!"

"He can't, Saracho. I'm pumping all this over the emergency broadcast system from the Justice Center." My words fell upon him like a tumbling tombstone. His eyes became wild, manic, as he stared at the deep black space where my face once was. "You cannot stop me. More importantly, you cannot stop the truth."

Saracho stared at me, eyes wide and hand locked on his gun. Then he turned and ran off camera, which automatically followed him as he gathered his men. I hit more buttons, and a recording spun up to speed, transmitting across Persephone on every frequency, every channel. Files squeezed into data streams and pumped into the atmosphere. Used for emergency defense plans, government disaster relief signals, and critical updates to the populous, it force-fed my message to every computer, handheld, laptop, phone, and entertainment unit. There the data reassembled, and began to speak.

"People of Persephone: Your world has been in turmoil for months. People, your people, have bled and died. Now it is time for you to know why. The sad truth is all of your misery, all of your pain, is because of two thefts."

The Key to Damocles

Beneath my voice, another signal went out. Deep beneath Saracho's feet, desperate men whispered prayers and activated remote detonators. Walls atomized, and the entire building shook like a giant with a fever. Men poured through the holes into the sub-basement. They were only thirty meters from the elevator control rooms, and it was the simplest thing to dart through deserted passageways there. Mercenaries would have taken one look at the controls and blown them up. But these weren't mercenaries. These were citizens of Persephone, and they carried badges.

They had all memorized the police lockout codes, used in case of hostage attacks, and one of their number input them now. Every elevator in the place paused, blinked twice, and then descended to the lobby, there to wait until released. Saracho and his men were in the corridor, staring at the elevator display panels as it happened.

> "The first theft begins with The Knights of Earth..."

Saracho threw a fit into his radio, demanding the elevators be put back online. Of course, he wasn't screaming at his own people, and if channel 311 security had been interested in helping him at all before, they surely were not now. The former police were speaking to the current police officers, and neither really had much desire to get in a gunfight for the Director of an agency that had been no help up until now.

> "...and so the chaos turned you against each other: poor against rich, politician against citizen, actor against shop owner, Latin against African. All of your pettiest grudges provided fuel for a fire that has consumed your planet and left you to live in ashes. They were free to get what they came here for..."

I watched the police band carefully waiting for him to be rebuffed by the street cops in the employ of Channel 311. I was waiting for the basement team to begin the long, hard climb to

James Daniel Ross

the newsroom. I was waiting for Saracho to call for his fliers. I heard his orders for pickup, and the confirmed reply. He and his last, few Agents bolted for the roof.

"...but they were not the only ones with plans to use the chaos."

I pressed a button and my voice flooded the police band, too.

"I always thought Saracho was working for L/V/D, trying to steal the planet wholesale for the movie house, but that wasn't it. L/V/D was being held hostage by his armed Agents. In truth, Saracho was tired of taking orders, so he used the chaos to his advantage. He found a dissident who wanted to play *El Presidente...*" *El Toro's image lit up screens, but it was his half-panicked, half-whining voice that slapped the population awake. Those that saw his face did not see the brave revolutionary leader. They saw a boy playing God, caught pulling the wings off of flies.* "We didn't set any of the bombs. We never did anything illegal. Saracho's men did that."

Off camera, my voice came in, making it disturbingly like an interview. "He set the bombs? Did he tell you when it was happening?"

Toro shook his head, his smile dying as his brow contracted. "No. The bombings started before he found me."

"He came to you?"

He nodded, swelling further with pride. "I had been running a pirate network site for years, lambasting L/V/D for discrimination against Latinos."

Saracho's pace slowed, his endurance attenuated by years behind a desk rather than in the field. He brought his radio to his lips, but all he heard was my voice.

The Key to Damocles

"Yes, *El Toro* was a patsy for the Director, acting as a figurehead for a revolution that did not exist. Did Saracho plan to arrest and execute him, or simply pull the strings from the shadows?"

Outside, slewing through the pouring rain, *The Succubus* raced just above street level, massive exhaust vents cooking the highway dry as our shadow passed. In the cockpit, Doe yanked on the collective control, popping above the buildings like a flying spider. Six bright sparks leapt from the wings.

"I think he meant to watch the polls and just join the winning team. But suddenly I was too close to *El Toro*, too close to the truth. I have to hand it to him, Saracho did not hesitate..."

Saracho tossed away the radio and began shouting orders to everyone within reach. The Agents continued upward, alternatively pulling and pushing their boss. Kilometers away, three PISs fliers became high velocity debris. Doe rocked out of the canyons between abandoned office buildings and pushed the throttle to the stops.

Battle scenes came next, visceral scenes that jumped and blurred, clearly clipped from HUD cameras. Enemy soldiers shot at the cameras with laser rifles and rocket launchers, completely disregarding the safety of people in the buildings on all sides. The data screen kept freezing, zooming in on the PIS logos. The audience watched breathlessly, wincing at rocket detonations and grenade explosions. They looked at the office buildings on every side, and wondered who cowered there, imagining it was outside their own doors. Of course, it was footage from the flat town, but they didn't need to know that yet.

"...He was, however, a little late."

Another transmission played out on millions of screens. The fish-eyed camera that had made the recording did not provide the best visual, but the woman screaming in MexiCali was unmistakable. The tall, lanky man kneeling next to her over the body of their friend looked disturbingly like Christ. The big, scary men in black fast-response armor, the imposing rifles were perfectly costumed villains. The PIS logo was highlighted in gruesome detail as they opened fire. The screams were over quickly, but they reverberated across Persephone like a tectonic shift. They gunned down the woman without hesitation. "But it didn't stop him from trying—"

The cloud of Agents stopped cold around Saracho. A few in the back were trying to push the whole lot forward. The director began roaring for progress, but many of the police officers were watching over the police band HUD. They saw the same thing as everyone else.

The Agents burned the woman to the ground, then turned their guns to the long-haired techie handcuffed on the floor. He did not die well. He begged and cried before they murdered him too. The last thing they did was shoot the camera on the floor.

Saracho struck one of his men and pushed two others over. The crowd of them continued up the stairs, but at every landing a few more Agents dropped back, lingering a little too long as Saracho struggled higher and higher up the staircase. Like a comet entering the atmosphere, Agents peeled off and were left behind.

The director didn't notice. All he could see was my face. All he could hear was my voice…and the terrified beating of his heart.

"The Knights of Earth caused death and despair across your world. I am sorry to say the one man tasked with fighting them went into hiding. He only emerged to forge an alliance with a figurehead that would terrify you into compliance. All these

491

things have been done so that Saracho could emerge and play hero to you all. He would have ruled you like an emperor, and you would have thanked him for it..."

Saracho and less than a dozen Agents burst onto the roof, rain pummeling him and his men with merciless fists. The sky was alive with lightning and the thunder was so close it felt like mortar fire. Bright blue flames marked the position of the flying craft and the outlaw lawman allowed himself a triumphant smile for a split second. Then he saw the craft was way too big to be a police shuttle. It was hovering dozens of meters up instead of sitting on the landing pad.

"...but I promise you, justice is coming."

And with that, my recorded voice went silent. On the roof, the scream of aeroline turbines, roaring sky, and insane rainfall combined into the music of war itself. It built into a crescendo as Saracho looked left and then right, and then everything seemed to hush as searing lights turned the falling sheets of water into a wall of white lace.

"Hello, Mister Director. Glad you could come." Saracho recognized my voice, and I could see his jaw quiver with the force of his hate, caught between a howl of rage and a sob of despair. I continued, voice amplified by my helmet. "You are all under arrest. Place your weapons on the roof, and you will be taken into custody."

Two Agents dropped their weapons to the roof, the rest of them were visibly considering it. And just like that, it seems like I'd won, but I hadn't. The universe is never so neat, clean, or easy.

The people had just been shown Saracho was a traitor, but it wouldn't end there. There were hundreds of politicians from the planetary government still hiding in L/V/D. It was too much to hope for that all of them would be tossed out. Some of them would return to power. Some of them would owe Saracho favors. Others would consider him special, one of the ruling elite, and none of them would want to see him punished. It would only make them more accountable for actions they would much sooner forget.

Two more Agents dropped their guns, but Saracho began to smile like a jackal. He knew what I knew. I had no more right to arrest him than a dog. I wasn't a citizen of Persephone, so I couldn't even make a citizen's arrest. Anything I did now would just muddy the waters and make his conviction that much harder. He gingerly, slowly removed his suit coat, exposing his favorite negotiator in a holster.

Truth be told, there was little chance he would ever face true justice for what he had done. Someone had to make sure he wasn't alive and free, a cancer inside Persephone as it recovered from its wounds. It couldn't be Tony. He was the law. It couldn't be the policemen, or militia... it wouldn't be one of the old guard of politicians or one of his Agents... they were part of this mess, drowning in it. It had to be me. It had to be now.

The rest of the Agents disarmed, and I stepped forward, dropping my C^2 helmet to the roof. Footstep built upon footstep until I was barely seven meters away. It was at that moment that I could see every line on his face constrict. He squinted against the bright lights behind me, the rain coming down, but still clearly identifying my shorn-dreadlocked silhouette. He actually smiled at me, reveling in his secret hope for freedom as he began to reach for his gun slowly, using only two fingers.

I closed my hand on the butt of my pistol, snapping off the restraining strap as my other hand rose dramatically to my chest. The ripping sound of Velcro caught his attention and made him pause. He squinted again. I angled my body so my front caught a blade of light.

A brave bronze shield glinted on my chest, given molten glory by the silver droplets that polished it. He could identify it easily enough, but had he been closer, he would have seen the eagle, the scales, and arrows. In stark relief, the black enamel letters jumped out at him, the badge number of 888 and the name Rook. He saw the badge, and assumed exactly what I wanted him to, that he was about to be arrested, for real.

His mouth moved, but there was no sound.

I tightened my grip.

The Key to Damocles

His insides boiled, his limbs shaking, the little murmur escaping like the echoes of an earthquake which had not yet arrived. "No…"

My mind blanked. Everything came down to this moment. Anarchy or stability, infamy or justice, it all came down to the next heartbeat and the speed of my metal laden fist.

All sound died in the world, even as the storm surged, even as the engines roared, even as men flanked us on every side, he and I were alone in our own private time line.

And then it came. His face became a rictus of rage. His hand enclosed the butt of his pistol. His voice erupted with such force it caused him to tremble and mixed his spittle with the rain. It was a single word, a denial of reality and promise of death. "NO!"

Suddenly, the curtains of rain became a hail of comets, caught between seconds as lights lend brightness to every microcosm of water. My hand yanked gun clear of holster. He flipped off his gun's strap and began to pull, barrel seeking me with a hungry mouth. My gun came up. His arm straightened. My sights aligned. His hands slapped together around the butt of his weapon.

My plasma gun bucked once, hard.

Blood and flesh vaporized instantly, and Saracho's gun tumbled from nerveless fingers. His trachea carved out by several thousand degrees of liquid light, the director collapsed. He struggled and fumbled, flailing to draw breath through a throat fused into a solid charred mass. A clap of thunder announced his death.

The rain screamed harder at the earth below. The *Angels* turned our lights off. We retreated to *The Succubus*. We lifted off into the outraged sky. Now it was over. Now I had won.

Now I could go home.

CHAPTER 38: PACKING UP

Like a Persian prince of old, I marveled at the magic of the rain from the roof of the Justice Center. Like a beautiful tribal princess in a wedding dress, the brown, silty soil of New California had given birth to billions of flowers. Rich, green grass reached for the sun, covering bloodstains as vines crept up and sought to drag the hulks of cars into their graves. Spores buried deep inside the rough-textured walls became curtains of moss that covered posters, graffiti, and the scars of bullets past. It was only a momentary respite from the heat and sand, but sometimes you can live a lifetime in a moment like this. It gives you courage for the times in between.

The *Angels* were on loose liberty, able to come and go at will. Our home for a week had been the Justice Center, a necessity since we needed to schedule a refuel for *Deadly Heaven*, and ships carrying hundreds of thousands of tons of nuclear enriched fuel do not come into war zones unless they have to. Thankfully, Haven had just reclassified Persephone from 'open anarchy' to 'unstable'. Ships were coming in from across the colonized worlds, drawn like flies to a corpse by the smell of profit. The Intergalactic Bank reopened relations, and the military was in orbit to keep things calm up there. As soon as the politicians and Lomen decided who was in charge, they'd come down and help keep order in New California.

I snorted, Welcome to the party, guys.

In other news, Saracho was dead. *El Toro* was dead. Silver and Carver were very, very dead. In the movies L/V/D produced, this is where you'd get a glorious sunset, dramatic music, and scrolling credits. *At least I got the sunset, dammit*, because this really wasn't the end to everything; it was only the beginning.

Many cities had major damage from riots, explosives, and a lack of basic services. Almost all of New California looked like it had been bombed. The world's economy had only half the power of simply a year before. L/V/D was still producing movies and bringing in money to the economy, but after the constant demonization, it was unlikely Lionel would help out more than the bare minimum. *Can't say I'd do that much.*

The Key to Damocles

Out of the 'old guard' politicians, only a handful were able to slither back into temporary positions of leadership, but it would be years before they were trusted with more than a paperclip inventory. *Toro* was right about one thing... belief is the most powerful thing. Now people had a choice; they could believe in the new government when it finally formed, or they could continue living as city states. Either way was fine with me as long as everything stopped blowing up. I'd done my job.

The media, likewise, was crippled. Advertisers, faced with falling sales, had pulled their money. They bought less expensive ads on venues that reached more people, such as on the blogs, newsfeeds, and programs of the pirate newscasters. Already Alberto Alberez was richer than he had ever imagined. He was going all day and night, splitting his time between filling his newsfeed with stories and finding other newscasters to help. Soon he would have a clean, professional staff looking for news at all hours and putting it up as fast as possible to hook those addicted to such things. He'd be in a race with everyone like himself, and competition would become fierce. Rather than inspiring better work, fact checking would become shoddy in return for speed. In short, he'd be just like the people who he replaced. If Persephone was lucky, it would take a good, long while. The way things were going, it would be sometime next week.

Thankfully, the population had learned their lesson here as well, and it would be generations before the media could play kingmaker again. Hopefully by then, they would rediscover their job was to report the news, instead of creating an echo chamber for their opinions. Stranger things had happened.

The door to the roof opened and closed, gravel shifting underneath shoes as Tony cleared his throat politely. "Good morning, Captain."

I glanced back at him, amazed at how much better he looked after a week of uninterrupted sleep. "They haven't made you *El Presidente* for life yet?"

"Nah." He strolled forward, hands in the pockets of his street clothes. Uniforms were in short supply, and he had probably put his back into the pool. He really didn't need one anymore; everyone on Persephone knew his face. "Well, they've tried, but

I've never really felt the need to be anything more than a Captain."

I laughed. It sounded cleaner, more whole, than I felt inside. "I know how you feel, Tony."

A few seconds, each heavier than the last with unsaid words, passed between us. Finally, he screwed up the courage. "You're leaving aren't you?"

I nodded. "Yep. The team has played enough, and really we can't do any more damage around here."

"Well, the last week has been a welcome kind of exciting, I'll agree." He chuckled. "But I think we could do with more of that kind of damage."

I shrugged, smiling sadly. "It's time."

He nodded, and fell silent. At the beginning of their liberty, I gave the *Angels* a hundred grand of their pay and let them loose. With nothing to do, and loads of stress to slough off, the credits had gone through their grubby little fists like water. They had created demands, and people had come forward to meet with supply. It had kick-started the economy in this little area and given people money for the bare necessities. It was nothing more than a drop in a well, but hopefully the people who had braved New California once to bring them the goods and services my team had wanted would do it again and be followed by more. Still, my team needed the rest of that money for equipment and training if not family and dreams. I sighed. "What happens to Carlos? And the unbondables, for that matter?"

"Well, I am going to throw the book at our erstwhile Agents. The mercenaries, uh, unbondable, will be delivered to the military for trial as soon as they get their asses down here. Any way you cut it, their futures are going to be cut pretty short." Tony leaned over the edge of the Justice Center, saw nobody below, and spit.

"And how about you?"

He shrugged, getting that embarrassed look akin to a teenager being praised by a teacher. "Everyone wants me to run, and not for the governorship of New California. They want me to run the whole damn planet. I just don't know."

"This planet has no right to ask anything more than the service you have already given to it." I turned to him, amazed at how short he was... just a little fireplug of a man with a tightly trimmed beard and barrel chest. In my memory, he was always a giant. I shook his hand. "But I believe you'd do a fine job, Captain Lomen."

His eyes sparkled with moisture, but he just smiled and nodded. I gave him a salute, and he returned it. I left him looking out over his city, watching life scab over the signs of death.

I walked down the first set of stairs and then decided I had done enough walking for the next month. I caught the elevator deeper into the Justice Center. I leaned against the back wall and relaxed. I closed my eyes and Saracho's face sprang unbidden to my mind. Pale and bloated, he mouthed curses at me...

My eyes snapped open, dispelling him like a dream. No, you don't, you sonofabitch. You don't get to haunt me. I saved millions from the hell you would have created. You had no more right to your life than any other murderer, traitor, or tyrant. I closed my eyes, and he was gone. I knew he'd be back just like all the others. I accepted that fact as the price of doing business.

I took a deep breath and the doors opened. The halls were a little more lived in than the designers had ever envisioned, with refugees filling every possible space and more showing up every day. Underneath the professional smells of paper and running electronics, there was a definite funk of unwashed bodies. Small bits of litter were beginning to collect in the halls, and every executive suite had been staked out for the large, plush couches that could be found therein.

New arrivals were being moved to the buildings on every side of the Justice Center. Without the constant attacks, this place was becoming a truly safe haven. Someone had homemade templates, and they were using spray paint to stencil 'REMEMBER WEST LOT' onto every flat surface and piece of clothing.

Pride. Pride will heal wounds and cement these people together. It was a good sign, and I felt that much better about leaving.

Thompson caught up with me around the next corner. "Captain! Captain! Can I have a word in private?"

The voice was mine but the words were my Captain's, with her name cut-and-pasted with mine. "Goddammit, Thompson! I gave you time off to go have some fun. You're going to be worth a fart in the wind if you don't learn to go relax once in a while. You're good at your job; I get it. Now stop trying to impress me with how *fragging* efficient you are. You are going to burn out on me."

"Captain, I had a conversation with Grisham." I closed my eyes and thought, *Oh, grit*, very loudly as she continued. "I asked him, well, I wondered out loud about what would've happened if you didn't make it back from the roof of Channel 311 and—."

"—and he told you that if I died, control of the *Radiation Angels* and all the team's holdings would be transferred to you. Yeah, I recorded my last will in kind of a rush." She stumbled to a stop in the middle of the hallway, staring at me like an alien being. *So, this is what's been eating at you the whole week.* I found an empty office and steered her in. Once the door was shut, I held up a hand to forestall her questions. "Logan doesn't want the team; he's had plenty of opportunity. My family doesn't want it. Nobody else could have completed the mission and kept men alive. It was you. It is still you. Either you can live with that, or you can't. If you can't, you just have to let me know."

"You're comfortable with the only thing between me and a multi-million credit spacecraft and one of the most prestigious names in mercenary circles being your death?"

"Shouldn't I be?" I waggled my eyebrows at her. "Besides, don't thank me yet; you still have to pass Officer's Candidate School. You've got lots of cash, so you are going to pay for it yourself, and if you are not up to snuff, OCS will chew you up and shit you out. The next two weeks will be about studying, preparation and memorization. By the time you are done, you might want to shoot me. For now, go relax, we're going to lift off in a few hours."

And without another word, I left her there, speechless, to consider the whole new shape of her universe. I found Logan and Archer outside, cannibalizing abandoned fliers to get a few more working for the inhabitants. The cyborg waved and then shoved his grease-covered silver hands deep into the guts of the dead beast. He loosened bolts with his metal fingers, took out the fly-by-wire computer wholesale and then gently set in the replacement. By the time I reached them, he had tightened down the bolts and Archer was reconnecting the wires to the rest of the system.

The Key to Damocles

Logan turned to me, with a little less snap than I was used to. I took a deep breath. "Sergeant, we will be lifting off in two hours. Do you have enough cash in your account to get yourself fixed?"

I could see him looking into his future and wondering. He was wondering if the lack of structure and action would begin his decent into failure and madness. Like some prehistoric fish, he had to keep moving, had to keep working, to outpace the demons of his past. He nodded, slowly, sadly.

"Good, because after training, refitting, restocking, and hiring a few more bodies, I'm thinking of returning to my ranch to do some workups before our next job."

All eight of Logan's eyes snapped into focus, doing their very best to bore into the very center of me. His deep voice seemed to rumble up out of the ground. "But you are retired, Captain."

I motioned to the busy street on every side. "Do I look retired to you, Master Sergeant?

"No, Captain. Sorry, Captain."

"Not at all, Sergeant. Now, make sure everyone followed orders and is sober, packed, and with no extra bodies attached." Logan saluted and moved off, but I stopped him with a single word. "Sergeant?"

He stopped and looked over his shoulder.

"Do you see them?" I motioned to the street on every side, pointing to people at random. *They are alive because of you.*

He nodded. A tightness in his cybernetic shoulders released, and he moved off like a man who knows precisely where he is and what he is doing. *The bastard, I only get to fake that walk.*

The moment was almost ruined by Archer asking, "What was that about?"

I took a deep breath. "Always remember your promises, Sniper. They are important."

He took that as well as could be expected. At least he wiped the sneer off his lips before he asked, "Hiring new people, sir?"

I took a deep breath. "Yes, Sniper."

"I... I, uh... I wanted to say—"

"Apology denied, Sniper. You have been a massive pain in my ass from the moment we entered danger until long, long, long after it was over. You are tactless, lazy, and a drain on the morale of the team." I met his eyes with mine, drawing myself up to my full height and letting every bit of contempt I felt for him show as I lowered my voice to a whisper. "The first is fine, the other two are not. I will fix these flaws in you, Archer. Moreover, I swear the next time you question one of my orders on the heat of battle, I will gun you down."

Archer's eyes went wide and he swallowed hard. "Next time?"

I nodded, but I was frowning. "You still have a job, Sniper."

I turned to leave, but a single word slithered out and hooked me back into the conversation. "Why?"

I did not turn to face him. "You carried Lopez all the way back to the shuttle, even though you knew there was a crazy bastard with a gun chasing you, even though you knew the whole ship was going to slip into the sun, and even though you knew I would never make it to the shuttle in time. You saved your partner's life, and I figure that's not a bad place to start for building a good soldier."

And then I walked away, back into the Justice Center and away from the already sweltering heat of the day. I made my way down into the bunker beneath the Justice Center. I found my room and began packing the little bits of equipment that had managed to escape my pack: clothes, C² unit, my laptop, a knife, a book, four magazines of ammunition, toiletries, and my quasi-official police badge. I had them mostly fit into my bag when a knock at the door startled me. *Idiot, this place is safe, now.* I took two steps and opened it.

There stood Miss Cody. We just stood there and stared for a few moments because, honestly, I could not think of anything to say. She was such a mix of fragile and powerful. Hurt, but healing, I had watched this tiny woman stand up to the bad end of guns armored in nothing but willpower.

I stepped back from the doorway to give her personal space, but she followed me in, wrapping her arms around me as far as they would go. I returned the hug gently. She began to tremble, and I let her go but she hung on determinedly until the shivers stopped. She let go when she decided to, not when her pain decided she should.

With two women like her in my command, I could conquer the known universe.

Her whisper blended into the silence so cleanly, I almost missed it. "I needed to say thank you for saving my life."

The Key to Damocles

My heart was hammering. "That's funny, Miss Cody. I had the same thing to say to you"

She made one of those blended laughing and sobbing noises before backing off and wiping at her nose with a tissue. "You say that a lot."

I took three steps back and sat on the bed, hands in plain view, voice low and tender. "A few weeks ago, in the medical center of the police station, I told you to be a hero, and that's exactly what you did."

Tears broke free and raced down her face. "I'm no hero."

"You are magnificent. You've survived things that would kill most people." I looked her directly in the eyes, trying to lower all my walls so she could see me, really see me. "You've shown bravery, loyalty, and kindness. It's going to hurt for a long time, but you are going to survive."

She nodded, but reluctantly. "But now you're leaving..."

I stood slowly, took three deliberate steps across the room, and cupped her face in my hands. "I did not save you. You saved you. I have been running all over this planet, dodging missiles, bullets, explosions, light, and heat. I have hidden, I have run, and I have fought when I could. All the while, you've never been free of your demons for one moment. You have fought every second of every day.

"I am not your hero, Miss Cody. You are mine." I let her go and gave her space again. She moved forward, stood on tip-toe, and kissed my cheek. I smiled sadly at her. "You can do this."

She nodded, then she handed me an envelope. "Good bye, Captain Rook." And she left.

People blame war for hardening a mercenary. They are right. Some people blame the hardships, and the training, or being cooped up inside a metal can hurdling through space from place to place. That's true as well. But the worst thing, the absolute worst thing, was leaving before she was completely on her own two feet. Mercenaries usually only get to see the cut, not the suture. They get to see the coup but not the elections. We leave before happiness really gets time to set in because long before that nobody wants to pay us anymore. I knew I was going to leave this planet and never see Miss Cody again. Even if we struck up conversations over the quantum net, such things never last; they always trickle away in the end, leaving a dry ditch where a friendship used to be. I would worry about her long into the night for the rest of my life. I sighed and shouldered my bag.

My new MercTool beeped. I answered it and Logan's voice came out of the microspeaker. "Captain, I have found Doe. He is unable to perform his duties."

I glanced at the letter in my other hand and saw a familiar symbol. "All right, I'll fly. Go lock him in the brig. We'll cut his pay and assign him some *grit* work to do as punishment. Everyone else ready to go?"

"Affirmative."

I tore open the letter with my teeth, spitting out a shred of envelope before I could say, "Perfect. Liftoff in three hours. Rook, out."

I dropped the MercTool into my pocket and my eyes scanned over the paper.

> 'Grandma used to say the most important things should be written by hand. I hate the fact there is no delete key for pen and paper.
>
> I am still not sure what happened because it feels different. I want you somehow, in some way, near me. I feel trapped and alone, but only because you are not here. I have never needed anyone, and I still don't, but I feel weaker when you are away.
>
> I will meet you for drinks on Haven.
>   -Kei O'Leary'

I took a deep breath to steady myself, my mind filled with a cloud of doubt and unease that amounted to, *This is going to get complicated.* For just a second, I thought wistfully remembered the safety of dodging bullets, but when I left the Justice Center, there was a spring in my step.

For just this second, I knew precisely where I was, who I was, and what had to be done. I was working again. I was a Captain again.

And most of all, I wasn't faking it.

EPILOGUE: FAMILY

My eyes stung, and even when I closed them, the preflight charts swam in my vision. *Check fuel status... check. Warm up test of nuclear fuel igniters... check.* Discipline is a hard-won trait of a solider, and it must be constantly maintained. Running through the seventy-five items on the list took time, but aircraft are much like firearms. The moment you take them for granted, someone dies. I'd rather follow the list, thank you very much.

Doe was in the brig in the back; I could hear him singing a German *brauhaus* shanty... *or does it have to be about an ocean to be called a shanty?* I'd have to think up a punishment of the boring variety, rather than painful. He had needed to blow off steam like anyone else, but had gotten precious few chances during this mission. Orders were orders, and I had to impress upon him the need to follow even those he found harsh.

I sighed. Test control surfaces... check. Check aeroline cell rotation... check.

The rest of the *Angels* were saying their goodbyes. They should be here in thirty minutes, and this third run of the preflight procedure would be done in five.

Boots clanked on the metal grate floors in the cabin of *The Succubus. Someone's early...* it's not that unusual. Mercenaries are used to putting down on planets, living through thirty-two flavors of hell and then leaving just as the victory party starts. Leaving cleanly, quickly, is easier for all involved.

I finished a system check on the gauges, again, which came up all green, again, when a two-toned hand clapped on my shoulder.

"Ready to fly, *jefe*?"

I turned to stare at the face of Electronics Warfare Officer Manuel Ortega. My nostrils flared and my lips compacted into a tight line. "What the hell are you doing here, Ortega? You caught a flight to the compound days ago."

He put on an easy smile as fake as my ribcage and flopped down into the copilot's chair, sighing with relief. "Well, as I see it, I've left you without an *EWO*. You flew all this way to come and help me out, the least I can do is—."

I went back to flipping dials and checking my chart. "Get off my boat, Ortega."

What followed was three seconds of shock broken only by switches cracking like knuckles. "Captain, I owe you."

"You owe me jack and shit, *EWO*." I continued running the chart, the number of boxes shrinking fast. "I came here because you asked. I did the job that needed to be done. I even sent you a bill. You did your part and now it's over."

"But Captain—"

I checked off the last box and stowed the clipboard in its holder. "It's time for you to go home, Ortega."

He was hurt. He was abandoned. He was afraid. The stupid *sonofabitch* didn't even know why. I sighed and took off my headset, putting it on the console and rubbing my eyes fiercely. When I looked at him again, I saw his mother's temper beginning to rumble up his neck, bringing a rich color to his cheeks. "Ortega, you've got a family that needs you."

"All the *Angels* have family of one kind or another."

I could have punched him in the face right then. "But this is the only way they can support their loved ones. I know there can't be mountains of credits left, but there should be enough to pay the taxes on your property and maintain it for future generations.

"You served your time. You rolled the dice. You didn't just win a little you got the whole *fragging* jackpot, a mercenary's dream. Go. Get a job. Find a plump wife and have kids. Stay with your family, Manuel. Because... if you go out you probably won't come back. You are not going to get that lucky again."

Manuel sank back into the chair, swiveling it back and forth nervously like a teenager taken to task. "I feel like I'm letting the team down, Captain."

I slapped the console and got up. Ortega followed suit on sheer reflex and then trailed behind me as I walked to the dropship's starboard boarding hatch. I flung it open, and just beyond the edge of the roof I could see a sea of people, milling about. "Look. Just look at them. Sure, they're celebrating today, but if you think this thing is over, then you are sadly mistaken.

"There is a legion of assholes just looking to hump this city for a little money, power, or both. Someone's got to stay and make sure this place gets put together correctly. Someone's got to make sure we didn't bleed for nothing." And as I stared into his eyes, I could see him give way.

His shoulders slumped and his head bowed, but there was just a little residual fight inside of him, moving on pure inertia. "What about you, Captain? What about your family?"

Something tight and angry constricted inside my chest. "I'm from Roh, Ortega…"

He shook his head, "You can't hold that against them—."

I set my jaw. "Don't be a *jacka*, Ortega. I didn't disown them; they disowned me."

Our eyes met, mine hard and hurt, his wide and unbelieving. "Do they know what you've done, I mean everything you've done, sir?"

"I'm a mercenary. That's all they needed to know."

And an uncomfortable silence loomed between us, a void he had to fill. "You would make any family proud, Captain."

"No Ortega, I wouldn't." I sighed. "There's been too many years without contact. What contact there is has been short and angry. Maybe if I'd listened a little more, tried to explain instead of bluster… They want nothing of me… I'd save you that, Ortega."

And deep inside himself, he chewed on that. He'd be doing it for the rest of his life, unless I miss my guess. He reached out to shake my hand. "Goodbye, Captain."

I took it and pumped it hard. "You don't have to call me Captain, Ortega."

Finally, finally, when Ortega looked at me, I saw a man. "Yes, sir, I do."

And then he disembarked *The Succubus*. He would never set foot on her again.

As Ortega reached the stairway into the building, the rest of the team appeared. Hugs and handshakes were exchanged all around as Logan caught my eye above the heads of the rest.

He shrugged slightly. *How did it go?*

I nodded grimly. *He's taken care of.*

His head lowered, staring at me intently. *How are you?*

I hooked my thumb toward the door. *Shut up and get in.*

The *Angels* boarded, and I turned to marvel at the whole, dirty, uncivilized lot of them. This small group of mercs had flown across the galaxy and had stopped the rape and pillage of an entire planet. There was no thanks that could ever suffice;

they'd collect precious little of it in any case. They'd come, they'd done the job, and I was proud of them. As strange as it might seem, that was enough. I blinked back tears as I pushed the throttles forward.

Below, by the staircase, was Captain Lomen. He saluted smartly.

I saluted back as the engines screamed with power. *The Succubus* leapt into the sky, a prehistoric dragonfly laden with *Angels* and devils, the laughing and crying, the brave and the fearful. Soldiers. My soldiers.

Radiation Angels.

LEXICON

Bioweapon - A weapon composed, in whole or part, of a living organism. Germ warfare and some poisons are just two examples.

Body Swapping - A criminal activity where a clone of a known person is grown, then swapped for the real thing. Normally, the clone has very little personality and only serves to delay pursuit until all hopes of stopping the kidnapping are lost.

Cathlist - A Christian denomination that grew up in the 23rd century. It combines many of the tenants and rituals of Catholicism, but does not give any leadership to a pope.

Citizen Militia - A citizen militia is a group of civilians who band together in times of national crisis in order to maintain the life of their society and protect their state, nation, or planet from harm.

Corvette - A Corvette is a medium-sized spaceship with a compliment of fifty to three hundred men. It is a deep space craft, capable of traveling between solar systems.

Deadwood - Deadwood is an ancient theatrical term referring to unsold tickets at the end of a performance which would then have to be destroyed. In the time of *The Radiation Angels*, it is slang used by actors and refers to anything useless and wasteful.

Drop-And-Rock Security System - A series of miniature, armed, non-mobile robots that are carried into an area, dropped, and turned on. They are programmed to recognized friendly personnel, as well as threaten, then disable, then kill intruders.

ETC - Electro-thermal Chemical. This ammunition uses a charge of plasma to push a projectile down a rifled barrel faster and further than old-style gunpowder.

The Key to Damocles

Fast Mover - Mercenary slang for any supersonic flying craft.

Field Craft - Military and Intelligence term denoting the skills required to successfully pursue a mission.

Five by Five - Military transmissions are rated by signal strength and clarity on a scale from one to five. Five by five means perfectly 'loud and clear'. It can also be used as slang to mean an enthusiastic affirmative.

Fragging/frag/frayged - During the war in Vietnam, soldiers unhappy with their commanders would roll fragmentary grenades into the offender's tent, killing them. This vile act of treachery has become the king swear-word amongst mercenaries.

Grit - This is a swear word derived from Mars, where grit would cause malfunctions in machinery and kill many people.

Gypsy Ship - Gypsy ships are playgrounds for mercenaries. Stocked with hundreds of employees, they provide a wide range of chemical, personal, and monetary services designed to help mercenaries blow off steam and separate them from their credits. They go from war zone to war zone in order to be where the money is.

Hard Point - A reinforced point on a vehicles frame that can then sustain the weight and recoil of a heavy weapon. Such items might include heavy machine guns, rocket launchers, bomb racks, and so on.

Integrated Personality – Many robots have only a base operating system and set of subroutines. More expensive models, mostly those meant to interact with people constantly, are also given a personality. This difference engine hurtles through complex algorithms based on human psychology so that the robots can more fully interact with their owners.

Ion Dust Grenades – These contain a small, explosive charge that fragments the compressed dust charge and then charges it. The charged silicate cloud fragments coherent light weapons such as lasers, and disrupts the electron ball projectiles of pushguns.

Jacka – A compressed swearword, made by lopping off the double s from the end.

Jaw Jacking – Speaking about personal affairs while on the clock.

Jimmy – Once meaning to pick the lock on a car door, now it is used as a police swearword.

Knights of Earth – A secret society of people, similar to the Masons or the Knights of Columbus, that believes it is man's divine right to return to Earth.

L&D – Stands for Load up and Dust Off. Mercenary shorthand for, "Grab your stuff and let's go."

Laws of War – The Laws are a complex document made to ritualize combat to a certain extent, and to reign in the worst excesses by providing standardized rules and punishments for wartime behavior. Similar to the Geneva Convention.

LIDAR – Light Detection And Ranging, similar to RADAR, but using light, and in some cases coherent light, as a base.

The Key to Damocles

Lieutenant/Flight - A specific rank given to flight crews. This is so a flight officer has superior rank onboard a spacecraft while a grunt has superior rank on the ground.

Martyr Mission - Any such mission where success is doomed due to overregulation, mission creep, or interference from higher ups.

MexiCali - A language composed of English and Spanish.

Mind Screen Theater - Mind screen theaters plug the patron into a sensory net that makes them feel like they are part of the action.

MuRR - Multi-Role Rockets. There are dozens of combination rockets that have a two to five stage warhead that combines the killing power of anti-personnel and/or anti armor explosives with specialty warheads such as fragmentary, gas, fuel-air, thermite, and so on.

Nerve Manipulator - A nerve manipulator can emit radiation that shuts down the chemical producing ends of a nerve.

Newsies - Merc slang for a news man, woman, or thing.

Nine Millimeter Migraine - Merc slang for being shot in the back of the head with a small caliber handgun.

Pain Box - Nerve Manipulators that are altered to excite nerve endings.

Plasteel - A combination of natural and synthetic polymers that very closely replicates steel cables, plating, etc.

Principal - Slang for any target, contractee, or other person vital to a mission. Usually a noncombatant.

RADAR - Radio Detection And Ranging uses radio waves to detect and track objects.

Screamer Chain ™ Locks - Screamer Chain locks are impregnated with high performance speakers and tiny batteries. If the circuit is cut, then the speakers blare at a deafening 120 dB.

Smartchip Translators - Inside of many electronic devices are translators that will take incoming words and seamlessly synthesize the voice into another language.

Snail Drum Magazine - An ammunition storage device that holds so many bullets it is curled like a snail's shell.

Straight Board - Old style ships have a board to tell where there is danger during explosive decompression. Any open hatches are show with O's all closed hatches are show as dashes. Thus, a board showing all dashes is a 'straight board'.

Suicide Kings - A popular card game that involves using numbered cards to 'murder' face cards.

Sy-Vine™ laser pistol. - A stylish, if somewhat impractical, laser pistol favored by people who never see dirt, mud, *grit*, or blood.

Talent Cloning - Talent cloning involves getting the genetic material of a superstar, cloning a child, and then releasing them as a 'new' version of the old star once their career has come to an end.

Toolbot - A simple maintenance robot that can carry out repairs.

Whiplash - A complex, fast-paced card game that fluctuates wildly depending on the cards in play. One can be ahead and then behind from hand to hand, with the only sure loser being the guy in the middle.

White Knight Syndrome - An unofficial mental disorder in which a person so badly wants to be a hero he will ride to save anyone from harm, regardless of need or the advisability of doing so.

Willpowerless™ Dispenser - A small, hardened box that dispenses dangerous or addictive medication only in tune with the prescription.

WOC/WOCing - An actor's curse. It stands for With Out Contract. Generally used in the same way a mercenary uses *frag*.

James Daniel Ross first discovered a love of writing during his high school education at The School for the Creative and Performing Arts in Cincinnati, Ohio. In those early days, in addition to this passion, he was an actor, computer tech support operator, infotainment tour guide, armed self-defense retailer, automotive petrol attendant, youth entertainment stock replacement specialist, mass market Italian chef, low priority courier, monthly printed media retailer, automotive industry miscellaneous task facilitator, and ditch digger!

James began his writing career in simple, web-based vanity press projects, but his affinity for the written word soon landed him a job writing for Misguided Games. After a slow-down in the gaming industry made jobs scarce, he began work on his first novel, *The Radiation Angels: The Chimerium Gambit*. Soon after came the sequel, *The Key to Damocles*, followed by other novels in the sci-fi/fantasy genre: *Snow and Steel, The Last Dragoon, The Whispering of Dragons, The Echoes of Those Before*, and many novellas and short stories. He shares a Dream Realm Award with the other authors in the anthology, *Breach the Hull*, and two EPPIE awards with those appearing in *Bad-Ass Faeries 2* and *3*.

James' books can be found on Amazon.com and at many retailers across the country. James himself can be found on facebook. Most people are begging him to go back to ditch digging.

In a world beset by nightmares, another is coming. Two of the mightiest nations in the world are clashing in a war that will shake the Great Veddan River Valley to its core. The fae elves and the bronze dwarves look upon one another as foreign and alien, their conflict fueled by dark powers and bigotry. Pride and misunderstandings foil peace at every turn, and two star-crossed lovers shall suffer as their people descend into bloodshed.

Shandahar is a cursed world. People will live and die. Wars will be fought, kingdoms built, discoveries made. For centuries, history will proceed apace... and then everything will come to a grinding halt and start all over again.

Shandahar is a world brimming with darkness, filled with no promise of a future but one. A prophecy. Spoken by the renowned seer, Johannan Chardelis, there is a divination that tells the coming of someone who can stop the curse. The snag? They have failed four times already.

Enter a world swirling with mystical realms and bloody battles, with enchanted forests and crowded cities where things are not always as they seem. Enter the World of Shandahar.

Doomed by his forbidden love, discarded by the crown, forgotten by the people, a disgraced hero rises from the ashes to combat the rising darkness. Accompanied by a novice priestess of the God of Death, this armored savior will crash headlong into the ranks of the undead. As the legions of the unliving surround and entrap him, he faces the dark truths of his own failures and discovers the limits of his warrior will.

Picture a hero.

I bet he's tall, muscular, and chiseled... forthright and chaste with bright, shiny armor... takes on all challengers face-to-face... lots and lots of honor?

Yeah. I am not that guy. Am the antithesis of all of those things.

In this world, with so much gold at stake, with the most powerful people in the kingdom taking notice...

That shiny hero? Yeah, he dies.

I am the guy that can get the job done.

I am Fox Crow.

Imagine living over one hundred years without a home, without a family, without responsibility. Imagine being alone in the wilderness with nothing but memories of the long ago past. Imagine dreaming of the day you might find something worth living for... worth dying for.

Elvish Jewel

Visit the website at
www.winterwolfpublications.com
for

Breaking News
Forthcoming Releases
Links to Author Sites
Winter Wolf Events

Made in the USA
Columbia, SC
28 August 2024